Queer Universes: Sexualities in Science Fiction

Liverpool Science Fiction Texts and Studies

Editor David Seed, *University of Liverpool*

1. Robert Crossley *Olaf Stapledon: Speaking for the Future*
2. David Seed (ed.) *Anticipations: Essays on Early Science Fiction and its Precursors*
3. Jane L. Donawerth and Carol A. Kolmerten (eds) *Utopian and Science Fiction by Women: Worlds of Difference*
4. Brian W. Aldiss *The Detached Retina: Aspects of SF and Fantasy*
5. Carol Farley Kessler *Charlotte Perkins Gilman: Her Progress Toward Utopia, with Selected Writings*
6. Patrick Parrinder *Shadows of the Future: H. G. Wells, Science Fiction and Prophecy*
7. I. F. Clarke (ed.) *The Tale of the Next Great War, 1871–1914: Fictions of Future Warfare and of Battles Still-to-come*
8. Joseph Conrad and Ford Madox Ford *The Inheritors*
9. Qingyun Wu *Female Rule in Chinese and English Literary Utopias*
10. John Clute *Look at the Evidence: Essays and Reviews*
11. Roger Luckhurst *'The Angle Between Two Walls': The Fiction of J. G. Ballard*
12. I. F. Clarke (ed.) *The Great War with Germany, 1980–1914: Fiction and Fantasies of the War-to-come*
13. Franz Rottensteiner (ed.) *View from Another Shore: European Science Fiction*
14. Val Gough and Jill Rudd (eds) *A Very Different Story: Studies in the Fiction of Charlotte Perkins Gilman*
15. Gary Westfahl *The Mechanics of Wonder: The Creation of the Idea of Science Fiction*
16. Gwyneth Jones *Deconstructing the Starships: Science, Fiction and Reality*
17. Patrick Parrinder (ed.) *Learning from Other Worlds: Estrangement, Cognition and the Politics of Science Fiction and Utopia*
18. Jeanne Cortiel *Demand My Writing: Joanna Russ/Feminism/Science Fiction*
19. Chris Ferns *Narrating Utopia: Ideology, Gender, Form in Utopian Literature*
20. E. J. Smith (ed.) *Jules Verne: New Directions*
21. Andy Sawyer and David Seed (eds) *Speaking Science Fiction: Dialogues and Interpretations*
22. Inez van der Spek *Alien Plots: Female Subjectivity and the Divine*
23. S. T. Joshi *Ramsey Campbell and Modern Horror Fiction*
24. Mike Ashley *The Time Machines: The Story of the Science-Fiction Pulp Magazines from the Beginning to 1950*
25. Warren G. Rochelle *Communities of the Heart: The Rhetoric of Myth in the Fiction of Ursula K. Le Guin*
26. S. T. Joshi *A Dreamer and a Visionary: H. P. Lovecraft in his Time*
27. Christopher Palmer *Philip K. Dick: Exhilaration and Terror of the Postmodern*
28. Charles E. Gannon *Rumors of War and Infernal Machines: Technomilitary Agenda-Setting in American and British Speculative Fiction*
29. Peter Wright *Attending Daedalus: Gene Wolfe, Artifice and the Reader*
30. Mike Ashley *Transformations: The Story of the Science-Fiction Magazine from 1950–1970*
31. Joanna Russ *The Country You Have Never Seen: Essays and Reviews*
32. Robert Philmus *Visions and Revisions: (Re)constructing Science Fiction*
33. Gene Wolfe (edited and introduced by Peter Wright) *Shadows of the New Sun: Wolfe on Writing/Writers on Wolfe*
34. Mike Ashley *Gateways to Forever: The Story of the Science-Fiction Magazine from 1970–1980*

Queer Universes

Sexualities in Science Fiction

Edited by

WENDY GAY PEARSON,
VERONICA HOLLINGER,
AND JOAN GORDON

LIVERPOOL UNIVERSITY PRESS

First published 2008 by
Liverpool University Press
4 Cambridge Street
Liverpool L69 7ZU

This paperback edition published 2010

British Library Cataloguing-in-Publication data
A British Library CIP record is available

ISBN 978-1-84631-135-2 cased
978-1-84631-501-5 limp

Typeset by Koinonia, Manchester

For Joanna Russ and Samuel R. Delany
and for Eric Garber and Lyn Paleo
with gratitude and admiration

Contents

Part III: Disordering Desires

Part IV: Embodying New Worlds

Acknowledgements

The editors would like to thank *Science Fiction Studies* for permission to reprint Wendy Gay Pearson's 'Alien Cryptographies: The View from Queer' (*SFS* 26.1 [Mar. 1999]: 1–22) and Rob Latham's 'Sextrapolation in New Wave Science Fiction' (*SFS* 33.2 [July 2006]: 251–74). We are very grateful for *SFS*'s support of the *Queer Universes* project. Thanks also to John Greyson, for permission to use stills from his film *Zero Patience*, and to Anthony Cond, our editor at Liverpool University Press, for his unfailing interest and enthusiasm.

Notes on Contributors

Sylvie Bérard is Assistant Professor at Trent University in Peterborough, Ontario, where she teaches Québec literature and culture. Her scholarly research includes women's science fiction, feminist writing, and Québec literature. With Suzanne Grenier, she has translated novels by English-Canadian sf and fantasy writers Leona Gom and Nancy Kilpatrick. As a writer, she has published numerous short stories in Canadian and foreign magazines. In 2002, she received the Aurora award for best Canadian sf short story in French for 'La guerre sans temps' (published in Québec magazine *Solaris*). In 2005, she was awarded the Grand Prix de la science-fiction et du fantastique for her sf novel *Terre des autres* (Alire, 2004).

Guy Davidson is a lecturer in the English Literatures Program at the University of Wollongong, Australia. He has published on late nineteenth-century British fiction, and twentieth-century Australian and American fiction. He is currently working on a book on commodity culture and same-sex desire in contemporary US literature and cinema.

Kelley Eskridge is a fiction writer, essayist, and screenwriter. Her short stories have been published in the United States, Europe, Australia, and Japan. She has won the Astraea Award and several of her stories have been finalists for the Nebula and James Tiptree, Jr awards. Her first novel, *Solitaire* (2002), was published by HarperCollins Eos and is currently being adapted for film by Cherry Road Films. Her first collection of short stories, *Dangerous Space*, was published by Aqueduct Press in 2007.

Joan Gordon is Professor of English at Nassau Community College in New York and the reviews editor for *Science Fiction Studies*. She is the co-editor of *Blood Read: The Vampire as Metaphor in Contemporary Culture* (University of Pennsylvania Press 1997) and *Edging into the Future: Science Fiction and Contemporary Cultural Transformation* (University of Pennsylvania

Press 2002), both with Veronica Hollinger. She is a past president of the Science Fiction Research Association and winner of the SFRA's Clareson Award for outstanding service. She has published widely on science fiction, including Starmont Readers' Guides to the science fiction of Joe W. Haldeman and Gene Wolfe.

Nicola Griffith (nicolagriffith.com) was born in England and now lives with Kelley Eskridge in Seattle. She has written five novels, most recently *Always* (2007); co-edited the *Bending the Landscape* series of anthologies, and won various awards (Lambda, Tiptree, Nebula, World Fantasy, etc.). Her most recent book is *And Now We Are Going to Have a Party: Liner Notes to a Writer's Early Life*, a multi-media memoir ('a do-it-yourself Nicola Griffith home assembly kit' — Garry K. Wolfe).

Veronica Hollinger is Professor of Cultural Studies at Trent University in Peterborough, Ontario. She is a co-editor of *Science Fiction Studies* and, with Joan Gordon, co-editor of *Blood Read: The Vampire as Metaphor in Contemporary Culture* (1997) and *Edging into the Future: Science Fiction and Contemporary Cultural Transformation* (2002). She has published many articles on science fiction, including on feminist science fiction, cyberpunk, and postmodern technoculture. She is a winner of the Science Fiction Research Association's Pioneer Award.

Nancy Johnston is a writer, teacher, and academic. Her short story, 'The Rendez-Vous', appeared in *Bending the Landscape, Original Gay and Lesbian Writing: Science Fiction* (1988). She teaches Women's Studies and Writing at the University of Toronto.

De Witt Douglas Kilgore is the recipient of the Science Fiction Research Association's Pioneer Award for Excellence in Scholarship and the author of *Astrofuturism: Science, Race, and Visions of Utopia in Space* (University of Pennsylvania Press 2003). Born in St Louis, Missouri, he is Associate Professor of English and American Studies at Indiana University. He and his family live in Bloomington, Indiana.

Rob Latham is Associate Professor of English and American Studies at the University of Iowa and a past director of Iowa's Sexuality Studies Program. A co-editor of *Science Fiction Studies* since 1997, he is the author of *Consuming Youth: Vampires, Cyborgs and the Culture of Consumption* (University of Chicago Press 2002). He is currently working on a book on New Wave science fiction.

Patricia Melzer is Director of the Temple University Women's Studies Program in Philadelphia. Her research interests focus on the connections of (popular) cultural texts and feminist and queer theory. She is the author of *Alien Constructions: Science Fiction and Feminist Thought* (University of Texas Press 2006), which explores feminist theories in sf texts. She is co-editor of a special issue of *Femspec* on 'Gender and Technology in Science Fiction Film'. Her latest research examines transgender identities in popular culture, focusing in particular on film and science fiction.

Helen Merrick is a lecturer in the faculty of Humanities at Curtin University. Her research focuses on feminist science fiction and feminist science studies, with publications appearing in *The Cambridge Companion to Science Fiction* (2003) and *The Joy of SF* (2007), and forthcoming in *The Routledge Companion to Science Fiction* and *On Joanna Russ* (Wesleyan UP). With Tess Williams, she co-edited the collection *Women of Other Worlds: Excursions through Science Fiction and Feminism* (University of WA Press, 1999). She is on the editorial boards of the science fiction journal *Extrapolation* and of *Transformative Works and Cultures*.

Graham J. Murphy is interested in critical interrogations of post/human embodiment in science fiction, cyberculture, and popular culture. He has had a book published on Ursula K. Le Guin and his articles have appeared in *Science Fiction Studies, Extrapolation*, and *Foundation: The International Review of Science Fiction*. He is co-editor of *The Irish in Popular Literature in the Early American Republic: Paddy Whacking* (Edwin Mellen 2000). He is currently adjunct faculty with the Cultural Studies Program and the Department of English at Trent University (Peterborough) and also teaches part-time at Seneca College (Toronto).

Wendy Gay Pearson has published numerous articles and book chapters on queer theory and its application to speculative and science fiction, as well as on questions of contemporary Canadian film and literature, sexual citizenship, and same-sex marriage. Her recent publications include 'Postcolonialism/s, Gender/s, Sexualitie/s and the Legacy of *The Left Hand of Darkness*: Gwyneth Jones' Aleutians Talk Back' in *Yearbook of English Studies*, '(Re)reading James Tiptree's "And I Awoke and Found Me Here on the Cold Hill's Side"' in *Daughters of Earth: Feminist Science Fiction in the Twentieth Century*, ed. Justine Larbalestier (Wesleyan University Press 2006) and '"Whatever That Is": Hiromi Goto's Body Politic/s' in *Studies in Canadian Literature*. She is currently an Assistant Professor in Film Studies at the University of Western Ontario (London, Canada).

Introduction: Queer Universes

Wendy Gay Pearson, Veronica Hollinger, and Joan Gordon

> Now, my suspicion is that the universe is not only queerer than we suppose, but queerer than we *can* suppose... I suspect that there are more things in heaven and earth than are dreamed of, in any philosophy.
>
> — J. B. S. Haldane, *Possible Worlds and Other Essays* 286

> If there can be a modernity without foundationalism, then it will be one in which the key terms of its operation are not fully secured in advance, one that assumes a futural form for politics that cannot be fully anticipated, a politics of hope and anxiety.
>
> — Judith Butler, 'The End of Sexual Difference?' 180

Signs of the (queer?) times. Two Michaels legally marry each other in Toronto, while the Vatican pronounces homosexuality 'objectively disordered' and lesbians 'anti-human' (Congregation; Butler, *Undoing Gender* 190). Newspaper and TV images show 4,000 lesbian and gay couples lining the steps of San Francisco City Hall for their own legal marriages (shortly followed by those marriages' annulment in the State of California), while other photographs circulate through the global lesbian and gay media witnessing the hanging of rural Iranian teenagers Mahmoud Asgari and Ayaz Marhoni for sexual acts they were unaware were criminalized under Iranian law.[1] An Italian newspaper proclaims that tolerance for homosexuality has led to a proliferation of genders in the US (male, female, homosexual, lesbian and transsexual) (Butler, *Undoing Gender* 183), while American fundamentalists claim that 9/11 is God's punishment on the US for allowing homosexuality, feminism, abortion, and the ACLU.[2] Court victories are celebrated in South Africa, Spain, Canada, the Netherlands, and Denmark, entrenching equality and basic human rights for all people regardless of sexual orientation, while Matthew Shepard, a young college student, is beaten, tied to a fence in Laramie, Wyoming, and left to die. At least Shepard's murder is national news, unlike that of 15-year-old Sakia Gunn, an African-American lesbian stabbed to death as she waited at a bus stop in New Jersey; the media neglect of Sakia's death, like its near silence on the executions of gay children in Iran, reminds us that sexuality never exists as a discrete category, but is always inflected by class, gender, race, religion, and nationality.

In science fiction, as in life, sexuality is a complicated and remarkably intransigent subject of inquiry, one whose material consequences can be ignored only at the peril of both individuals and cultures. Representation matters. In sf, indeed, bodies also matter, even at those times when they appear to have failed to matter or – often simultaneously, as is so frequently the case in cyberpunk – to have transcended matter. And yet sexuality in sf so often catches us by surprise: we may think, as readers and scholars, that it is not represented at all or, when we do catch a glimpse of it out of the corner of our generically conditioned eye, we may blink at it in bemusement, wondering what, after all, a spaceman who lusts after his Captain is doing in a nice little story of starfaring life – as in Theodore Sturgeon's 'The World Well Lost' (1953). But then, as Michel Foucault has so famously remarked, sexuality was – and no doubt still is – caught in the double binds of its active repression and the concomitant and endless compulsion to speak its details. Who would have imagined, when sf was a fledgling genre in the early nineteenth century, that issues around sexuality and gender would become, if not the greatest cause of conflict in the modern world, still extraordinarily fraught areas of human existence and thought, ones with sometimes extreme corporeal consequences? Who would have imagined, as they thumbed the pages of Mary Shelley's *Frankenstein* (1818), that that very novel would pave the way to establish the interrogation of issues of gender and sexuality as central to sf from the beginning? For it was, after all, only in the late twentieth century that readers and critics alike really came to notice what was sexual – and perhaps even what was queer – about Mary Shelley's tale of the man and his monster. Sex, gender, and sexuality have material consequences for both Victor and the Creature: the realization of the reproductive potential in creating a mate for his monster leads to her destruction before she is even brought to life, and ultimately to the deaths of all those whom Victor loves. Indeed, one of the most strikingly queer features of *Frankenstein* is the novel's extraordinary anxiety about the material outcomes of heterosexual relations. It is, perhaps, one of the most powerful effects of queer theory that it enables us to locate and identify the diverse anxieties and issues invoked by the representation of sexuality in sf.

Thus we begin this introduction with a few of many examples that remind us that the subject of queer theory – the role of normativity and Cartesian thinking on human sexualities, both as actual practices and as epistemologies – exists within a field of conflicting discourses, each of which has material effects on the everyday lives of real people. At the same time, the extent to which conflicts over the meanings of sexual acts and desires and their association with discourses of normality, propriety, and morality have become central to the self-definition of individuals, groups, and nations testifies to Eve Kosofsky Sedgwick's far-reaching assertion that 'an understanding of virtually any aspect of Western culture must be, not merely incomplete, but damaged in its central substance to the degree that it does not incorporate a critical analysis of modern homo/heterosexual definition' (*Epistemology of the Closet* 1). This collection takes Sedgwick's claim seriously.

Science fiction notoriously reflects contemporary realities back to us through the lens of a particular type of imagination, one associated with the future, with the potentials of technology, and with the important idea that life does not remain static; what we know today may be entirely different tomorrow. In thinking about the application of queer theory to science fiction, what is apparent is not only sf's ability to think outside mimetic reproductions of contemporary reality, but also its capacity to fulfil at least part of Michel Foucault's call to 'free thought from what it silently thinks, and so enable it to think differently' (*Use of Pleasure* 9). Wendy Gay Pearson has noted that queer sf narratives tend to be those that exceed requirements to reproduce, in Darko Suvin's words, the world of 'human senses and common sense' (qtd. in Pearson, 'Alien Cryptographies' 14); these are narratives that extend Suvin's argument about cognitive estrangement precisely to those areas which a focus on the science of science fiction tends to elide: the very world in which 'science' takes place, the world of the bodies and social systems that enable scientific endeavour. 'Cognitive estrangement', in and of itself, however, does not seem sufficient either to produce queer depictions of the world (or universe) or to think thought itself differently, particularly when what is being estranged is not necessarily related to the issues of gender, sexuality, and corporeality that seem to be the *sine qua non* of queer theory. Indeed, viewed as a matter of 'empirical surfaces and textures' (Suvin, qtd. in Pearson, 'Alien Cryptographies' 14), sf may not appear to be very estranged at all in terms of the social, cultural, and personal warp and weft of these brave new worlds. Cognitive estrangement may be a relatively small bump in the otherwise straight road to an undifferentiated future, but it is linked in a fundamental way to Foucault's call to queer thought itself. In this sense, perhaps, science fiction cannot help but be a little queer.

A 'straight' history of queer theory is an obvious impossibility, although such invariably teleological attempts tend to start either with Michel Foucault's notorious pronouncement, in the introductory volume of the *The History of Sexuality* (1976; trans. 1978), of the historical moment that produced the homosexual as a species, or with the term's invention by feminist film theorist Teresa de Lauretis and the exemplary collection of articles published in 1991 as 'Queer Theory: Lesbian and Gay Sexualities' in *differences: A Journal of Feminist Cultural Studies*. As William Turner's study of queer theory has pointed out, however, its definitional slipperiness and the inappropriateness of a search for the field's origins suggest that the more apt approach is a genealogical one. Such an approach would point as much to the work of American (lesbian) feminist theorists and historians, such as Carroll Smith-Rosenberg, Blanche Wiesen Cook, Lillian Faderman, and Gayle Rubin, as to Michel Foucault; as much to feminist theorizing of the relationship of gender and sexuality as to gay male historians such as Jeffrey Weeks, David Halperin, and Jonathan Dollimore; as much to histories of sexuality, including Foucault's, as to the contemporary theorists most associated with queer theory, such as Eve Kosofsky Sedgwick, Judith Butler, Teresa de Lauretis, Lee Edelman, and Michael Warner. When we attempt to conceptualize the rhizomatic links between these various approaches, a few things become evident: queer theory has arisen in part as a result of the move from thinking of sexuality in binary terms (Rubin's good versus bad sex, for example) to understanding it within the larger social and political context; that is, through discourse (Turner 88). It has made this move as part of a general critique not only of the way in which binary thinking underwrites most modern epistemologies of gender and sexuality, but also as part of a postmodern project of rethinking Cartesian systems of knowledge. A significant emphasis within queer theory involves exposing the ways in which ideas of the normal, particularly as expressed through heteronormativity, constrain people's lives – and not just their sexual lives – in remarkable ways; in concert with the critique of heteronormativity, queer theory returns to Foucault to examine the ways in which heteronormativity is enforced through panoptical encitements to self-discipline and the reshaping of the individual to fit statistical and discursive norms. Finally, queer theory participates in a debate about the political efficacy of theory in general and, more particularly, about the degree to which critical investigation, subversive practices, and queer acts are able to have material consequences in the 'real world'. As Judith Butler has pointed out,

> The task of all these movements [lesbian and gay, transgender, intersex, queer and feminist] seems to me to be about distinguishing among the norms and conventions that permit people to breathe, to desire, to love, and to live, and those norms and conventions that restrict or eviscerate the conditions of life itself... What is important is to stop legislating for all lives what is livable only for some, and similarly, to refrain from proscribing for all lives what is unlivable for some. (*Undoing Gender* 8)

If we then take as the central task of queer theory the work of imagining a world in which all lives are livable, we understand queer theory as being both utopian and science fictional, in the sense of imagining a future that opens out, rather than forecloses, possibilities for becoming real, for mattering in the world. We begin to understand the importance of sf as a genre for exploring these very possibilities, as well as for interrogating the consequences of societies and futures in which conditions render the lives of many unlivable – sometimes in unbearably literal ways.

Some years ago, two of the editors of this present collection contributed to one of the earliest critical discussions of queer theory's affinities with science fiction in a special section of *Science Fiction Studies* (Mar. 1999), which included Wendy Gay Pearson's 'Alien Cryptographies: The View from Queer' and Veronica Hollinger's '(Re)reading Queerly: Science Fiction, Feminism, and the Defamiliarization of Gender'. In many ways *Queer Universes* is a continuation and an expansion of that earlier work, which is why we have included Pearson's Pioneer Award-winning essay here as a theoretically astute framework for the essays and articles that follow. In its focus on sexualities, *Queer Universes* is certainly interested in the politics of representation, that is, in how science fiction has represented/imagined human (and other) sexualities and genders in its fictions of the past century. More than this, however, *Queer Universes* is a queer project, one committed to the perspectives and interests of a queer cultural politics.

In the context of sf, we can understand some of the variations possible in the deployment of queer, both as an interrogative mode and as a political one, by considering the differences between Joanna Russ's *The Female Man* (1975) – which focuses on the struggle to establish lesbian and feminist identities and sexualities within the constraints of a culture of compulsory heterosexuality – and Ursula K. Le Guin's *The Left Hand of Darkness* (1969) – which, through a radical imagining of human life *without* gender, explores gender as a cultural construction that is at once coercive and contingent. Judith Butler's theoretical work, on the cusp of feminism and queer theory, suggests the potential for queering our reading of feminist issues in science fiction, at the same time as it suggests queer's support for core elements of the feminist project. A statement of Sedgwick's is particularly resonant in this context: '[the] study of sexuality is not coextensive with the study of gender; correspondingly, antihomophobic inquiry is not coextensive with feminist inquiry. But we can't know in advance how they will be different' (*Epistemology of the Closet* 27). Nor can we know in advance the various ways in which they might support each other.

Queer theoretical approaches, alongside feminist, postcolonial, postmodern, and critical race theories, allow critics to make visible the naturalized epistemologies of sexuality, gender, and race that underwrite the most conservative sf, as well as to explain some of science fiction's most striking attempts to defamiliarize and denaturalize taken-for-granted constructions of what it means to be, and to live, as a human. Indeed, the most imaginative and challenging works of sf are so far ahead of much critical theory that Hollinger and Joan Gordon argue in their introduction to *Edging into the Future* that 'the challenge for contemporary science fiction criticism and theory is to keep up with a popular genre that is itself in a state of constant flux and that is often far ahead of its critics in terms of its sociopolitical and ethical explorations' (2). Queer (re)readings of classic feminist sf texts, for example, can lead to a fresh appreciation not only of the extent to which some sf stories have always challenged the technologies of compulsory heterosexuality, but also of the extent to which contemporary sf imagines alternative ways of living in the world as a sexual/ized subject.

Science fiction – especially literary science fiction, the focus of this collection – is intimately concerned with the question of how people live in the world and what makes the world livable for them. Often sf answers these questions – or extends the sequence of interrogation – by postulating alternative (often future) societies and cultures, affected by alternative, perhaps foreseeable, alterations in science and technology. These science-fictional 'thought experiments' in alterity coincide with critical theory along a number of axes.[3] As a subgenre of sf, for example, cyberpunk fiction and its progeny are both informed by and often resistant to Haraway's feminist cyborg theory and other contemporary work on the meanings of bodies and sexualities, including theorizations of the posthuman; lesbian and gay sf exists in perpetual dialogue with non-essentializing modes of conceptualizing sexuality within the genre; writers such as Samuel R. Delany, Nalo Hopkinson, and Hiromi Goto, whose texts are both racialized and sexualized, deploy complex narrative techniques that limit the usefulness of simplistic readings of their works along a single line of inquiry. The result is a field that is coming to understand that knowledge of social systems and ontological questions is as necessary to any conception of alternative (future) societies as is knowledge of science and technology per se. At the same time, in keeping with its epistemological mandate, science fiction continues to explore the increasingly complex and influential role of technoscience in the construction of both individual subjects and social structures.

There has not been, to date, any truly significant efflorescence of research into sexuality in sf, although there is by now a very notable body of published research about gender in sf, developed for the most part through feminist criticism and through studies of the roles of women and women authors in the field.[4] In contrast, the only anthologies of critical work on sexuality in science fiction were published more than twenty years ago; these are editor Donald Palumbo's *Erotic Universe: Sexuality and Fantastic Literature* (1986) and *Eros in the Mind's Eye: Sexuality and the Fantastic in Art and Film* (1986). The most comprehensive published body of work on alternative sexualities in science fiction to date has been Eric Garber and Lyn Paleo's *Uranian Worlds: A Guide to Alternative Sexuality in Science Fiction, Fantasy, and Horror* (1983; rev. 1990), an annotated bibliography that includes both positive and negative representations of homosexuality and bisexuality in a wide variety of genre texts. Since the mid-1980s, however, only rarely have there been any substantial attempts to focus on alternative sexualities in science fiction.[5] One of the consequences of this lacuna has been that, as with the study of race in sf, there has been a break between those who approach sexuality in sf texts bearing in mind both the history of sf and of sf criticism and those who come to the work of individual sf authors from other fields, such as African American or lesbian and gay studies. It is our hope that *Queer Universes* will help to bring these various textual approaches into dialogue with each other.

This volume brings together an array of discussions about genders and sexualities by writer/scholars and scholar/readers with a broad range of expertise in the sf field. Their diverse readings are influenced not only by queer theory, but also by feminist theory, postcolonial theory, lesbian and gay studies, critical race studies, and a variety of other critical tools for interrogating the topic. Some of the articles are historical, aimed at recuperating a history of sexual representation that has, to date, largely been obscured by the widespread impression that there was no sex in science fiction in a past usually conceived as a 'Golden Age' of innocent childhood (even for its adult readers). Other articles are contemporary in focus, examining the ways in which current writers of sf respond both to popular cultural apprehensions and to academic investigations of sexuality. We have grouped these discussions into four sections. The first of these, 'Queering the Scene', centres around Pearson's 'Alien Cryptographies', a careful mapping of some of the ways in which queer theoretical perspectives can intersect with a range of sf texts to produce new readings of science fiction that are both relevant and suggestive. The figure of the alien, not surprisingly, is at the centre of Pearson's (re)-reading, which includes detailed analyses of two very different treatments of the alien/queer as the figure who moves invisibly through the territories of heteronormativity: John W. Campbell's 'Who Goes There?' (1938) and Tom Reamy's 'Under the Hollywood Sign' (1975). This section also presents an essay/dialogue by critically acclaimed writers Nicola Griffith and Kelley Eskridge, 'War Machine, Time Machine', in which they look backwards to recall their various discoveries of both science fiction and queer identities and forwards to their own trajectories as readers and writers of (sometimes transgressive) science fictions about genders and sexualities and subjectivities.

Our second section, 'Un/Doing History', looks at some moments in the history of sf through the lens of contemporary critical approaches to sexuality. In 'Sextrapolation in New Wave Science Fiction', Rob Latham investigates the new emphasis on 'adult' narrative in sf of the 1960s and 1970s, opening with the challenge of the New Wave's pre-eminent editor, Judith Merril, who contended in 1966 that it is 'long past time for some of the same kind of hard-headed speculative thinking that science fiction contributed to space flight and atomics to be done in [the areas of] interpersonal psychology and sexology' ('Books' 26). In 'Towards a Queer Genealogy of SF', Wendy Gay Pearson investigates the possibilities for constructing a queer genealogy of sf in order to unsettle 'the empire of certainty' (Greyson, *Zero Patience*) established by an enlightenment episteme which values particular forms of rationality, history, science and knowledge. Pearson argues that, 'If we focus on the ways in which much queer work relies on various attempts to examine what it means to be human and to have a livable life, concerns that, given the contemporary episteme cannot help but be inflected by questions of gender and sexuality, then our genealogy must draw widely from both fictional and critical/academic work' (99). The third essay in this section, Guy Davidson's 'Sexuality and the Statistical Imaginary', offers a detailed reading of Delany's classic 'ambiguous heterotopia' *Triton* (a.k.a. *Trouble on Triton*, 1976) as 'an exemplary postmodern document' about the proliferation of sexual desires in the context of contemporary capitalism. Davidson's argument is that the 'increased flexibility of capital is correlated with an increased flexibility in modes of selfhood. In *Triton*, plasticity of identities and desires is also a central feature of the future world that Delany renders with characteristic vividness and intelligence' (101). Finally, Graham J.

Murphy proposes a queer reading of some well-known cyberpunk fiction, notably William Gibson's classic *Neuromancer* (1984). Although cyberpunk has traditionally been read as an especially heteronormative and masculinist genre, Murphy argues – taking account of Judith Butler's discussion about the ideological defensiveness of heteronormative penetration – that the 'stray penetration' recurrent in Gibson's novels induces a heteronormative 'systems crash' in these exemplary cyberpunk fictions.

Our third section, 'Disordering Desires', opens with Veronica Hollinger's 'Something Like a Fiction', which considers a range of sf stories, from the 1930s to the present, in which sexuality intersects with, is framed by, and/or incorporates the technological, especially as these intersections have been allegorized in the figure of the cyborg. In particular, Hollinger's discussion valorizes Joanna Russ's great lesbian-feminist satire *The Female Man* as 'a novel about conjunctures, intersections, and sexual encounters that are monstrous, hybrid, perverse, and – above all – political' (152). In 'And How Many Souls Do You Have?', Patricia Melzer investigates the way in which technologies of the body enable sexual alterities in the erotic sf anthologies edited by Cecilia Tan. Tan's anthologies bring together a diverse collection of writers whose stories construct versions of the technobody in order to literalize the scenarios of sadomasochism, bondage and discipline, and a variety of other non-normative sexual practices. Melzer examines 'how technology denaturalizes not only bodies (and thus gender), but also sexual *desires* and practices' (164). The third essay in this section is Sylvie Bérard's 'BDSMSF(QF): Sadomasochistic Readings of Québécois Women's Science Fiction'. Bérard's contemplation of the polymorphous perversity of feminist sf writers – in this case, three contemporary Québec writers – concludes that, 'as they write and expose their most intimate and extreme images and fantasies, these writers place themselves in the same state of vulnerability that they impose on their characters when they throw them onto the stage of a fictive BDSM performance' (196).[6] Bérard develops her ideas about speculative sexualities at the intersections of embodiment and performance, representation and discourse.

The final section in *Queer Universes* is 'Embodying New Worlds'. The interview and two essays in this section concentrate on the impossibility of disentangling discourses of sexuality from those of race and gender in the imaginative effort to construct desirable futures. Nancy Johnston interviews Nalo Hopkinson, a Caribbean-Canadian sf writer whose novels, short stories, and edited anthologies have attracted much critical acclaim in the past decade. In their lively and provocative conversation, Hopkinson illuminates some of the ways in which, in Johnston's words, she 'employs myth, archetype, speculation, and potential technologies to imagine worlds where her characters can transform or transcend their bodies and invent futures where individuals are not alienated by race, colour, sex, gender, or class' (202). In the first of the two essays in this section, 'Queering Nature', Helen Merrick takes a step beyond the queering of human or even human–alien relationships to examine how queer ecofeminist theory provides a productive reading strategy for feminist sf texts in which 'nature' itself is denaturalized. Concentrating on two novels by Amy Thomson, *The Color of Distance* (1995) and *Through Alien Eyes* (1999), Merrick re-visits 'the loaded space of "the natural"' in order to 'consider how "queering nature" might further question normative notions of sexuality and gender' (216). In the final essay of the collection, De Witt Douglas Kilgore asks, 'Must any future order, whether on Mars or elsewhere, recapitulate a racialized heteronormativity? Can we imagine a peaceful and just society only as the outcome of a reproductive order that requires a firmly rooted hierarchy of racial and sexual identities?' (233). He finds some answers in an examination of the utopian trope of 'the coming race' in Kim Stanley Robinson's *Mars* trilogy (1993–97). Robinson's fiction takes the reader back to queer theory's challenge to read the racialization and gendering of bodies as inseparable from their sexualization, yet, at the same time, his trilogy moves towards a utopic vision of a future in which the painful limitations of the protagonists' present produce future alterities that cannot be so easily controlled by discursive or ideological strategies. As Kilgore concludes, we do not find the future in Robinson's trilogy; 'instead we discover a text that invites us to dream of escaping from heteronormative whiteness' (249). And we get an inkling of how a queer futurity might be lived.

All the essays and articles here are informed by queer perspectives, even as some of these discussions look at queer sex, some at straight sex, and some at forms of sexuality that cannot be contained by that binary, including sadomasochism and BDSM. All are informed by the proposition that the ways in which we understand sexuality shape every aspect of culture, both 'real' and speculative. None assumes that there can be any one sex/uality that is the norm in human affective relations, in spite of the discourses of normative heterosexuality that insist otherwise. Locating queer theory as a challenge to heteronormative epistemologies, Pearson has insisted on its commonalities with science fiction, as both historical and contemporary practice:

> sf has a long history, dating back at least to Mary Shelley's *Frankenstein*, of questioning systems of thought, particularly those we now label metanarratives (science, history, and so on), even as it appears to – and sometimes does – valorize notions of scientific method, objectivity, and

> progress. Queer, with its denaturalization of master narratives and its movement towards subcultural and subaltern understandings of texts, operates, by analogy, on some of the same levels as does sf. ('Alien Cryptographies' 18)

Some of these intersections of queer theory and speculation are our focus in the pieces that follow.

Notes

1. In this particular case, Iran also violated an international law which prohibits the execution of people who were minors when the crime was committed, a law to which Iran is a signatory.
2. The most famous of these statements was made by Jerry Falwell in a broadcast with Pat Robertson. Falwell's exact words were 'I really believe that the pagans, and the abortionists, and the feminists, and the gays and the lesbians who are actively trying to make that an alternative lifestyle, the ACLU, People For the American Way – all of them who have tried to secularize America – I point the finger in their face and say "you helped this happen"'. ActUP NY has a transcript of this conversation at http://www.actupny.org/YELL/falwell.html.
3. See, for example, the substantial arguments developed by Carl Freedman in his *Critical Theory and Science Fiction* (2000).
4. Some of the best recent studies include Brian Attebery's *Decoding Gender in Science Fiction* (2002), Jane Donawerth's *Frankenstein's Daughters* (1997), and Justine Larbalestier's *The Battle of the Sexes in Science Fiction* (2002).
5. We have already mentioned *SFS*'s special section 'On Science Fiction and Queer Theory'; the Autumn 2002 special issue of *Foundation: The International Review of Science Fiction* on 'Gay and Lesbian Science Fiction' is also noteworthy.
6 'BDSM' is a polysemic acronym, including references to bondage and discipline and to domination and submission, as well as to sadomasochism.

Part I

Queering the Scene

Alien Cryptographies: The View from Queer

Wendy Gay Pearson

> Fiction, then, can be divided according to the manner in which men's relationships to other men and their surroundings are illuminated. If this is accomplished by endeavoring faithfully to reproduce empirical surfaces and textures vouched for by human senses and common sense, I propose to call it *naturalistic fiction*. If, on the contrary, an endeavor is made to illuminate such relations by creating a radically or significantly different formal framework… I propose to call it *estranged fiction*.
>
> — Darko Suvin, *Metamorphoses of Science Fiction* 18

1. Introduction: Fear of a Queer Galaxy

On November 25, 1998, the memberships of the USS Harvey Milk and the Voyager Visibility Project (offshoots of the lesbian and gay sf group, the Gaylaxians) issued a call for a boycott of the then soon-to-be-released *Star Trek: Insurrection*. After nearly two decades of lobbying the producers of the various *Star Trek* shows and movies for the inclusion of a lesbian or gay character[1] in a cast intended to represent all types of humans (including a variety of racial and ethnic types, as well as both sexes[2]) and quite a miscellany of aliens, the group's membership has finally, it seems, had enough. Curious as it might seem at first glance, sf shows seem to be the last hold-outs in a medium that is rapidly accommodating itself to the idea that there really are lesbian and gay people in the 'real' world that television claims, however peculiarly, to reflect (in precisely that mode that Suvin labels 'naturalistic').

Spokespeople for the Voyager Visibility Project note, trenchantly enough, that despite the addition of visible lesbian and gay characters to non-sf television shows, 'it is just as important as ever to show that gays and lesbians will exist and will be accepted in the future'. The heteronormative assumptions behind much science fiction, both cinematic and literary, are very neatly exposed by the circular reasoning with which the producers of *Star Trek* reject demands for visibly non-straight characters: homophobia, they say, does not exist in the future as it is shown on *Star Trek*; gay characters therefore cannot be shown, since to introduce the issue of homosexuality is to turn it back into a problem; in order for *Star Trek* to depict a non-homophobic view of the future, it must depict a universe with no homosexuals in it.[3] Clearly, logic is not a prerequisite for would-be television gurus.

Nevertheless, while I certainly acknowledge that a visible gay or lesbian character on the cast of a *Star Trek* show would be a politically astute move for those whose day-to-day politics are focused on an inclusionary, rights-based approach to ameliorating the conditions in which lesbian and gay people live, it is worth asking whether the inclusion of a gay character on a show that presupposes an already heteronormative view of the human future can be said to 'queer' that future in any significant way. If a lesbian officer is shown on the bridge, for instance, or a gay male couple is shown holding hands on the holodeck, either might certainly be an instance of 'cognitive estrangement' (to borrow Suvin's term) for many audience members, but neither instance would necessarily be queer. Of course, the producers will have to use a little – and one might suggest that it would only take a very little – imagination in showing us that their new lieutenant, shall we say, is lesbian, without making her sexuality into a 'problem'.

Moving from a consideration of *Star Trek* to sf in general, I suggest that the presence of a lesbian or gay character, while not *per se* a radical or subversive strategy, may change one thing, for a particular reader, the reader who is unused to – and is perhaps searching for – a gay/lesbian presence within sf. In this case, the naturalization of a lesbian or gay character within a plot that has nothing explicitly to do with sexuality may, temporarily, function as a *novum* for this reader, just as the incidental revelation in Heinlein's *Starship Troopers* of Johnny Rico's blackness did for Samuel Delany.[4] In this case it is not so much the character as the character's environment that produces cognitive estrangement, since the character goes unremarked within his world and is not marked as different, either racially in the case of Rico or sexually in the case of our putative gay/lesbian character. It is precisely this revelation that the Voyager Visibility Project wishes the producers of *Star Trek* to provide for its viewers: the vision of a future in which queerness is neither hidden nor revealed *as difference*, but is simply there. Given the ubiquity of political, religious, and social commitment to the continual reinscription of heteronormative 'family values', this strategy may be queerer and more subversive than one might at first think.[5]

For the remainder of this essay, I want to explore what might be implied when one combines the terms 'queer theory' and 'science fiction'. This contemplation will circulate around two quite different strategic interventions of 'queer' into the world of sf – one is the performance of a 'queer reading' and the other is the recognition of a 'queer text'. In speaking of queer readings, I want to make it clear that this is not necessarily a strategy most usefully applied to already queer texts; similarly, I want to suggest that the inclusion of gay and lesbian characters or issues does not make a text queer. The answer to my earlier question – what *would* queer *Star Trek*? – presumes, then, a movement beyond the inclusionary towards a radical re-writing of the assumption within the show of the naturalness, endurance, and fixity of our current understandings of sexuality and its relationship both to the sex/gender dyad and to sociocultural institutions. To return to my *Star Trek* example one final time, the portrayal of a marriage between, say, Lieutenant Tom Paris and Ensign Harry Kim would certainly be gay – probably in both senses of the word – but it would not necessarily be queer.

What, exactly, do I mean by 'queer?' Or, as an esteemed elderly colleague of mine was heard to say, after reading my partner's MA thesis proposal, 'Isn't queer a bad word?' Of course, queer *is* a bad word. Despite the particular joy with which both academics[6] and activists (often they are the same people) have reappropriated it, for the majority of gays and lesbians 'queer' is still an insult, too often accompanied by bottles, fists, or the blows of a baseball bat. Because queer theory is a politically engaged form of academic work, most people immersed in the field are only too conscious of the ethical implications of this reappropriation. Queer resonates not only with its pejorative usage, but also with its mundane connotations – odd, strange, eccentric. In fact, the first definition in my dictionary explains it as 'deviating from the expected or normal'. Any attempt to define 'queer' within a postmodernist theoretical milieu must take into account the context through which we come to understand this deviation: is the deviation itself a misunderstanding by society at large of the fact that we are all human, that lesbians and gays deviate from the normal *only* in terms of our choice of romantic and sexual partners, a difference which is itself understood in this formulation as minor, even inconsequential? Or does queer deviate from the 'normal' in ways that are radical and subversive, dedicated to exposing and challenging an ideologized teleology that reaches beyond sexual attraction to reveal the deeply un-natural and constructed nature of our understandings of biological sex, the performative nature of gender roles, and the sociocultural institutions founded upon this ideology? Or, to put it in its simplest possible terms, is queer a politics of identity or a politics of difference?[7]

My answer to this question is dependent on my own sense of where queer comes from: a dissatisfaction with both the universalizing (all gays are alike) *and* the segregating (gay men and lesbians are different) style of 'identity politics' influenced by an ethnic model of gayness; the late twentieth century's intellectual shift to a more contingent, discursive, and localized understanding of the production of knowledge; and AIDS. The construction in the West of AIDS as a disease identified with homosexuality and the concomitant rise of an overt and death-dealing homophobic discourse reinforced the existing tendencies towards political engagement and consciousness on the part of those theorists, critics, and activists whose work has been gathered under the rubric of queer – even when that term has not always been used by the individuals themselves. Nevertheless, queer remains, both within the academy and among gays and lesbians in general, very much a contested term. As Annamarie Jagose points out in her survey of queer theory's origins and meanings: 'Given the extent of its commitment to denaturalization, queer itself can have neither a foundational logic nor a consistent set of characteristics' (96). Queer's very slipperiness, however, its tendency towards instability and its pleasure in resisting attempts to make sexuality signify in monolithic ways, are all parts of its appeal. Furthermore, queer suggests a move not just towards a different conception of sexuality, but also towards a different understanding of subjectivity and agency. Lee Edelman notes, in 'The Mirror and the Tank', that

> [to] the extent that we are capable of identifying those junctures where the gay subjectivity we seek to produce recapitulates the oppressive logic of the culture that necessitated its emergence, we have the chance to displace that logic and begin to articulate the range of options for what might *become* a postmodern subject; we have the chance, in other words, to challenge, as Andreas Huyssen suggests postmodernism must, '*the ideology of the subject* (as male, white, and middle-class [and we must add, as he does not, heterosexual]) by developing alternate and different notions of subjectivity'. (111)

How, we might ask, does sf allow us to develop alternative notions of subjectivity? What practices of representation have developed within the genre to allow for the expression of a subject who is not male, white, middle-class, and heterosexual? To see the potential within the genre for postmodern and, specifically, queer subjects, we need only look at the works of Samuel R. Delany and Joanna Russ. As with each of these writers, sf provides for the potential queer author more than a possible field in which to represent an alternative subjectivity. Its very popularity, its resistance to interpellation within the 'mundane' field of literature, provides tools for the author who wishes to avoid the dangers of mimesis that have typically hampered gay and lesbian writing in the naturalist mode. The Cartesian subject of realist fiction always risks reincorporation back into a naturalized and faithful reproduction of 'empirical surfaces and textures vouched for by human senses and common sense' (Suvin 18).

Furthermore, sf has a long history, dating back at least to Mary Shelley's *Frankenstein* (1818), of questioning systems of thought, particularly those we now label metanarratives (science, history, and so on), even as it appears to – and sometimes does – valorize notions of scientific method, objectivity, and progress. Queer, with its denaturalization of master narratives and its movement towards subcultural and subaltern understandings of texts, operates, by analogy, on some of the same levels as sf. As Earl Jackson points out, '*Science fiction* offers a tradition of representational formalization of a worldview in which the subject is not the cause but the effect of the system that sustains it' (102; emphasis in original). This insistence that the subject is the effect of the system neatly recapitulates the imbrication of alternative narrative strategies with dissident subjectivities, with a refusal of the Cartesian subject. This resonates for me with precisely the strategic rationale behind Samuel Delany's call to resist attempts to reclaim sf as 'literature'. In Jackson's words,

> Delany's theoretical blueprints for and his own examples of the kind of critical fiction that the science fiction writer can achieve revalorizes the 'fictive'. The specific importance Delany places on the paraliterary differences of the genre at once constitute a challenge...to the dominant obfuscating obsession with 'authenticity', while providing eloquent theoretical grounding for that challenge as well as for textual practices that prioritize specification over referentiality, the production of meaning over the repetition of 'Truth'. It is science fiction's foundational infidelity to the 'real world' that affords the fictive world the status of a critical model. (125)[8]

In the remainder of this essay – which is literally *un essai*, an attempt, to see how sf and queer may illuminate each other – I hope to bring some of this 'theoretical grounding' to bear on the actual practice of sf as it has evolved over the twentieth century. In so doing, I am going to suggest a variety of models for understanding the intersections of queer with sf at the level of the text. These may include, first, the sf narrative that is not overtly queer, but that can be read analogically within a specific historical context and sensibility; second, what one might call the 'proto-queer' text that, although not queer itself, effects a kind of discursive challenge to the naturalized understanding of sexuality and its concomitant sociocultural surround; third, the text that is coded as queer, but in such a way as to hide in plain sight – this is the narrative equivalent of the 'open secret', the one which everybody knows, but no one wishes to call attention to, at least not within the specific historico-cultural milieu in which it was written; and finally, the overtly queer text, the text which questions the 'naturalist fiction' that sex and gender and sexuality are matters of 'human senses and common sense'.

While this list may have the appearance of being categorical and complete, I want to insist that these 'categories' are nothing more than tentative and temporary attempts, readings-in-process of a subject (and subject matter) that is itself in process. None of these readings, then, is necessarily authoritative, nor can they take place outside a historical and cultural context, since what is hidden from one audience is plainly visible to another, and what can easily be seen from one perspective is indecipherable from another viewpoint. Like 'queer' itself, my discursive strategy in this essay will require movement backwards as well as forwards, will prove on occasion slippery and even fractured in its attempt at narrative, and will remain, no doubt, contestatory and contested.

2. (E)strange(d) Fictions: Who Goes There?

> Each of us with an eye on the other to make sure he doesn't do something – peculiar. Man, aren't we going to be a trusting bunch! Each man eyeing his neighbors with the grandest exhibition of faith and trust – I'm beginning to know what Connant meant by 'I wish you could see your eyes'. Every now and then we all have it, I guess. One of you looks around with a sort of 'I-wonder-if-the-other-*three*-are-look'.
>
> — John W. Campbell, Jr, 'Who Goes There?' (108)

I once asked my science-fiction class, during a seminar discussion of *The Left Hand of Darkness* (1969), whether they could draw any parallels between the construction in the novel of Estraven as a traitor[9] and the history, recent at the time Ursula Le Guin wrote the novel, of the House Committee for Un-American Activities. What, they responded, was a House Committee for Un-American Activities? I asked if any of them knew who Joseph McCarthy was – and received eighteen perfectly blank looks. What did the phrase 'commie pinko queer' mean? Well, they could parse parts of it – 'commie' was a communist and 'queer' was, well, you know – but they could not put the parts together. What could being communist possibly have to do with being gay, or vice versa? And what did either have to do with *The Left Hand of Darkness*?

Queer how things have changed, isn't it? And now – belatedly – I should warn you that discussions like this, of sexuality and particularly of sexuality in the context of the fluidity and semantic sensitivity of queer theory, inevitably lead to bad puns and worse jokes. The stories invoked within the complex field of attempting to understand how we exist in the world as sexual beings are fraught with *double entendres*, contradictions, misapprehensions, and (un)faithful reiterations – so much so that one might, in fact, be tempted to agree with Leo Bersani when he argues that, at heart, most people really do not like sex (95). Certainly we fear its power, just as we fear being exposed as different. But unlike the differences of race and biological sex, sexual difference is often invisible.[10]

I would like to offer, as my first example of a possible application of queer theory to sf, a reading of John W. Campbell's classic 'Who Goes There?'(1938) against the cultural anxiety that enveloped ideas about homosexuality in the era surrounding World War II. At its height, this anxiety was related to a widespread desire to return to a vision of pre-war morality and lifestyle,[11] in part by persuading women to return to the home, and in part by repudiating a practice of unspoken but official tolerance – within fairly strict limits – for gays and lesbians in the military and in government service.[12] The backlash was spectacular, exacerbated as it was in most of the Western world by both xenophobia and anti-communist propaganda. It is also one of those historical events that exhibits particularly well the imbrication of misogyny and homophobia: both the women and the queers had to be put back in their place. At the same time, the need to reassert heteronormativity was reflected in cultural production by a proliferation, particularly within sf, of both stories and movies which demonized the Other – already a prevalent theme within the genre. While these sf tales are normally viewed as allegories of the dangers of communism, they can also be read as warnings of the dangers of homosexuality to the emergent nuclear family: whereas in Nazi Germany, the Jew and the homosexual were metonymically the same person,[13] in the US and Canada, the communist and the homosexual were seen as representing so clear and present a danger to the American way of life as to render them virtually indistinguishable.[14]

However, in order to carry out such a policy, or to police it, one must be able to identify 'the enemy'. Women, except for the occasional passing butch, were relatively easily identified. But how does one recognize a 'homosexual'? The problem of how to identify the alien in our midst, the queer who could pass, remained fraught both for governmental institutions and for 'ordinary' people. Lee Edelman, in his study of the discursive contradictions underwriting the conceptualization of sexuality in this time period, points to the ways in which, on the one hand, queerness was envisioned as always already written on the body, while, at the same time, queers were feared in part because of their ability to 'pass' ('Tearooms and Sympathy' 151–56).

Under these circumstances, it is hardly surprising to find a proliferation of stories and films fixated on the danger of the alien who is able to assume human guise and travel unseen amongst us, wreaking havoc on the nation and destroying the family. Among films, Don Siegel's *Invasion of the Body Snatchers* (1956) is probably the best known, although the first film version of Campbell's story, retitled *The Thing* (1951), certainly merits an honourable mention. Just as *Frankenstein*'s tale of the monster created from within can be read in a multitude of ways that focus on the revelation of different kinds of monstrous births – in at least one of which it can be read as an originary story about the parent's, especially the father's, fear of producing a queer child (queer as different serving always synecdochically to bring into view queer as *sexually* different) – so 'Who Goes There?' serves as a near perfect example of the way in which the story of the alien who passes as human derives from the precise confluence of anxieties that serve to claim, *at the same time*, that homosexuality is always written on the body and that it is always able to pass.

In 'Who Goes There?' the alien – and a very nasty alien it is, too, with an immutable drive to conquest that may be part guilty imperialist conscience and part fear of the Other – has been frozen into the ice of Antarctica for twenty million years. A team of researchers finds the alien ship, retrieves the solitary frozen specimen, and sets out to thaw and study the apparent corpse. That the alien is not innocently dead is presaged by the dreams of various members of the all-male team; even frozen, it appears to be able to exert some sort of telepathic and perhaps suggestive pressure on the human mind, luring men into unconsciously betraying both themselves and their species.

The revived alien takes over the bodies of other species, merging with them and consuming their physical being, so that each in turn becomes the Other. The alien imitation of the 'normal' man is so perfect, however, that it remains undetectable by all the tests that the men are initially able to devise. They know that some of them have become monsters, but they do not know which. The threat is internalized, as all of these apparently human males are involved, one way or another, in a race to discover a test that will reveal (that is, make visible) the monstrosity lurking in the guise of human before the alien is able to muster enough strength to escape Antarctica and conquer the remainder of the planet. The tone throughout the story is minatory, every scene replete with the unseen but omnipresent threat: 'An air of crushing menace entered into every man's body, sharply they looked at each other. More keenly than ever before – *is that man next to me an inhuman monster?*' (118).

The conversion from human to alien is figured in bodily terms that are reminiscent of the sexual act. The men, caught in the monster's gaze, are passive victims of its alien seductions – Connant, for example, stares into the living red eyes of what is supposed to be a corpse but it seems to him 'of no more importance than the labored, slow motion of the tentacular things that sprouted from the base of the scrawny, slowly pulsing neck' (95); he puts up no resistance, psychological or physical, to his absorption by the alien. The actual moment of alien takeover is never shown to us, taking place discreetly 'off camera'; yet it is figured in terms of both consumption and consummation: the alien inserts a part of its substance into the men, taking them over completely. Contacts with identifiable versions of the alien are depicted in terms of violence of very specific types: the men burn it with a fiery probe, they fall upon it and virtually tear it to pieces which they then cauterize, and they attack Blair – the first convert and last survivor – with yet another equivalent of the red-hot poker:[15]

> The huge blowtorch McReady had brought coughed solemnly. Abruptly it rumbled disapproval throatily. Then it laughed gurglingly, and thrust out a blue-white, three-foot tongue. The Thing on the floor shrieked, flailed out blindly... crawled and howled. (123)

The alien seduces men into submission to its will and then uses their appropriated bodies as the means by which to assimilate the remaining men. The men, some of whom are already aliens in disguise, argue about its imitative abilities, concluding that a perfect imitation 'would take a superhuman skill':

> 'It would do no good', said Dr. Cooper, softly as though thinking out loud, 'to merely look like something it was trying to imitate; it would have to understand its feelings, its reactions. It *is* unhuman; it has powers of imitation beyond any conception of man... no [human] actor could imitate so perfectly as to deceive men who had been living with the imitated one in the complete lack of privacy of an antarctic camp'. (102)

The fear of the perfect imitation, undetectable even within an environment as intimate as the camp, resonates with the fear that the gay male can imitate 'real' men so perfectly as to pass undetected in the most masculine of environments. The imitation should be detectable – written on the body of the gay man pretending to be straight – yet he remains undetectable within the military, the government, and – most frightening of all – the family.[16]

The alien is also unable to reproduce and is portrayed as having, by necessity, to recruit its forces by converting the normal in literally physical ways – consumption and appropriation – into the monstrous. In addition, what gives the monstrous alien away in the end is its selfishness, the one thing that distinguishes it from the valorous altruism of real humans. McReady explains that every part of the alien is a whole – even its blood once it is split off – with the result that, being too selfish to sacrifice itself for the good of the species, the new part will strive to preserve itself: 'the *blood* will live – and try to crawl away from a hot needle'.[17] There is a resonance here with the populist conception of the gay man as selfish, a conception which may have arisen, in part, because he is seen as refusing to share his genes and perform his male role in perpetuating the species, but which may also be partially a bowdlerization of Freud's theories of the role of narcissism in the psychosocial construction of the male homosexual.

Not only is there an extremely dark homoerotic tone underwriting both the construction of and the threat against this closed all-male society (traditionally the one environment in which homosexual activity is most likely to take place among men who do not define themselves as gay), but the threat is also conceived in terms that replicate the particular rhetoric with which the heteronormative forces of the political and religious right have chosen to characterize the threat of the (male) homosexual: he is endlessly but inexplicably seductive; he cannot reproduce and so must convert in order to continue his species; he is the monster who comes from within, since he is, by necessity, produced by apparently normal heterosexuals; and he is able to vanish and to remain nearly undetectable, free to work his wiles against all of those institutions Americans hold most dear.[18]

There are powerful resonances between the historical understanding of dissident sexuality, particularly homosexuality, from the turn of the twentieth century through to the beginning of the gay liberation movement and the construction of the alien in this story. Nevertheless, I do not mean to suggest that this reading of the story is necessarily more authoritative than or precludes other potential readings. It does serve, I think, as a useful example of how that peculiar, imprecise thing we have come to call 'queer theory' can illuminate the connections between, on the one hand, a particular perspective on our sexual ontology and its origins and, on the other, an sf story about the dangers of aliens who can pass invisibly in the midst of 'normal' people. Not surprisingly, it is Blair, the first alien convert, who argues for a viewpoint not based on an attempt to naturalize a normative ideological formation, when he tells the other men that they 'are displaying that childish human weakness of hating the different' (94). Given the events of the story, 'hating the different' would appear to be just what the doctor ordered.

3. Alien Nation: Visualizing the (In)Visible

> [It] is a central purpose of art, in conjunction with criticism, to expand the realm of conscious choice and enlarge the domain of the ego. It does this by making manifest what was latent, a process that can be resisted, but not easily reversed. And so even those who dislike what I have had to say may yet find it useful as a warning of how things appear to other eyes...
>
> — Thomas M. Disch, 'Embarrassments of Science Fiction' 155

Cultural constructions of visibility operate like magic: they make certain things disappear, or appear only in very particular contexts. Let me tell you a story. Once, about a decade ago, on a long and boring car ride with a young woman I scarcely knew, I found myself running out of topics of conversation. It was all too obvious that everything that interested me bored her. Her descriptions of her fiancé, on the other hand, bored me, but might, I thought, at least give us some commonality on an aesthetic level. So, as we waited at a stop light, I pointed out a particularly lovely young man. She perked up, gazed in the direction of my pointing finger, and finally said, with much puzzlement, 'Where?'

'Right there,' I said, 'at the bus stop.'

'I don't see anyone.'

'Sure you do – that good-looking black guy...'

And at that moment I looked at her blonde hair and contemplated the story of her Norwegian husband-to-be and finally figured it out.

You see, now I've told you a story. It is one that functions – as sf itself often does – on the level of analogy. On an academic and intellectual level, we are generally conscious – I hope – of race and racial issues. It is no longer completely improbable to us that a young white woman, someone who probably would describe herself as not at all racist, would be unable to see a young black man in this context.[19] We understand this story. It is less clear to me that we – that is, all of us – understand the other story, the one by which queer people in plain sight escape the heterosexual or, perhaps more precisely, the heteronormative gaze. This is the other half of the story: while 'Who Goes There?' replicates the concern with the gay man (or lesbian) who 'passes' invisibly within the larger society, other queer people, their history and their cultural production, remain invisible and unrecognized, even when that invisibility comes at the cost of a wilful act of blindness.

Now I can theorize this peculiarity of the heteronormative gaze in reference to feminist theorizing of the gaze[20] itself or – in a useful analogy to heteronormativity – to work by people like Richard Dyer on the visual and cultural meanings of whiteness, or to the larger discursive strategies of post-colonial theory. Furthermore, I can also explain the invisibility of queerness within the text, specifically, by reference to the work of critics and theorists such as Alan Sinfield, who have laboured to make visible the invisible and to demonstrate the usefulness and importance of reading from a subcultural position, whether it be queer or racial, ethnic or gendered, a matter of class or location. Such theoretical constructions are useful, perhaps essential, to what I'm calling queer theory, since they help to explain the seemingly quixotic inability of heteronormative institutions (which largely includes academia itself and also, I'm sorry to say, often includes sf, both readers and critics) to see anything queer in a text, an image, or the world itself.

Thus, on the one hand, a queer reading can be a reading against the grain, where one looks at a text from what is clearly a subcultural position: often that involves reading the text through the cultural and historical milieu in which it is written; that milieu is not, however, understood in hegemonic terms, but rather through the historical and sociocultural perspectives afforded by the reader's subculture. On the other hand, a queer reading may set out either to reveal or to recuperate what is already in some sense a queer text, usually a product of a history in which writing as a gay man or as a lesbian was impossible or dangerous. Such queer readings also provide alternative understandings of texts that cannot be labelled gay or lesbian, since those subject positions were not available to their creators. Thus, for example, we queer certain, indeed many, Renaissance texts. This does not, however, imply that their authors are 'queer' or gay/lesbian or even homosexual, since those categories are all modern; it does imply, though, that we can recognize within the texts the traces of an alternative or dissident sexual subjectivity that may be revealed through close and careful reading within both a historical context and a theoretical framework. Such a reading is delineated, for example, by Earl Jackson when he attempts to map the strategies by which deviant subjectivities can be represented within the text. Jackson notes the necessity for a decoding practice, a cryptography of the text, which is historically contingent:

> Like the Renaissance sodomite, the nineteenth-century 'Uranian' relied on phallocentric mythographs of masculine self-overestimation to disguise his fantasies – he sought a visibility through which he could remain unseen. This defense allowed the writers or artists to elude surveillance while conveying their hidden meanings to those whose desires enabled them to read the codes. (51)

While it is possible to argue both that such subterfuge was historically necessary – and may still be necessary for those desiring to have their work commercially published, at least in some fields – and that it was a self-defeating strategy in terms of a nascent homosexual identity politics, such encrypting of meaning should not be understood as necessarily subversive. Both Sinfield and Jackson note the containment by hegemonic forces of coded texts: one can be a little subversive so long as one remains below the synaptic threshold at which the dominant regime is forced to take notice. Furthermore, as Jackson notes, 'Although the perverse resignification of dominant masculine iconography provided a cryptography for an "outlaw" community, its mimesis of patriarchal autoaffection was too well executed to disturb the dominant meanings of those expressions' (51).

The mimetic reproduction of a hegemonic vision of the world is itself a historically contingent process, in the sense that codes that are indecipherable to one decade or age or to one set of people may become obvious to another. Thus, for example, we have masculinist readings of the stories of James Tiptree, Jr – Alice Sheldon's male pseudonym and alter ego – that are wholly lacking in irony. Tiptree was praised for 'his' understanding of the male psyche and texts that, to us, are not only obviously but almost paradigmatically feminist were understood totally within the domain of a reading practice that rendered women invisible. Tiptree's works were not only not read as feminist but were defined – and not only by Robert Silverberg, although he seems to have been the only person unfortunate enough to put what appear to have been widely held opinions in print – as arising from a clearly masculine understanding of the world. Not only does Silverberg refer to Tiptree's prose (having, ironically, just cited 'The Women Men Don't See') as 'lean, muscular, supple', but he also insists that 'there is, too, that prevailing masculinity about both [Hemingway and Tiptree] – that preoccupation with questions of courage, with absolute values, with the mysteries and passions of life and death as revealed by extreme physical tests, by pain and suffering and loss' (xv). Men, it seems, did not see *any* of the women in 'The Women Men Don't See'.

In a not dissimilar way, purely feminist readings of 'Houston, Houston, Do You Read?' may not account for, or have any interest in, either the necessary lesbianism of these future women or the construction of the Andys as transgendered. Andy is variously described, mostly by Bud, the sexually aggressive male (of the three, one of the others is figured as a patriarch – literally, the name of the father – and the other, the narrator, is probably homosexual), as 'a boy', as having 'no balls at all', as 'a dyke', and as a woman with excess androgen (thus the name). Yet a reading that foregrounds only the gender relations within the story is one that, in a sense, makes *men* central once again. The story is then read as a sad parable of the impossibility of heterosexual women and men being able to create a viable world together, since Tiptree, it seems, has already damned the men as innately violent, domineering, patriarchal, and sexually aggressive (although none of those constructions explains the narrator). The positive, loving, and intimate relationships between the women, the fact that they have survived and prospered, that they have, in fact, become 'humanity', are seen as less important, in such a reading, than the failure to repatriate heterosexuality. Yet demonstrating the viability of a successful, happy, and entirely non-heteronormative world seems quite queer to me. Surely the story's assertion that heteronormative relationships are irredeemable argues not so much for a feminist uprising in which all men will be slaughtered as for a rethinking of the ideological and sociocultural presuppositions that make it impossible to imagine relationships across the sexes outside the limited regime of what one might call the 'heterosexual imaginary'.[21] Is it then possible to consider 'Houston, Houston, Do You Read?' as a queer text, as well as a feminist one? Can it be both? I raise these questions not to answer them, but to suggest to the reader some of the potential ways by which one might perform a queer reading of this text.

4. Becoming Alien, Becoming Homosexual: From Cryptography to Cartography

> 'Under the Hollywood Sign', I think, is a perfect example of that one quadruple somersault from the highest bars that Tom could manage again and again, but which Reamy-clones never seem able to pull off. In this piece, as I say, we can hear the singular voice of Tom Reamy, singing a dangerous song of primal fears so deep and yet so commonplace that

> we automatically reject them, precisely because they may be universally shared. No one likes to imagine him- or herself as a potential point-beast ready to run with the slavering pack.
>
> —Harlan Ellison, 'Introduction' to *San Diego Lightfoot Sue* xiii

I want to turn in this section of my essay to a story that was first published in 1975 and that was not, I suspect, read at the time as primarily a gay text or a text about either homosexuals or homosexuality, Tom Reamy's 'Under the Hollywood Sign'. Reamy died in 1977, at the age of 42, having published only a handful of sf stories and one novel, *Blind Voices* (1978), that is more horror than sf. Reading between the lines of Harlan Ellison's introduction to the posthumous collection of Reamy's short stories, *San Diego Lightfoot Sue and Other Stories*, I deduce that Reamy was probably gay himself. If not, it is evident in the stories – especially 'Under the Hollywood Sign' and 'San Diego Lightfoot Sue' (which won the 1975 Nebula Award for best novelette) – that he was remarkably familiar with the gay idiom of the time. Either way, it does not matter a great deal, since a text's queerness cannot be said to reside in the sexual identity of its author. Yet having said this, I am aware of having, yet again, opened up the question of the ways in which 'queer' can be construed variously as belonging to, being seen in, or being read into the text, the author, or the reading. 'Under the Hollywood Sign', for all its being, I suspect, relatively unknown within the world of sf criticism, may prove a particularly fruitful (and, yes, the pun is deliberate) example of the ways in which queer theory can effect a re-reading – and not just of the text, but also, perhaps, of the heteronormative reading protocols that have constrained earlier readings. In this case, I will be reading 'Under the Hollywood Sign' in part for its peculiarly (un)faithful reiteration of the trope of the invisible alien; as such, I will be reading it against the ghosts of earlier readings – difficult as those traces are to discern – both of the story itself and of that other story I have set up here as exemplary of the trope, Campbell's 'Who Goes There?'.

'Under the Hollywood Sign' tells the story, in first-person narration, of a self-identified heterosexual LA cop, Lou Rankin, who sees and becomes obsessed with a group of near-identical and extraordinarily beautiful red-headed young men who lurk in the background of vehicle crashes and other sites of lethal violence (and who are, in the end, revealed as aliens who feed on the life energies of dying humans). Invisible to everyone else, the young men exert a peculiar fascination on Rankin, to the extent that he eventually kidnaps one of them and takes him to a borrowed cabin in the foothills. There he chains the young man up and attempts to make some sort of contact with him. These attempts consist at first of highly unsatisfactory question and answer sessions; after three weeks, the narrator resorts to a violence that quickly becomes sexualized. It soon becomes apparent, however, even to the narrator, that the young man is not remotely what he seems. In fact, the narrator has interrupted some form of alien life cycle, which results in the stillbirth of a winged creature described (as the young man had earlier been) in terms reminiscent of traditional depictions of angels. After the death, the narrator returns to LA, where he finds his partner's wife, whose sexual attentions he has been trying to avoid, hiding in his apartment. The partner, Carnehan, turns up while they're having (reluctant, on the narrator's part) sex, kills the wife, knocks out the narrator, drives him to the Hollywood Hills, and eventually dumps him out on the hillside under the Hollywood sign, shoots him in the gut, and leaves him to die. Unable to acknowledge that he is dying, the narrator attempts to crawl to safety – only to look up and find himself surrounded by four more of the beautiful red-headed young men who 'look at [him] the same way Carnehan looks at an apple he's been saving for a special occasion' (66).

From the very first sentence – 'I can't pinpoint the exact moment I noticed him' (40) – the story foregrounds the paradox that these exceptionally beautiful, and therefore one would think noticeable, young men are visible only to the narrator. Part of the crowd of gawkers around the site of a nasty traffic accident, the young man is seen, apparently, only by Rankin. The narrator makes three specific observations: first, that he has been seeing but not seeing the young man: 'I suppose I had been subliminally aware of him for some time' (40). Then, he notes that the young man does not react the same way as the rest of the crowd: 'That's one of the reasons I noticed him in particular. He wasn't wearing that horrified, fascinated expression they all seem to have. He might have been watching anything – or nothing' (40). And finally, the narrator makes an observation that situates the story firmly within the realm of the sexual, although he does so by denying that very interpellation: 'Don't get the wrong idea – my crotch doesn't get tight at the sight of an attractive young man. But there's only one word to describe him – beautiful' (41).

The story thus circulates from the beginning around three related issues: the question of visibility, as it is expressed through the narrator's ability to see the aliens; the sexual identity of the narrator, who, although self-identified as heterosexual, has an immediate and overwhelming sexual response to the aliens; and the identity of the aliens themselves, which is only slowly unveiled, as the objects of the narrator's gaze slip from an initial identification as beautiful young men to a sense that there is something profoundly different about them to the final revelation that they are, in fact, an entirely alien life-form – or, to be more precise, that they represent a stage, a kind of chrysalis, in a profoundly alien lifecycle that has nothing at all to do with human wants, desires, or identities. Because the aliens are never explained – never even overtly identified within the story *as aliens* – the story hesitates on the borderline between sf and fantasy/horror: a scientific explanation would tip it one way, a supernatural one would tip it the other. Furthermore, there is a marked refusal within the text to make a definitive pronouncement on the issue of the narrator's sexual identity. Instead, the text plays with conventional notions of homosexual/heterosexual difference, never fully locating the narrator at a specific point on the psychosexual map of the homo-hetero divide. It does so, furthermore, within the framework of an outlaw cryptography, a series of codings, of in-jokes, that are only indeterminately available to the presumed heterosexual audience of sf. How many straight readers, I wonder, were familiar in the late 1970s with *The Advocate*, the US national gay magazine in which, among other things, Pat Califia gave explicit sexual advice to gay men?

In 1984, on the only occasion that I have taught 'Under the Hollywood Sign' to my science fiction course – it has since gone out of print – I found my students divided into two distinct camps: on the one hand, the majority, who saw only the most obvious signs of queerness in the text, assumed that, had the story really been about homosexuality, it would have been expressed by some other metaphor; on the other hand, I had several students from the nearby Bible College in the class, for whom the story was, it appeared, perfectly clear. Fundamentalists to the core, these particular students objected vehemently to the story's inclusion on the syllabus, claiming that it was both pornographic and blasphemous. Both responses exemplify particular cultural assumptions about the representation of homosexuality in literature – the one, used to a reading protocol founded on assumptions of universality and 'Truth', finds the homosexuality in the story insufficient in itself, so that it must be about something more 'universal', which is inevitably then something more heterosexual; the other, used to a reading protocol that weighs everything against the 'literal Truth' of the Bible, reads (and judges) the story against both a particular moral standard and a particular iconography, in which an angel, for example, can only be an angel and a homosexual can only be evil. Both interpretations locate the story at specific, albeit different, positions on the cultural map, positions which say a great deal about our sociocultural beliefs about queerness, if very little about queerness itself – or about the text.

As an intervention into or a rewriting of the story that reveals the menace of the alien passing invisibly amongst us, 'Under the Hollywood Sign' reverses many of the standard tropes that inform 'Who Goes There?'. The monstrosity of these aliens, if it exists at all, resides not in their deformity, their ugliness, or their insatiable appetite for conquest; however, although these aliens are, by human standards, extraordinarily beautiful – 'all the artists for the last thousand years have been trying to paint that face on angels, but their fumbling attempts never came close' (54) – they are not necessarily 'good'. As it becomes clear that the aliens need to feed on the life-energy of dying creatures in order to complete their metamorphosis (into winged beings who are even more obviously angel-like than their 'human' forms), it becomes equally clear that they are somehow causing the sudden increase in human deaths. As Cunningham, the pretty cop who is normally on 'Pansy Patrol', says to the narrator: 'What got into people last night, anyway? Seems like everybody was trying to get themselves killed' (52). Thus, while the alien of 'Who Goes There?' is never figured as anything but monstrous evil, the aliens in Reamy's story are much more morally ambiguous. Furthermore, because, on the one hand, they are marked as 'queer' by the text – compared with the 'pretty boys' in the gay bars, as well as to Cunningham and even to Rankin's partner, Carnehan, in a reproduction of the stereotype that certain men are too beautiful to be straight – and, on the other hand, they are marked as angelic and described in terms of a kind of beautiful neutrality, as if they are above the pettiness of human concerns, these aliens are only ambiguously interpellated as either monsters or angels. Metonymically, they fail to serve as warnings of the invisible 'passing' Other, whether communist or homosexual, since not only does the text provide the reader with no clear way to judge the relative value of a human life against the birth of an alien/angel, but the narrator's remorse at the winged creature's death and his comparison of the angelic disinterested beauty of the alien with the fleshy demands of Carnehan's wife suggest that the aliens/Others may be the true norm against whom humans, the not-Other, are revealed as lacking.

In addition, the text's refusal to disambiguate Rankin's overt sexual attraction to the apparently male aliens (they have penises, but use them neither to urinate nor for sex) and his repeated assertion of himself as a heterosexual man, call into question the very heterosexual/homosexual dyad by which the twentieth century came to understand and to differentiate forms of sexual attraction.[22] At the same time, both the style of narration, reminiscent both of hard-boiled detective stories and of the 'lean, muscular, supple' prose of Tiptree, and Rankin's position as a cop mark him as clearly male, disrupting the presupposition that effeminacy is a prerequisite for the experience of masculine same-sex desire. The text does not disallow the reading that suggests that Rankin has been, all along, a repressed homosexual; however, by making the discourse of repression overt in the conversations between the cops, and specifically between Cunningham, of 'Pansy Patrol' fame, and the police psychologist, the text suggests both that such a repression is universal – Cunningham suggests the psychologist is gay, Carnehan reads *The Advocate*, the narrator concludes that Cunningham probably *is* gay – and that it is inadequate to explain either the specificity of the narrator's desire for the aliens or the extent of his obsession. In constructing Rankin as the most masculine of men, the cop, the story also reveals the curious imbrication of the police, especially the vice squad, with their prey – pretty Cunningham goes out on 'Pansy Patrol' with a padded crotch, Carnehan chuckles over an anti-cop joke in a gay magazine, both Cunningham and the narrator reveal an obsession with penis size, and all of them are familiar with the bars and restaurants, with the gestures and idiom of the gay subculture. Masculinity, it would seem, does not automatically equate to heterosexuality. Furthermore, the very location of the story in LA, where everyone's first reaction, when the narrator asks if they've seen the aliens, is to talk about actors, grounds the story within a notion of performance: under the Hollywood sign, masculinity is most obviously a role played with varying degrees of verisimilitude. Or, as Judith Butler notes in 'Critically Queer': '[i]nsofar as heterosexual gender norms produce inapproximable ideals, heterosexuality can be said to operate through the regulated production of hyperbolic versions of "man" and "woman". These are for the most part compulsory performances, ones which none of us choose, but which each of us is forced to negotiate' (22).

As with 'Who Goes There?', the construction of the masculine as the object of the gaze creates a profound uneasiness. Rankin's ability to *see* the aliens is nearly indistinguishable from his desire for them, a desire which is figured nearly as much in terms of wanting to see and to be seen, to be acknowledged, as it is in overtly sexual terms. After he rapes the alien for the first time, Rankin holds the alien's face and forces him to respond, to be present:

> 'Don't hide from me. It doesn't do any good. I can see you. I can see you!' He swam to the surface and looked at me. 'Did you enjoy it? Did you even feel it?'
>
> 'Yes.'
>
> 'Did it feel good? Did it hurt?'
>
> 'Yes.' (60)

The alien's responses to the narrator's questions, as to his actions, settle nothing. On the one hand, they can be interpreted within the standard conventions of pornographic writing, in which the description of anal penetration in terms of 'hurts so good' has become a cliché; on the other hand, they indicate the alien's near-complete disengagement with anything human, as he strives to complete his birth. The alien's transformation, the end of his life cycle, produces a moment of cognitive dissonance that resonates both in terms of sf and in terms of the deconstruction of our assumptions about gender and sexuality, as this apparent male quite literally attempts to give birth, an attempt that fails only because the narrator has prevented the alien from gathering enough life energy – an intervention which the narrator sees as tragic, but which, ironically, has no doubt saved the lives of humans.

It is possible then to read 'Under the Hollywood Sign' as a text in the process of becoming queer; initially accessible through a kind of outlaw cryptography, the signs by which its queerness are produced have become more familiar to the 'general population' through the proliferation of a visible gay and lesbian subject. It has become harder for the reader, however attached ideologically to a heteronormative reading protocol, to dismiss anything queer within texts as 'a rag of extraneous meaning that had got stuck onto them' (Sinfield 63).[23] Consequently, a queer reading of Reamy's story might chart the movement from cryptography to cartography, from decoding a text whose signification is only apparent to the chosen few to locating its insights into the sexual epistemology of the culture on the map of our own sexual ontologies. Thus, both the narrator and the object of his obsession remain, in a sense, indeterminate within the text itself: it is through our reading that the narrator becomes homosexual (or not), just as it is through our reading that the beautiful young men become either aliens or angels. The quality of their otherness can only be understood as a doubling effect, just as the queerness of the text depends on the reader's particular subject position and willingness to indulge in different reading protocols. The aliens/Others are both ineluctably masculine and, like Tiptree him/herself, not masculine at all, since the mere fact of their otherness equates them synecdochically with the female, the black, the queer. As Jackson suggests, the subject of the sf story is 'not the cause but the effect of the system that sustains it' (102); in 'Under the Hollywood Sign', the narrator's subjectivity is an identity-in-process, an effect of a system that can be variously understood, depending on one's worldview. In the end then, I locate the text's queerness not in a determination that the narrator *is* gay, because he desires and finally rapes the alien, but rather in the way the text itself calls into question the very system which effects the narrator as a gay subject.

5. Conclusion: An Alien Cartography

> A text's subversive potential is not dependent upon its generic innovation, but on how it maps and motivates the antagonisms constituting the subject(s) of representation, and on how it transfigures and recathects the available forms of cultural expression... This rewriting is coextensive to the articulation of gay male identities-in-process as these deviant subjects confront culture and enter into representational agency within it. The most radical representational practices of deviant subjects not only challenge the official versions of their lives, but also transvalue the notion of deviance, and interrogate the mechanisms and meanings of representational practices – including their own.
>
> — Earl Jackson, Jr, *Strategies of Deviance* 44

I have argued in this essay that a queer reading is performative in itself and that it is, in the long run, less about content – we have already considered the lack of queerness of gay and lesbian content within mimetic representations – than about worldview. Queer readings are informed by a desire to understand the text both in terms of its potential for representing dissident sexual subjectivities outside of a Cartesian understanding of the subject and in terms of the text's engagement with a specific historico-cultural understanding of dissident sexualities and of the place of such sexualities within the sex/gender system that regulates and constructs normative – and thus also non-normative – ways of being-in-the-world as a sexed and sexual subject. When the questions raised by the formulations 'queer reading' and 'queer text' are brought to bear on sf, what is revealed is a complex and contradictory fictional arena. On the one hand, there is the particular aptness of sf, as a non-mimetic form of writing, to produce stories in which sexuality does not need to be understood in ways 'vouched for by human senses and common sense' and to interrogate the ways in which sexual subjectivities are created as effects of the system that sustains them. On the other hand, there are also the variety of ways in which most sf texts, regardless of their identification as 'estranged fictions', are completely unselfconscious in their reproduction of the heteronormative environment in which they were written.

A queer reading may then work through a range of different strategies – from decoding the outlaw cryptographies that have hidden – and may still hide – issues of sexual difference (often in plain sight) to delineating the specifics that may make a particular text queer, to disinterring the many and peculiar ways through which the dominant Western conception of sexuality underlies, is implicated in, and sometimes collides with sf's attempt to envision alternative ways of being-in-the-world, ways which are always, no matter how deeply their signs are hidden, already about being-in-the-world as a person with a sex, a gender, and a sexuality. The subversive potential of sf as a mode through which non-Cartesian subjectivities can be represented is a function precisely of sf's ability to create a 'radically or significantly different formal framework' (Suvin 18), of its very estrangement from the mimetic attempt of naturalistic – or mundane – fiction to reiterate faithfully a teleological understanding of humanity's being-in-the-world, to represent the subject as the cause rather than the effect of the system. Thus, sf's 'foundational infidelity' (Jackson 125) to the world 'vouched for by human senses and common sense' at one and the same time makes it possible – although obviously not inevitable – for sf to tell alternative stories – other stories, alien stories – of both sexual ontologies and the systems that sustain and create them. Sf narratives may, seen from a queer viewpoint(s), provide a map or chart of those alien spaces – whether inner or outer – in which queers do, have, and will exist. Queer sf provides spaces to go beyond simply writing gay men and lesbians into uninterrogated heteronormative visions of both present and future and may, at its best, answer Eve Kosofsky Sedgwick's call to bypass the old familiar routes 'across the misleadingly symmetrical map… fractured in a particular historical situation by the profound asymmetries of gender oppression and heterosexist oppression' and, instead, to engage in 'the more promising project [which] would seem to be a study of the incoherent dispensation itself, the indisseverable girdle of incongruities under whose discomfiting span, for most of a century, have unfolded both the most generative and the most murderous plots of our culture' (*Epistemology of the Closet* 90).

Notes

1. Henry Jenkins has a useful discussion of this movement in the final chapter of *Science Fiction Audiences*, 'Out of the Closet and Into the Universe'. The history of the involvement of the Gaylaxians with *Star Trek* and the formation of the Voyager Visibility Project can be found online at http://www.gaytrek.com/history.html.
2. There is, of course, some argument as to whether humans do indeed come in only two biological sexes. For a comprehensive discussion of this issue, see van den Wijngaard's *Reinventing the Sexes*.
3. These arguments can be found online in copies of the correspondence between the producers of *Star Trek* and the Voyager Visibility Project that are documented at the Gaytrek web page (http://www.gaytrek.com).
4. This now well-known story is told by Delany in 'Shadows': 'What remains with me, nearly ten years after my first reading of the book, is the knowl-

edge that I have experienced a world in which the *placement* of the information about the narrator's face is *proof* that in such a world much of the race problem, at least, has disappeared. The book as text...became, for a moment, the symbol of that world' (94–95).

5. As Lauren Berlant and Michael Warner have pointed out with reference to the political climate in the US, this reinscription is not merely the policy of right-wing fundamentalists but reflects a broader sociopolitical climate 'whose highest aspirations are marriage, military patriotism, and protected domesticity'. They add that '[it] is no accident that queer commentary – on mass media, on texts of all kinds, on discourse environments from science to camp – has emerged at a time when United States culture increasingly fetishizes the normal. A fantasized mainstream has been invested with normative force by leaders of both major political parties' (345).
6. There is sometimes a tendency among people whose only exposure to queer theory is through academia to forget that, like earlier theorizations of same-sex and/or dissident sexualities, 'queer' is not merely about playfulness and fluidity, but also about an active political engagement in the realpolitik of queer people's lives. One might think, to take only one example, of the two major threads of political engagement that run through Eve Kosofsky Sedgwick's work – the need to create a world that is safe for queer kids and the desire for an ethical, humane, and sex-positive response to AIDS. See, for example, her *Epistemology of the Closet* and 'How to Bring Your Kids up Gay'. The fact that queer theory is so heavily imbricated in the study, theorization, and practical and political response to AIDS is itself an indication of the extent to which 'queer' does not and, I think, should not exist purely as an intellectual construct whose primary feature is its *jouissance.*
7. Annamarie Jagose has a useful discussion of the meanings and contestations of 'queer' in chapters 7 and 8 of *Queer Theory* (72–126), as does Michael Warner in his 'Introduction' to *Fear of a Queer Planet.*
8. Delany has frequently argued this position. See, for example, 'Science Fiction and "Literature"' and 'The Semiology of Silence: The *Science-Fiction Studies* Interview'.
9. For an examination of this construction in both *The Left Hand of Darkness* and Eleanor Arnason's *Ring of Swords,* see my 'The Queer as Traitor, the Traitor as Queer.'
10. The difficulty of ascertaining who is and who is not homosexual, within a conceptual framework that renders the homosexual/heterosexual dyad as *the* axis of difference, preoccupies science, which seeks 'objective' proof of this difference, first through psychoanalysis, then through a variety of supposedly accurate physiological tests (such as the RCMP's infamous 'fruit machine'), and most recently through the drive to discover the 'gay gene'.
11. Like all 'Golden Age' narratives, this one also imagines an era that never did exist; one might trace several genealogies for this particular cultural anxiety – one, at least, that tracks back to the Bolshevik Revolution of 1917, and another that recalls that World War I also had its Rosie the Rivetter and her equivalents, whose labour freed men for military service. Yet another trace might chart much the same territory as Christopher Isherwood's *I Am A Camera* and its cinematic offspring, *Cabaret.*
12. For a discussion of gays and lesbians in the military during World War II, see

Allen Bérubé's 'Marching to a Different Drummer'.

13. I do not, obviously, mean this literally, although the rhetoric of the time (from the early 1930s to the late 1950s) suggests that some of the people persecuting Jews, communists, and homosexuals saw them as being literally the same and not just as occupying the same structural position as threats to the white (Aryan), male-dominant, and heterosexual social structure.
14. See both chapter 4 of Sinfield (60–82) and Lee Edelman's 'Tearooms and Sympathy'.
15. Think of Marlowe's *Edward II*.
16. See Lee Edelman's 'Tearooms and Sympathy' for a discussion of this formation.
17. Today it is impossible not to think of AIDS in the context of the role that blood plays in determining who is human and who (what) is the alien Other; in the West, where AIDS has been popularly conflated with the figure of the homosexual, 'bad blood' becomes a marker not of one's HIV status but of one's queerness (which, as an aside, explains why lesbians, who have a very small incidence of AIDS, are widely presumed to be as much at risk – and as much a danger – as are gay men).
18. We can see how the figure of the vampire might also serve to carry the same burden of monstrosity in this context. See, for instance, Ellis Hanson's 'Undead' for a critical discussion of the ways in which AIDS and vampirism have become conflated in popular discourses since the onset of the AIDS epidemic.
19. There is, of course, that other improbability to be taken into account: that I, as a self-described dyke or queer, should recognize a beautiful young man when I see one. For some people, including some gay people, that, too, defies explanation.
20. It is interesting to note, in regards to the gaze, the unease generated among the male characters in 'Who Goes There?' once they become the objects of each other's gaze; they spend a huge amount of time staring at each other, and even talking about the way in which they look at each other ('Your eyes – Lord, I wish you could see your eyes staring – ' [104]). Theoretically, of course, the object of the gaze is always a sexual object – and cannot be a (heterosexual) man. To quote Laura Mulvey, '[a]ccording to the principles of the ruling ideology and the psychical structures that back it up, the male figure cannot bear the burden of sexual objectification' (27–28).
21. I first encountered this useful phrase in an eponymously named article by sociologist Chrys Ingraham; it indicates a worldview that cannot imagine certain relationships as 'heterosexual', even when they occur between two people of opposite sexes. At its most heteronormative, the heterosexual imaginary cannot conceive of either a sexually aggressive woman or a sexually passive man, still less of a heterosexual man who wishes to be the receptive partner in anal sex. Anything outside of the heterosexual imaginary is thus conceived as either a perversion or a fetish.
22. Eve Kosofsky Sedgwick's introduction to *Epistemology of the Closet* gives a good historical overview of contemporary understandings of this development: 'It is a rather amazing fact that, of the very many dimensions along which the genital activity of one person can be differentiated from that of another... precisely one, the gender of object choice, emerged from the turn of the

century, and has remained, as *the* dimension denoted by the now ubiquitous category of "sexual orientation"' (8).

23. The quote is part of Laurence Lerner's response to the idea that gay readers might read W. H. Auden's poems for some sort of gay meaning. Sinfield notes that 'Lerner allows that there will have been gay readers. "That Auden was a homosexual is well known, and it is perfectly possible, even likely that some of his friends winked when they read his love poems and gave an extra smirk... But in doing this they were not reading the poems; they were noticing a rag of extraneous meaning that had got stuck onto them... They, like Sinfield, were unwriting them"' (Sinfield 62–63).

War Machine, Time Machine

Nicola Griffith and Kelley Eskridge

> [It] is quite possible for a work of literature to operate as a war machine upon its epoch.
>
> — Monique Wittig, *The Straight Mind* 69

> Yes, but is it art?
>
> — Anonymous

Nicola

The golden age of queer sf is 20. Or maybe it was the 1970s. Or perhaps it was in France. It's all relative, like the notion of 'queer' itself.

My golden age began in Scotland, when I was 20. My girlfriend and I were sleeping on a friend's floor, travelling about a bit, absorbing life – and lots of hash. A woman handed me a book, saying, 'I hear yeez like the wee aliens and shite. Have ye read any with gur-uls before?' I have a vague memory of glancing at a blue-ish cover before returning to the serious business of reducing my brain to a microdot. But at some ungodly hour of the morning, I opened the book – Sally Miller Gearheart's *The Wanderground* – and fell into it.

It blew me away. For a 20-year-old escapee from Catholic World, where the consensus was that I was going to hell, it was visionary dynamite. Under the sunlight of story, the essentialist feminist theory I'd read but not embraced flowered into a magical paradise.

The early 1980s were a time when I was being thrown against the wall by members of the Special Patrol Group,[1] and harassed by local plods simply for being a dyke, when many women I knew were at Greenham Common fighting for world peace (and I was just fighting). *The Wander-*

ground explained to me how and why the Bad Men would get their comeuppance. I hadn't even realized I needed validation, but suddenly here were women like me rising above their challenges, being wise and kind and strong and, more to the point, victorious.

I began an indiscriminate, desperate search for lesbian sf. I vacuumed up the output of Onlywomen Press (Caroline Forbes's *The Needle on Full, The Reach and Other Stories* edited by Lilian Mohin and Sheila Shulman, etc.), moved on to The Women's Press (Josephine Saxton, Jody Scott, Sandi Hall, Lisa Tuttle, Rhoda Lerman), and then Virago (Zoë Fairbairns). I loved them uncritically.

By 22 or 23 I moved from hash to snorting amphetamine sulphate, and from Gearheart to lesbian and feminist work by Joanna Russ and Monique Wittig, Marge Piercy and Virginia Woolf. There wasn't enough of it, but I was hooked. I found Tiptree, then Gwyneth Jones and Vonda McIntyre, Suzy McKee Charnas and Elizabeth A. Lynn. Eventually I graduated to the crack of Marion Zimmer Bradley imports (*The Shattered Chain, Thendara House*).

In real life I'd started to grow marijuana and sell speed to ensure my own supply, and it slowly dawned on me I could also generate my own supply of lesbian sf. I began to write.

My first attempt at a story, 'Women and Children First', was meant to be witty and ironic: a spaceship hurtling through the void, an accident, a lantern-jawed hero-captain who says, 'To the lifepods. Women and children first!' The women say, 'Okay', and merrily abandon the ship, ending up on an uninhabited planet and founding a woman-centred society, where everything would be beautiful and perfect.

But when I starting writing – when I really started to think – was When It Changed.

I imagined as fully as possible each woman and child landing on this uninhabited planet. Why are they travelling in the first place? What are their fears and dreams? What luxuries will they miss, what challenges will they welcome? Which fellow passengers will they admire or loathe? I imagined the women disagreeing, then squabbling, then fighting. I imagined the little boys growing up and wondering why their mothers' friends hated and feared them. I imagined what would happen when the little girls started fancying the little boys. And, phhtt, no more lesbian feminist paradise.

Epiphany through writing is more addictive than opiates, more of a rush than speed. The story became a novel. I finished the novel and immediately started another, set on the same planet but many hundreds of years later. I found that by this time there were two civilizations: the women-only side of the planet and the mixed-gender side. People from both sides were silly and vain and smart and kind and vicious and generous. By mistake, I had aimed the lesbian war machine not at my epoch but at my own assumptions; I had discovered that the idea of essentialism is monumentally silly.

Kelley

A very different personal history brought me to the same conclusion. I grew up the child of white civil-rights activists in the American South in the 1960s, surrounded by my parents' friends and associates – black, latino, white, gay, straight, priests and hippies and drug addicts and feminists and slumlord attorneys – and as a result I've never cottoned to essentialism. I certainly don't care for the emotional labelling that so often goes with it: *black people are just looking to take advantage of white folks* or *what happened to make you hate men?*, or (my personal head-scratching favourite of those applied to me) *how sad you can never have children*. I find such things stupid and reductive, and I'm not partial to being reduced.[2]

My mother was a grammar-school librarian and both my parents read for pleasure. I grew up surrounded by books. The stories I loved best always involved danger and growth: a character choosing, or being compelled, to put herself at risk, to go out into the cold and deal with what she found there. To find her own strength and discover her own power. Alexei Panshin's *Rite of Passage*, David Palmer's *Emergence*, Joan Aiken's *The Wolves of Willoughby Chase*, even *The Wolf and The Dove* by romance writer Kathleen Woodiwiss (with the first sex scenes that ever turned me on). Stories that compelled me because they spoke to me of people who were brave and smart and sexual and tough and *interesting* in ways that I wanted to be too.

Like Nicola, I began in my twenties by writing what I wanted to read (which was much more along the lines of baroque Tanith Lee imitations than Sally Miller Gearheart-like utopias). And like Nicola, I found it wasn't enough. I had to write what I hadn't read yet, and on some level they had to be stories that would make me feel brave and smart and sexual and tough and interesting. That's what stories were for.

It was this that drove me to apply to the Clarion writing workshop in 1988. And that's When It Changed for me. I fell in love with Nicola and with writing, both of which were dangerous and intense and so exciting. And I began to have my assumptions about who I was, as a person and a writer, ripped away.

Samuel R. Delany was one of our teachers. He was fairly impatient with us – a bunch of wide-eyed, white, mostly middle-class not-exactly-kids, many of whom saw writing as the necessary process to the goal of getting published. One day he went off on us for having worldviews the size of grapes, for imagining everyone in our futures as white, middle-class, and polite (except for the dangerous characters, who were allowed to be gay or black as long as they died or were otherwise redeemed). Seriously, this is what many of us were writing. I remember one student in the workshop who wrote a lesbian character that looked and talked exactly like Nicola, because she was the only out lesbian he had ever met. And he didn't understand why she might be offended. But Delany did, and he challenged us to do better. To take (although he did not put it this way) some fucking risks.

Red flag to a bull. I offered one of my stories up for dissection. *Tell me what assumptions I'm making,* I said, and he gave me an impassive look and answered, *Are you sure you want me to do that?* An hour later I was in tears, mortified by my assumptions and even more so by my utter lack of awareness of them. Here I was, with all my liberal childhood credentials, my race and class consciousness, my experiences of poverty and powerlessness, my carefully forged autonomous identity, my hip new still-emerging bisexuality, revealed as fatuous – I may have been some of those things as a person, but as a writer I was straight, white, resolutely privileged, protective of the cultural status quo, and embarrassingly safe.

It's one of the most miserable experiences I've had as a writer, and I'll always be grateful for it. I have no idea if Chip would approve of my work now, but he would certainly find it different.

After Clarion I found new things to read. Nicola introduced me to the science fiction that had steered her into writing. I found most of it inscrutable or uninteresting – it didn't speak to my experience the way it did to Nicola's. I offered her some of my formative favourites – Panshin's *Rite of Passage*, Barbara Hambly's *Darwath* trilogy – and she found them as alien as chick lit. I tried lesbian fiction (speculative and not) from my local feminist bookstore: I felt hemmed in by the overt separatism of some (was I supposed to start hating men now?), and most of the rest were variations of coming-out stories that bored me silly. Eventually I hunkered down with Theodore Sturgeon, Robert Heinlein, and Marion Zimmer Bradley, all of whom wrote a different kind of coming-out story – more of coming-in stories at heart, about people coming into themselves. These stories did what the lesbian stories couldn't – offered me ways to explore new ideas about myself in the context of straight people as well as lesbian people. I needed that to chart my way.

Nicola

The line between safe and dangerous – our explorer's path, our way – creeps with time.

Genre, art, and queerness all lie in the eye of the beholder. When it was first published, Joanna Russ's 'When It Changed' (1972) was for most people blindingly, mind-bogglingly queer. Now – partly because Russ's novella was so brilliant that it changed the sf cultural landscape – it's not. A world of women who love (and hate) each other about to fall apart because the men have found them? These days, in some circles, it might be considered almost reactionary.[3]

My first two novels, which I think of as sf, are not regarded as particularly queer by the self-identified queer community. The literary community doesn't think they're art. And they are certainly not seen as Real SF by the Grand Old Men of the mainstream sf community. One famous writer chatted to me briefly after an award ceremony.[4] 'Well,' he said, 'I suppose *Ammonite*'s not bad, for a piece of sub-genre.'

I couldn't have written *Ammonite* without the trail-blazing of Russ and Le Guin and Wittig. But even though the path already existed, many people told me it would be impossible to get my book published. I got my first taste of how things would go when I sent the manuscript to a former teacher (not Chip) for a blurb. He phoned me up:

'Nicola, this is a rattling good read, but no one will buy it. I know publishing. This is too freaky. There has to be at least reference to men.'

'No,' I said, 'there doesn't.'

'Well, can't the women dance around the fire in fake beards once a month and sorta ritualistically remember all that they've lost?'

'No,' I said, awed by his obtuseness. He couldn't accept that these women were fully human in, of, and by themselves, not in comparison to or competition with men. He didn't get it.

But others did. The manuscript got multiple offers and was published by Del Rey without fanfare in 1993. And then, oh-ho, the letters (this was before email) began to flow from disgruntled readers. Like my former teacher, most of this Angry, Tunbridge Wells cohort simply couldn't wrap their heads around the notion of women as human. I'd honestly had no idea people would find it so difficult. For me, the gender thought-experiment was a by-the-by, an offshoot of the real story: of Marghe and of differing peoples' response to change.

My first review, in *Locus*, from one of the dyed-in-sf-wool reviewers (he might scorn the word 'critic' as being too highbrow) lauded the book while bemoaning the lack of men: how much better the book might have been if only Marghe had had a brother. Reviews in the sf columns of major news journals – *The New York Times Book Review, Los Angeles Times, New Stateman* – praised the book. The LGBTQI (known in our house as the quiltbag) press did not deign to notice. After all, it wasn't a book about being a lesbian. No one had to actively choose to be a dyke and then agonize over that choice, and suffer the slings and arrows of homophobic fortune, because everyone on the planet was a girl. Besides, it had a spaceship on the cover. It was sci-fi rubbish.

I did my best to ignore all this; I was busy working on *Slow River*.

Not long after I sent the *Slow River* outline to Fran, my agent, she called:

'This is not a selling outline.'

'Why not?'

'Well,' she said, 'in *Ammonite* Marghe had a girlfriend because she had no choice, poor thing. But why does Lore like girls?'

'Because she's a dyke, Fran,' I said, and I fired her.

When the galleys were ready, I took a handful to OutWrite, the lesbian and gay writing conference, and I literally couldn't give them away.

'Oh, I don't read stuff like that,' said one review editor.

'Like what?' I said.

'Rockets and bug-eyed monsters.'

'No rockets,' I promised. 'No monsters – except the human variety.'

'No,' she said. 'I don't read sci-fi.'

So I moved on to the next critic.

'Oooh,' she said, 'you wrote *Ammonite*!'

'That's right.'

She looked at the *Slow River* galley. 'But why do you call your stuff sci-fi?'

'Well, actually I call it sf, but, anyway, that's what it is.'

'No, no. Sci-fi is terrible, so I don't like it, but I like your book, so it's not sci-fi.'

I am not making this up.

Then *Slow River* came out, and this time the mainstream press reviewed the book outside their sf round-up columns, but they couldn't resist saying, *Oooh, this transcends the genre!* None of them understood why I didn't take this insult to one of my favourite genres as a compliment. One sales rep even confided, after several drinks, that he thought I'd invented a new tense. It took me a while to understand that I had fucked with his sense of what was proper to such a degree that he felt I must have altered language itself. I honestly didn't know whether to laugh, cry, or buy another round.

The genre reviews of *Slow River* were mostly concerned about the 'fact' that in the novel all I did was write about lesbians, that all of my books were about lesbians, that there were no heterosexuals in my books at all, ever, and that this was, well, it was wrong. (You could practically see their veins sticking out.) Once again, I was astonished.[5] While there are a lot of lesbians – or at least lesbian sex – in the book, there's also a lot of straight sex. Yet these reviewers simply didn't see it. It reminds me of that famous experiment: put ten doctors or engineers or any other traditionally male profession in a room, seven men and three women. Most observers will say the gender split is about half and half. Make it six and four, respectively, and observers will say there is a majority of women.[6] The Other takes up more space than the Norm.

As I've climbed the publishing prestige ladder, from mass market 'science fiction' to hardcover 'near-future fiction' to 'a novel of suspense' to 'a novel' (categorizations that are outside my control), reviewers have stopped whingeing about lesbians and are noticing instead that there's something funny about the way I tell stories. When I started to get questions about this oddness, I invented a name for it: narrative reverse-labelling technique.[7]

According to labelling theory, if you label someone as, say, a criminal, regardless of whether or not they are criminal, you and others will perceive them to have the traits associated with the criminal, and treat them accordingly. After being treated as a criminal for long enough, the subject will see no harm in acting like one. A self-fulfilling prophecy. In my fiction, I simply excise heterosexism and remove labelling based on sexual orientation. Being a dyke is unremarkable. Literally. In fictional terms, this changes the world.

Kelley

One of Delany's lessons at Clarion was that you can't just turn a sexual or gender paradigm on its head and call it more inclusive. Narrative homosexism is simply lazy, a way of 'making theme' by turning the status quo upside down and stepping aside with a Vanna White-like flourish of arms: look, it's the *uoq sutats*! It makes straight people the weirdos! Isn't that daring? Now the gay people will treat the straight people badly. That'll teach 'em.

I despise conscious theme, the great battering ram on the literary war machine. It subverts story. It renders characters nearly non-dimensional. It makes for some truly terrible dialogue. Good writers smile a polite 'no' when the theme tray is passed around, and instead allow theme to emerge from a well-told story about people who engage us because their choices, fears, and hopes seem real, even if they are as strange to us as the surface of Pluto.

It's vital for people who live outside of the dominant culture to find themselves reflected in positive ways within that culture. When those images don't exist, we create them. It's important and essential. But the goal should be to expand the boundaries of art, not establish new and increasingly granular rules and categories (never-het-dykes, bears, BDSM femmes, Log Cabin leathermen...) by which to label one another. I want people to write stories about strong women, people of colour, people of varied sexual orientation or physical condition, in order to make space in the cultural discussion for such people – not to set up a gay and lesbian table in the corner, as my stepbrother's first wife did at their wedding reception so Nicola and I 'would have people to talk to'. We didn't go to the wedding. I don't want to talk only to or about gay or lesbian people. Sexual expression is not that much of a bridge-builder these days: in person and in text, I'm too lesbian for some people, too straight for others, and not sf enough for most of whoever's left. And I don't care. I want my identity to be expansive, not reductive.

But then there's *queer*. An interesting word. An expansive word. *Queer* is not a word that assumes everyone at the table is the same. *Vive la différence*, it says.

I don't call myself queer any more than I call myself lesbian, but I'm more and more prepared to think of what I write as queer. That's partly because *queer* functions as a meta-descriptor for me, the word itself implying relativity, fluidity, defiance of categories. I feel free to define it any way I want.

People sometimes remind me that, as a writer, I ought to be hip to the notion that words have a specific meaning. They have a point: but at the heart of a bias towards constructed identity, which I have, is the notion that personal experience *is* truth, and sometimes more important than the wider cultural construct. I do respect the meaning of words: and I think that part of *queer* is the expansion and reconstruction of meaning, including the meaning of queer itself.

As a writer, I accept the definition of queer writing as writing that expresses culturally non-standard sexual activity and identity. But I'm coming more and more to see that queer embraces the subtle differences as well as the obvious ones. And I believe that queer writing is *anything* that extends and legitimates the possibilities of sexual and gender identity beyond the writer's personal comfort zone.

If I create specific, particular humanity in a character whose sexual or gender expression makes me uncomfortable on some level, then I believe I've done a piece of queer writing, whether or not it's obvious to anyone else. If a straight-down-the-middle woman writes a straight woman character who does something even a little bit outside the writer's own sexual or gender boundaries – wears naughty underwear to work, or looks at a man's trouser bulge before she looks at his face – and if she writes it well enough to take herself and her readers there, then she's writing queer. Even though for most self-identified queer people, it wouldn't be a blip on the radar.

And so not all queer writing is quiltbag, and neither is all quiltbag writing queer. This is certainly true in speculative fiction: there are enough gay or lesbian sf writers crafting stories that reflect their own experience of sexuality and gender these days that it's no longer in and of itself a brave new thing to do. I think this is nothing but good: much better for such works to be seen as part of the greater genre gene pool than as anomalies. All respect to the writers whose courage and talent opened this space for the rest of us.

And now I think it's time to let go of calling words on a page *gay* or *lesbian* as if those terms made the words any more or less important, any more or less art. But it's easy for me to say that: I'm comfortable taking my work into mainstream straight space because there's much about my work that is straight, just as there's much about it that isn't. Like Nicola, I don't make an effort to explain or justify the sexual identity of characters. And since my work is more personally than politically queer, it threatens only the most easily threatened of readers and critics.[8]

The works of mine that most people most readily categorize as 'lesbian' – *Solitaire* and 'Alien Jane' – are some of my least queer writing. I don't believe I ever wrote anything consciously (personally and textually) queer until I began to explore a character called Mars, whose stories are told from the first-person voice and whose gender is never specified.

It's not that Mars is genderless, but that gender isn't an issue in Mars's expression of self, or in the way that others respond to Mars. And Mars isn't meant to be a puzzle for readers to solve, but a space into which any reader can fit themself. I know gender exists, and so does gendered behaviour, but beyond it is the basic human stuff: love, fear, joy, sex, pain, hope, courage, confusion… I don't believe there are 'like a woman' or 'like a man' ways to feel these things, and it's a joy to find the *human* ways to bring these experiences to Mars and watch them unfold.[9] And in so doing, I discover all kinds of ways I've never thought of before to be brave and smart and sexual and tough and interesting. Some of them make me a little uncomfortable, a little vulnerable. Some of them may change how I view my own sexuality, my own ideas of gender. And that's queer.

Nicola

If all we write is the war machine, and then the war changes – if the front moves – we're left stranded waving our sword in the middle of someone's picnic. There's embarrassment all around. We creep away pretending not be a lunatic. However, if the blade is decently scabbarded in story – in particular characters experiencing specific situations – we might be asked to sit and eat a sandwich and share in the new peace. If we avoid the cliché and get particular, readers will see relevance in our work, still get a kick out of our words, still admire the artistry of our blade when we whip it out and let it glint in the sun. They might even want to touch it.

At a family dinner in the UK recently, various relatives – some older, but mostly younger – were kibitzing about movie stars. 'Whoa,' one nephew said, 'she's got a pair of…' at which point his mother shot him a look and he closed his mouth. Kelley chimed in about Johnny Depp[10] and the family blink-rate went up. They didn't know what to say. You can bet, though, that they all did think about it later, and talk about it when we weren't there. To some degree, then, simply by existing and walking and talking, Kelley and I function as a war machine on the more insular reaches of our epoch. This is all very well, in fact it's often enormous fun, but when it comes to our fiction, we aim higher. We aim for it to be art, too.

Art is fiction that is beautiful, appealing, of more than ordinary substance and cultural longevity. It speaks to us across time. If we assume that good fiction deconstructs cultural cliché by writing about individual, particular characters in individual, particular situations, and if we define as queer any fiction which destabilises the assumptions that underpin the construction of sexual identity, then all really good fiction whose particulars include reference to sex and gender can't be anything other than queer. War machine and time machine.

Notes

1. The SPG were a controversial unit of the London Metropolitan Police, who travelled about Brixton in an armoured troop carrier. They were a major factor in the 1981 Brixton riots. They certainly made me feel like rioting when I was down there.

2. For the record, I don't call myself a lesbian writer. I don't even call myself a lesbian. I live in a committed relationship of nearly twenty years with Nicola, and would crawl on my belly like a reptile to beg her forgiveness for having mad sex with Johnny Depp if I ever got the chance. And yet what's the point of correcting people? *No, no, I'm not a lesbian!* is defensive at best, and offensive at worst, and I don't feel either way about this part of me.
3. Don't send me an indignant email. Or at least please read my essay 'Living Fiction, Storybook Lives' before you go off like a firecracker.
4. Not as famous as he was, though, ha ha.
5. Perhaps I am a little dim. I just don't seem to learn...
6. Nope, I can't cite my sources. But I read about it when I was about 20, if that's helpful...
7. I will freely admit to the possibility of reinventing the wheel here, but I didn't have time to make enquiries and trawl the literature. The microphones (okay, more often the phone or keyboard) were in my face; I made something up. If there's a real, academe-speak term for this, please don't snicker – just tell me.
8. Among these is a reviewer at *Publishers Weekly* whose unnecessarily snarky comment in 2002 about the primary love relationship in my novel *Solitaire* was an obvious and clumsy attempt to flag the book as 'lesbian' for the rest of the fearful. Thankfully, one finds less of that sort of sloppiness in *PW* these days.
9. It's also interesting that many readers and reviewers don't notice the lack of pronouns, and happily assign gender to Mars. I've seen Mars discussed as both male and female, and therefore as both straight and gay, depending on the stated gender of the character Mars is relating to sexually in any particular story.
10. If I inadvertently gralloched Mr Depp with my shiny blade, I admit I would not feel the need to beg for anyone's forgiveness.

Part II

Un/Doing History

Sextrapolation in New Wave Science Fiction

Rob Latham

In her 1985 essay 'The Virginity of Astronauts', Vivian Sobchack argues that science fiction film has persistently refused to deal with human eroticism, exiling sexuality to the extent that it manifests only as unconscious pathology. The classic icons of the genre – monsters and mutants, alien invasion and possession, technological mastery or impotence – emerge in her analysis as neurotic symptoms, materializations of the forces of repression that lurk beneath the antiseptic surfaces of its futuristic sets and the Ken-doll banality of its space-jockey heroes. Her study is devoted largely to classic sf films of the 1950s, and one wonders how she might apply her psychoanalytic methods to the more risqué movies of the 1960s and 1970s, such as *Barbarella* (1968) and *Flesh Gordon* (1974). Perhaps she would view such films as an epochal 'return of the repressed', an explosion into conscious awareness of the hidden libidinal energies that have always animated the genre. Capitalizing on the freer climate for sexual expression within contemporary popular culture, such Space Age sex farces might be seen as traducing the chasteness and moral seriousness of traditional sf cinema, deriving much of their comic charge precisely from a counterpoint between the puritanical rectitude of 1950s-era sf and the decadent excesses of the youth counterculture.

In a review of the comic-book version of *Barbarella* in the March 1967 issue of *The Magazine of Fantasy and Science Fiction*, Judith Merril playfully defended the 'valid modern phenomenon' of the sexy single girl, as incarnated in the eponymous heroine, over against the 'under-sexed high-minded Boy Scout of the space patrol' one might normally expect to find in similar sf stories ('Books' 3/67, 25). Yet she acknowledged that hers was probably a minority taste, at least among traditional fans, for whom *Barbarella*'s cheerful ribaldry might seem dreadfully unserious – or, as Merril winkingly implied, vaguely threatening to the adolescent males who make up sf's core audience. In the same review, Merril also praised John Barth's quasi-sf novel *Giles Goat Boy* (1966) for its sophisticated handling of sexual material. In essence, she deployed a highbrow postmodernist novel and a lowbrow pop-cultural comic, both of which deal with sex bawdily and unapologetically, to critique the middlebrow tameness and asexuality of most genre sf. 'It is time', she claimed, 'and long past time, for some of the same kind of hard-headed speculative thinking that science fiction contributed to space flight and atomics, to be done in [the areas of] interpersonal psychology and sexology' (26).

Merril was, of course, one of the most visible – and voluble – apostles of the New Wave in 1960s' sf, and this review may be seen as a volley in her ongoing battle to force the genre to 'grow up', to shed the legacy of its pulp past and embrace contemporary realities. Her review shows that this programme featured demands not only for a greater ethos of aesthetic experimentalism but also for more 'adult' forms of content, including sexuality. Indeed, one of the central ways the New Wave was experienced, in the US and Britain, was as a 'liberated' outburst of erotic expression, often counterpoised, by advocates of the 'New Thing' (as Merril called it), against the priggish puritanism of the Golden Age. Yet this stark contrast, while not unreasonable, tends ultimately, as do most of the historical distinctions drawn between the New Wave and its predecessors, to overemphasize rupture at the expense of continuity, effectively 'disappearing' some of the pioneering trends in 1950s' sf that paved the way for the New Wave's innovations. Moreover, following an insight of Michel Foucault's, it is probably wise to be suspicious of a simplistic 'repressive hypothesis', an assumption that taboos surrounding sexual expression automatically operate to silence discussion of sex rather than to sustain and propagate it.[1] Even Sobchack's Freudian argument, with its emphasis on sublimation, shows that sf, willy-nilly, is always treating sexual topics, perhaps most powerfully when it seems to be primly avoiding them.

On the other hand, while it is certainly worth recalling that Freud's theory of repression involves not merely the psychic cancellation of forbidden data but also, in hydraulic compensation, the unconscious production of neurotic symptoms, I definitely do not wish to understate the true neutralizing power of literary censorship in sf magazine culture prior to the 1960s. Though some Golden Age authors have denied the existence of constraining taboos during the pulp era – Lester del Rey, for example, has argued that he 'never had any magazine reject any story with sex in it' ('Art or Artiness' 85) – there is plenty of testimony by reminiscing writers who either encountered direct resistance to their handling of controversial topics or else practised self-censorship in order to avoid editorial interference in their work. Harry Harrison frankly acknowledged in 1964 that sf writers 'all censor our work for the magazines... We have been so broken to the pulp habit that we cannot relax even if we want to... We have been taboo-ridden too long and seem incapable of accepting sex and bodily functions as a normal part of life' ('We Are Sitting' 42).

Those who refused to self-censor were subjected to the merciless pruning of editorial blue pencils. Tom Purdom has recounted how his 1957 story 'Grieve for a Man' was bowdlerized by the editor of the magazine *Fantastic Universe*: the story features a bullfighter battling a robotic bull, with the assembled crowd cheering for the machine; as written, the matador at one point thinks to himself: 'Well, let them get an erection out of that if they want', which the editor changed to: 'Let them get young again out of that if they want to' (9). A more famous example of such meddling was Frederik Pohl's modification of Harlan Ellison's 'I Have No Mouth, and I Must Scream' (1967) prior to its publication in *If*, where a character who was 'big in the privates' like 'a giant ape' and had 'an organ fit for a horse' was referred to instead as 'like an animal in many ways'.[2] Given the anatomical specifics of these alterations, it is unsurprising – if not exactly forgivable – that some of the more macho young writers of the 1960s should have been infuriated by this symbolic gelding of their work; as Norman Spinrad rather feverishly complained in 1968:

> What does [all this censorship] do to writers? Those who can cut it in the big world out there – like Bradbury and Vonnegut – leave while still in possession of the contents of their scrotums. Others are sufficiently anesthetized by the novocaine of in-group egoboo that they submit to the castrator's knife. There are those who remain men and remain within the field and do the best they can within the limitations and suffer nothing worse than broken hearts. ('Totem and Taboo' 10)

Not all writers, of course, were quite so tamed. Women such as C. L. Moore and Leigh Brackett had been infusing their planetary romances with a decadent sensuality for many years without apparent threat to the ostensible masculinity of their *noms de plume*. And Thomas Scortia has written of how enterprising punsters, throughout the 1940s and 1950s, tried to sneak off-colour jokes or other smutty references past John W. Campbell's resident censor at *Astounding*, editorial assistant Kay Tarrant. Probably the most famous success story in this regard was George O. Smith's 1947 tale 'Rat Race', with its reference to 'the world's first ball-bearing mousetrap', which later turns out to be a tomcat – according to Scortia, this game was called 'slipping one past Kay' (13). Some of Campbell's admirers in the field – such as Harrison, for instance – have attempted to absolve the editor of culpability for the excessive chasteness of his magazine, blaming it instead on the priggish Ms Tarrant (see Harrison, 'Letter'); but there can be little doubt that Campbell himself had, in this area as in so many others, quite firm and eccentric views of what was acceptable and what was not. In his editorial for the October 1965 issue of *Analog*, he defended himself against charges that the material he published scanted important human drives such as erotic desire, opining that '[a]chievement, personal worth, is a more universal motivation of Man than hustling the handiest female into bed' (160), and going on to list the truly great writers whose work had long endured despite its lack of prurience, such as Shakespeare![3]

Not all Golden Age stalwarts shared Campbell's view that sex was a seamy distraction from the exalted heroism of the best sf; certainly, Robert Heinlein's work during the 1960s grew increasingly preoccupied with sexual matters, culminating in the embarrassing debacle of *I Will Fear No Evil* (1970), in which a rich old man's randy brain is transplanted into the nubile body of his female assistant.[4] But the split between Old Guard and New Wave, coinciding as it did with an unparalleled period of erotic openness in the broader culture, inevitably came to involve fraught exchanges regarding the growing explicitness of contemporary sf's depictions of sexuality.[5] I will examine some of the more significant of these exchanges shortly, but first I would like to revisit a moment during the early 1950s when it seemed to a number of contemporary observers as if the walls against tabooed material in sf were finally coming down. This moment tends to get lost in all the furious combat of the subsequent decade, when New Wave authors' calls for a fully 'mature' sf often traded on a caricatured portrait of the genre as naively juvenile prior to the advent of their fearless avant-garde. This is not to diminish the significance of the New Wave's militancy, in the areas of gender and sexual politics especially, but rather to show how a few bold writers and editors of the 1950s broke some of the paths that the New Wave's champions would bravely tread a decade later.

During the early 1950s, a handful of stories were published in the magazines that dealt explicitly with sexual topics long ignored by the genre, often treating their material with a Freudian slant that gave to sf's heroes a lurking, dark unconscious previous incarnations had generally lacked.[6] These tales include, in order of publication: Fritz Leiber's 'The Ship Sails at Midnight' (1950), in which an alien female becomes resident muse – and bisexual lover – to a group of young bohemians; Leiber's 'Coming Attraction' (1950), a stark portrait of an atom-bomb-ravaged future crawling with sadomasochistic subcultures; Philip José Farmer's 'The Lovers' (1952), which boldly affirmed the human–alien miscegenation that many pulp covers had only hinted at; R. J. McGregor's 'The

Perfect Gentleman' (1952), in which a repressed young woman stranded alone on a planet grows a prospective lover from a seed; Sherwood Springer's 'No Land of Nod' (1952), a post-apocalypse tale in which a man breeds with his own daughter in order to continue the human race; Theodore Sturgeon's 'The Sex Opposite' (1952), in which a hermaphroditic symbiote forms a kind of *ménage à trois* (albeit a platonic one) with a heterosexual couple; Sturgeon's 'The World Well Lost' (1953), a tale of gay aliens whose telepathic influence draws out the suppressed homoeroticism linking two male buddies; Farmer's 'Mother' (1953), a creepy story of a mom-obsessed neurotic who is adopted by a conch-like alien, becoming at once its child and its lover; and Idris Seabright's (a.k.a. Margaret St. Clair's) 'Short in the Chest' (1954), in which mandatory sexual relations between members of the armed forces serve as a mechanism for ensuring Cold War harmony.

Significantly, with the exception of 'Coming Attraction', which was featured in the second issue of *Galaxy*, none of these stories appeared in the three major digests of the period (including also *Astounding* and *The Magazine of Fantasy and Science Fiction*). The others were either published in the pulps *Startling Stories* and *Thrilling Wonder Stories*, which were on their last legs at the time, or in second- and third-tier digests just struggling to establish themselves: *Fantastic Stories*, *Fantastic Universe*, and *Universe*. In short, the magazines with the highest profiles in the market tended to shy away from this sort of material. John Brunner has reported that Farmer's 'The Lovers' was rejected by H. L. Gold at *Galaxy* with the note: 'I'll publish this if you can get rid of the sex – I run a family magazine!' ('Interference' 24). Even more disturbingly, Campbell not only rejected Sturgeon's 'The World Well Lost' but is rumoured to have written to other editors warning them against publishing it.[7] As Farmer has commented:

> We had a field wherein, theoretically, the writer was unlimited in choice of subject matter, wherein he had the whole cosmos to roam... Yet the writer was far from being unlimited. He avoided any sex except for the inclusion of the dummy figure of the professor's daughter or an occasional superfemale who was almost always evil... Perhaps the hero and the [heroine] kissed as the story ended, and red Mars sank in the background, but this did not take place often. ('Reap' 7)

An exchange of letters between Sturgeon and Springer regarding the latter's 'No Land of Nod', published in *Thrilling Wonder Stories* in 1953, indicates the repressive editorial climate of the field and the impatient chafing of ambitious authors in the face of it. According to Sturgeon, Springer's story was a failure not because it went too far in its depiction of father–daughter incest, but because it did not go far enough: given a post-apocalypse situation, in which not only is the survival of the species at stake but also prevailing social codes have been literally wiped out with the rest of humanity, the story's hero would not have been as wracked with hesitancy and guilt as Springer depicted. 'Taboos need to be broken', Sturgeon wrote, 'either because they are bad in themselves or because of this odd quirk in human beings that makes it necessary to prove they *can* be broken. But when you break 'em, break 'em clean... [If] science fiction is to remain the viable genre it is, it must be capable of exploration in other frameworks – objectively, and all the way' ('Taboos Need Breaking' 139). Springer's reply in a subsequent issue is revealing: rather than defend the story against Sturgeon's critique, he described the difficulties he had writing and publishing it. A gathering of authors with whom he discussed the basic plot had been excited by the idea, agreeing it addressed an important topic, but had claimed that the story would be 'impossible to sell' – a judgement later affirmed by a number of editors, whose collective verdict, according to Springer, was 'too hot to handle' (134). The sense of pulled punches that Sturgeon complained of was, Springer admitted, a quite calculated gamble to get such incendiary material into print.

One might assume, given this context, that writers eager to shatter taboos were facing not only censorious editors but also puritanical readers who – as Albert Berger has quoted one long-time fan – 'read science fiction to stimulate [their] intellect[s], not [their] gonads' (281). Yet while there was general agreement that the sexually themed stories of the early 1950s were obviously 'controversial', the feedback in the letters pages of *Startling* and *Thrilling Wonder* responding to Springer's 'Nod' and Farmer's 'The Lovers' and 'Mother' was almost uniformly positive, praising the authors' maturity and skill in handling difficult themes. Editor Samuel Mines expressed some amazement that 'nobody called us to task for printing' Springer's story, saying he had expected a storm of protest ('Reader' 135), while John Brunner wrote anticipating attacks by 'nasty little minds' ('We're Glad' 130) on 'The Lovers' that never really materialized.[8]

There were some complaints, of course, such as the following diatribe from one C. M. Morehead (Reverend):

> That *Mother* thing by Farmer made me gag... Should I wish to read about the tendency of some adults to retreat into 'the womb of the world' I'll read text-books on psychology. I certainly don't need it in my recreational reading! ... Shortly after finishing [the story] I was seized with an attack of the flu accompanied with violent seizures of vomiting, [sic] I think *Mother* had something to do with it. (135)

But most correspondents were pleased to see such imaginative handlings of unusual topics, claiming they proved the genre's intellectual boldness and fertility of imagination. One reader praised Mines 'for advocating more mature stories in which sex is allowed to appear in its true light: as an important and essential part of life on this or any other planet' (Corley 131). Poul Anderson, who was just beginning to establish himself as one of the more promising young talents in the field, saluted Farmer for producing, in 'The Lovers', a tale in which sex is treated straightforwardly as a 'biological phenomenon, with no pornography at all. Let's face it', he continued, foreshadowing Merril's brief a decade later, 'babies are not found under cabbage leaves, and there's no reason why the science-fiction writer shouldn't extrapolate the facts of reproduction as he does those of physics and neurology and the other sexless sciences' (135). Like Brunner, Anderson also predicted a flood of complaints from 'prudes and old women', which he feared could have the effect of dissuading Mines from publishing more such tales in future; yet at the same time he acknowledged that the story was the talk of his Minneapolis fan club, where everyone was 'raving about it' (135).

This sort of response validated Mines's own view, expressed in his editorial for the issue of *Startling* featuring 'The Lovers', that sf should be 'about people first and gadgets second': 'It must contain the basic requirements of drama, it must be well told, it must depict real people, it must be as sincere in its emotional values as in calculating the speed of a space ship operating on ultra-galactic drive'. While foreseeing 'squawks' from readers who will 'hate [the story] to pieces', Mines defended such experiments as being essential to revitalize the field, drawing in more sophisticated readers by 'boldly tackling subjects undreamt of ten years ago' ('Ether' 6). Clearly, Mines – along with Brunner and Anderson – should have shown more faith in the fans: on the strength of 'The Lovers' and 'Mother', Farmer was named Best New Author at the first Hugo Awards convention in Philadelphia in 1953.

The point of rehearsing all this background is to indicate that a quite developed discourse regarding taboos and censorship – focused especially on their impact in hindering the artistic growth of the field – had emerged during this period, well before the advent of the New Wave. It is also worth stressing that this debate, and the venturesome stories that emerged from it, was made possible in large part because the period from the early to the mid-1950s was a seller's market for authors; in 1953 alone, 181 issues of 37 different professional magazines were published in the US and Britain, overseen by some two dozen editors, many of whom could afford to take chances with young writers and controversial content in search of a niche in the burgeoning scene. By the end of the decade, however, the boom was over: all the pulps were gone, and the digests had dwindled to a handful of titles controlled by only five editors – Campbell (at *Astounding*), Gold (at *Galaxy* and *If*), Robert P. Mills (at *F&SF*), Cele Goldsmith (at *Amazing* and *Fantastic*), and John Carnell (at *New Worlds, Science-Fantasy*, and *Science-Fiction Adventures*). Campbell and Gold in particular had settled into constricting routines, their risk-taking impulses subordinated to the necessity of providing more or less predictable fare, while Goldsmith's and Carnell's magazines had begun to suffer sharply declining sales. As the new decade dawned, there was a widespread sense of malaise in the field, effectively captured in the title of Earl Kemp's 1960 Hugo-winning fanzine, *Who Killed Science Fiction?*[9]

In the midst of this painful contraction, sf authors began to debate the possibility of founding a writers' union, in order not only to advance their financial interests but also to establish standards for editorial interference in their manuscripts. The newsletter *Proceedings of the Institute for Twenty-First Century Studies*, which appeared between 1959 and 1962, became the main forum for what were sometimes contentious exchanges regarding the degree of aesthetic autonomy writers should legitimately expect in their work, with the discussion turning on occasion to the topic of editors' unilateral expurgation of hot-button content. According to Farmer, Campbell and Gold routinely rejected 'controversial stories based on sex because they found them personally disgusting and disturbing', but they were doing no more than reflecting the current state of the field:

> the *average* s-f reader doesn't really want disturbing or thought-provoking stories, he wants entertainment. The average and even superior editor knows this, and he prefers to entertain the reader. Bob Mills is an exception, but even he is taking a poll of his readers to determine if they wish controversial stories. If the majority says no, then it's Good-bye to s-f magazines for me, both as a reader and writer. I can continue to write innocuous stories, and probably will now and then because I need the money, but my heart won't be in it. (qtd. in Cogswell 139; emphasis in original)

Given this depressing climate, some authors gazed wistfully at greener pastures, pondering the merits of abandoning the field in favour of other, less fettered genres or the broader 'mainstream'; a few, such as Harlan Ellison and Robert Silverberg, had already begun penning soft-core potboilers for fly-by-night paperback houses such as Ember and Nightstand (though they did not brag about this in the newsletter).[10]

Yet Farmer soldiered on, managing to place his delirious tale of a future fertility cult, *Flesh* (1960), with the Galaxy novels series. This book appeared alongside Ballantine's collection *Strange Relations* (1960), which gathered 'Mother' and several other path-breaking stories from the 1950s, and the following year saw publication of a novel-length version of *The Lovers*. Indeed, the growing book market for sf became a site where the editorial shibboleths of the magazines could potentially be transcended. Sturgeon's novel of a hermaphroditic utopia, *Venus Plus X*, which had been unable to find a periodical home in the US (it was serialized in *New Worlds*), was brought out in paperback in 1960. Other older writers who had a lurking streak of ribaldry began to loosen the reins in their novels – for example, Leiber (*The Wanderer* [1964]) and Edgar Pangborn (*Davy* [1964]); and this is not to mention the ongoing spectacle of Heinlein's libidinous conversion. But it was Farmer, renowned as the pioneer taboo-breaker from the previous decade, who often figured as the touchstone for those eager to see sf shed its legacy of strait-laced proscriptions. In a 1964 fanzine article, Charles Platt – who would soon join the editorial coterie at *New Worlds*, the flagship of New Wave innovation – argued that Farmer's work, despite its 'casual American style of hack writing' ('Strange' 35) and the occasional lurid coarseness of its treatment of sexual themes, was breaking important ground in the field: 'by its originality and deliberate disregard of commonly accepted limits of plot and action', Farmer's 'biological experimentation and off-colour sexual ideas' could conceivably inspire a fresh generation of writers 'to produce work of better overall quality' (38).

When Michael Moorcock took over the helm at *New Worlds* in the summer of 1964, improving the 'overall quality' of sf was one of his main goals. Convinced that the genre had for too long consisted of 'boys' stories got up to look like grown-ups' stories' ('Play' 123), Moorcock brought to the task not only a hard-won knowledge of contemporary sf's shortcomings drawn from a long apprenticeship in British fandom, but also a reputation for pugnacious activism on behalf of 'outlaw' writers.[11] He had been featured as a correspondent in a November 1963 exchange in the *Times Literary Supplement* regarding the work of William S. Burroughs, where he had defended that author against a reviewer who denounced his novels as sordid and obscene. Moorcock's championing of Burroughs continued in his debut editorial for *New Worlds*, which claimed that wildly audacious books like *The Ticket That Exploded* (1962) and *Nova Express* (1964) were precisely 'the SF we've all been waiting for', while acknowledging that many traditional fans would be put off by their widespread 'description of sexual aberration and drug addiction' and their 'frequent use of obscenities' ('New Literature' 2). Burroughs's importance for the genre, in Moorcock's eyes, lay not merely in his experimental form, his radical break with conventional modes of narration, but also in his relevance to the current times, with their sceptical questioning of authority and pursuit of fresh experiences. As a subsequent *New Worlds* editorial opined,

> Since SF is growing up... [,] the form must be reshaped and new symbols found to reflect the mood of the sixties... It is no good living in and off the past these days – no good living *in* the world of writers like Heinlein and *off* their terms, symbols, backgrounds and even ideas. The age that formed them is past... Quite often the moral assumptions found in a story of the fifties can be virtually meaningless to today's new generation... ('Symbols' 2–3, emphasis in original)

Yet despite his commitment to boldness and novelty, Moorcock soon discovered that the longstanding conservatism of sf magazine culture was not so readily transcended. After the September 1964 issue of *New Worlds* ran Langdon Jones's story 'I Remember, Anita...', in which the narrator broods intensely over an erotic relationship brutally terminated by the outbreak of nuclear war, an angry reader wrote in to protest against the work's 'downright pornography', warning the editor not to 'forget the circulation of this magazine among young eager readers, who wants [sic] something else than trash just good enough to be sold under the counter' (Van Gastel 125). Moorcock's brusque reply that he was 'not publishing a magazine for schoolboys' (126) probably came back to haunt him in the summer of 1967 when another bawdy tale by Jones, 'The Time Machine', prompted the magazine's printer to refuse to produce the July issue, thus forcing the editor to scramble for replacement copy (Moorcock, 'Introduction' 20). The libidinal rhetoric in 'Anita' had been relatively mild, eschewing stark anatomical references in favour of the evasive blather of pseudo-literary erotica – 'the loin-heat that...suffuse[d] my abdomen', 'the straining symbol of my passion', etc. (75–76)[12] – but 'The Time Machine' upped the ante with its graphic depiction of intercourse between the protagonist and his menstruating lover, a taboo the sf magazine was apparently not prepared to break.

These flare-ups were minor, however, compared to the furore that erupted when *New Worlds* began serializing Norman Spinrad's *Bug Jack Barron* in the December 1967 issue. The novel, strongly influenced by Burroughs's fiction and the theories of Marshall McLuhan, portrays a near-future, media-saturated society in which the eponymous hero, a TV talk-show host, suavely seduces not only the mass audience but also an array of young women, in scenes sprinkled liberally with the lingo of 1960s' eroticism: 'fuck me into the mystic circle of power where it's all at... make me real with your living-color prick... ball me with your image, baby, and I'll ball you with mine' (36, 38). Initially written under contract to Doubleday, the manuscript was rejected by their sf editor, Lawrence Ashmead, who judged the book to be '"unpublishable" in its original form' due to both its sexual explicitness and its chaotic counter-culture language (Spinrad, 'The *Bug Jack Barron* Papers' 13) – making it precisely the sort of hip, unconventional work that Moorcock was seeking for *New Worlds*.

Unfortunately, the magazine's distributor, and the powerful bookshop chain W. H. Smith and Sons, found the serial obscene and refused to stock the offensive issues, putting a major crimp in the journal's shaky finances, which had only recently been shored up by a grant from the British Arts Council. To add insult to injury, a Tory representative in the House of Commons stood up and demanded to know 'why public money was being spent on filth' by the Arts Ministry (Moorcock, 'Introduction' 21). During a visit to the offices of W. H. Smith's, Moorcock was told 'that they would rethink their decision' if he agreed to 'modify the magazine's contents and "kill" the Spinrad serial', which he angrily refused to do (22). It was only under pressure from the Arts Council that Smith's relented and lifted the ban, but *New Worlds* had already received a financial blow from which it never entirely recovered.[13]

When *Bug Jack Barron* was finally published in the US, in a 1969 paperback edition from Avon, it provided more fodder for what was by then a clamorous debate regarding the growing salaciousness of contemporary sf. Defenders of the novel praised its 'energy and sincerity' as a realization of the New Wave's commitment to aesthetic originality and social relevance (Pringle 6), arguing that its sexual explicitness 'must have its place in any reasonably comprehensive portrayal of adult human characters' (Singleton 4); as one reviewer commented, 'there'll be no going back to the "safe" subject matter and the "fit for children" writing dictated by the magazines and many pocketbook publishers' (Geis 17). Critics of the book – such as Samuel Mines, erstwhile editor of the path-breaking pulps of the 1950s – complained about its pervasive profanity, the '*needless* overdone vulgarity which some writers without taste apparently think is realism' (Mines, 'Four-Letter' 18; emphasis in original). To Donald A. Wollheim, former member of the Futurian fan group and current sf editor at Ace Books, Spinrad's 'nauseous epic' was 'depraved, cynical, utterly repulsive and thoroughly degenerate and decadent', proof positive of the essential nihilism of the New Wave. 'It may even win the Hugo – who knows? – but it's garbage just the same' (5).

As these stern remarks indicate, the battle lines being drawn between the self-styled guardians of traditional sf – whose 'wondrous visions' were in danger of being eclipsed by the New Wave's 'stylistic claptrap and downbeat' themes (Wollheim 4) – and the proponents of what Merril called 'The New Thing', an unconventional, countercultural mode of sf writing, often overlapped with a heated debate regarding the ethical and aesthetic merits of overt representations of sexuality. The enemies of the New Wave frequently stereotyped the movement in terms of its allegedly 'sick' obsession with outré forms of sex: one Old-Guard fan claimed that every character in a New Wave story 'must have a sex problem', making the fiction resemble a series of psychiatric case histories (Brazier 5), while John J. Pierce, the most indefatigable polemicist for traditional sf among 1960s' fans, argued that New Wave fiction tended to treat 'the sexual impulse as basically neurotic or even psychotic... bedded in a context of cruelty and disgust' ('Letter' 45). In an essay entitled 'The Devaluation of Values', Pierce went on to argue that the New Wave attitude towards sex was not liberatory at all but rather nihilistic: 'There are plenty of hang-ups, but no joy; lots of explicit description, but no love. The "New Thing" writers don't say in so many words that sex is "dirty", but they manage to convey that impression' (10).

For their part, the New Wave's defenders mocked the sublimated tameness of old-style sf, where 'intersexual relationships did have their place, though always in a hearty familial way, and offstage to boot' (Harrison, *Great Balls* 46–47). Brian Aldiss, reviewing Old-Guard author James White's novel *The Watch Below*, derided the book's 'prissy' timidness: 'All references to sex seem to set [the story's] bold seafaring men "close to panic." They can hardly mention uh menstruation or uh fornication without stuttering' ('Review' 31). '[All] the Simon-pure Asimovs and Heinleins', Aldiss remarked in another context, 'falsified by admitting no worlds below the belt' (*Shape* 63–64). Harlan Ellison, in a sharp exchange with Pierce regarding the alleged degeneracy of contemporary sf, claimed his opponent's position was 'precisely the stand a blue-nosed Puritan would take in the face of such overwhelming changes' as were sweeping through society in the 1960s ('Letter' 48). In short, both sides in the debate basically accused their opponents of displaying some form of sexual pathology, whether puritanical repression or neurotic desublimation.

The theatrical hysteria of this controversy, which consumed the field during the late 1960s and early 1970s, had its dress rehearsal in the furious hype surrounding Ellison's 1967 anthology, *Dangerous Visions*. In an effort to blunt the censorious influence of the magazines, a handful of sf authors during the mid-1960s explored the possibility of launching book series containing all-original short fiction, in the hope of inviting risk-taking work that might otherwise go unpublished. The first series to appear was Damon Knight's Orbit, which premiered in 1966; by the early 1970s, a number of such franchises – Harry Harrison's NOVA, Robert Silverberg's NEW DIMENSIONS, Terry Carr's UNIVERSE – were offering strong competition to the traditional magazines, which were compelled to liberalize their editorial policies as a result.[14] But none made the splash within the genre that *Dangerous Visions* – and its 1972 companion volume, *Again, Dangerous Visions* – did.

Part of the reason for this was the unique personality of its editor. A quarrelsome presence within fandom for over a decade and an unparalleled master of aggressive self-promotion, Ellison built up a huge anticipation for his anthology through breathless letters to fanzines and barn-burning talks at sf conventions. In a Guest of Honour speech at the San Diego Westercon in July 1966 – later published as 'A Time for Daring' – Ellison offered a typically contentious assessment of the present state of the field: it had become safe and stale, and was rapidly driving its best writers into the arms of the literary mainstream, where figures such as Burroughs and Vonnegut were already being celebrated for producing an audacious new brand of sf. 'These people have left us for the very simple reason that they're too big and talented to be constrained by our often vicious, often ungrateful little back water eddy' (33), the sf 'ghetto' whose confining walls were patrolled by a handful of narrow-minded, cosily incestuous gatekeepers. As a result, 'we've been leaching the vitality out of our best writers... [W]hen they write something new and fresh and different and inventive, we don't know where they are' (33). *Dangerous Visions* was geared to provide a welcoming market for just such material – specifically, for fiction the magazines would not publish because of prevailing taboos and prejudices. As Ellison's introduction to the volume trumpeted: 'no one has ever told the speculative writer, "Pull out all the stops. No holds barred, get it said!" Until this book came along' (xxiv).

Containing thirty-three stories, many of them franker in their treatment not only of sexuality but of politics and religion than the average output of the sf magazines, *Dangerous Visions* was without doubt the publishing event of the decade in American sf. Thanks to Ellison's constant, belligerent shtick – which continued in the form of long, button-holing headnotes to the stories – it was impossible *not* to have an opinion about the book; indeed, the enterprise was essentially designed to provoke outrage among conservatives since, if it failed to do so, the editor's diagnosis of the field's paralysing stuffiness would have been obviated. And there is no question that the usual suspects were suitably provoked: Wollheim, for instance, complained about Ellison's persistent 'attempts to shock sensibilities rather than to charge the imagination... a reflection no doubt of the notorious sewers of Hollywood he unfortunately has to dwell in'. Philip José Farmer's contribution in particular – 'Riders of the Purple Wage', an ambitious Joycean punfest simmering with intrafamilial eroticism – Wollheim dismissed as 'thirty thousand words of Freudian nonsense' (6). And an article in Pierce's fanzine, *Renaissance*, griped about the 'degenerate antiheroes' infesting the stories and their many 'sex scene[s] described in detail – preferably perverted' (Schweitzer 10). Yet sf fans largely embraced the book, awarding it three Hugo awards, including a special one to Ellison for editing it.

What is perhaps most interesting about the genre's collective reaction to *Dangerous Visions* is the fact that, as Pamela and Ken Bulmer pointed out in a perceptive review, the book's 'revolutionary' purpose depended 'entirely on the degree of prejudice amongst its readers' (9). If one was primed to be offended by an unapologetic statement of atheism or a scene of brother–sister incest, then the stories would have their intended effect; if not, then it was sometimes difficult to assess their merits simply as stories. Indeed, even some champions of the emerging New Wave were disappointed by the book's insistent commitment to taboo-breaking rather than to elevating the aesthetic standards of the field, as if the two goals were necessarily conjoined. In Merril's view, the result was to 'substitute shock for insight' ('Books' 12/67, 33); as Aldiss tartly remarked: 'the artificially-sustained "family" values of the magazine ethos' did make the stories 'appear quite shocking; but it was rather like shocking your maiden aunt with ribald limericks' (*Trillion* 298). Ellison's in-your-face editorial policy, his calculated rabble-rousing, made it rather too easy to stereotype the fiction in the book, as Philip K. Dick hilariously proved in a brief fanzine article entitled 'The Story to End All Stories for Harlan Ellison's Anthology *Dangerous Visions*':

> In a hydrogen war ravaged society the nubile young women go down to the futuristic zoo and have sexual intercourse with various deformed and nonhuman life forms in the cages. In this particular account a woman who has been patched together out of the damaged bodies of several women has intercourse with an alien female, there in the cage, and later on the woman, by means of futuristic science, conceives. The infant is born, and she and the female in the cage fight over it to see who gets it. The human young woman wins, and promptly eats the offspring, hair, teeth, toes and all. Just after she has finished she discovers that the offspring is God. (47)

Still, despite its tendentiousness, *Dangerous Visions* was an important landmark in the genre, marking a point of no return for the treatment of controversial topics; in its wake, efforts to suppress uncomfortable content became increasingly unsustainable. As a result, the erotic frankness of books such as *Bug Jack Barron* grew progressively more acceptable, despite the complaints of the Old-Wave crowd.

In the remainder of this essay, I would like briefly to anatomize three significant and at times overlapping ways in which sf's new sexual openness was expressed during the late 1960s and early 1970s. The first of these – the feminist critique of normative gender roles and sexual relationships, whose key literary achievements include the short fiction of Alice Sheldon (a.k.a. James Tiptree, Jr) and Joanna Russ's novel *The Female Man* (1975) – has received extensive coverage in the extant scholarship and thus requires little summary. What I want to stress here is the way that feminist sf served as a kind of conscience for the New Wave movement, seeking to ensure that the genre's newfound aesthetic freedoms would be used with some degree of moral accountability. In many cases, feminist sf built upon – and ethically complicated – the genre's quasi-Freudian experiments of the 1950s: several of Sheldon's stories – such as 'And I Awoke and Found Me Here on the Cold Hill's Side' (1971) or 'Love is the Plan, the Plan is Death' (1973) – can be read as corrective extensions of Farmer's pioneering tales of inter-species desire, drawing out the fetishistic exoticization of otherness lurking within them. More obviously, feminist sf writers served as a counterweight to the more or less explicit misogyny of the sexual revolution: for example, when Ursula K. Le Guin reviewed C. W. Runyon's forgettable 1971 novel *Pig World*, a tale of near-future dystopia rife with gratuitous sexual description, she complained about the crudely objectifying way female bodies were evoked. As she remarked: 'freedom from censorship, and the resulting advent of sex to science fiction, are altogether good. I hope we never take one step back towards prudery'; but 'where there's freedom there's responsibility', and the male sf author should strive to depict his women characters as somewhat more than 'a pair of styrofoam boobies' ('Thea and I' n.p.).

The difficult balancing act Le Guin is negotiating here – acknowledging the progress achieved in overcoming censorship while bemoaning the resulting excesses – points to the generally fraught response of second-wave feminism to the eruption of sexual liberalism during the 1960s. As Alice Echols has observed, the growing erotic openness of the 1960s 'increased women's sense of sexual vulnerability by acknowledging women's right to sexual pleasure while ignoring the risks associated with sexual exploration for women' (289). The '"male" sexual revolution', in Ruth Rosen's words, 'needed to be redefined in terms that would ensure gender equality, not exploitation' (144) – and this redefinition is precisely what feminist sf set out to accomplish. In the frankness of their sexual representations,

Sheldon's stories, for example, could not have been published ten years earlier, yet their explicitness is never gratuitous but rather is precisely driven by a conviction that the untrammelled expression of male lust is a potential catastrophe for the species. Russ's *Female Man* excoriates the heterosexist assumption that women should make their bodies available for casual sex to any desirous male, yet it also uses the new sexual freedom to explore graphically lesbian sexuality: 'It would be delightful to have erotic play with Elena Twason; I feel this on my lips and tongue, in the palms of my hands, all my inside skin. I feel it down below, in my sex' (147). This complex dialectical response to the epochal liberations of the period is one of the most profound legacies of feminist sf.

A second way the genre responded to the lifting of the ban on explicit content, as Le Guin's comments about *Pig World* indicate, was the proliferation of various forms of sf pornography. While Runyon's novel was put out by a mainstream sf line (Doubleday, which only a few years earlier had rejected *Bug Jack Barron*), a host of books were released by porn publishers exploiting the popularity of science-fictional settings or themes. Often, these were one-shot efforts by authors merely dabbling in the genre – e.g., Hughes Cooper's *Sexmax* (1969), in which libidinal revolutionaries battle a controlling dystopian regime[15] – but in a number of cases, the novels were produced by well-established sf authors and fans, sometimes under pseudonyms, for speciality imprints such as Midwood, Bee-Line, and Brandon House. Andrew J. Offutt and Richard E. Geis were the most prolific of these sf pornographers, generating titles such as *Fruit of the Loins* (1970; by Offutt as 'John Cleve'), about a spaceman who returns to a female-only Earth and becomes a walking sperm bank, and *The Sex Machine* (1967; by Geis), in which the eponymous time-traveller from an erotomaniac future dutifully services a bevy of twentieth-century women. These plot descriptions suggest that the vast majority of these books were predictable male fantasies thinly veiled in sf trappings. As Gabe Eisenstein observed in a review of George Shaw's *Astrosex* (1971), the tale's futuristic scenario was basically used 'to pack in more and better sex scenes than could be justified logically in a contemporary setting' (R5); thus, the appeal was primarily to a porn audience rather than to sf readers – a point emphasized by Richard Delap in a review of Geis's 1969 novel *Raw Meat*: 'The eroticism crowd will probably dig it, but the sf group will only sigh [and] shake its collective head' ('SF/Sex' 29).

Yet there were, during this period, some thoughtful efforts to fuse sf and pornography. Offutt's novels *Evil is Live Spelled Backwards* (1970) and *The Great 24-Hour THING* (1971) were more serious attempts to develop sexual possibilities out of science-fictional premises than were the books released under his John Cleve byline, with the former title projecting the social fallout from the invention of a powerful chemical aphrodisiac. Offutt coined the term 'sextrapolation' to describe the planning that went into these works ('Extrapolation' 27) – which he attempted to market to sf publishers, only to be rebuffed (Offutt, 'Grumlin' 5). The ideological significance of 'sextrapolation' was recognized by Alexis Gilliland in a 1970 essay, 'The Pornography of Science Fiction', where he argued that a true synthesis of porn and sf could proliferate erotic possibilities that transcend mundane experience, generating visions of polymorphous otherness in a kind of 'non-linear or branched-chain orgy' (141).

Without question, the works that went furthest towards accomplishing this heady goal were the novels released during the late 1960s by Essex House, a short-lived publisher of ambitious erotica. These included Hank Stine's *Season of the Witch* (1968), a more serious take on transgender themes than Heinlein's *I Will Fear No Evil*, in which a convicted rapist is compelled to expiate his crime by being transformed into a woman, and Philip José Farmer's *The Image of the Beast* (1968), a phantasmagoric tale of hermaphroditic aliens who sexually humiliate and prey upon a hard-boiled detective. Though both stories contain an abundance of graphic imagery, they are hardly fodder for male masturbation fantasies since they use their science-fictional set-ups precisely to lay bare the pathologies of rampant machismo. While one would be hard-pressed to call them feminist, they certainly escape the strictures of Le Guin's critique of *Pig World*. Also, thanks to Essex House's shrewd packaging and marketing – including striking cover designs and afterwords by major sf authors (Ellison in the case of Stine's novel, Sturgeon in the case of Farmer's) – the books managed to reach and engage a fairly broad sf audience.[16]

The third way in which sf adapted to the climate of sexual openness in the 1960s and 1970s basically involved non-pornographic forms of 'sextrapolation': projecting future trends based on current sexual mores or inventing novel sexual practices and relationships. An excellent example of the former option is Robert Silverberg's 1973 story 'In the Group', which satirizes 1960s' countercultural attitudes in its portrayal of therapeutic group sex channeled and enhanced by biotechnological interfaces. Many such tales depict the accelerating reification of sexuality as attractive, sophisticated machines come to assume increasingly intimate roles in everyday life: Robert Sheckley's 'Can You Feel Anything When I Do This?' (1969) involves a love affair between a housewife and her new high-tech vacuum cleaner, while Ian Watson's 'The Sex Machine' (1970) depicts a soda-vending kiosk whose transactions with consumers are explicitly erotic. Though not exactly a work of science fiction, J. G.

Ballard's 1973 novel *Crash* is perhaps the best-known instance of this trend, with its corrosive vision of denatured humans bleakly coupling with – and through – their cars. Probably the most celebrated New Wave story that deals with an 'alien' form of sex is Samuel Delany's 'Aye, and Gomorrah...' (1967), which creates a new, futuristic fetish in its depiction of the fraught connection between castrated spacers and worshipful 'frelks'; while the tale obviously riffs on contemporary sexual arrangements (rock-star groupies, homosexual cruising), the spacer–frelk relationship achieves a level of truly estranging otherness that cannot readily be recuperated into existing sexual paradigms. A number of New Wave works – such as Silverberg's *Son of Man* (1971) and Sheldon/Tiptree's 'All the Kinds of Yes' (1972) – deal with sex between humans and gender-bending aliens, though if we consider these as allegories of bohemian bisexuality, they might be seen as examples of the trend of extrapolating existing sexual models.

Sextrapolation in all its varieties became such a common staple of New Wave sf that the 1970s saw the publication of four theme anthologies devoted to the subject: Joseph Elder's *Eros in Orbit* (1973), Thomas N. Scortia's *Strange Bedfellows* (1973), Douglas Hill's *The Shape of Sex to Come* (1978), and Michael Parry and Milton Subotsky's *Sex in the 21st Century* (1979). Some of these books reprinted the pioneering fictions of the 1950s alongside fresher efforts, thus affirming a continuity between the decades that the New Wave's champions (and detractors) sometimes wilfully obscured. Indeed, Sheldon's 'All the Kinds of Yes' reads like a soft-core update of Fritz Leiber's 'The Ship Sails at Midnight' and Sturgeon's 'The Sex Opposite', and a number of other tales of alien sex from the 1960s and 1970s stand squarely in the footprints of Farmer's 'The Lovers' and 'Mother'. The New Wave debate regarding sex in sf not only persistently touched base with Farmer's work but often, as we have seen, centrally involved Farmer himself. When Stanislaw Lem set out to write a magisterial overview of the topic – 'Sex in Science Fiction', published in the Australian fanzine *SF Commentary* in 1971 – he saluted Farmer as 'the one man to whom we owe so much' (5), though he went on to chastise his 1950s stories as scientifically implausible, which led to an angry exchange with Farmer in subsequent issues.

Leaving aside the question of whether the biological possibilities outlined in 'The Lovers' and 'Mother' are convincingly rendered or not, what is most interesting about Farmer's reply to Lem is his evident deep pride in his achievement: as he testifies, his landmark feats of sextrapolation 'gave me a great joy, an intellectual near-orgasm... What differentiates the sf writer from the writer of other types of fiction is an intellectual joy in creating well-thought-out and original worlds' – a delight Farmer went on to compare with the dolphin's vibrant play in the ocean ('Letter' 22). This ludic sense of liberated energies lies at the core of New Wave sextrapolations as well, even when they are tinged with Freudian satire and neo-Gothic grotesquerie (as Farmer's 'Mother' certainly was). While sometimes sniggeringly adolescent, seldom politically correct, and often marked by now-dated sexual-political rhetoric, sf of the 1960s and 1970s made possible a new frankness about sex in the genre that the magazine culture of previous decades had at best muted if not censored outright. The libidinal genie had escaped from the bottle, and there was no putting it back in again.

Notes

1. See Foucault's *History of Sexuality, Vol. 1* (17–49).
2. Compare the magazine version (26) with the restored text in Ellison's collection (7, 11), where an authorial introduction acknowledges that the story 'got a little too rough for *If* in spots' (2).
3. For a critique of this specific editorial, see Perry, who castigates Campbell for 'want[ing] to eliminate sex as an ingredient of great and enduring literature' (9). See also the exchange of letters published in Lewis, where Campbell responds to the accusation that he persistently cleaned up authors' prose to protect younger readers 'from the evils of sensual pleasure' (14).
4. For an early assessment of this shift in Heinlein's writing, see Steele. Fan reviews of *I Will Fear No Evil* expressed shock at the novel's heavy-breathing prurience: see Edwards, who called it 'a very sick book' (31), and Boyer, who considered it 'worthless' and 'depraved' (14).
5. For a study of the general easing of literary censorship during the postwar period, see de Grazia; a more broad-based survey of sexual mores in the 1960s is given by Allyn.
6. Attebery and Larbalestier have shown in great detail how sf, from the pulp era onwards, was deeply engaged with the exploration of gender relationships and 'sex role' issues; the overt representation of specifically sexual acts, desires, and fantasies, however, was generally interdicted.
7. The source for this fact is Scortia, though he only identifies 'an editor for whom [Sturgeon] had been doing a great deal of work' (63); the inference that this was Campbell seems clear enough. According to Scortia, the editor of *Imagination*, after receiving Campbell's missive, 'out of sheer spite very nearly bought the story but finally decided against it, the temper of the times being what it was' (63).
8. This lack of widespread outrage contravenes the prevailing view that 'The Lovers' in particular was received by fans as somehow beyond the pale. For example, Douglas Hill, editor of an anthology of erotically themed sf, *The Shape of Sex to Come* (1978), asserts that 'tirades poured in from the prudes, the repressors, the usual sort of folk who form censorship committees' (9); yet a perusal of the letters pages of *Startling* during 1952 belies this claim, as Mike Ashley has recently pointed out (14–16). It should be said, though,

that, for all their trafficking in themes of incest and species crossbreeding, 'No Land of Nod' and 'The Lovers' were still operating within the borders of heterosexuality. It is likely that Sturgeon's 'The World Well Lost', with its homoerotic focus, was more overtly outrageous in context: long-time fan Richard Delap, reviewing Thomas Scortia's 1973 anthology *Strange Bedfellows* (which includes Sturgeon's story), remarked on the genre's lingering silence regarding this 'touchy item', which 'seems to embarrass the shit out of most people' ('Tomorrow's Libido' 6).

9. Earl Kemp, incidentally, was a longtime editor and publisher of erotic literature, hiring slumming sf authors to churn out copy for Nightstand Books in the early 1960s before eventually being indicted by the Nixon Justice Department in 1971 for releasing – along with erstwhile sf editor William Hamling – a bawdily illustrated edition of the Report of the Presidential Commission on Obscenity and Pornography. For more information on Kemp's career, see Hemmingson.
10. The prolific Silverberg released a flood of porn novels under several pseudonyms, with titles such as *Party Girl* (1960) and *Beatnik Wanton* (1964); he also wrote a number of works of popular sexology under the byline 'L. T. Woodward' (see Silverberg's 'My Life as a Pornographer').
11. For more on the emergence of the New Wave out of 1960s' British fan culture, see my '*New Worlds* and the New Wave in Fandom'. For an overview of the New Wave movement as a whole, see my 'New Wave'.
12. Colin Greenland discusses the controversy spurred by Jones's 'Anita' in Chapter 3 of *The Entropy Exhibition*, his fine critical study of *New Worlds* (see 23–25); the chapter, entitled 'Love Among the Mannequins', offers an insightful analysis of the magazine's handling of gender and sexuality under Moorcock's editorship.
13. During the few years left to it, the journal continued to tackle controversial topics – including a special 'Does Sex Have a Future?' issue in March 1970. According to Greenland, Brian Aldiss was sometimes known to refer to the journal as 'Lewd Worlds' (33).
14. Just three years after Ellison's 'I Have No Mouth, and I Must Scream' was shorn of its genital references when published in *Galaxy*, the magazine serialized Robert Silverberg's 1970 novel *The World Inside*, with its unflinching depiction of a hyper-urbanized, sexually 'liberated' society. In one episode, a future historian muses on the squeamish puritanism of his twentieth-century forebears: 'Such importance placed on mere words? Jason pronounces the odd monosyllables aloud in his research cubicle. "Fuck. Cunt. Fuck. Cunt. Fuck." They sound merely antiquated. Harmless, certainly' ('Throwbacks' 44). Gardner Dozois has observed that it was almost as if Silverberg were remarking: '*look what I'm getting away with saying in Galaxy!*' (13; emphasis in original).
15. For a discussion of *Sexmax*, see Broege (112–14).
16. A number of fanzines in the US and Britain reviewed the Essex House titles enthusiastically: see Delap, 'Tomorrow's Libido'; Offutt, 'SF & F for the Big Kids'; and Platt, 'Non-Category Fiction'. In 1968, Samuel R. Delany wrote a hard-core novel, *Equinox*, that he hoped to place with Essex House, but the press folded before negotiations could begin. Eventually released by Lancer Books in 1973 under the title *The Tides of Lust*, the book is an extreme erotic fantasy in the tradition of Sade and Bataille, but it is not, except in the very loosest sense, a work of sf.

Towards a Queer Genealogy of SF

Wendy Gay Pearson

> Genealogy as an analysis of descent is thus situated within the articulation of the body and history. Its task is to expose a body totally imprinted by history and the process of history's destruction of the body.
>
> — Michel Foucault, 'Nietzsche, Genealogy, History' 148

> Genealogy makes no presumptions about the metaphysical origins of things, their final teleology, the continuity or discontinuity of temporally contiguous elements, or the causal, explanatory connections between events. Instead, genealogy can be seen as the study of elements insofar as they are already interpreted, a study aimed at unsettling established models of knowledge and epistemological presumptions involved in the production of history, philosophy, and morality.
>
> —Elizabeth Grosz, *Volatile Bodies: Toward a Corporeal Feminism* 145

A Livable Life?

It comes down to this: in a world where so many of us are unable to find a home, a place which is both materially and affectively livable, should we not all be able, at the very least, to find a home amongst the seemingly infinite planes of the imagination? And where else are such imaginative worlds to be found – the air breathable, the water potable, the crops edible, the houses built, and the furniture waiting to be rearranged – if not in science fiction? And if what is making our lives unlivable in the present has to do with the construction, regulation, and normalization of sexuality, with its concomitant effects upon sex, gender, race, and so on, then surely we may look to sf to posit worlds in which it is possible both to live differently and to think differently about how we live. If, indeed, what makes life unlivable for us is the way in which our world's understanding of gender and sexuality categorizes us as incomprehensible, insane or even inhuman, is not science fiction one of the places we might turn to find our own humanity even in the very figure of the alien her/him/itself?

The purpose of this chapter is to investigate the possibilities for constructing a queer genealogy of sf. Such genealogies rest upon particular reading strategies, including those which I originally discussed in 'Alien Cryptographies', as ways of reading which might help us to 'see how sf and queer may illuminate each other' (18). Any queer genealogy of sf, then, must take account of the possibility for queer readings to do more than simply locate analogies, decipher coded meanings, retrieve supposedly hidden or subcultural generic histories, and identify overtly queer texts. Such genealogical practices, as Elizabeth Grosz argues, aim 'at unsettling established models of knowledge and epistemological presumptions involved in the production of history, philosophy, and morality' (145). The history that is unsettled by genealogical readings of sf incorporates generic history, including the history of constituting and delimiting generic boundaries. This is a topic I will consider in more detail later in this chapter when I examine how sf texts, such as Ursula K. Le Guin's *The Left Hand of Darkness* (1969), position sexuality, in particular, as a lens through which to refract the potential to be recognized as human, the capacity for a livable life, and the possibility of asserting agency and subjectivity. The centrality of sexuality, and especially queer sexualities, thus links works of obvious sf – including *The Left Hand of Darkness*, Geoff Ryman's *The Child Garden* (1990), and Theodore Sturgeon's *Venus Plus X* (1960) – to texts that seem on the surface to be at most liminally science-fictional, such as Hiromi Goto's *The Kappa Child* (2002) or John Greyson's film *Zero Patience* (1993). Queer readings of these texts not only function to discern the ways in which each forms part of a queer genealogy of science fiction, but, beyond this, to apprehend the ways in which they operate synergistically to construct that very genealogy through the reciprocal connectivities such readings identify.

Reading sf queerly, we queer it as much as we are queered by it. As readers, we become different through the act of reading, of opening ourselves to the flow of possibilities, of new ideas, of new bodies. And it is on the body – whether human body, alien body, virtual body, body politic, body of work, body of writing – that queer exerts its greatest effects. But it is also the body (in all of these senses) that is threatened by queer's potential disintegration in the face of a defensive and frighteningly powerful heteronormative hegemony over lives and meanings. To read queerly, to construct queer genealogies, is not then a simple or apolitical task, but one that is fraught with potentials for meaning-making, for laying oneself open to various kinds of disciplinary power, both discursive and material, and for locating the very queer kinships among and within sf texts that work to undo the discursive and material conditions that make it hard to find livable worlds, even in the imagination.

Undoings: Queering the Politics of Origin

> Genealogy does not pretend to go back in time to restore an unbroken continuity that operates beyond the dispersion of forgotten things; its duty is not to demonstrate that the past actively exists in the present, that it continues secretly to animate the present, having imposed a predetermined form to all vicissitudes. Genealogy does not resemble the evolution of a species and does not map the destiny of a people.
>
> —Michel Foucault, 'Nietzsche, Genealogy, History' 148

That the Foucauldian idea of genealogy is also intimately connected with the ways in which many critics and theorists have come to think about gender and sexuality is evident in Judith Butler's citation of Foucault at the beginning of her first book, *Gender Trouble* (1990), where she notes that exposing 'the foundational categories of sex, gender, and desire as effects of a specific formation of power requires a form of critical inquiry that Foucault, reformulating Nietzsche, designates as "genealogy"'. Butler adds that

> [a] genealogical critique refuses to search for the origins of gender, the inner truth of female desire, a genuine or authentic sexual identity that repression has kept from view; rather, genealogy investigates the political stakes in designating as an *origin* and *cause* those identity categories that are in fact the *effects* of institutions, practices, discourses with multiple and diffuse points of origin. The task of this inquiry is to center on – and decenter – such defining institutions: phallogocentrism and compulsory heterosexuality. (viii–ix, emphasis in original)

If centring on and decentring the foundational institutions of patriarchy and heteronormativity is the task of genealogical inquiry, as Butler argues, how then do we create a genealogy of queer sf? Certainly one way is to follow Butler's paradigm, that is, to concentrate our inquiry on works which critique those institutions, practices, and discourses which have defined the ways in which gender and sexuality are rendered culturally intelligible or unintelligible, just as particular embodied expressions of gender and sexuality are made to constitute their possessors as inside or outside the borders of the normal and the human. This is a theme which Butler has taken up throughout her work, but most particularly in her recent study, *Undoing Gender* (2003). Yet another approach would be to look at those forms of cultural expression which naturalize certain forms of gender and sexuality. Revealing the heteronormativity of such works frequently involves exposing representations of sexuality *per se*. Eve Kosofsky Sedgwick argues that heterosexuality is so discursively preserved from scrutiny – and thus from representation *as* sexuality – that it comes to be 'consolidated as the *opposite* of sex'. She further states that the 'making historically visible of heterosexuality is difficult because, under its institutional pseudonyms, such as Inheritance, Marriage, Dynasty, Family, Domesticity, and Population, heterosexuality has been permitted to masquerade so fully as History itself – when it has not presented itself as the totality of Romance' (*Tendencies* 10–11). Indeed, the queer project of revealing heterosexuality to itself has become sufficiently commonplace that it now seems a little like shooting fish in a barrel; if I were to mix my metaphors, I might add that, in this respect, learning to see heterosexuality-as-sexuality is a little like perceiving the vase between the faces: once seen it can no longer not be seen. What makes this a difficult proposition is that there are many people who do not want to see it.

For the purposes of our queer genealogy, however, the more useful project may perhaps be the interrogation of the historical and cultural conditions that made it possible for heterosexuality to position itself as its pseudonyms – that is, as Butler notes, to interrogate heteronomativity as a range of '*effects* of institutions, practices, discourses with multiple and diffuse points of origin' (*Gender Trouble* ix). Such a project must indeed be inherently genealogical, since it takes up Foucault's proposition that genealogy not only marks a view of the past that looks for beginnings, rather than for a single origin, and that tracks these beginnings in ways not necessarily linear or progressive, but also situates itself 'within the articulation of the body and history. Its task is to expose a body totally imprinted by history and the process of history's destruction of the body' ('Nietzsche, Genealogy, History' 148). Queer genealogies of sf, then, are engaged as much in a process of un/doing history as they are of un/doing gender. Indeed, the process of undoing is inseparable from the process of doing, since the former depends upon the latter; if we can return momentarily to Butler, it would seem that that undoing may be less a refusal than a failed iteration, even where that failure is, to some extent, deliberate and agential.

In *Undoing Gender*, Butler focuses on the connection between doing – or failing to do – gender and being able to live in the world. Her work here is 'about the experience of *becoming undone* in both good and bad ways. Sometimes a normative conception of gender can undo one's personhood, undermining the capacity to persevere in a livable life. Other times, the experience of a normative restriction becoming undone can undo a prior conception of who one is only to inaugurate a relatively newer one that has greater livability as its aim' (1; emphasis in original). Given the extent to which gender is conflated with sexuality in contemporary thought, either because gender is seen as an effect of (hetero)sexuality or because it is understood as the same as sexuality (so that gay people, for example, are seen as having become another gender entirely), Butler's argument points to the extent to which the doing of gender regulates, enables, and limits the capacity to have a livable life and to be recognized as human.[1] Butler adds that

> [if] part of what desire wants is to gain recognition, then gender, insofar as it is animated by desire, will want recognition as well. But if the schemes of recognition that are available to us are those that 'undo' the person by conferring recognition, or 'undo' the person by withholding recognition, then recognition becomes a site of power by which the human is differentially produced. That means that to the extent that desire is implicated in social norms, it is bound up with the question of power and with the problem of who qualifies as the recognizably human and who does not. (*Undoing Gender* 2)

The connection that Butler makes between the concept of doing gender and of being undone by it, or by its recognition or misrecognition, and the possibility of being seen as human is an important one in terms of understanding the exploration of gender and sexuality within science fiction – which is, after all, so often about what it means to be human. It is, for example, the very crux of Le Guin's *The Left Hand of Darkness*, where the ways in which the Gethenians fail to do gender – since biological sex, for Gethenians, is a temporary state rather than a permanent identity – makes them seem inhuman to the Terran narrator, Genly Ai. By contrast, the ways in which Genly does gender, as a being in a state of permanent *kemmer* or potential sexual arousal, a state seen by Gethenians as a form of perversion, renders him less than human to most Gethenians. The question of humanity is literalized in the novel, and in science fiction generally, by the creation of alien races with different biologies, bodies, and cultures; the embodiment of gender, the notion that one is shaped in particular ways by one's sexual biology, is fundamentally challenged by the Gethenians in ways that are profoundly linked to the question of normativity and the problem of recognition. Genly, for example, almost invariably misrecognizes the Gethenians by trying to impose a normative Terran gender schema onto Gethenian behaviour, stereotyping particular traits as 'masculine' or 'feminine' in ways that are meaningless on Gethen. Genly's talent for misrecognition works on both macro and micro levels, as he misunderstands both Gethenians in general and individual Gethenians, notably Estraven. As the novel traces Genly's slow assimilation into Gethenian culture, it also tracks a kind of undoing of gender – or at least of Genly's perception that gender is immutable and immanent – and an alteration in Genly's perception of who is and is not human.

Le Guin, as other critics have noted, marks the novel's emphasis on Genly's function as a perceiving subject through the pun in his last name, Ai/eye/I.[2] The eye that sees and the I that sees cancel each other out for most of the novel, as Genly's assertion of his particularly Terran subjectivity prevents him from recognizing others as human, first Estraven and the Gethenians, then his own shipmates and colleagues, who appear to him at the end of the novel as aliens, as perverts. If seeming to have two genders but only one sex (or should that be one gender, but two sexes?) renders the Gethenians inhuman at the start of the novel, at the end it is still gender and, especially, sexuality that humanize or dehumanize for Genly Ai: 'But they all looked strange to me, men and women, well as I knew them. Their voices sounded strange: too deep, too shrill. They were like a troupe of great, strange animals…' (296).[3]

What *The Left Hand of Darkness* does not address is how Genly comes to his assumptions that humans are naturally bi-sexed, that gender is a function of sex, and that sexuality is determined by both sexes in a perfectly binary fashion. While Le Guin's work has become increasingly sophisticated in its approaches to these issues, particularly sexuality, and while *Left Hand* remains a remarkably powerful thought experiment about the effects of binary sex/gender systems and what might happen if they were removed, the novel examines the effects of such a system rather than considering the system itself *as* effect. What Genly's 'before and after' states of mind have in common is that they still categorize certain ways of doing gender and sexuality as wrong and therefore perverse. This links them through psychiatric discourse to the nineteenth-century classification of the homosexual not merely as a species, but as one that is intrinsically diseased, whether mentally or physically. For Genly, in fact, the perverted or diseased nature of the improper performance of gender marks itself as a visceral reaction against the body itself. Genly's colleagues are 'great, strange animals… great apes with intelligent eyes, all of them in rut, in kemmer', phrases which locate them as merely related to, but also quite clearly *not*, human – and, moreover, which specifically implicate their sexuality, their permanent and unnatural kemmering, as that which renders them inhuman (296). Genly's experience is a process of disorientation and reorientation that is *explicitly sexual*; it is about what acts he perceives bodies to be capable of, with whom, and when. As Sara Ahmed points out, 'If the sexual involves the contingency of bodies coming into contact with other bodies, then sexual disorientation slides quickly into social disorientation, *as a disorientation in how things are arranged.* The effects are indeed uncanny: what is familiar, what is passed over in the veil of its familiarity, becomes rather strange' (162; emphasis in original). It is precisely this contingency of bodies, the possibility, if not the fact, of sexual contact, that situates Genly's disorientation as to who is and who is not human firmly in the corporeality of the sexed and sexualized body. Thus the resolution of the novel is not simply the incorporation of the Gethenians into the human, but the displacement from the human of all other Ekumenical races. In this sense, despite the productive potential of the Gethenians for the imagination of and continued investigation into the possibilities of thinking sex/gender differently, the association with first one set of bodies and anatomies, then the other, with perversion and thus with conceptions of non-heterosexuality as diseased, works not so much to undo heteronormativity in the novel as to instate the possibility of Genly's interpellation into a form of 'hermaphronormativity', to coin a term. And in *The Left Hand of Darkness* as Le Guin first imagined the people of Gethen, the hermaphronormativity of the Gethenians was itself strictly heterosexual, thus rendering the distinction between different expressions of normativity entirely moot.

Blinded by Science? Appearances and Disappearances

> People continually sneezed, summer or winter. They were always ill, with virus... Because of advances in medicine, acceptable patterns of behaviour could be caught or administered.
>
> Viruses made people cheerful and helpful and honest. Their manners were impeccable, their conversation well-informed, their work speedy and accurate. They believed the same things.
>
> —Geoff Ryman, *The Child Garden* 1

It may perhaps be more obvious that *The Left Hand of Darkness* is science fiction than that it is queer; indeed, one might argue that *Left Hand*'s queering of gender is partial, more productive *in posse* and in the discussions that it has inspired than in the actual novel. Alternatively, one might opine that while Genly's inevitably flawed view of the Gethenians causes a reversal of his own affiliation with the human, rather than a queering that would instate a non-binary acceptance of both Gethenians and Ekumenicals, the greater queerness of the novel lies always in what Genly *fails* to see: first the queer humanity of the literally alien bodies of the Gethenians, then the newly queered humanity of his original compatriots. Genly has very little history and virtually no understanding of the processes of interpellation and subjectification in which he is caught up. By contrast, John Greyson's *Zero Patience*, a musical film about AIDS, is superficially difficult to recognize as generic sf, yet deeply informed by contemporary critical theory and remarkably clear about the constitution of the subject through empiricism and enlightenment science. Like Geoff Ryman's novels *Was* (1992) and *Lust* (2001), *Zero Patience* is remarkably science-fictional for something that is apparently more fantasy, magic realism, or ghost story than it is sf. However, the storyline of *Zero Patience* is as dependent upon science, as illustrative of contemporary anxieties about it, and as focused on revealing its effects on the interpellation of individuals as healthy or diseased, homosexual or heterosexual, as any queer science fiction text might be. Indeed, as I will discuss shortly, *Zero Patience* has much in common not only with *Was*, but also with Ryman's *The Child Garden*, a much more obviously science-fictional work.

Zero Patience begins by introducing the spectator to the historical figure of Sir Richard Francis Burton (John Robinson), who survives as the chief taxidermist for the Museum of Natural History in Toronto by means of an unfortunate encounter with the Fountain of Youth. Burton is engaged in constructing a Hall of Contagion for the Museum; discovering that he has lost his 'King Tut', the 'Dusseldorf Plague Rat', to financial cutbacks, Burton searches for an alternative spectacle around which to centre his exhibit. A suggestion arrives magically by way of the epidemiological cluster study which first identified AIDS as a sexually transmitted disease, folded into a paper aeroplane. Burton unfolds it and traces out the connections to arrive at 'Patient Zero' (Normand Fauteux), Greyson's deeply ironic recasting of the idea that one individual – identified by journalist Randy Shilts in his book *And the Band Played On* (1987) as a Québécois flight attendant named Gaëtan Dugas – introduced AIDS to North America. Bursting into song, Burton convinces the Museum director that rebuilding the exhibit around Patient Zero will not only make it a success, but will also play its part in rebuilding the 'empire of certainty' that had put the European race 'on top' through its devotion to empirical science. As the story progresses, however, Burton encounters the ghost of Zero, whom only he can see, and undergoes a radical reorientation which sees him engaged in revealing, instead of exploiting, the particular media spectacle that scape-

Figure 1: Miss HIV, floating among Zero's blood cells, sings about the identification of HIV as the cause of AIDS. Film still courtesy of John Greyson.

goated Zero. Burton's reorientation has a threefold cause: his desire for Zero, his growing love for him, and (ironically) his increasing conviction that the epidemiological cluster study which 'identified' Zero as the AIDS version of Typhoid Mary involved bad, or at least misinterpreted, science. The film ends with both the science and the media thoroughly discredited, in part through a musical number sung by Miss HIV (Michael Callen), in which the personified virus points out that Zero's participation in the cluster study did not prove that he was the first person in North America with HIV, but rather saved lives by proving that the virus could be sexually transmitted and so instituting a regime of safer sex.

Roger Hallas argues that Foucauldian genealogy functions as a critical tool to construct a reading of *Zero Patience* that 'historicizes the spectacle of AIDS through a defamiliarization of its contemporary self-evidence, situating it in relation to the historical context of nineteenth century scientific positivism, the colonialist construction of the other, and the concomitant emergence of technologies of mass spectacle' (18–19). Indeed, the topic of AIDS cries out for critical reading precisely at these levels – the legacy of scientific positivism that constructs AIDS as an object of scientific inquiry and the relentless production of already racialized, gendered, and sexualized scientific and populist discourses about disease and abjection; the refutation of what is taken as self-evident, in particular the notion that AIDS was (and is) a 'gay disease' or an 'African disease'; and the deconstruction of mediated spectacles of disease, perversion, and otherness. *Zero Patience* achieves these levels of critique by re-situating the story of 'Patient Zero' as the target of musical parody intertwined with a trans-historical, loosely science-fictional romance between a 174-year-old eccentric, if not actually mad, scientist and a very sexy ghost. Burton (1821–90) was an explorer, scientist, Fellow of the Royal Geographic Society, writer, and translator whose work was notoriously centred around questions of sexuality – particularly through his translations of the *Kama Sutra* and *The Arabian Nights*, his studies of penis size, his investigations of Asian brothels and practices of homosexuality, and his 'Sotadic Zone' theory that sodomy could only flourish in warm climates. The direct implication of enlightenment science and the use of the controversial figure of Burton situates *Zero Patience* as both queer and queerly science-fictional, in ways that are tangible through practices of genealogical reading. Such practices might note, for example, similarities between Burton's obsessive scientific pursuit of and, in truth, creation of Zero as a monster to exhibit in his Hall of Contagion and Victor Frankenstein's compulsion to create his own particular monster; both Frankenstein's reanimation of the creature constructed from parts of corpses and Burton's attempts to make Zero visible are directly related to a desire to defy death, particularly the death of loved ones.

Indeed, if we return to Brian Aldiss's famous, if somewhat controversial, definition of 'science fiction [as] the search for a definition of mankind and his status in the universe which will stand in our advanced but confused state of knowledge (science), and is characteristically cast in the Gothic or post-Gothic mould' (*Billion Year Spree* 8), we might consider *Zero Patience* to be far more science-fictional than it appears at first glance. Allowing for a somewhat more inclusive notion of humanity, we can certainly note that *Zero Patience* is concerned with the ways in which sexuality is used to render some people less than human. Greyson's film looks in particular at the way in which AIDS literalizes the constrictions of an unlivable life and the creation of monsters and also grants permission for the expression of extreme, indeed sometimes genocidal, homophobic public discourses.[4] Furthermore, *Zero Patience* not only examines the definition of humanity in contemporary North American society, it does so specifically in relation to science – and the science of AIDS, even in 1993 when the film was released, can scarcely be figured as anything but an 'advanced but confused state of knowledge'. Finally, the presence of Patient Zero as a ghost visible only to Burton certainly situates the film within the Gothic mould (or 'mode', as Aldiss later revised his definition to read). Moreover, Greyson's use of the Gothic is entirely ironic, particularly since the entire film is, in a sense, a rebuttal of Shilts's supposedly non-fictional work. Hallas trenchantly notes that, '[for] Shilts, [Dugas] is a one-dimensional scoundrel from a gothic novel and an emblem of gay lifestyle in the post-liberation era, obsessed with his own pleasure and vanity' (21). Greyson's approach is not a simple reversal. Indeed, rather than redeeming Zero, as becomes Burton's eventual goal, Greyson allows Zero to point out that this aim falls into the same trap as did the vilification by Shilts and the media: it denies him his humanity as a complex 'real' person and recasts him as a figure in someone's Gothic fiction, whether as villain or hero. As Monica B. Pearl points out,

> New Queer Cinema [of which *Zero Patience* is exemplary] is less interested in the story – in something that renders the virus coherent – than in something…that provides another way of making sense out of the virus, that does not placate and does not provide easy answers – that reflects rather than corrects the experience of fragmentation, disruption, unboundaried identity, incoherent narrative and inconclusive endings. ('AIDS' 33)

Pearl's comment applies as much to the figure of Zero as it does to the inherent meaninglessness and ambiguity of the virus itself. Poised between life and death, Zero functions as a virus in the Derridean sense, one of several signifiers of undecidability. Derrida argues that the virus is 'a parasite that disrupts destination from the communicative point of view – disrupting writing, inscription, and the coding and decoding of inscription – and which on the other hand is neither alive nor dead' (Brunette and Wills 12). It is the very undecidability of Zero's existence as both ghost and lover, like the undecidability of the neither living nor dead virus itself, that links the film to the Gothic via other exemplars of the horrors of indeterminacy, notably the vampire, the golem, and the zombie. Both Zero and the HIV virus 'can therefore be understood as *différance*, existing in the tension between life and death and yet at the same time a deferral of death – and, perhaps, of life' (Pearson, 'I, the Undying' 188). Such indeterminacy is horrific precisely because it contravenes the Western need for a narrative and, specifically, for a story of origins, a story that identifies where the virus comes from and whom to blame for it. Yet, as Pearl notes of the film's discursive response to Shilts, 'At the beginning of the AIDS crisis was Zero. Nothing. There was no beginning… [C]oming up with any one beginning was just another way of telling the story' ('*Zero Patience*' 142). Pearl does not make the connection between Greyson's refusal of the discourse that marks Zero (Dugas) as the origin of North American AIDS and the film's genealogical pedagogy; this is, however, clear both in the film itself and in Roger Hallas's excellent article on the topic.

To return momentarily to the topic of *Zero Patience* as sf, however, I conclude that it is certainly possible to argue that, despite the fact that science fiction is not one of the genres usually identified by film scholars in *Zero Patience*'s generic mix, the film's characteristics fit closely enough with Aldiss's definition of sf. So, too, does the fact that one of the major targets for satire and parody in *Zero Patience* is the scientific community, exemplified primarily by pharmaceutical companies, Burton himself, and the director of the Museum. However, the film's not wholly gentle handling of the ACT-UP group which protests against the indifference of the medical establishment involves a larger interrogation of the societal anxieties caused by technological and scientific discoveries – such as the identification of Zero as *the* beginning, or 'primum mobile', which invoked public fear of gay men as *the* source of the disease, and the fear that drug-testing protocols and corporate greed will withhold potentially life-saving medications from the dying in the name of either research or profits; such investigation is also one of the hallmarks of even the most solidly generic sf.

That the film itself uses genealogical reading practices to create its specific exposure of scientific blindness, media hype, and the greed of pharmaceutical companies further links science and sexuality via Foucault's particular concept of genealogy as a practice whose 'task is to expose a body totally imprinted by history and the process of history's destruction of the body'. What could be more exemplary of this process than a text such as *Zero Patience*, which literalizes both the body imprinted by history – Zero's body and all those marked by Kaposi's and other such signifiers – and the process of history's destruction of that body, a bodily disintegration of which Zero, as a ghost, undergoes a performative iteration at the end of the film, when he is rendered as only an image on a giant screen (an obvious pun on the fact that all he or any film character can ever be is an image on a giant screen) and even that disappears as he blows cigarette smoke onto the water sprinklers, shorting out the very mediating technologies which had so spectacularized him as both human body and infectious body (that is, as virus).

If knowledge is viral, as Jacques Derrida suggests, then the textual return to AIDS in queer fictions of many kinds represents one approach to the construction of genealogies of sf: it links the clearly science-fictional,

Figure 2: Zero begins to disappear as water shorts out the monitor. Film still courtesy of John Greyson.

such as Ryman's *The Child Garden* and Elizabeth Hand's *The Glimmering* (1997), to the less obviously so, such as *Was*, *Lust*, and *Zero Patience*, to the borderlands of slipsteam, fantasy, and magic realism, such as Peg Kerr's *The Wild Swans* (2001) and Samuel R. Delany's 'Tales of Plagues and Carnivals' (1984). In *The Child Garden*, Ryman constructs his own genealogical pedagogy, not unlike John Greyson's. Indeed, teaching and learning are foregrounded in the novel, as is their relationship to disease, through the very means by which they are transmitted. This is a pedagogy whose subject is Western cultural assumptions about disease, assumptions that, as Foucault points out, derive from the same mutations in social and conceptual structures that produce modern ideas about race, about sexuality, and about biopower in its more general sense. The HIV virus, like the syndrome it causes, comes to signify both excess meaning and meaninglessness (thus Greyson's direct linkage of it to Zero: the virus is Zero, nothing, but, *pace* Monica Pearl, also something – just as Zero is more than a ghost, more than a cipher for the competing discourses of recrimination and recuperation). Furthermore, while it is possible, as Pearl does, to read Burton as a figure for Shilts, Burton's own curiously

Figure 3: Singing about decentring phallogocentrism and compulsory heteronormativity: 'If the arsehole ain't so special, then the phallus can't be either; patriarchy would crumble if we started getting wiser'. Film still courtesy of John Greyson.

viral indeterminability – he was, after all, 'infected' by apparent and entirely uncanny eternal youth – suggests that it is considerably more useful to understand Burton as being, like Zero, a kind of proof of the futility of the search for *the* beginning, the source. In other words, the film establishes queer genealogy as an alternative to mainstream histories of AIDS, histories which, like Shilts's, can only see it in the light of narratives of origins and blame. In both *The Child Garden* and *Zero Patience*, the linkage of viruses to pedagogy and pedagogy to genealogy teaches the reader that disease cannot be defined simplistically, that histories can have no singular beginning, that all stories have more than one interpretation, and that the *pharmakon*, the cure, may also be a disease or toxin at the same time.[5] Each text, moreover, exposes these connections within an explicitly anti-patriarchal context: *The Child Garden* because the Consensus must learn its lessons directly from the protagonist, Milena Shibush, and not from a male authority, and *Zero Patience* through direct references to the involvement of patriarchy in the toxic discourses which have rendered life sometimes literally unlivable for those with HIV/ AIDS.

Milena is an orphan who grew up in an English 'child garden' (orphanage) after her immigrant mother's death. Initially resistant to the viruses which infect every infant with language and the knowledge of their society, Milena is finally infected when she is ten – on the brink of adulthood in her world, where the cure for cancer has reduced the human lifespan to thirty years. Because she is so ill, however, Milena misses the other adulthood rite of her world, the Reading which initiates all citizens into the Consensus by placing a model of each into the world's governing body. Reading, however, is also the process by which the Consensus rids itself of 'diseases' such as lesbianism, so Milena lives in terror both of the viruses that made her so ill and of the possibility that the Consensus will decide to Read and thus to cure her, a process that involves infecting her with viruses that will change her personality, her behaviours, and even her DNA – and that is thus itself a form of genetic engineering which implicitly refers to the contemporary possibility that identifying a 'gay gene' might result, not in more tolerance, but in a 'cure' for homosexuality.

Milena can only understand the possibility of being 'cured' as making her into somebody she is not. 'She was doomed always to fight to be herself' (3), something which differentiates her from her colleagues in the theatre troupe in which Milena 'acts'. Milena's assignment as an actor is deeply ironic, in part because she is so bad at being someone else, in part because, in a world in which homosexuality is defined as 'Bad Grammar', Milena is assigned to cross-dress, in a reversal of Shakespearean practice, as Constable Dull in a production of *Love's Labour's Lost* performed before three-year-old orphans whose viruses have already given them the complete memory and understanding of the play. Everyone is bored, actors and audience alike, because Milena lives 'in a culture that replicate[s] itself endlessly but never [gives] birth to anything new' (8). Milena is condemned to wear hideous floppy boots because the Consensus's production of the play recreates the original production – and nothing can be changed from the original. This is a reinstatement of the author not only as living, but as textual God; the Consensus has no place for Roland Barthes. If this were not enough evidence of the Consensus's obsession with historical accuracy and with reinstating single authorized interpretations of a text, Milena eats in a café frequented by young people who call themselves 'Vampires of History' and whose 'virus-stuffed brains [give] them the information they [need] to avoid anachronism' (8). The Vampires take their obsession to great lengths, even avoiding the sunlight on which every other Consensus citizen feeds (adapted to photosynthesize, a process which turns everyone purple), and thus, like the actors, being forced to rely on scarce and expensive real food in order to remain authentically pale.

Reading, learning, and cutural hegemony are central to *The Child Garden* and also intrinsically joined to questions of identity, subjectivity, and sexuality by the role of Reading in making children into good adult citizens. They are also linked by the identification of Milena's love of other women as 'Bad Grammar', a linkage which identifies language with desire and proper grammar with normality. Milena thinks that she may be the last person in the world suffering from resistance until she meets Rolfa, the Bear Who Loves Opera. Genetically engineered to mine the Antarctic, Rolfa is a 'Polar Bear', the slang term for her tribe of GEs. All GEs live outside the Consensus, which positions them as less than human and as alien (in the American style that places that label on non-citizens). Like Milena, however, Rolfa is an entirely liminal character whose family disapproves of her because she loves opera more than mining and profits. She is also a lesbian – perhaps the only one in the world beside Milena. Milena meets Rolfa in the Graveyard, a clear signal for the uncanniness and indeterminacy of the two characters; the Graveyard, built into the underside of a bridge, is a storage place for discarded costumes, providing yet another appropriately Gothic set of textual markings (discarded costumes, bridges, the darkness of the room, the strangeness of windows in a bridge) for the characters' liminality and thus for their queerness in this world in which queer people are literally unable to exist.

When Rolfa hands Milena the score for Gustav Mahler's *Das Lied von der Erde*, Milena, who knows the notes by heart, is disappointed by its familiarity and shocked by the waste of paper. Indeed, when Rolfa notes, sarcastically, that the reading of music surely provides no difficulty for her, Milena agrees in all innocence. She does not understand when the Polar Bear remarks sardonically that 'you haven't *learned* how to read music. If you haven't learned it, it isn't yours' (16). Indeed, it takes Milena the entire course of the novel to understand what Rolfa means by this. When Rolfa's family exile her for her obsession with music, Milena talks the Consensus into agreeing to Read Rolfa and make her a citizen, able to photosynthesize and to work as an opera singer. Ironically, of course, this infects Rolfa with the Consensus's viral knowledge, leaving her unable to create original music; it also leaves her unable to sing because, as she says when she and Milena finally meet again, no one is going to cast a Polar Bear as 'a delicate Chinese heroine in a classical Beijing piece' or even as 'Desdemona in *Otello*' (316). In yet another comedy of misunderstanding, Milena discovers Rolfa's lesbianism just as Rolfa is infected with the viruses that will cure her; Rolfa, in turn, assumes that Milena, like every other human being, has already been Read and cured. They become lovers very briefly, while Rolfa's viruses take hold, only to be irrevocably separated as Rolfa loses both her interest in women and her music. In a final ironic twist, after Rolfa's Reading, Milena discovers that Rolfa has scored Dante's Comedy as an opera and she becomes determined to produce it, to introduce something genuinely new into the viral culture of the Consensus. Addressing herself to Rolfa in her mind, however, Milena realizes that

> you won't be here to hear, Rolfa. You won't be able to hear it. You'll be someone else. You'll be like a ghost, Rolfa. I'll see you walking through the Zoo, but you'll be dead, undead. I'll hear you sing, but it won't really be you. All of this may have been a comedy, Rolfa, but it hurts, it hurts like slapstick full in the face. So it wasn't a high comedy, my love. I would call it low. (96)

'A Low Comedy' is, of course, the subtitle of *The Child Garden*, thus making explicit the connection between the farce of Milena's life in the Consensus and the world in which Ryman writes. It also links *The Child Garden*'s genealogical pedagogy, its reflection on the necessity of learning for oneself, of reading and interpretation, and of resistance, to Greyson's comedic efforts in *Zero Patience*, particularly the very low comedy indeed of the infamous 'Butthole Duet', where Burton's and Zero's animated anuses sing to each other about the positioning of anal sex within homophobic AIDS discourse in a series of clever, critically informed, and witty lyrics (the mocking line 'the rectum's not a grave', for instance, references the title of Leo Bersani's best known article on AIDS, reiterating Bersani's own discursive critique).

Just as Burton does not understand his lover, Zero, mistakenly assuming that Zero is as interested in his historical reputation as is Burton himself, Milena does not understand Rolfa. Not only does Milena not realize Rolfa's reciprocated desire for her, she also misses the point that Rolfa's operatic scoring of Dante, *Winnie the Pooh*, the Bible, Proust, and Shakespeare 'wasn't meant to be performed. It was all more original than that. It's lazy just to listen to music – Rolfa had said that and [Milena] didn't understand' (351). Rolfa's scores are not a new form of opera, but a new form of book, something which the citizens of the Consensus, whose ability to read music is virally infected from infancy, ought to be able to read as easily as they can read English. They are not, however, the work's intended audience, something else which Milena also misunderstands.

When Rolfa writes on the text 'FOR AN AUDIENCE OF VIRUSES', she appears to mean it literally. Milena has the Consensus score it and then produces it for them, giving us the extraordinary spectacle of an operatic version of Dante performed as holograms beamed from space into the world's skies. However, Milena's production leaves Rolfa indifferent, not only because Rolfa is herself a different person from the person who scored the text or even because Rolfa is now indifferent to any love offering from Milena, but also because Milena has entirely missed the point. The score is intended not for the infected, but for the infecting agents, the viruses themselves. Rolfa's 'new kind of book' does for the viruses the same thing that Milena's peculiar ability to alter DNA does: it unravels and recreates viruses as something entirely different. At its most concrete, it might seem that one works on the corporeal level, on disease in its literal sense, the other on the discursive level, on disease at the level of language and hermeneutics – except that, of course, the corporeal and the discursive cannot be so neatly separated. It is necessary to change both, and to change the one in the other, to queer the world. Thus only through a change in the viral DNA of the Consensus, a DNA that is both corporeal and textual, can that world become queer, can it be helped to change its singular and heteronormative discourse into an ironic unfolding of multiple possibilities. As Milena fumbles through her attempt to survive in the Consensus, change begins to unfold around her: a mutated virus causes some people to be unable to speak, except in song; another changes people into Bees, able to Read (and unable not to Read) everything organic. Milena becomes the virus that sets the selves of the Consensus free, granting its 'last and most secret wish' (385).

This is not the work of a hero, in any sense; Milena continually gets it wrong, particularly as she labours to produce Rolfa's operatic version of Dante. Rolfa's desire to write for an audience of viruses produces a text that Milena comes perilously close to undoing when she stages a performance of the first two books. Similarly, Burton, the author of fifty books, cannot understand that Zero does not want to write a book, even the book of his own life and death, does not want to be famous, does not even greatly care about being blamed for the arrival of AIDS in North America. Zero wants to live, to love, to get laid. His desires are much more directly rooted in the body than are Burton's. For all four characters, however, though they come to it from very different routes, freedom lies in not accepting the dominant reading of the world, of asserting a type of vampiric subjectivity which, as Allucquère Rosanne Stone argues, 'sees the play of identity from the metalevel, sees the fragrant possibilities of multiple voice and subject position, the endless refraction of desire' (*War* 182). A kind of viral or vampiric identity, a position of undecidability, links Milena with Rolfa, with Zero and with Burton. All are in one way or another uncanny within the framework of their own world's conception of normality – and that uncanniness is also, in every case, a refraction of their cultural and sexual queerness. A kind of genealogical pedagogy thus imbricates viral subjectivity with practices of reading and interpretation, suggesting that we are interpellated by our own reading practices, that we become who we are by the ways in which we interpret the world, indeed that seeing the world queerly makes us queer.

As *The Child Garden* so thoroughly and, in some ways, so literally demonstrates, we construct genealogies through our reading practices. Queer readings produce queer genealogies, and vice versa. In this sense, genealogy is to history what Kristeva's concept of intertextuality is to allusion, a way of understanding relationships between texts outside a binary conceptual world that necessitates our deciding what is important and what is unimportant, what is a 'good' reading and what a 'bad' reading, what – in the terms of *The Child Garden* – is 'Good' Grammar and 'Bad' Grammar. Barthes long ago proclaimed the death of the author, yet practices of textual exegesis still find authority and intent in that reanimated corpse, proclaiming the superiority of reading practices that recognize intertextuality in its non-Kristevan sense. In such a world, sexuality in sf, whether literary or cinematic, can only be inserted there by the deliberate gesture of author/director/creator. The author's vitality may be questionable, but 'his' authority as a generator of textual meanings lives on, circumscribing the possibility for reading outside the conventionally prescribed orientations. Genealogical readings, by contrast, allow us to link texts in ways that resist hegemonic narratives of both importance and adequacy; they are, in this sense, exceptional, always excessive, positively queer. Ryman literalizes this in *The Child Garden* by making Milena a lesbian, but also by making her lover, Rolfa, a literally larger-than-life character whose very existence demonstrates her always already excessive queerness.

Indeed, although I have thought for a long time about what Ryman means when he has the Consensus declare Milena's lesbianism to be 'Bad Grammar', about what her ability to pull apart and reconstruct viral DNA demonstrates about discourses of disease and health, and about the role of the viral knowledge in constraining interpretation, I had not considered these factors in terms specifically of genealogical pedagogy until I began to consider them in the light of Roger Hallas's reading of *Zero Patience*. However, if we put together Milena's role in teaching us the dangers of how we think about disease with the teaching function of viruses in the novel, we arrive at precisely the kind of genealogical pedagogy that Hallas identifies in the film. In other words, reading *The Child Garden* in the light of *Zero Patience* provides a new and illuminating way of understanding the former while emphasizing the role of science both in the film and in the creation of the problematic discourses that it targets for parodic deconstruction. In this sense, both Greyson's film and Ryman's novel are themselves viral, inserting necessary degrees of indeterminacy and undecidability into a culture of already excessive certainty – both Ryman's science-fictional one and Greyson's more apparently mimetic one. Both genealogical pedagogies have at their heart an interrogation of what it means to be stuck in a world where one's humanity is rendered culturally incoherent and where one is denied the possibility of a truly livable life. Indeed, towards the end of *The Child Garden*, a dying Milena, being mined by the Consensus for her cancers, thinks,

> There always is a Consensus. We always do what it wants us to do because we are part of it and it is part of us. We are embedded in it, and so we obey the logic. We are born, we have to eat, we are left alone and we have to survive in the ways that are open to us. We obey the logic of love and sex and of health and disease of ageing and infancy and death. If we escape one framework, we move into another. If we make a new framework, we imprison our children in it. We have always fought to escape the Consensus and have always done its will. We fight and obey with one motion. (383)

The indeterminacy of *The Child Garden*'s ending – does Milena set the selves of the Consensus free or are we all always caught up in some Consensual framework or other? does Milena die or is she alive in some eternal Now? – seems entirely appropriate to its viral comedy. If no story of origins is possible, then neither is a story of endings. As Elizabeth Grosz argues, '[g]enealogy makes no presumptions about the metaphysical origin of things, their final teleology' (145). As readers, we neither know where Milena comes from nor exactly what happens to her – nor even precisely what effect she has had on her world. To know these things would be to abandon genealogy for traditional history and to recentre notions of progress and purposive evolution. Like Zero, Milena disappears, but the finality of that disappearance allows for a number of potential readings. Ryman ends the novel with the statement that the whole truth is 'the third book [of Dante's Comedy], beyond words or low imagining. Leaving Purgatory will have to be comedy enough' (388). Again, the comparison to *Zero Patience* is remarkable: it finishes with Zero singing (in the rain of the fire extinguishers), 'I'm not the first, but I'm still the best. Make me true, make me clear, make me disappear – make me disappear'. Thus the film finishes with the refusal of originary narratives, but it also links truth and clarity to the indeterminacy of Zero's disappearance. What does it mean for him to disappear? The spectator cannot know, other than that it is the only possible fulfilment of Zero's desire for truth and clarity, since Zero appeared in response to the proliferation of lies and obscurity, some of which were incidental and some of which were caused by a culture of fear, homophobia, and greed. For Zero, too, it seems that leaving the Purgatory – that is, the utter and utterly viral indeterminacy – of his reappearance on Earth will have to be comedy enough. Both the film and the novel have 'expose[d the] body totally imprinted by history and the process of history's destruction of the body' and their queer genealogies have become visible, even as the bodies they identify disappear.

Linking *The Child Garden* and *Zero Patience* to *The Left Hand of Darkness* is the central question of humanity: how do we define the human given our 'advanced but confused state of knowledge (science)'? Queer theory answers this question through the very genealogy that connects these texts to each other. As William B. Turner notes in *A Genealogy of Queer Theory*, Foucault's work on genealogy and identity poses a threat to those orders of knowledge most dependent on attempting not only to define the human but also on having historically placed specific limits on the possibilities for definition under the very rubric of universality. For Turner,

> [the] threat Foucault's work posed stemmed from the challenge he offered to the universalizing impulse that underlies this epistemological and ethical framework. Scientific knowledge serves as our epistemological gold standard, even for historians…, because scientists elaborate universal laws – generalized statements about how the world works that provide some measure of predictive certainty. Foucault suggested that we assign considerable epistemological and ethical value to science because of the historical a priori that govern the modern epistemes. The human sciences, on this view, simply will not admit of elaboration in terms of universal laws, even though the episteme requires that human scientists strive to provide precisely that form of justification for their work. They can only answer the questions the episteme poses for them. (184–85)

Address Unknown: Dis/locating Queer Utopia

Theodore Sturgeon's *Venus Plus X* explores the problem that contemporary epistemologies of gender and sexuality have indeed rendered life nearly unlivable for many, while forcing others to contort themselves into specified moulds in order to survive in a culture which has created an unbridgeable abyss between male and female. Sturgeon literalizes this debate by positing a world in which nuclear warfare has become an inevitable result of the battle between the sexes, even though it does not directly involve men fighting women but rather occurs as the generalized effect, as I shall explore shortly, of a world lacking in balance between masculine and feminine elements. This element of sex or gender warfare is extremely explicit in the novel and is the element that Justine Larbalestier tackles in *The Battle of the Sexes in Science Fiction*. Larbalestier anchors her reading of *Venus Plus X* through a comparison to other 'hermaphrodite narratives' such as *The Left Hand of Darkness*, *The Disappearance* (1951) by Philip Wylie, and *Proud Man* (1933) by Katherine Burdekin (a.k.a. Murray Constantine). The designation is apt because *Venus Plus X* contrasts two worlds, the contemporary world of the human narrator, Charlie Johns, and the secret hermaphroditic world of the Ledom (whose name is very obviously 'model' backwards) in which Johns finds himself after his warplane crashes in the mountains.[6] The overall theme of Larbalestier's book means that, in evaluating Sturgeon's depiction of the hermaphroditic Ledom, she is already primed to look for examples of conflict between the sexes rather than, say, questions of the extent to which the Ledom queer human anatomy and thus also human identity. Thus Larbalestier argues that in each of these hermaprodite narratives, 'hermaphroditism or androgyny is transformed from a problem that must be surgically corrected [as intersex is today] into a possible solution to the problem of difference between men and women' (92).[7] Yet Larbalestier sees few of these novels as managing to make good on their promise of imagining a livable world for a humanity not divided into two sexes, genders and, inevitably, sexual orientations.

In particular, Larbalestier's reading of the failure of *The Disappearance* to realize its apparent project of gender equality affects her reading of *Venus Plus X*. Larbalestier notes the protagonist's eventual appreciation in *The Disappearance* of the 'long-standing blunder of our species... The fact is, *no such thing as "man" or "woman" exists*; one sex without the other had neither past nor future and is but death' (qtd. in Larbalestier 84; Wylie's emphasis). The incoherence of this quotation indicates the extent of Wylie's ambivalence, since he refers first to undoing gender, but then reverts to an idea of gender complementarity – the 'separate but equal' version of gender discourse that dates back to Rousseau. Moreover, since it is the men who realize this and who announce it to the women and since the women return to being the males' helpmeets, the revelation that there is no difference between the sexes seems short on actualization.

Noting Sturgeon's acknowledgment of Wylie – and indeed his direct quotation of *The Disappearance* in *Venus Plus X* – Larbalestier seems to come to Sturgeon's novel expecting to find a similar failure to imagine a genuinely balanced and egalitarian society, even though all of its inhabitants share the same reproductive anatomy. Larbalestier notes that even the legend of Hermaphroditus fails to invoke a genuine transcendence of gender or even gender equality, since the story involves the subsumption of the nymph Salmacis into the male body of Hermaphroditus; in the process, the acquisition of Salmacis's femaleness makes Hermaphroditus less than a man while also obliterating Salmacis, whose very name disappears. Larbalestier notes that '[if] woman is lack, and man is the one, then their unity will result in the woman vanishing altogether, or in the woman becoming a man. The Ledom are a version of men, but not a version of women' (99). Partially undoing this conclusion, however, Larbalestier ends her discussion by asking, 'if Hermaphroditus is only another kind of man why has "he" been so consistently obliterated, renamed, ignored, or punished under the law? Why is the human bisexual visitor to a world of hermaphrodites so horrified?' (99).

These are good questions, of course, and they work to problematize the contention that hermaphrodites involve either a loss or a gain for masculinity, but a total dissolution of the female. The larger question for me, however, is the extent to which they are applicable to *Venus Plus X*. Are the hermaphrodites in *Venus Plus X* really, as Larbalestier puts it, only 'men with additional female parts' (98)? In some senses this question is hard to answer because, like *The Left Hand of Darkness*, *Venus Plus X* filters the reader's knowledge of the Ledom through the not very perceptive eye of Charlie Johns. The Ledom have no breasts when not lactating; the silky 'sporran' covering the Ledom's genitals deprives Charlie of other clues to their nature. As a result, the Ledom all look like men to Charlie – men with uteri. But is Charlie's perception of the Ledom the one the reader is meant to adopt? After all, Charlie is not the brightest light, especially in the world of the Ledom, and the novel finishes by revealing that Charlie is not really Charlie at all, but Charlie's memories impressed by the cerebrostyle onto the brain of Quesbu, the Ledom's 'Control Natural' – the unaltered Ledom whom they keep literally as a control in relation to the experiment that the Ledom themselves represent.

Charlie is created because the Ledom need to find out what will happen if they reveal themselves to humanity. At first, Charlie's reactions seem entirely positive; he is happy with, indeed enamoured, of Ledom society while he thinks that their hermaphroditic anatomy is the result of a random mutation, yet he is horrified to learn that it is the result of deliberate surgical intervention on all newborn babies. When Mielwis asks Charlie Johns what 'homo sap.' would do if it met the Ledom, Charlie's response is, 'We'd eliminate you down to the last queer kid... and stick that one in a sideshow' (152).[8] The Ledom's anatomy may eliminate sexual difference and gender roles, yet it is a slur about sexuality that Charlie reverts to when he decides that do-it-yourself hermaphroditism is simply perversion. The scientist, Mielwis, sadly concludes that '[h]umanity has never obtained its optimum ability to reason, its maximum objectivity, until now, because it has always plagued itself with its dichotomies' (155).

In my reading of the novel, which is quite different from Larbalestier's, the question of whether hermaphroditism subsumes women into men remains relevant, but in a slightly different way. Because Larbalestier reads *Venus Plus X* in the context of the battle of the sexes, the hermaphrodite bodies in the novel can only be read in terms of the degree to which they successfully intertwine male and female, a notion that presupposes that there is some genuine, essential difference between men and women. This, of course, returns us to Butler's argument: in order to write about gender or sexual difference, one has to accept their terms, which makes it difficult to avoid reifying them. Both biological sex and gender have a discursive reality with extraordinary material consequences, consequences one can rarely avoid no matter how clearly one recognizes that the underlying discourses are relatively transient cultural phenomena. If the hermaphrodite is one way of undoing gender, then perhaps we need to think of hermaphroditism outside the intertwining of male and female. One way to do this is to multiply genders, as is the case with feminist biologist Anne Fausto-Sterling's now infamous argument – which is also the basis for Melissa Scott's novel *Shadow Man* (1995) – that there are at least five sexes; another way is to accept that hermaphrodites signify a balance between the sexes; yet another is to suggest that some uses of the figure of the hermaphrodite work better than others to undo gender and, indeed, that if there is a balance to be found it is to be sought in that very undoing, the refusal of both masculine and feminine. The very terms of Larbalestier's work, however – the battle of the sexes – seem to mean that her reading of *Venus Plus X* is about *doing* gender, not undoing it. If what the Ledom are supposed to be doing is gender equality, thus making women and men equal, then they represent as much of a failure as Wylie's novel. The point seems to be that men and women cannot be equal as they are; some transformation is required, whether into Ledom or into something else. Sturgeon is utterly pessimistic about the time span required for homo sapiens to learn to be Ledom without becoming Ledom. The failure, it seems to me, is the desire to return to the bisexual model rather than accepting the Ledom as a queer and wholly optimistic future. This is both a triumph of the contemporary episteme and a failure to recognize Sturgeon's own slightly peculiar version of genealogical pedagogy, a pedagogy he instates in the novel through his use of the work of Gordon Rattray Taylor, a British writer and Freudian who was originally trained as a natural scientist.

While most – although certainly not all – of sf's attitudes towards sex, gender, and sexuality in the 1950s and 1960s were based on an acceptance of the normality and naturalness of (largely) American attitudes of the time, Sturgeon treats these topics in *Venus Plus X* with the same seriousness as any other science. In other words, he does his research. Much of his argument is based on Taylor's *Sex in History* (1954), a book which was very popular in the 1960s and early 1970s, when there was an overall dearth of scholarship on the history of sexuality.[9] Taylor argues that attitudes towards sexuality vary according to whether a 'matrist' or 'patrist' culture dominates a particular epoch; matrist cultures tend to be pro-sex but, at their extreme, disorganized and prone to random violence, while patrist cultures are anti-sex, violently repressive, and authoritarian.[10] Taylor's argument, which Sturgeon takes up, is summed up in Taylor's author's note to the second edition:

> there has been a marked extension of sexual permissiveness. Lack of super-ego restraint also manifests as violence, the rejection of the father as a revolt against authority... But it is a balanced integration of the matrist and patrist elements that marks a healthy and constructive society. Soon we shall be as far from that happy mean on the matrist side as we formerly were on the patrist side. Eventually, I imagine, a violent reaction toward austerity and control will occur. How we can halt the pendulum in the middle – that is the burning question. (*Sex in History* 10)

Sturgeon's reliance upon Taylor, whose book on sexuality was published six years before *Venus Plus X*, provides some important clues as to how he represents sexual issues in the novel. Like Taylor and judging from his portrayal of Charlie's (and the 1960s' reader's) apparent contemporaries, Herb and Smitty, who babysit, shop, do the dishes and use a variety of barely masculinized cosmetic products, Sturgeon seems to believe that 'the present period inclines to the matrist side... Perhaps it has reached a point a little more than half-way' (Taylor 285). In *Venus Plus X*, however, the Ledom illustrate the point at which Taylor's pendulum reaches its perfect balance. Charlie's inclination towards genocidal violence upon learning that the Ledom's hermaphroditism is a product of surgery is thus associated with Taylor's notion of patrism, which tends toward highly organized collective violence; the Ledom, by contrast, remain a model of balance, even if it is one which has to be reached artificially. Sturgeon, in fact, anticipates Shulamith Firestone's argument that equality between the sexes will remain impossible so long as women bear babies and men do not.[11]

Reading *Venus Plus X* through Sturgeon's use of Taylor's *Sex in History*, one cannot help but see the Ledom as a model for an alternative society in which gender as we know it has quite literally been undone. The hermaphroditic Ledom illustrate precisely that point at which the pendulum between patrist and matrist societies may be not only halted but maintained in balance. Whether this is a practical solution is another matter. It is useful to remember, however, that the 1950s and 1960s, despite considerable anxiety about the effects of technology, particularly nuclear technology, also consistently looked to science and technology for solutions. Taylor, like many of the science fiction writers of the period, expected the future to develop at an ever-increasing pace. In another work, *The Biological Time Bomb* (1968), Taylor predicted that medical technology would include 'an extensive transplantation of limbs and organs by the year 1975, man-animal chimeras by the year 2000, or functioning disembodied brains shortly thereafter' (qtd. in Gudding 538). Given such a view of the speed of technological change, it is possible to argue that some form of technological intervention into human gender (whether the creation of a hermaphrodite race or the externalization of reproduction) is no more unlikely or unbelievable – indeed, perhaps considerably more credible – than Taylor's chimeras and disembodied brains.

As a result of all this, when I read *Venus Plus X*, I see the novel propounding the necessity to produce a stable, egalitarian, and inevitably genderless society. Sturgeon's postulate here, like Firestone's, assumes that human biology combined with societal attitudes renders the attainment of equality virtually impossible. Something has to change and that something, in this novel at least, is reproductive anatomy. The result is a society that Charlie Johns, despite his conservative, not terribly perceptive twentieth-century attitudes, temporarily sees as ideal: 'I think you're the most remarkable thing ever to hit this old planet, you Ledom'. Asked whether he approves of the Ledom, he replies 'I should say I do!' (135). Charlie's change of mind about the Ledom anatomy reflects one of Sturgeon's major themes throughout his career: the fear of difference. From short stories such as 'The Sex Opposite' (1952) and 'The World Well Lost' (1953) to *More than Human* (1953), Sturgeon tackles topics of difference and what he understands as the unfortunate, but apparently natural, human response to it. Like gender, fear of difference is something humanity must outgrow in order to develop as a species. Of course, gender *is* very frequently understood as difference, although not in exactly the same ways everywhere or everywhen. To eliminate human fear of sexual difference, in *Venus Plus X* Sturgeon eliminates difference itself. The result seems to many readers utopian; more importantly for the creation of a queer genealogy of sf, however, it links the novel rather obviously to the sub fusc queerness of *The Left Hand of Darkness* and, through it, to the much more overt queerness of many other sf works, including *The Child Garden*, and thus ultimately to *Zero Patience*.

I will conclude by noting that it is now unlikely that any reader will come to *Venus Plus X* except through a reading of *The Left Hand of Darkness*. While it might be possible to do a close reading of Sturgeon's novel outside the context of Le Guin's Gethenians and Genly's reaction to them, such a reading would lack both genealogical and generic context and would seem highly incomplete. I would argue, however, that all readers will bring to bear not only their experience with *The Left Hand of Darkness*, but a whole generic context, both of works dealing with hermaphroditism and androgyny, of feminist and queer sf, and of the genre as a whole – including its permeable borders and the various crossings those borders permit. Thus while Larbalestier may read *Venus Plus X* in the context of Sturgeon's references to Wylie's *The Disappearance*, I might read it in the context of the genderless figure from Japanese mythology that the nameless female narrator encounters in Hiromi Goto's *The Kappa Child*, a work that is more speculative than science fiction, or in contrast with Candas Jane Dorsey's genderless alien, Blue, in *A Paradigm of Earth* (2001), who arrives in Canada as a blank slate and has to be raised 'human'. Dorsey reverses the more common narrative in which the stranger-in-a-strange-land is a Terran (human) who must learn the ways of an alien culture; in this case, the alien must learn Earth – indeed, it is 'hard-wired' for this task, regardless of its own desires and sense of belonging. Both works reveal something of the changes that can be wrought on the particular paradigm of undoing gender that Sturgeon investigates in *Venus Plus X*.

As well as thinking through the generic connections that might contribute to our queer genealogy of sf, however, we also need to recognize the important role that contemporary thinking about gender and sexuality plays in these works. Sturgeon makes obvious use of Taylor – his *Sex in History* is the only work on sexuality that is included in the sources listed in the novel's postscript (along with *The Disappearance*), just as Piercy clearly takes some of her ideas from Firestone's *The Dialectic of Sex* and Melissa Scott in *Shadow Man* explores Fausto-Sterling's hypothesis that humans should be recategorized into five genders. Contemporary sf novels are thus permeated by the thought of critics such as Michel Foucault, Judith Butler, Eve Kosofsky Sedgwick, and so on. Thus our queer genealogy has to include both contemporary and historical work on issues of gender and sexuality. If we focus on the ways in which much queer work relies on various attempts to examine what it means to be human and to have a livable life, concerns that, given the contemporary episteme, cannot help but be inflected by questions of gender and sexuality, then our genealogy must draw widely from both fictional and critical/academic work. The lines we draw may not be neat, but they may be the more productive for that. And as we proliferate genealogies – for each of ours will be different – we may enter into dialogues not only with each other but with contemporary epistemological and ethical approaches to questions of identity, subjectivity, history, and science. In the process, perhaps we can begin to imagine wider possibilites for what it means to be human, to undo some of the constraints on being recognized as such, and, we might hope, to make it impossible for the Charlie Johns of the world to judge others less than human and thus not worthy of life.[12] The question is, will we have to become Ledom to achieve this utopia?

Notes

1. Butler cites an article in an Italian newspaper, *La Repubblica*, which argues that tolerance of homosexuality in the US has led to the creation of five genders (*Undoing Gender* 183).
2. For example, Donald Theall notes the pun in 'The Art of Social-Science Fiction: The Ambiguous Utopian Dialectics of Ursula K. Le Guin' (257).
3. The argument that Gethenians have two sexes depends entirely on our acceptance that men and women have different sexes; to themselves, the Gethenians would obviously appear to be single-sexed and Terrans would appear not as duals, but as halves, horribly incomplete and perhaps mutilated.
4. Sedgwick, in particular, has investigated the way in which homophobic discourses that proliferated in the early years of the AIDS crisis drew on and mobilized a 'utopian' genocidal vision of a world without homosexuals. See 'How to Bring Your Kids Up Gay'.
5. For a more detailed reading of Ryman's play with the problematics of disease and cure, see my 'Science Fiction as Pharmacy: Plato, Derrida, Ryman'.
6. Sturgeon is remarkably coy about his naming practices in the novel (see the 'Postscript' 160); by contrast, it is likely that the reader will identify Philos with '-phile', meaning loving, and will see the name of the Ledom as an indication that they are to be taken as a model for an alternative way of being in the world, an alternative which begins with the reinscription of biological sex on the body and which works its way through sexuality and religion to all aspects of social and cultural life.
7. I am not fully convinced that 'hermaphroditism' and 'androgyny' are interchangeable terms; the former refers ineluctably to biology, while the latter covers a wider territory that ranges from biology to obviously cultural factors

such as fashion. One could argue, I suppose, that 'hermaphroditism' refers to variations in sex, while 'androgyny' provides alternatives in the realm of gender.

8. Charlie's reaction reflects the current cultural divide over homosexuality, where the line between the belief that homosexuality is inborn and the belief that it is a free choice also marks the line between tolerance and intolerance.
9. Taylor's work is rarely read today and seems to be regarded as eccentric, in part because of its use of Freud and in part because of its attempt to reach a totalizing theory of sexuality. For postmodernists, in particular, the application of a single all-encompassing theoretical model to explain everything about human sexuality is inimical.
10. Taylor defines matrists as mother-identified and patrists as father-identified, but he applies the terms generally to specific cultures and historical epochs. There are subtle differences between these terms and the more common 'matriarchy' and patriarchy'.
11. In *The Dialectic of Sex* (1970), Firestone argues that women's repression under patriarchy results from biological difference and advocates that women seize control of the means of reproduction, particularly cybernetic and in vitro technologies as an alternative to 'natural' childbirth. She also advocates the abolition of the nuclear family in favour of community living, a suggestion that Marge Piercy also explores in *Woman on the Edge of Time* (1976).
12. It is important to recognize Sturgeon's point here: it is the Charlie Johns of the world who appoint themselves judge, jury and – sometimes – executioner. It is consoling to believe that one needs a Hitler for genocide to take place, rather than recognizing the capacity for 'ordinary' people, people such as Charlie and thus such as the reader, to conceive and to act on such judgements.

Sexuality and the Statistical Imaginary in Samuel R. Delany's *Trouble on Triton*

Guy Davidson

1

In common with most of his work, Samuel Delany's science fiction novel *Trouble on Triton* (1976) is subscribed with a tag providing the geographical and temporal co-ordinates of its composition – in this case, 'London, Nov. '73–July '74'. Asked in an interview whether this particular tag has 'some organic significance', Delany replies: 'It's been my contention for some time that science fiction is not about the future. It works by setting up a dialogue with the here-and-now, a dialogue as intricate and rich as the writer can make it' ('Second *SFS* Interview' 343–44).[1] In this essay, I want to pursue some of the ways in which *Trouble on Triton* might be seen as engaging in dialogue with the here-and-now of its composition – a here-and-now that, if we accept one influential periodizing analysis of commodity culture, is also our own. *Triton* is written at that point in history in which economic stagnation in the West necessitates significant changes in the organization of capital – changes that have been collected together and described under the rubric of postmodernity. From the early 1970s – or, in David Harvey's more precise formulation, from 'around 1972' (vii) – there is a gradual and uneven, but nonetheless momentous, shift from the Fordist dispensation of the previous postwar decades, under which mass production entailed standardized products and mass consumption, to a more mobile and flexible regime of accumulation, under which economies of scope supplant economies of scale, resulting in a seemingly unrestrained proliferation of 'niche' consumer options. For many theorists of postmodernity, this increased flexibility of capital is correlated with an increased flexibility in modes of selfhood. In *Triton*, plasticity of identities and desires is also a central feature of the future world that Delany renders with characteristic vividness and intelligence.

Due to a range of fantastic technologies, citizens of Triton can transform virtually any aspect of their person that they please – including aspects that, in our own world, are generally perceived to be fixed or essential, such as gender, race, and sexual orientation. *Triton* thus suggests a hyperbolic extension of contemporary consumer capitalism, in which, it has been claimed, the notion of a core self has been discarded as postmodern subjects deliriously shop for new identities in a 'supermarket of style' (Polhemus). In proposing correspondences between Delany's fiction and some of the central claims of commentaries on postmodernity, I do not mean to suggest, however, that *Triton* simply endorses the 'schizophrenic' tendencies of post-Fordist capitalism – tendencies often seen in postmodern theory as deleterious. Instead I suggest that in *Triton*, as in much of his other writing, Delany powerfully conveys a sense of *both* the progressive *and* the regressive possibilities inherent within contemporary commodity culture, so that this novel in particular and his work in general might be thought of as exemplifying the kind of intellectual project called for by Fredric Jameson, in which it becomes possible to grasp 'the demonstrably baleful features of capitalism along with its extraordinary and liberating dynamism within a single thought' (*Postmodernism* 47).[2]

It is primarily through its account of the multiplicity of sexual desires on Triton that the novel develops its account of the potentials of contemporary capitalism. Triton is a world relieved of 'twentieth-century style sexual oppression' (99), which has seemingly no taboos on consensual sexual behaviour, and which accommodates a bewildering array of sexual identity types – an exponential expansion of our own society's division of the population into the relatively attenuated taxonomy of homosexual, heterosexual, and (perhaps) bisexual. The myriad erotic persuasions of Triton are catered to in a range of clubs, bars, and similar venues: to take just a couple of examples, there are mentions of an 'establishment that cater[s] to under-sixteen-year-old girls and fifty-five-year-plus men' (248) and of places where one 'can manacle eighteen-year-old boys to the wall and pierce their nipples with red-hot needles', or indeed 'ice-cold ones' (99). Though the commercial aspects of life on Triton are not foregrounded, the panoply of venues in which different erotic tastes may be pursued clearly invokes the commodified sexual culture of the postmodern Western metropolis (and here it is perhaps worth noting the near-coincidence of the advent of postmodernity 'around 1972' with the appearance of one of the most spectacular examples of commodified sexual culture – the vibrant and comparatively visible urban gay subculture of the post-liberation decade).

Triton's representation of a proliferative economy of urban erotic styles dovetails with the argument developed by a number of theorists that the formation of sexual minorities is entangled with the growth of consumer capitalism. For instance, in his influential essay 'Capitalism and Gay Identity', John D'Emilio contends that the changes to traditional social arrangements wrought by capitalism – importantly, increasing urbanization and a new emphasis, for both men and women, on self-determination rather than responsibility to the family – have enabled the production and increase of homosexual individuals. By implication, this argument can be extended to the formation of other sexual minorities, such as s/m practitioners. However, in invoking the work of scholars such as D'Emilio at this point, I am complicating my suggestion that Delany's representation of sexual diversity may be correlated with the postmodern moment. For the work of D'Emilio and others pinpoints this shift in sexual identity formation at the turn of the twentieth century – the period of the early stages of commodity capitalism rather than its contemporary manifestation, that is, the period of modernity rather than postmodernity.[3] The complication makes evident one of the most vexed issues associated with the periodization of capitalism. If sexual diversity can be read in one critical context as symptomatic of modernity and in another as an indication of the postmodern present, this suggests that postmodernity is in important ways continuous with modernity rather than a decisive break with it. In what follows, I maintain a sense of the heuristic usefulness of the distinctions between modernity and postmodernity, while also attempting to keep in sight some of the important continuities between these formations. I find helpful here Harvey's argument about the 'interpenetration of opposed tendencies in capitalism as a whole' (342), according to which there is within both Fordist and post-Fordist capitalism 'never one fixed configuration, but a swaying back and forth' between 'modern' and 'postmodern' characteristics such as 'centralization and decentralization, … authority and deconstruction, … hierarchy and anarchy, … permanence and flexibility' (339). If *Triton* is an exemplary postmodern document, it is so in part because it registers the interpenetration of modern and postmodern elements: at the same time that it attests to the condition of postmodernity, the book evinces the persistence of modern elements of culture and – in particular – identity.

The swaying back and forth between modern and postmodern conceptions of identity is crystallized in the novel's connection of sexuality to what I call *the statistical imaginary*. The phrase is intended as a shorthand term for an entrenched mode of perception that is intimately related to the operations of capitalist culture, in both its modern and postmodern permutations. As theorists such as Ian Hacking and Mark Seltzer argue, in modernity and postmodernity statistical thinking is a significant determinant of selfhood: in important respects, people understand both their own identities and those of others in terms of statistical categories or types (Hacking; Seltzer esp. 82–84 and 93–118). Collaterally, the desire of individuals, including sexual desire, is also bound up with the statistical imaginary. The interrelation of sexual identity, sexual desire, and statistics is a central concern of *Triton*. It is an advanced version of our own statistical thinking that makes possible the multiple sexual types of Triton; on Triton desire itself can be scientifically rendered as sets of figures that indicate the range of erotic preferences. By pointing up the ways in which statistical discourse facilitates the constitution of types and the fixing of desire, Triton gestures towards the role of that discourse as a technology of the disciplinary society as well as its (arguably not unrelated) role as an instrument for the analysis and promotion of consumption. However, if statistics enables the distinctively 'modern' reification of individual identity, and therefore the regulation and control of individual bodies that has been such a source of anxiety for post-Foucauldian criticism, it is also the paradoxical case that statistical thinking tends to encourage the proliferation of categories – the production of ever more refined types, preferences, and commodities that leads to the distinctively 'postmodern' fragmentation and lability of identity.

Critics have tended to read *Triton* as endorsing this postmodern libidinal play and, beyond this, a postmodern politics of difference. *Triton* is often understood as a postmodern variant of the literary genre of the utopia, in which social difference, generally flattened in the traditional examples of the genre, is incorporated and, indeed, valorized. Despite Delany's own insistence that the novel should not be seen as a utopia, the critical tendency is understandable. As Delany concedes, the social system of Triton is clearly meant to be 'an improvement on our own' (*Triton* 323). Moreover, the novel is subtitled 'An Ambiguous Heterotopia', and thereby designated as a counterpoint to Ursula K. Le Guin's *The Dispossessed: An Ambiguous Utopia* (1974); Delany's use of the term *heterotopia* has usually been seen as gesturing towards the novel's distinctively postmodern emphasis upon and celebration of social difference.[4] But *Triton* celebrates this tendency of postmodern culture only up to a point; this is, after all, an *ambiguous* heterotopia. *Triton*'s valorization of postmodern heterogeneity is complicated by several narrative and formal elements, including its reliance upon a central convention of the realist novel – that is, its focus upon what Lukács calls 'the problematic individual', who experiences himself as being at odds with his social environment (*Theory* 78). Unusually for a novel that supposedly works within the utopian tradition, the narrative of *Triton* explores the romantic and psychic tribulations of its protagonist, Bron Helmstrom, rather than the details of the social totality; however, the novel also, as Tom Moylan points out, deploys the celebrated insight of 1970s' feminism about the connection of the personal and the political (Moylan 175), so that its account of Bron's misadventures obliquely signals the framing structures of Tritonian society. In important respects *Triton* – like much of Delany's later science fiction and consistent with the tenor of much of his critical writing – is critical of the perceived ideology of what Delany, in an appendix to the novel (as elsewhere), calls 'mundane fiction'. Indeed, *Triton*'s two auto-critical and self-reflexive appendices enable Delany to eschew the 'closing cadence' that he associates with conventional realism, as well as constituting significant expressions of the novel's ambivalent relation to the possibilities embodied within Triton society.[5] However, it is, in my view, most importantly through its deployment of the realist novel's standard concern with – to borrow Walter Benjamin's words – the 'profound perplexity' of 'the solitary individual' (87) that this heterotopia is rendered ambiguous. A throwback to late twentieth-century male chauvinism, Bron is a misfit on feminist, non-patriarchal Triton, and it is from his jaundiced point of view that we view his adopted society's sophisticated social and sexual arrangements. Although Bron is clearly intended as an unreliable point of focalization, his centrality to the representation also has crucial countervailing implications for our understanding of the possibilities of postmodern capitalism that the novel explores. And it is in his relation to my two titular concerns that these implied criticisms of postmodern potentials are worked out: in the representations of Bron's plight we most fully discern the intersection of sexuality and statistics, and the manifold political effects that this intersection entails.

2

On Triton the 'subjective reality' of its citizens is held to be 'as politically inviolable as possible' (225–26). Consequently, Triton embraces an ultra-liberalism that, in accordance with Darko Suvin's argument about the cognitive estrangement effect of the sf utopia, has the effect of bringing into relief the limitations of the purported pluralism of early twenty-first-century democracies (see Suvin esp. 58–62). Not only is there a diversity of erotic orientation that exceeds our own, there are also 'forty or fifty different sexes and twice as many religions' (99). The individual's choice in this seeming paradise of libertarianism is promoted and enabled by those technologies that allow quick and easy transformations of body type, gender, race, and sexual orientation. Sam, for instance, is a strapping black man who used to be a 'sallow-faced, blonde, blue-eyed...waitress' (126) attracted to other sallow, blonde, blue-eyed waitresses who (so it seemed to her) desired only black men; availing herself of the technological capabilities of satellite society Sam has become the black man desired by her own objects of desire. Bron, on the other hand, remains plagued by ineffable discontents and stubbornly resistant to the panacean possibilities of Tritonian society, asking, in 'profound perplexity': '[W]hat happens to those of us who *don't* know [what we like]? What happens to those of us who have problems and don't know *why* we have the problems we do? ... [W]hat about those of us who only know what we *don't* like?' (104). In the last third of the novel, after his girlfriend, the Spike, rejects him, Bron decides that he does know what he wants: the submissive woman who is the counterpart of his deluded macho self-image. Eventually recognizing the slim likelihood of ever finding a woman who embodies his sexist definition of proper femininity, Bron decides to become that woman himself. He also has his sexual desire 'refixed' at one of the popular clinics devoted to this purpose so that he will now desire men. These decisions paradoxically and somewhat comically exemplify Bron's devotion to masculine bravery. As he tells another of his housemates, Lawrence: 'There are certain things that have to be done. And when you come to them, if you're a man... you just have to do them' (231). In a society in which submissive women are a rarity, Bron sees his self-transformation, grandiosely, as a means 'to preserve the species' (232). But the sex change does nothing to make him (or her) feel any happier; in fact, it exacerbates Bron's isolation, so that the narrative ends with him/her in the depths of existential despair and, according to Delany's own commentary on the novel, teetering on the brink of psychosis ('Second *SFS* Interview' 338).

If fluidity of identity is a hallmark of postmodernity, then Tritonian society seems at first sight eminently postmodern. On Triton, the social identities of gender and race have been radically de-essentialized, decoupled from the bodies that are generally supposed visibly to indicate them. As Edward Chan notes, in the novel, gender and race are largely rendered as (one might almost say *reduced to*) 'surfaces', or configurations of 'visible markers' (Chan 190), and thereby aligned with the more obviously cosmetic, and even more easily rearranged, significations of identity such as dress and adornment. (The diversity and rapid turnover of sartorial fashion is, in an intensification of our own capitalist culture, a highly visible strand of everyday life on Triton; on a visit to the less socially progressive Earth, Bron is struck that there seem to be only 'three basic clothing styles' [135].) However, while it is true, as Chan argues, that the account of identity and social difference in the novel works to deconstruct assumptions about the essential nature, and therefore the enduring importance of, identity categories, there are also significant aspects of the representation that qualify this account. Notably, for instance, Bron comes to realize that simply changing his gender through technological intervention can never transform him totally into a woman, in the sense of providing him/her with a feminine subject position that is grounded in a personal history. As a counsellor at the gender reassignment clinic points out to him/her after his/her transformation: '*Being* a woman is ... a complicated genetic interface. It means having that body of yours from birth, and growing up in the world, learning to do whatever you have to do...with and within that body. That body has to be yours, and yours all your life. In that sense, you will never be a "complete" woman' (251).[6] The reference here to the significance of an underlying embodied history complicates the emphasis on the superficiality and fluidity of identity that elsewhere characterizes the novel, suggesting a continuity of the person not unlike that associated with the 'centred subject' of modernity (Jameson, *Postmodernism* 15).

The persistence of such an idea of personhood is still more strikingly apparent in the novel's representations of sexual identity – one of the aspects of individual existence, like gender and race, commonly thought to be core or essential but one, unlike them, not all that readily detectable as a set of 'visible markers' (in spite of the anxious cultural insistence that sexuality – or, more accurately, homosexuality – should be locatable in the visual register).[7] In modernity, the invisibility of sexuality is co-implicated with its status as a secret buried within the individual, significant aspects of which (so psychoanalysis teaches) may be inaccessible even to the individual him- or herself. Arguably, it is sexuality rather than gender or race (or indeed any other class of selfhood) that is in the modern era located as the deepest substratum of the personality – which is not, of course, to say that sexuality is always or even generally the most socially or politically significant permutation of identity.

One of the pleasures of the realist novel as it has developed since the eighteenth century is that it offers us an illusory knowledge of the secret domain of sexuality within others; the capacity of the novel to give us access to the consciousness of others – that is, characters – in a way that is not possible in real life is always in some sense an access also to the mysteries of those others' erotic lives.[8] In *Triton*, which focuses on the vicissitudes of Bron's sexual desire, Delany exploits this capacity adroitly. The pleasure of knowing another's sexual desire that the novel affords may be given a further frisson when the protagonist (like our 'real life' selves) is ignorant of or disavows his or her own sexual feelings and their implications – when the central consciousness through which the narrative is filtered is 'unreliable', as Bron's manifestly is. Although Bron insists that he knows his own desire (for a submissive female and then, once he has changed his sex, for a macho male), the narration makes it abundantly apparent that things are not this simple, providing a complexly layered account of the self-deceptions and self-justifications that accrue around Bron's experiences of his unsuccessful pursuit of his co-worker Miriamne, his abortive relationship with the Spike, and his/her muddled attempts to pursue men once he has been transformed into a heterosexual woman. Through this detailed unfolding of Bron's erotic conciousness (or lack of erotic consciousness, or erotic bad faith) the novel creates the sense of a complicated, but internally consistent, identity.

In its representation of other characters' sexualities, as well, the novel seems almost to retreat from the radical implications of its suggestion that identities are not essences. Sam, for instance, retains his desire (for white women who desire black men) despite his change of race and gender.[9] In the case of Alfred, Bron's adolescent housemate, there is the same hinting at an authentic erotic identity. Alfred's persistent experiences of impotence and premature ejaculation with women lead him to think that he might (really) 'be' gay, and he duly undergoes refixation. He tries on his new desire for six months, but his troubles continue, even though he is 'horny for men all right'. Eventually Alfred asks to be refixed so that he once again desires women: 'Let me at least like what I *like* liking – you know? – whether I mess up or not' (80). Even the Spike, one of the novel's most enthusiastic proponents of Triton's somatic and psychic makeovers, after being refixed so that she can reciprocate the feelings of a woman who is sexually interested in her, gets refixed again so that she can go back to her desire for 'tall, curly-haired blonds with high cheekbones' (77). With all three characters, then, there is a sense in which an underlying sexual orientation remains as the essence of selfhood, no matter what pyrotechnics of libidinal reconfiguration Tritonian technology makes available. Indeed, the scenario of sexual refixation is itself structured by a tension between fluidity and reification rather than exemplifying a straightforward expression of the former, for while the scenario suggests that desire may be easily rechannelled, it also insists that it is precisely, scientifically identifiable.

I probably need to clarify what I mean by making these observations about the tendency of the novel to adhere to a modern notion of sexuality as essence, given the prejudice within contemporary literary and cultural theory against ideas about the fixity of identity. I do not mean to say that this aspect of the novel is in any way a 'failure', either aesthetically or politically. On the contrary, what I want to suggest is that the novel's retention of a conventional conception of sexuality is part of what makes it a compelling narrative. As Eve Kosofsky Sedgwick's work has so richly shown, in the modern era sexuality constitutes a force field within which our cognitive relations – with ourselves, with others, and with texts – are importantly organized and galvanized.[10] In its insistence upon underlying sexual essences in the characters, and especially in its detailed rendering of Bron's sexual interiority, *Triton* enables possibilities of readerly recognition and identification, even though these possibilities may be, as we shall see (in critical contexts at least), disavowed.

3

Some critics have suggested that the focus on Bron's individually distinctive psyche is an appropriate means of representing a utopian world in which the individual is the primary social unit. What is seen as Bron's failure – or at best his pathos – lies in his inability to take advantage of the possibilities offered by Tritonian society to accommodate the 'subjective reality' of its citizens. For Michelle Massé, for instance, characters such as Lawrence, the Spike, and Sam, who take advantage of the multifarious choices on offer, 'stand as models of creativity and flexibility', providing an instructive contrast with Bron's increasingly rigid adherence to a mythic masculine ideal and his concomitant self-idealization ('Expectations' 61). Similarly, Tom Moylan argues that Sam is a 'counter-example' to Bron within the 'emancipatory political structure' of Triton, in which freedom, and its inherent risks, are radically guaranteed to the individual: for Moylan, Sam is a 'self-actualized person (185), the '"good-looking, friendly guy" that Bron could be if he let himself develop' (186). However, as Chan points out, the characters' subjective realities are never purely individual but always fashioned in the context of their alignment with various social groups (187). *Triton* is, in fact, preoccupied with the classification of people in terms of *types*.[11] On Triton, the concept of the type is the primary means through which social identity and social interaction are managed; and it is primarily through his resistance to typing that Bron's discontents are manifested. Bron 'hate[s] being a type' in this society in which, as both the Spike and Lawrence assert at different points, '*every*one' is a type (5, 67, emphasis in original). His fellow citizens are happy to improvise their identities within the parameters of various categories; as Lawrence puts it, 'The true mark of social intelligence is how unusual we can make our particular behavior for the particular type we are when we are put under particular pressure' (5). Bron, by contrast, seeks to differentiate himself from others, to mark himself out – in keeping with his investment in the ideology of stand-alone masculinity – as a unique individual. But even in his attempts to elude classification, Bron is captured within the logic of social typology. Bron tells Lawrence that 'I rather pride myself on occasionally doing things contrary to what *every*one else does', to which Lawrence replies 'That's a type too' (6). Much later in the narrative, Bron's counsellor at the gender reassignment clinic tells him that 'life under our system doesn't generate that many serious sexually dissatisfied types. Though, if you've come here, I suspect you're the type who's pretty fed up with people telling you what type you aren't or are' (220). So entrenched is the idea of the type that Bron himself resorts to it in order, paradoxically, to convey his own supposed uniqueness: '*I've* always prided myself on being the type who does the things no one else would be caught dead doing' (243).

For Chan, this preoccupation with the type means that the novel in fact 'subtly forecloses on the category of the individual' (190). If *Triton* depends on the realist convention of the 'problematic individual', it simultaneously undermines the ideological potency of this idea – and the form of the realist novel that depends so heavily upon this idea – by insisting on Bron's assimilation to the system of social typing. The novel's attention to social types is also the means through which it critically engages with postmodern capitalism's disposition of human experience in terms of commodified 'niches'. As in Jean Baudrillard's classic analysis of consumer society, on Triton individual differentiation is paradoxically only possible by identifying with a group – something alternately denied and (inadvertently) acknowledged by Bron. Analysing the ways in which the advertising of mass-produced commodities deceptively appeals to the desire for individuality, Baudrillard concludes that in consumer society the only way 'to differentiate oneself is precisely to affiliate to a model, ... to a combinatorial pattern of fashion, and therefore to relinquish any real difference, any singularity' (88). For Baudrillard, the phenomenon of defining one's identity through consumption in this way indicates the demise of the modern subject: 'The "person" as absolute value, with its indestructible features and specific force, forged by the whole of the Western tradition, as the organizing myth of the Subject – the person with its passions, its will, its character (or banality) – is absent, dead' (88).

But while Delany's rendition of the determination of individual identity by the group certainly resonates with Baudrillard's discussion of consumer society, he does not, of course, share Baudillard's unrelievedly lugubrious view of the implications of this phenomenon, nor does he join Baudrillard, and other critics of postmodernity such as Fredric Jameson, in a lament for the passing of 'the Subject' – for, despite Baudrillard's ironizing capitalization, and despite Jameson's careful hedging about whether the centred subject was ever a reality rather than 'an ideological mirage' (*Postmodernism* 15), nostalgia for the unified – and unique – individual clearly subtends their accounts of postmodern commodity culture. In fact, Delany has explicitly challenged Jameson's assertions on this issue, arguing 'that any time when there was such a notion of a centered subject, not only was it an ideological mirage, it was a mirage that necessarily grew up to mask the psychological, economic, and material oppression of an "other"' (qtd. in Dubey 201).

Delany is interested in *Triton*, as elsewhere, in the ways in which social categories help construct subjectivity: his often cited meditation on himself as a black man, a gay man, and a writer in *The Motion of Light in Water* (1988) could perhaps be nominated as the paradigmatic exemplification of this concern.[12] Baudrillard sees this phenomenon of the determination of the subject by categories as obviating the possibility of political action. As he puts it, the affiliation to the group encouraged by consumer society makes impossible 'concrete, conflictual relations with others and the world' (88); even more trenchantly, he claims that '[no] revolution is possible' in fully developed consumer society – or rather that 'revolutions take place every day at that level, but they are "fashion revolutions", which are harmless and foil the other kind' (94). Delany, by contrast, tends to see recognition of the role of social categories in the determination of identity as an extension of political possibilities rather than as a constraint upon them. This attitude obviously aligns Delany with the 'post-'68' orientation of postmodern theory towards the valorization of social difference. In his comments on *Triton*, Delany makes the alignment explicit, stating as justification of his opposition to the 'large-scale social engineering' of utopian thinking that '[the] "good life" simply cannot be mapped out wholly within the range traditionally described as the political. Indeed, the post-modern notion of the political has probably changed as much as anything else since 1968' ('Second *SFS* Interview' 331). Admittedly, when Delany makes his explicit claims about the productive effects of identity categories ('black man, gay man, writer') he does not do so with specific reference to the context of consumer culture. But if commodity logic is indeed the reigning logic of postmodern culture, then these kinds of politicized identities are never easily disentangled from the operations of consumption (though neither, of course, should the former simply be equated with the latter). With its descriptions of the urban market of sexual niches, *Triton* makes the intersection of identity with the commodity vividly apparent.

4

Attempting once more to define his own uniqueness, and in that attempt inadvertently succumbing once more to the inexorable logic of the type, Bron declares to Lawrence: 'Maybe I'm just that odd and inexplicable point oh oh oh oh oh one percent they call an individual' (121). Bron inadvertently succumbs here because there is an obvious contradiction between his self-designation as the member of even a statistically rare class of person and the intended rhetorical effect of his use of statistics – to establish his uniqueness. Bron's very use of statistics indicates his immersion in, rather than his separateness from, the society from which he feels alienated, for statistical discourse is an integral element within the novel's representation of Triton's life-world. Statistics functions not only to define social types but also to map such phenomena as the tallies of war casualties and cultural differences across historical periods. Talk about 'figures...estimates...and...predictions' (120) is one of the chief means through which the 'science' in this science fiction novel is conveyed, as well as being seamlessly woven into the idiom of the characters (as in Bron's declaration to Lawrence).[13] The novel's preoccupation with statistics indicates that this future society has maintained and indeed intensified what Joan Copjec, in a summary of the nineteenth-century development of statistics, calls 'the passion for counting' (169). Most significantly for my argument, though, statistics functions in the novel to define sexuality and to bring into relief the problematic nature of Bron vis-à-vis sexuality as it is disposed on Triton.

For if Bron is not unique, he is, by the statistical standards that govern Triton society, abnormal. He suffers a logical-erotic perversion – that is, male chauvinism. As Lawrence explains to him:

> Fortunately, your particular perversion today is extremely rare. Oh, I would say that maybe one man out of fifty has it – quite amazing, considering that it once was about as common as the ability to grow a beard. Just compare it to some of the other major sexual types: homosexuality, one out of five; bisexuality, three out of five; sadism and masochism, one out of nine; the varieties of fetishism, one out of eight. So you see, at one out of *fifty*, you really are in a difficult situation. And what makes it more difficult – even tragic – is that the corresponding perversion

> you're searching for in women...is more like one out of five thousand. (213)

The perversion is rarer in women, Lawrence asserts, because of the recentness of their emancipation from patriarchal oppression: 'Women have only been treated...as human beings for the last – oh, say sixty-five years; and then, really, only on the moons; whereas men have had the luxury of such treatment for the last four thousand. The result of this historical anomaly is simply that, on a statistical basis, women are just a little less willing to put up with certain kinds of shit than men' (212). The kind of woman that Bron thinks he desires, Lawrence declares, is 'very, very rare', maybe even 'nonexistent' (213): a woman unaffected by the nightmare of patriarchal history who can enjoy the 'logical masochism' (strictly distinguished by Lawrence from '*just* sexual' masochism [213]) of being treated as a lesser being.[14]

In spite of its determination to cater to the subjective realities of its citizens, then, Triton society proves unable to accommodate the freakishly outmoded reality of Bron. The lack of fit between Bron's desire and Triton's pluralism indicates the complex relations between the statistical imaginary and the simultaneously repressive and productive capacities of capitalism. Since its inception, statistics has entailed a doubled movement towards both social inclusion and exclusion, or towards normalization and diversity; a brief detour through salient aspects of the history of statistics will help bring into relief these bivalent tendencies of the statistical imaginary, which deeply inform *Triton*.

One of the foundational elements of modern statistical thinking was the work of Adolphe Quetelet on the bell-shaped curve that emerged when characteristics amongst human populations were plotted on a graph. Quetelet extrapolated from this phenomenon the famous idea of the average man, regarding deviations from the average as error. While Quetelet's concept of the average man proved to be fruitless, his work on the bell-shaped curve was ultimately scientifically productive, beginning 'the process by which error law became a distribution formula, governing variation which was itself seen to have far greater interest than any mere mean value' (Porter 7). Statistical thinking therefore is linked to an attention to heterogeneity within human populations; as François Ewald states, '[in] statistics, there are never any real constants – only differences of various sorts' (158). The dissolution of stable entities into a range of differences that statistical thinking entails is highlighted in the scene of Bron's sexual refixation, in which a numerical read-out is first made of his 'sexual deployment template' (227). A male and a female technician debate 'just how...[Bron's] basic configuration map[s] up with the rest of the population'. 'It's the majority configuration, isn't it?', asks the male; to which the female responds, 'There *is* no majority configuration' (228). While the 'base pattern' of Bron's desire is 'ordinary', what the read-out shows is a superstructure of preference that is 'entirely individual': for instance, the female technician tells him there is on his print-out 'a node line…running through from small, dark women with large hips to tall fair ones, rather chesty' and that the print-out also indicates that he 'must, at one time, have had some quite statistically impressive experience with older women, that was on its way to developing into a preference' (a result of Bron's employment as a prostitute on Mars before his emigration to Triton) (228). The male technician's retrograde suggestion that there is a majority or normative sexual identity (that is, male heterosexuality) is dismissed by the female technician's citation of the ways in which Bron's base pattern has ramified into a range of micro-orientations – the kinds of micro-orientations that Tritonian society both promotes and encourages.[15]

This link between statistics and social diversity is also evidenced by the fact that the development of statistics was, as Joan Copjec notes, in part a 'response to the various democratic revolutions which demanded that people be counted' (169). From one analytic perspective at least, statistics is associated with some of the most positive aspects of capitalist modernity: 'The interest in numbers was part of the modern state's concern for the welfare of its population, with whose well-being the state's was now intimately linked. What statistics calculated was the "felicity" of its citizens and what they aimed at was the indemnification against every sort of infelicity, every accident and misfortune' (Copjec 170).[16] The continuity between these statistically oriented democracies and Triton – perhaps the *ne plus ultra* of the Western liberal state which disinterestedly tries to provide its citizens with their own versions of the good life – is no doubt obvious.

Moreover, as Ian Hacking has demonstrated, statistics did not simply count various kinds of people, thereby enabling governments to cater to their various needs; by setting up categories it also brought classes of persons into being underneath those categories (Hacking esp. 223). Statistics does not simply attend to social diversity; it actively creates it. Here, though, the less 'felicitous' side of statistics also emerges. If Quetelet's idea of the average man had limited scientific purchase, the related conception of a statistically determined normality has proved to have far-reaching and sometimes deleterious effects. In its production of the norm, statistics is revealed as a key mechanism of Foucauldian 'discipline and punish[ment]'. (On the other hand, the creation of statistical categories of persons – such as homosexuals or criminals – also triggers the phenomenon of the counterdiscourse, whereby those groups classed as deviant can rally under originally pathologizing rubrics on their own behalf.) The less benign aspects of the statistical imaginary are invoked by certain vaguely sinister, even vaguely dystopian elements of life on Triton – the 'computer hegemony' where Bron works with its Taylorist 'efficiency index', the 'ego booster' booths in which citizens can access random selections of the state's surveillance files pertaining to themselves, and other indications of extensive (and secretive) government monitoring and control, such as the 'hysteria index', which (wrongly) predicts the probable number of people who will go outside when the Worlds sabotage Triton's sensory shield.[17]

There is one further aspect of the statistical imaginary that is germane to my argument about *Triton*, and that is the way in which statistics is associated with a degradation, not simply of the idea of stable identity, but of the more historically resonant notion of the individual. The political theorist Claude Lefort notes that with the institution of universal suffrage, paradoxically, 'social interdependence breaks down... the citizen is abstracted from all the networks in which his social life develops and becomes a mere statistic. Number replaces substance' (19). There is a certain parallelism between Lefort's account of the effects of democratization and Baudrillard's account of the disappearance of 'the Subject' ('the person with its passions, its will, its character [or banality]') from postmodernity, though there are also clear and important differences between the two. Lefort's historical reference, after all, is the institution of nineteenth-century democracy rather than postmodern commodity culture; also, what is lost for Lefort under the statistical regime is a sense of social locatedness rather than monadic self-containment. However, both these accounts trace the passing away of a 'substance' pertaining to the individual – with its concomitants of complexity and depth – and the arrival of a system of enumeration and categorization that submerges or indeed determines the subject. The opposition of category and subject that underpins the arguments of Lefort and Baudrillard is consistent with the epistemological orientation of statistics itself, which was from its inception informed by a distinction between predictable populations on the one hand and inscrutable individuals on the other. As Theodore Porter explicates, in its classic form statistics assumed that 'systems consisting of numerous autonomous individuals' 'could be presumed to generate large-scale order and regularity which would be virtually unaffected by the caprice that seemed to prevail in the actions of individuals' (5); as the scientific popularizer Robert Chambers proclaimed in relation to the new science in 1846, 'man is seen to be an enigma only as an individual, in mass, he is a mathematical problem' (qtd. in Porter 57).

Chambers's proclamation would seem to range statistics against the novel; for we have already seen that the novel derives much of its power from its access to that realm (of individual subjectivity, and, more specifically, of individual sexuality) that statistics deems an 'enigma'. In this, the novel participates in and in fact contributes to the resistance to categorization and regulation that has been a persistent countervailing impulse of the societies in which the statistical imaginary has taken hold: the cry of Patrick McGoohan's *Prisoner* – 'I am not a number' – is no doubt the most iconic expression of this impulse within the postmodern era. The realist novel might seem a particularly suitable form through which to express this resistance because of its characteristic construction of the complexity of the 'problematic individual', who is almost by definition at odds with the system of normalization that governs modernity and also postmodernity (for all its putative embrace of difference). Bron's self-proclaimed uniqueness is more delusion than reality; the novel points up the ways in which our experience of identity under statistical categories is not only unavoidable, but also may in fact be a means of achieving personal happiness. In so doing, the novel actually undermines the idea of 'the solitary individual' that sustains the classic realist novel and that Delany insists elsewhere is a pernicious ideological mirage. But in other ways, as we have seen, the novel depends upon this central convention of mundane fiction. Delany's deployment of the stock scenario of the realist novel – the tension between the individual and society – is an important means through which this ambiguous heterotopia achieves its ambiguity.

Moylan suggests that, 'by placing a twentieth-century male supremacist', the typical hero of many contemporary realist narratives, 'against the background of a society based on principles of equality and freedom', the novel 'exposes' that character type – and the political reality signified by it – under a critical light that reveals that character as no longer a 'hero' but rather a sad and fading figure of a dying social system' (190). While this is certainly how the text tends to be read by critics – and, according to Delany, principally how he intended it to be read – it is also the case, as Delany notes, that some readers (both men and women, he says) identify with this putatively despicable character ('Second *SFS* Interview' 333). While Delany seems slightly disconcerted by this reaction, it is surely not an unpredictable result of making Bron a Jamesian 'centre of consciouness'. I want to suggest here that in reading the novel, even if we do not experience the level of empathy that Delany reports in some readers, we are all required, simply because of our engagement with the conventions of the realist novel, to identify with him to some extent. While Bron may be a statistical abnormality by the standards of Triton society, we as novel readers are accustomed to sympathize, at least partially, with the abnormal or problematic individual. The carefully rendered vagaries of his desire and his consciousness ensure that he is surely a more compelling – if also perhaps a more objectionable – character than the Spike or Sam, whose 'flexibility' and 'creativity' some critics exhort us to admire. And if Bron is objectionable, he is also the only character we see in pain; and that pain casts a shadow over the ostensibly utopian brightness of Triton.[18]

The representation of Bron's inner life is the primary means through which the novel achieves what might be termed, in an extension of Suvin's formulation, a 'double cognitive estrangement effect'. That is, rather than the single level of defamiliarization encountered in more conventional utopias, the novel offers us two. The novel does not simply throw into relief the shortcomings of our present social organization by presenting us with a superior one. By filtering its depiction of Triton through Bron's objections, inchoate or lumpen though they may be, the novel also prompts readers to hesitate over the possibilities that Triton offers. Two moments from towards the end of the novel in which the statistical imaginary informs Bron's consciousness provide perhaps the most striking examples of this aspect of the text. In the first, the regendered Bron attempts to pursue her new sexual orientation at a bar, the lay-out of which is calibrated in order to cater to the different inclinations of its patrons: there are areas for those who want to approach, areas for those who want to be approached, and a 'free-range territory' (256). Bron, paralysed with indecision over what her own inclination should be, thinks to herself, 'What they need here, of course, is three counters: One for the ones who want to approach; and then one for the people who wouldn't *mind* being approached – but, no, that wasn't the answer… With a vision of the infinite regression of counters, each with fewer and fewer people at it, until she, herself and alone, stood at the last, Bron took her place at the center of free-range' (257).

Bron's vision of an infinite regression of choice indicates once more her aloneness, her inability to fit her desire even to Triton's accommodating dispensation. At the same time, though, her vision points up the tendency towards social fragmentation that is a possible effect of a culture – and an economy – based on the celebration and production of difference. It is surely not accidental that at the moment of her deepest psychic distress, which follows not long after this scene, Bron starts to obsess about the war between the Worlds and the Satellites – the large-scale, collective event that has barely impinged upon other Tritonians' individual pursuits of happiness.[19] The immeasurable pain caused by the war, which is rendered in the novel only as a statistical tally, is conflated with Bron's own pain; confusedly recalling Lawrence's estimation of the casualties on Earth, she dwells on the figures: 'hadn't [the Satellites] just killed three out of four, or five out of six' to keep the subjective politically inviolable? (277). Bron's state of mind at the closing of the narrative may, as Delany suggests, be psychotic, but the specificities of the representation here suggest the ways in which both large-scale and small-scale pain may be ignored in a society fixated on the blandishments of the immediate here-and-now. In focusing on Bron's interior erotic life, the novel meditates not only on the limitations and iniquities of our own social world but also on the shortcomings of the alternative world of Triton – an alternative world that is in fact an elaboration of the possibilities inherent in our own postmodernity.

Notes

1. As well as being one of its most eminent living practitioners, Delany is one of sf's most significant theorists, as demonstrated, for instance, in his collections of criticism, *The Jewel-Hinged Jaw* (1977), *Starboard Wine* (1984), and *The Straits of Messina* (1989). His influence upon contemporary sf – and particularly upon the attention to race and sexuality in the genre – is hard to overestimate. For insightful discussions of Delany's place in recent sf, see, for example, Broderick and Freedman.
2. Jameson's *Postmodernism, or, the Cultural Logic of Late Capitalism* provides the key discussion of postmodernity with which this essay is in dialogue. My understanding of the related, but not identical, category of post-Fordism is indebted to Latham as well as to Harvey. For studies that relate Delany's work specifically to postmodernity/postmodernism, see Broderick, Bukatman, Dubey, and Ebert.
3. For other arguments that associate the formation of sexual minorities with turn-of-the-twentieth-century commodity capitalism, see, for instance, Birken, Floyd (esp. 175–78), Gagnier. For arguments that emphasize the relations of sexual diversity to postmodernity, see, for example, Griggers and Wiegman.
4. See especially Moylan's reading of *Triton* as a 'critical utopia'; similarly, the novel has been characterized as a 'postmodern liberal utopia' (Easterbrook) and an 'open-ended utopia' (Somay). For an attempt to differentiate Delany's use of *heterotopia* from the usual understanding of utopia, see Chan. For Delany's rejection of a utopian reading of *Triton*, see 'Second *SFS* Interview', esp. 323, 327–31.
5. The quoted phrase is from a letter to Greg Tate, reprinted in *1984*, a selection of Delany's correspondence from that year: 'I [am] no longer interested in the closing cadence that ends so much narrative fiction' (268). The use of appendices is typical of Delany's novels from the late 1970s on and is an important enabler of the dialogism for which his fiction is well known. I

discuss the ambivalence of *Triton*'s appendices in n. 18, below. The dialogical intonation of *Triton* puts it at odds with the didactic imperative of the conventional utopia.

6. The awkwardness of pronominal reference is intended to indicate the extent to which Bron's bodily transformation is not matched by a shift in subjectivity. Interestingly, critics (and Delany himself in the *Science-Fiction Studies* interview) consistently refer to the post-transformation Bron using masculine pronouns, despite the fact that feminine pronouns are used in the novel.
7. The anxiety surrounding the invisibility of (homo)sexual identity is a major focus of queer theory. For an acute discussion of how the 'vast cultural project of bringing the [male] homosexual into the realm of representation... and especially into the realm of visually recognizable representation, must be mounted strategically in order to circumscribe the dangerously indeterminate borders of "homosexual difference"', see Edelman, *Homographesis* esp. 173–241; the quotation is from 199–200.
8. On the pleasures of reading character generally, see Gallagher, 'Trouble', esp. 293–94. For a suggestive elaboration of the idea that access to characters' eroticism may itself be erotically charged, see Gallagher's 'Immanent'.
9. This point is also made by Jeffrey Allen Tucker, who notes that 'interestingly, the object of [Sam's] desire...remain[s] the same, suggesting that only an exterior, sociopolitical identity has changed' (43).
10. In a general statement of this claim, Sedgwick writes: 'In accord with Foucault's demonstration...that modern Western culture has placed what it calls sexuality in a more and more distinctively privileged relation to our most prized constructs of individual identity, truth, and knowledge, it becomes truer and truer that the language of sexuality not only intersects with but transforms the other languages and relations by which we know' (3).
11. Chan provides the most substantial discussion of *Triton*'s preoccupation with the type, which is also more briefly noted by Fekete (137), Massé ('Expectations' 54–55), and Somay (35).
12. Like Lawrence in *Triton*, Delany in *Motion* sees categorization not as a constraint, but as providing the opportunity for improvisation; moreover, for Delany in his memoir, as for Lawrence, subjects are not fixed within single categories but may straddle – or purposively move across – types. For an acute discussion of this aspect of *Motion*, see Tucker 191–98.
13. For examples of the deployment of statistics in the novel's scientific or pseudo-scientific passages, see, for instance, the speech of the gender reassignment counsellor: 'left-handedness...has grown from five percent of the population to an even fifty'; 'studies from those years...show that the middle-class North American father spent, on average, less than twenty-five seconds a *day* playing with his less-than-year-old infant' (253); 'statistics show...' (254).
14. Lawrence's speech resonates with the point that the counsellor makes to Bron about how she/he can never be a 'complete' woman due to her/his lack of an embodied history of womanhood. For gender identity, on both collective and personal scales, history counts. It also counts in relation to sexuality: as Bron's read-out at the refixation clinic indicates, his sexual identity is in part at least a sedimentation of his erotic experiences. By contrast, the novel exhibits no interest in the historicity of race, which really does seem to be only a matter of 'visible markers', to use Chan's phrase.

15. Statistically precise parsing of desire is also a feature of Delany's later novel *Stars in My Pocket Like Grains of Sand* (1984), in which Rat Korga is calculated by the Web, a hyper-sophisticated system of information gathering, to be Marq Dyeth's 'perfect erotic object – out to about seven decimal places' (179).
16. Copjec cites Hacking's 'How Should We Do the History of Statistics?' (*I & C* 8 [Spring 1981]: 25), as the source of the term 'felicity'.
17. In his interview on *Triton*, Delany states that elements like these '[leave] the very notion of utopia pretty much shattered' ('Second *SFS* Interview' 328).
18. See particularly the closing pages of the main narrative, in which Bron suffers through a sleepless night, sure that the dawn '[will] never come' (275). The point I make here is also congruent with the words of Ashima Slade, the scholar whose life and work is the subject of the novel's 'Appendix B'. In words directly relevant to Bron's plight, Slade states: 'Our society in the Satellites extends to its Earth and Mars emigrants, at the same time it extends instruction on how to conform, the materials with which to destroy themselves, both psychologically and physically... To the extent that they will conform to our ways, there is a subtle swing: The materials of instruction are pulled further away and the materials of destruction are pushed correspondingly closer... [We] have simply, here, overdetermined yet another way for the rest of us to remain oblivious to other people's pain. In a net of tiny worlds like ours, that professes an ideal of the primacy of the subjective reality of all its citizens, this is an appalling political crime' (303).
19. Although the war, in which millions of civilians die, nags at the consciousness of several of the characters, it remains relegated to the background. The characters' general oblivion is matched by critics, who, distracted by Bron's personal failings, have generally failed to elaborate on the significance of this massive, if entirely off-stage, violence. A notable exception here is Jameson, who suggests that the war 'could stand as a comment on the violence implicit in Utopian closure as such' (*Archaeologies* 144).

Stray Penetration and Heteronormative Systems Crash: Queering Gibson

Graham J. Murphy

Even though literary cyberpunk is 'a product of the Eighties milieu' (Sterling x), it still continues to exert a cultural impact, as evidenced by ongoing critical attention, popularity, and dissemination of its motifs.[1] The key figure in cyberpunk lore is William Gibson and its key texts are Gibson's first trilogy, *Neuromancer* (1984), *Count Zero* (1986), and *Mona Lisa Overdrive* (1988).[2] In spite of its popularity, however, there have also been significant critiques of Gibson's fiction in particular and of cyberpunk in general. Nicola Nixon, in her influential feminist essay 'Cyberpunk: Preparing the Ground for Revolution or Keeping the Boys Satisfied?' (1992), argues that cyberpunk conceals 'a complicity with '80s conservatism' (231), a conservatism that can be interpreted as reinforcing traditional sexualities. In her essay 'Feminist Cyberpunk' (1995), Karen Cadora concludes that, with its focus on 'the male-dominated fields of computers, science, and sf, masculinist cyberpunk is ripe for the homoerotic. Sadly, fierce queens and flaming queers are absent from the pages of traditional cyberpunk. Indeed, cyberpunk is characterized by its rather rampant heterosexuality' (361).

Cyberpunk's rampant heterosexuality and patriarchal foundations are perhaps not surprising; after all, sf has a history of privileging male figures and, as Veronica Hollinger observes, sf remains 'an overwhelmingly *straight* discourse, not least because of the covert yet almost completely totalizing ideological hold heterosexuality has on our culture's ability to imagine itself otherwise' (24). Given the conventionally masculinist hetero-dominance of science fiction, can Gibson's seminal trilogy be queered? And why attempt something like this more than two decades after the publication of *Neuromancer*? Wendy Pearson argues that sf as a whole can benefit from queer's 'tendency towards instability and its pleasure in resisting attempts to make sexuality signify in monolithic ways... Furthermore, queer suggests a move towards not just a different conception of sexuality, but also towards a different understanding of subjectivity and agency' ('Alien Cryptographies' 17). I want to argue that a queer (re)reading of Gibson's *Neuromancer* sequence is the kind of move that might enable an expanded range of possible sexual(ized) configurations and understandings of the intimacies of gender, sexuality, and agency, configurations and understandings that stray from straightness.

In this project I offer a reading of Gibson's *Neuromancer* sequence as what Pearson calls 'proto-queer' texts. The 'proto-queer' text is one that 'although not queer itself, effects a kind of discursive challenge to the naturalized understanding of sexuality and its concomitant sociocultural surround' ('Alien Cryptographies' 19). A reading of this sequence as 'proto-queer' highlights an occasion and a location for the potential disruption of straight readings of gender and sexuality because 'the real aim of queer theory is to make possible a future in which society is radically restructured in order to invalidate fixed identities and deconstruct the Cartesian binarisms which automatically value white over black, male over female and straight over gay' (Pearson, 'Science Fiction' 157). In essence, proto-queering Gibson's fiction is a method of emphasizing that Gibson's cybernetic systems are neither *naturally* straight nor *naturally* queer. This opens up an occasion that, according to Pearson's theoretical construction of queer, highlights a productive instability that can be read as a resistance to monolithic significations of sexuality, a resistance that can also be mapped onto cyberculture and contemporary views of cyberspace.

Systems Crash: (Stray) Penetrating the Proto-Queer

The production and regulation in science fiction of sexuality which is monolithic in its heteronormativity can be tracked back to the conservatism of early sf narratives. In *The Battle of the Sexes in Science Fiction*, Justine Larbalestier is specific on this point; she demonstrates that battle-of-the-sexes stories often feature seemingly dangerous matriarchal social systems that need 'straight-ening' by the male protagonists. In Larbalestier's analysis, these narrative matriarchies can be read as queer spaces that resist heterosexual economies; thus, the stories and novels she discusses repeatedly depict patriarchy as shoring up its normative hetero-jurisdiction. She goes on to note that '[in] the process of rescuing the heroine from her matriarchal existence, the hero transforms her into a real woman'. This transformation and incorporation into 'the heterosexual economy is achieved through some kind of heterosexual penetration, usually a kiss' (40).[3]

The function of penetration in enforcing heteronormativity is not restricted to battle-of-the-sexes sf; rather, as Judith Butler makes explicit in her analysis of texts by Luce Irigaray and Plato, penetration is exactly what enables heteronormativity. It positions the male as the penetrator and the female as the penetrated – clearly, these are mutually exclusive positions. Butler questions the effects upon signification, however, if penetration were to stray from its heteronormative locus:

> if she were to penetrate in return, or penetrate elsewhere, it is unclear whether she could remain a 'she' and whether 'he' could preserve his own differentially established identity. For the logic of non-contradiction that conditions this distribution of pronouns is one which establishes the 'he' through this exclusive position as penetrator and the 'she' through this exclusive position as penetrated. As a consequence, then, without this heterosexual *matrix*, as it were, it appears that the stability of these gendered positions would be called into question. (*Bodies That Matter* 50–51)

In Butler's analysis of this hetero-matrix, stray penetration threatens the assumed impenetrability of the masculine by triggering 'a panic over becoming "like" her, effeminized, or a panic over what might happen if a masculine penetration of the masculine were authorized, or a feminine penetration of the feminine, or a feminine penetration of the masculine or a reversibility of those positions – not to mention a full-scale confusion over what qualifies as "penetration" anyway' (*Bodies That Matter* 51).

This full-scale confusion over penetration is a useful lens through which to revisit Gibson's *Neuromancer* sequence because the gender exclusivity that apparently separates 'masculine' and 'feminine' in Gibson's fictional worlds is made permeable through specific instances of stray penetration. First, city spaces such as the Sprawl and Chiba City are sites that perpetuate gender permeability, urban interstices occupied by monstrous entities that are in excess of heteronormative designations. This is particularly true in the proliferation of cyborg bodies and the elusiveness of heteronormative relationships. Second, cyberspace itself can be seen as a queer site. Although it has repeatedly been figured as a female 'body' undergoing heteronormative conquest by masculine console cowboys, it can also be read as possessing its own penetrative capabilities that can disrupt gender coding and potentially crash the gender(ed) matrix. Stray penetration saturates urban zones and the cyberspatial matrix and encourages the construction and deployment of Gibson's *Neuromancer* sequence as a series of proto-queer texts that edge beyond rigid heteronormative polarities.

Hot in the City Tonight: Proto-Queering the Urban

Stray penetration's invasion of urban sites colours the depiction of Molly Millions, the razorgirl of *Neuromancer* and *Mona Lisa Overdrive*. Critical discourse on Molly has been varied and contentious; [4] but what is of interest here are Molly's interstitial post/human qualities. Her status as penetrator is epitomized by the razorblades which can penetrate the flesh of other individuals and which solidify her role as street samurai. But nothing comes free in Gibson's fiction; in Molly's case, the price for her penetrative cyborg enhancements is her previous career as a penetrated meat puppet/prostitute. Yet Molly turns the table on the meat puppet business when, during one interlude, she kills her client. This dispatch is a baptism of blood because Molly emerges in *Neuromancer* as neither passive nor static: she tracks down Case in the urban Night City; she easily moves through the Sprawl; she breaks into the Sense/Net complex, despite a broken leg, to retrieve the Dixie Flatline; and she penetrates the Villa Straylight to extract the code that will enable the merger of the two artificial intelligences, Wintermute and Neuromancer. She moves through the urban, often forbidden, spaces of Sense/Net and the Villa Straylight, penetrating buildings, vaults, and security (guards). Urban zones are Molly's turf and, in *Mona Lisa Overdrive*, her return to the Sprawl is a return to form as she blends into the mass of bodies, protecting her ward, Kumiko Yanaka, while gliding through the multitudinous throngs.

In spite of Molly's centrality in *Neuromancer*, Claire Sponsler has criticized Gibson's characterization of the razorgirl. Specifically, she argues that Molly 'remains inscrutable to Case and therefore to us'; for Sponsler, the cyborgs in Gibson's fictions are 'undercut by a refusal to give them center stage as more than marginal freaks, a reluctance to grant them real narrative power' (52). This apparent inability to 'see' Molly – an inability Sponsler identifies as shared by both Case and the reader – is, however, also her figurative power and is a strength rather than a weakness. Her inscrutability and categorical elusiveness are epitomized by those iconic mirrorshades and the manner in which she reflects/avoids/controls the gaze of her fellow characters. This is particularly important because, as Brian Attebery argues in *Decoding Gender in Science Fiction*, gaze is a key to gender. In his analysis of pulp-era sf, Attebery concludes that

> women's eyes, like their bodies, are defined as something to be looked at, by men. They are typically described in terms of coyly dropped eyelids, sweeping lashes, luster, and soulfulness rather than acuity, focus, or force... The eyes of male characters in SF are given extended range and enhanced power by various mechanisms: microscopes, telescopes,

> spy rays, view screens. These in turn are sources of greater knowledge. Thus, the eye – or rather the symbolic representation of the eye – is both a marker of sexual difference and a sign of scientific prowess. (49)

While Gibson's *Neuromancer* sequence is clearly not pulp-era sf, Attebery's analysis is still useful as a means of reading Molly's relationship to sexual difference. Since Molly's eyes are always completely hidden behind her mirrorshades, the 'sweeping lashes, luster, and soulfulness' associated with pulp-era sf femininity have been sacrificed for the masculinized realms of enhanced vision and an extended visual range that allow her to actively perceive and engage the world beyond any kind of biologically restricted (that is, conservatively feminine) spectrum.

This engagement is particularly pronounced in Molly's interactions with Peter Riviera and Case, two male figures who are unable to capture her in their respective gazes. For Peter Riviera, the Judas of *Neuromancer*, this visual deflection is particularly pronounced because his unique abilities are based on visual deception; he has the ability to project holographic illusions that fool the visual senses. In one scene Riviera engages in a holographic theatrical performance, a stageshow based on perception wherein he builds a simulation of Molly only to have her satisfy his sado-masochistic desire for control as she strips him apart. Riviera can control only his holographic simulation of her; he is unable to possess the corporeal Molly through his gaze. In other words, he cannot see her seeing him. Rather, this techno-Narcissus can see himself only as a reflection of the mirrored lenses covering her eyes or as a production of his own holographic projections. This ocular frustration is played out when Molly is captured by 3Jane Tessier-Ashpool and Riviera, yearning to see the colour of her eyes, smashes one of her mirrorshades. This scene stages his gender anxiety: his masculinity is under threat because she is not subject to his masculine gaze nor can he follow her gaze and control it.

Riviera's frustrations are mirrored by Case as he too is unable either to control Molly's gaze or to keep her firmly in his sights. When Case first encounters Molly, she is following him but he is unable to see her: 'Behind sailors in short-sleeved khaki. Dark hair, mirrored glasses, dark clothing, slender… And gone' (14). Later, having fled from her by jumping out a second-floor window, Case looks up: 'a head appeared…backlit by the fluorescents in the corridor, then vanished. It returned, but he still couldn't read the features' (18). Finally, *Neuromancer* ends on a last note of visual failure: 'He never saw Molly again' (271). When it comes to the simstim (simulated stimulation) scenes, Case's ocular frustration is also evident. At one point Molly 'was moving through a crowded street, past stalls vending discount software… For a few frightened seconds he fought helplessly to control her body. Then he willed himself into passivity, became the passenger behind the eyes' (56). Then during the Straylight penetration, Molly is paying 'little attention to the cabinets and their contents, which irritated him. He had to satisfy himself with her disinterested glances…' (176).

In her reading of these scenes, Sharon Stockton finds the use of simstim to be a problematic representation,

> at best, an extension of traditional narrative omniscience and, at worst, a figurative celebration of rape. This penetrability is unidirectional: Case can penetrate or withdraw from Molly's mind; she has little access to his. He is described as 'riding' Molly's augmented body, a body thus constructed as subject to outside penetration and modification, not stable and autonomous as is his own. (601)

In spite of the apparently unidirectional penetration in these scenes, however, they also show Case as powerless in his role as passenger. Granted, he can disengage from Molly, but while jacked in he is unable to control her body and is repeatedly tethered to her gaze. Furthermore, these scenes also indicate that power is not the default of an apparently omniscient penetrator as Case's vulnerability is reinforced several times. First, Molly playfully taunts Case by stimulating her own nipple: 'She slid a hand into her jacket, a fingertip circling a nipple under warm silk. The sensation made him catch his breath' (56). Later, Case jacks into Molly moments after her leg has been broken during the Sense/Net run and flips 'into the agony of broken bone. Molly was braced against the blank gray wall of a long corridor, her breath coming ragged and uneven'. Unable to stand her pain, 'Case was back in the matrix instantly, a white-hot line of pain fading in his left thigh' (64).

Even though Case repeatedly enacts the techno-penetration of Molly's body, he lacks any power or agency afforded by that penetration. He is effectively impotent. Molly, on the other hand, moves beyond simply *seeing* the world; rather, she is a potent force *in* that complex world and she can be read as actively challenging tidy gender divisions. This is made evident in Gibson's designation of Molly as the action-hero of the novel; Case compares her to 'every bad-ass hero, Sony Mao in the old Shaw videos, Mickey Chiba, the whole lineage back to Lee and Eastwood. She was walking it the way she talked it'. Tellingly, her bad-ass appropriation of the masculine action hero is 'a performance. It was like the culmination of a lifetime's observation of martial arts tapes, cheap ones, the kind Case had grown up on' (213). Of course, there is the danger that Gibson's allusions to such iconic action-hero figures simply reduces Molly to a woman in man's clothing. In her essay on cyberpunk, 'Yin and Yang Duke It Out', Joan Gordon concedes that this type of reading risks becoming disempowering because it is 'the most facile and least thoughtful representation of the liberated woman' (198). On the other hand, Gordon argues that Molly is 'simply a human being in women's clothing, one of the two standard issue uniforms for the species' and 'for a woman to enter the human army as an average soldier with no distinction in rank, privilege, or job position is, on the covert level, a feminist act' (198).

Once again, Brian Attebery's work on gender codes provides a useful paradigm for enabling an even broader view of Molly and her challenges to the 'two standard issue uniforms'. Attebery writes that male/masculine and female/feminine are not the only ways of thinking about biological sex and gender designations; rather, 'within the gender code, certain ways of expressing maleness or femaleness can serve to destabilize the binary pair. Such disrupters include cross-dressing, homosexuality, and surgical alteration of the body. Any of these variations can serve as a third gender option, thereby changing the position of the other two' (8). The final variation – surgical alteration of the body – calls to mind Molly's surgical alterations: the mirrorshades covering her eyes; the surgically enhanced reflexes; and the razorblades housed under her fingernails. In Attebery's sense, Molly's cyborg enhancements position her as a third option that allows her to enact an uncanny performance of *each* of these gender uniforms. As this cyborg third gender option – she is neither solely male (penetrator) nor solely female (penetrated) – Molly's narrative and critical strength is the inscrutability that surrounds her and that enables her to function as a queer tool for critically violating heteronormative gender designations.

The stray penetration that informs my reading of Molly's narrative construction and performance in *Neuromancer* is mirrored in the stray penetration embodied in what I will term the 'hyper-masculine' in Gibson's novels. In 'The Fetishization of Masculinity in Science Fiction', Amanda Fernbach explores the relationship between techno-prosthetic fetishization and narrative depictions of masculinity. In particular, Fernbach argues that science fiction film often features the hypermasculine cyborg, exemplified in figures such as the Terminator and Robocop; she sees 'a tension in these narratives between representations of postmodern subjectivity and depictions of an old-fashioned and traditional action-hero masculinity that has not yet accepted its decentering' (235–36). I am arguing, however, that the hypermasculine is not seamless in Gibson's fictional universe; rather, there is an anxiety-ridden gap between *hyper* and *masculine* – it is, rather, hyper-masculine. As Baudrillard-inspired simulation,

Gibson's hyper-masculine is profoundly ambiguous in these urban zones because it embodies a masculinity that is achieved and/or maintained via surgical submission to penetration – is readily appropriated by razorgirl assassins like Molly. In other words, the instances of hyper-masculinity in Gibson's cyberpunk novels are, in Baudrillard's language of the hyperreal, maps with no definable territories to ground them or to provide stable reference points.

Neuromancer's Case, a character described at one point as a virgin, [5] is repeatedly faced with the disturbing ambiguity of such hyper-masculinity. For example, he meets with Wage, a shady character whose face was 'a tanned and forgettable mask. The eyes were vatgrown sea-green Nikon transplants... He was flanked by his joeboys, nearly identical young men, their arms and shoulders bulging with grafted muscle' (21). Later, when Case meets with the Panther Moderns, he is unsettled by Angelo: 'His face was a simple graft grown on collagen and shark-cartilage polysaccharides, smooth and hideous... When Angelo smiled, revealing the razor-sharp canines of some large animal, Case was actually relieved. Toothbud transplants. He'd seen that before' (59).

Other hyper-masculine simulations are presented by those characters who give up their flesh and go digital. In the opening paragraphs of *Count Zero*, corporate espionage agent Turner is blown apart by 'a kilogram of recrystallized hexogene and flaked TNT'. Death is forestalled, however, and Turner is stored in a 'ROM-generated simstim construct of an idealized New England boyhood of the previous century' while his meat remnants are placed in a support vat wherein a new body is cloned and grown on 'slabs of collagen and shark-cartilage polysaccharides' (1). In this hyper-masculine reconstruction, the masculinity attributed to a male body is clearly depicted not as an incontrovertible default but as a surgical process, a corporeal simulation to be later inhabited by the virtual(ized) Turner. Interestingly, not everything can be regrown, as '[t]hey bought eyes and genitals on the open market' (1). The features that must be purchased for the meat are telling: eyes, those sources of greater knowledge that, according to Attebery, have denoted male scientific prowess; and genitals, the penetrating phallus itself.

The loss of a (masculine) body is temporary for Turner. For *über*-wealthy antagonist Josef Virek of *Count Zero*, however, it is a permanent state of affairs. Marly Krushkova, a woman whose professional stature has been shattered by the inadvertent sale of an artistic forgery, is hired by the enigmatic Virek to discover the creative genius behind a series of new Cornell boxes, each of which is an artistic pastiche that is 'a universe, a poem, frozen on the boundaries of human experience' (15). As Marly discovers, meetings with Herr Virek are entirely digital. For example, a virtual Barcelona is the site of her first interaction with one whose 'wealth was on another scale of magnitude entirely' (12). Virek later reveals to Marly that his rare attendances at conferences or other public functions are achieved via hologram projections. Virek no longer has a coherent body as his genetics are breaking down and his cells have opted 'for the quixotic pursuit of individual careers' (16). To stay alive he has been 'confined for over a decade to a vat. In some hideous industrial suburb of Stockholm. Or perhaps of hell' (13). He has become the perpetual hyper-masculine simulation, a pure pattern lacking independent physical presence, the digital embodiment of masculinity increasingly divorced from corporeal form. In this sense, Virek is permanently performing the hyper-masculine; the masculine avatars which he adopts are compensation for his own loss of a masculine physicality.

Stray penetration and the hyper-masculine can also be seen as challenging the stability of heteronormative relationships. Tyler Curtain, for example, argues that '*Neuromancer*, not to mention *Mona Lisa Overdrive*, ends in...a reconstituted nuclear family as a way to secure the "humanness" of technology and the future of the matrix' (137). In Gibson's fictions, however, security is elusive and the *Neuromancer* sequence demonstrates that heteronormative pairings – that is, Curtain's nuclear family – are incredibly difficult to sustain *within* queer urban spaces and effectively remain an unrealized fantasy. In fact, problematic relationships are pervasive and heteronormative nuclear families emerge only when characters retreat from the urban sphere. Case is betrayed in *Neuromancer* by his lover, Linda Lee, while Molly eventually abandons him, disclosing that the relationship is taking the edge off her game. At the end of *Count Zero*, Angie Mitchell and Bobby Newmark are moving towards a romantic relationship, but at the beginning of *Mona Lisa Overdrive* the relationship has failed and they are separated. Finally, in the most telling examples, both Case and Turner must retreat from their familiar worlds to have any chance at heteronormative stability: Case finds a new girl (curiously named Michael) and, as Molly reveals in *Mona Lisa Overdrive*, eventually quits the hum of biz altogether to raise his four children. Turner also becomes a family man when he partners with his widowed sister-in-law, moves to the countryside, and becomes a father. Heteronormative pairings may take place but they appear incompatible with the stray penetration of Gibson's urban sprawls.

After failing to find stability in the urban zones, the heteronormative nuclear family might appear to retreat into cyberspace. Curtain argues that the 'authority set up in *Neuromancer* to police the boundaries of cyberspace, to make it safe for the phantasmatic family, as it were, are the Turing police'. He then draws attention to an 'offensive irony' that this force, named after gay British mathematician Alan Turing, is responsible for guaranteeing 'a queer-free cyberspace and the maintenance of normative subjectivity' (137). Curtain's assessment of cyberspace as queer-free is initially convincing. At the end of *Neuromancer* Case does see a digital family 'who stood at the very edge of one of the vast steps of data. Small as they were, he could make out the boy's grin, his pink gums, the glitter of the long gray eyes that had been Riviera's. Linda still wore his jacket; she waved, as he passed. But the third figure, close behind her, arm across her shoulder, was himself' (270–71). Similarly, the end of *Mona Lisa Overdrive* has the hetero-pairings of Bobby/Angie and Colin/Continuity joining the Finn in an expedition to the Centauri system. Nevertheless, the apparent inability of the nuclear family to retain its position within queer urban spaces is mirrored in the matrix as the queer effects of stray penetration inf(l)ect cyberspace itself and preclude unproblematic heteronormative closure. For example, despite the paradisal hetero-locale he shares with the deceased Linda Lee, Case rejects the computerized transcendence offered him by the Neuromancer AI. Even the nuclear family Case encounters online at the end of *Neuromancer* is suspect; after all, they are immaterial copies, digital simulations, certainly not the 'real' thing Case finds with Michael and the children. Similarly, *Mona Lisa Overdrive*'s hetero-ending is a wishful illusion. In a move towards disembodiment, Bobby leaves his body and uploads into an aleph, a pocket universe that is 'an *abstract* of the sum total of data constituting cyberspace' (210). When Bobby hooks the aleph into a cyberspace deck, it becomes a node within cyberspace, 'a plain white vertical column [that] appeared in the exact center of the display' (247). One cannot help but notice the hetero-phallic imagery of a large column featured in the centre of the matrix display. But while the aleph may be a data-phallus dominating the cyberspatial landscape, it is not the entirety of the matrix; it is merely a node. This aleph is within cyberspace but does not replace it. Also, the aleph's very existence relies on the offline world as Molly hooks the data construct into solar batteries to enable the continued existence of this cyber-world and its inhabitants. In sum, the figures at the end of *Mona Lisa Overdrive* parallel Case's and Turner's respective retreats as they must also retreat, this time from cyberspace-proper into an aleph, to give heteronormative closure its chance at success.

Skin Trade: Queering all the Matrixes

The queer obstacles to heteronormative closure throughout the novels extend to the online medium itself. Dani Cavallaro writes that 'a number of critics have proposed that cyberspace is indeed a body, despite its apparent immateriality, not only because of its commodified status but also because of its sensuous qualities' (102). Much discussion regarding the body of cyberspace focuses on the apparent 'femaleness' that emerges as a by-product of Gibson's choice of language. Lance Olsen explains that '[the] word *matrix* derives from the Latin for *womb*, which in turn derives from the Latin for *mother*. So while it is true that only males have access to cyberspace, it is equally true that what they have access to is a female region' (283). In her feminist critique, Nixon notes that women become cyberspace decks in Gibson's sequence, notably in *Count Zero*, and such instances demonstrate that '[not] only is the matrix itself mystified and feminized, but so are the means of entering it. Lucas tells Bobby...that certain women, voodoo "priestesses" called "horses", are metaphorical cyberspace decks... The cowboys can "mount" and "ride" such horses into the matrix' (227).

In spite of the etymology of 'matrix', however, these figurations of cyberspace as a penetrable female body can be directly challenged because Gibson's matrix repeatedly takes on the role of the penetrator. This is made particularly evident given the appearance of voodoo *loas*: in *Count Zero*, Turner sees Angie twice-possessed, penetrated by both Legba and Baron Samedi; also, Jackie, one of Gibson's only female hackers, becomes Danbala's horse. In both cases neither Angie's nor Jackie's body is ridden solely as access to the digital world; rather, a *penetrating* force emanating from the matrix rides their bodies to access the offline world. Homoerotic penetration also takes place as Bobby becomes a horse, his male body penetrated by the masculine *loa* of Baron Samedi. A parallel moment takes place at the beginning of *Mona Lisa Overdrive* when Angie feels the returning presence of a penetrating feminine *loa*, Mamman Brigitte. Such stray penetration indicates that Gibson's cyberspatial matrix evades simplistic gender coding; the voodoo *loas* and their penetrative riding haunt both offline and online realities where male and female spaces cannot be cordoned off from each other.

A cyberspatial matrix that is etymologically linked to a female body but takes on its own masculinized penetrative qualities is also suggested in the evocation of 'When It Changed'. Gibson's 'When It Changed' is a seemingly deliberate reference in *Mona Lisa Overdrive* to Joanna Russ's Nebula-winning feminist short story 'When It Changed' (1972). A narrative about an all-female utopia, Russ's story depicts the reappearance of males on the planet Whileaway and the return of masculinist sexism and misogyny. In *Mona Lisa Overdrive*, several references are made to a cyberspace-based 'When It Changed' as the event that forever transformed the cyberspatial matrix. The vodoo *loas* explain it to Angie:

> 'Only the one has known the other, and the one is no more. In the wake of that knowing, the center failed; every fragment rushed away. The fragments sought form, each one, as is the nature of such things. In all the signs your kind have stored against the night, in that situation the paradigms of *vodou* proved most appropriate.'
>
> 'Then Bobby was right' [responds Angie]. 'That was When It Changed...'. (257)

Descriptions of When It Changed lead Nixon to remark that Gibson's use of this phrase is 'referring, in effect, to when the matrix became an inhabited feminized world' (227). Apparently mirroring Russ's narrative, Gibson's When It Changed 'is also gender specific: the uncontrollable feminizing of the matrix, the uncheckable transformation of viral software technology into a feminine Other' (Nixon 227). Nixon parallels Russ's 'When It Changed' – a story of masculine intrusion and penetration – to Gibson's When It Changed – an uncontrollable feminizing of cyberspace that prompts Gibson's hackers to 'jack in' to the matrix to penetrate ICE (Intrusion Countermeasures Electronics), a 'sort of metaphoric hymeneal membrane which can kill them if they don't successfully "eat through it"' (Nixon 226).

Nixon's argument is compelling, but I want to suggest an alternative reading that strays from the heteronormative. The When It Changed of the hacker mythos is the merging of the Wintermute and Neuromancer AIs at the end of *Neuromancer*. As the events in *Count Zero* reveal, this AI synthesis is followed by fragmentation and the emergence of voodoo *loas*. The events in both *Count Zero* and *Mona Lisa Overdrive* occur after When It Changed, while the events in *Neuromancer* take place before this radical transformation and, in fact, lead up to it in the merging of Neuromancer and Wintermute at the novel's conclusion. But as Nixon describes it, Gibson's When It Changed is a feminizing of the matrix, a 'female infection and (viral) takeover of original masculine space' (227). Following this argument, all instances of 'jacking into' the matrix that precede this feminizing When It Changed viral takeover that occurs at the end of *Neuromancer* must therefore be a penetration of what Nixon has described as an original *masculine* space. In other words, if the When It Changed moment feminized the matrix, then all instances of male hackers penetrating a pre-When It Changed matrix – the entirety of *Neuromancer* – can be read as male penetration of an original masculine cyberspace. In an ironic (and more than likely unintended) fashion, the When It Changed described in *Mona Lisa Overdrive* retro-queers the first novel in the sequence by using references to Russ that redeploy *Neuromancer*'s own images of console cowboys 'jacking into' a (masculinized) matrix. The introduction of When It Changed in *Mona Lisa Overdrive* and its ties to the queer politics of Russ's 'When It Changed' consequently destabilize straight readings of cyberspace and offer multiple ways of reading it: 1) it is the feminine matrix of *Neuromancer* penetrated by hackers 'jacking in'; 2) it is the masculine pre-When It Changed matrix of *Neuromancer* penetrated by male console cowboys; 3) it is the feminine penetrating agent of *Count Zero* and *Mona Lisa Overdrive* that rides male and female hackers to access offline reality. In sum, a multi-faceted queering of Gibson's matrix can readily be deployed to destabilize monolithic readings of a straight cyberspace and straight readings of the *Neuromancer* sequence.

The Post/Human Problematic

The non-normative possibilities effected through the proto-queering of Gibson's fictions are not divorced from the critical interrogations taking place in cyberculture; after all, Gibson *is* cyberculture, or at least one crucial sector in this interpretive field. Michael Benedikt's *Cyberspace: First Steps* (1991), one of the earliest explorations of cyberculture, begins with Gibson's meditation 'Academy Leader'. Similarly, Allucquère Rosanne Stone argues that 'the single most significant event for the development of fourth-stage virtual communities was the publication of William Gibson's science-fiction novel *Neuromancer*', a text whose inhabitable cyberspace has served as the groundwork for 'a series of experiments in both the military and private sectors' ('Boundary Stories' 95). Finally, in his contribution to *Prefiguring Cyberculture*, Scott McQuire argues that *Neuromancer*'s success and influence should be read 'as symptomatic of a complex of social changes and cultural anxieties which is still far from exhausted' (167). Thus, a proto-queer project offers the opportunity to respond to and to re-envision overlapping genealogies of gender, sexuality, and cyberspace. In this manner a critical interrogation of Gibson's sf works as a means of critically engaging cyberculture, if we agree that sf is in 'a privileged position because of its generic interest in the intersection of technology, scientific theory, and social practice' (Csicsery-Ronay, Jr, 'SF of Theory' 388).

Standing at this intersection is the figure of the cyborg that in Gibson has been deployed as the inscrutable Molly and/or embodied as the ambiguous hyper-masculine. In *Cyborg Citizen*, Chris Hables Gray clearly demonstrates that cyborgs have moved well past the status of imaginative trope and 'are proliferating throughout contemporary culture, and as they do they are redefining many of the most basic political concepts of human existence' (19). In a witty subversion of popular culture, Gray suggests that '[men] may be from Mars and women from Venus, but there is the rest of the universe to think of' (158), a universe whose proto-queer potentials are explored in Gibson's fictions. In sum, I am suggesting that the proto-queer universes of Gibson and Gray position the post/human cyborg as a *problematic*, defined as a 'conceptual framework within which further research and analysis can be conducted' (Freedman xx), and this problematic operates at the levels of both 'reality' and 'fiction'. In other words, cyborgs and their multiple instantiations are conceptual articulations of the queer possibilities penetrating the post/human spaces between (and beyond) Mars and Venus.

A parallel reconsideration of the hetero-gendered matrix is also no academic exercise. It has broader implications for how we conceptualize cyberspace. Just as Gibson's *Neuromancer* sequence can be retroactively re-coded in a proto-queer manner, so too can stray penetration be used to (re)read early explorations of cyberculture in a proto-queer manner that enables a move 'towards a different understanding of subjectivity and agency' (Pearson, 'Alien Cryptographies' 17). For example, in 1994, Allucquère Rosanne Stone argued that the seduction of cyberspace is rooted in gender:

> The experience of unlimited power is both gendered, and, for the male, fraught with the need for control, producing an unresolvable need for reconciliation with an always absent structure of personality... It seems to be the engagement of the adolescent male within humans of both sexes that is responsible for the seductiveness of the cybernetic mode. ('Boundary Stories' 108)

Stone even goes so far as to identify the 'desire to cross the human/machine boundary, to penetrate and merge, which is part of the evocation of cyberspace' as an 'inarticulate longing of the male for the female' which can be characterized as '*cyborg envy*' ('Boundary Stories' 108). Finally, she brings this hetero-default into distinct relief when she writes that 'penetration is translated into envelopment. In other words, to enter cyberspace is to physically *put on* cyberspace. To become the cyborg, to put on the seductive and dangerous cybernetic space like a garment, is to put on the *female*' ('Boundary Stories' 109; emphasis in original).

Proto-queering Stone's analysis hinges on her explanation of cyborg envy. In other words, cyborg envy is used to gender cyberspace as a male penetration of the female; tellingly, this (adolescent) male penetration is ascribed to both sexes ('engagement of the adolescent male within humans of both sexes'), so that Stone's own analysis queers her heteronormative axis. On the one hand, all forms of entering cyberspace are equated to a heteronormalized male/female dynamic of cyborg envy; on the other hand, since the position of the penetrating 'male' is accessible to both sexes, gender demarcation is problematic. In a proto-queer reading of Stone's analysis, the female cyborg is simultaneously female and adolescently male. Similarly, the female cyborg body is coded as performance: cyberspace-as-female is worn, a cyborg garment. Alternatively, the male cyborg, in penetrating cyberspace, becomes 'female' by becoming the cyborg, the object of envy, and then puts on the cyborg garment to enter it. Thus, Stone's cyborg envy can be simultaneously straight and queer as the female cyborg taps into her adolescent maleness to penetrate the feminine; similarly, the male cyborg figuratively becomes the object of his own desire, desiring to penetrate the feminine and being penetrated by the cyborg in order to satisfy that desire. What appears as a relatively straightforward heteronormative interpretation in Stone's early analysis can quickly mutate into a reading of proto-queer identities and unstable subjectivities for the Internet age.

'Putting on the female' is a structural metaphor that was also deployed by Deborah Lupton. In her 1995 exploration, however, the female becomes more dangerous as computer hackers penetrate and plunder the fluidic computer networks, the loci of women, sexuality, and the maternal body:

> Computer users...are attracted towards the promises of cyberspace, in the utopian freedom from the flesh, its denial of the body, the opportunity to achieve a cyborgian seamlessness and to 'connect' with others, but are also threatened by its potential to engulf the self and expose one's vulnerability to the penetration of enemy others. As with the female body, a site of intense desire and emotional security but also threatening engulfment, the inside of the computer body is dark and enigmatic, potentially leaky, harbouring danger and contamination, vulnerable to invasion. (111)

Lupton's images are of a feminized cyberspace founded on engulfment, invasive contamination, and an enigmatic darkness; thus, she implicitly codes computer users, with their fear of enemy penetration and invasion, as male. Once the dominance of the male cyborg is challenged and the female cyborg is factored into the equation – a factoring that is more prevalent today than it was when Lupton's essay was first published – cyberspace and cyborgs are also readily proto-queered. Specifically, female surfers are symbolically proto-queered since they are metaphorically being engulfed by an intensely desirous and emotionally secure space that in its dark, enigmatic, and potentially leaky configuration is coded as feminine. In addition, female surfers can become penetrators as they delve into the computer's engulfing interiors. In this case, the female surfer who desires the feminine engulfment of cyberspace while simultaneously becoming the masculine penetrator to achieve such technologically mediated connection is marked by stray penetration. As with the stray penetration of Gibson's cyborgs and the cyborg space between Mars and Venus that Chris Hables Gray describes, proto-queer re-readings of Lupton's and Stone's studies, emblematic of cyberculture's early steps, continue to enable ongoing queer interrogations of cyberspace and the monolithic signifying practices that elide its multiplicity.[6]

I have been reading Gibson's paradigmatic *Neuromancer* sequence against the grain in a proto-queer manner that allows Gibson's three novels to take on new resonances for the twenty-first century. They also become part of an important task of pushing science fiction as a genre to resist its own 'overwhelmingly *straight*' discursive history and to 'imagine itself otherwise' (Hollinger, '(Re)reading Queerly' 24). The texts, penetrated by stray penetration, can be read as staging a loosening of signification in both urban and cyberspatial domains that helps to denaturalize heteronormativity and its concomitant ascription of gender roles. This de-naturalization bleeds into the broader cyberculture arena in which Gibson's fiction is firmly situated, an arena that continues to build on the theoretical considerations first outlined by theorists such as Stone and Lupton. In sum, proto-queering different facets of cyberculture enables ongoing dialogue as to the shape of the cyberspatial matrix, a shape that is neither naturally straight nor naturally queer. This proto-queer engagement will, one hopes, give birth to new ways to 'think ourselves outside the binary oppositions of a fictively totalizing [heteronormative] feminine/masculine divide' (Hollinger, '(Re)reading Queerly' 25).

Notes

1. In addition to cited sources, recent cyberpunk explorations include Pat Cadigan's *The Ultimate Cyberpunk*, Sabine Heuser's *Virtual Geographies*, Chad P. Barnett's 'Reviving Cyberpunk', William Irwin's *The Matrix and Philosophy*, Thomas Foster's *The Souls of Cyberfolk*, William S. Haney II's *Cyberculture, Cyborgs and Science Fiction*, and Stacy Gillis's *The Matrix Trilogy*.

2. For example, see Larry McCaffery's *Storming the Reality Studio* and George Slusser and Tom Shippey's *Fiction 2000*.
3. Examples of battle-of-the-sexes sf discussed by Larbalestier include Nelson S. Bond's 'The Priestess Who Rebelled' (1939) and Edmund Cooper's *Who Needs Men?* (1972). In Larbalestier's argument, heteronormativity in these stories is founded upon penetration: 'In both texts a kiss is the turning point in the conversion from matriarchy to patriarchy. In "The Priestess Who Rebelled" the kiss is the climactic, in every sense, moment and it occurs towards the end of the text' (60). Similarly, the Rura character in *Who Needs Men?* endures a rape only to discover 'that she likes it. Penetration is crucial to her becoming woman' (61).
4. See the essays by Joan Gordon, Lauraine Leblanc, and Nicola Nixon.
5. Case's virginity is established near the beginning of *Neuromancer* when he is taken by Molly to see the Finn. He is scanned by the Finn for technological augmentation and bodily modification; afterwards, the Finn remarks: 'Guy's a virgin... Some cheap dental work, is all' (49).
6. For another queer reading of cyberspace, see Shannon McRae's 'Flesh Made Word'. In her analysis of online relationships and identities, McRae concludes that '[if] boys can be girls and straights can be queers and dykes can be fags and two lesbian lovers can turn out to be both men in real life, then "straight" or "queer," "male" or "female" become unreliable as markers of identity' (80). More recently Nina Wakeford's 'Cyberqueer' posits cyberqueer as an articulation of cybernetic sexualities that emerges from the 'alliances between lesbian, gay, transgender and queer experiences and computer-mediated worlds' (410). In this sense Wakeford's cyberqueer offers interesting possibilities for subverting 'the assumed superiority of heterosexuality within the politics of representation, and [makes] evident the silences and those silenced by the new computer-aided logic of global accumulation' (409). See also Cleo Odzer's *Virtual Spaces*, Sherry Turkle's *Life on the Screen*, Claudia Springer's *Electronic Eros*, and Beth E. Kolko, Lisa Nakamura, and Gilbert B. Rodman's *Race in Cyberspace*.

Part III

Disordering Desires

'Something Like a Fiction': Speculative Intersections of Sexuality and Technology

Veronica Hollinger

> If gender is the social construction of sex, and if there is no access to this 'sex' except by means of its construction, then it appears not only that sex is absorbed by gender, but that 'sex' becomes something like a fiction, perhaps a fantasy...
>
> — Judith Butler, *Bodies That Matter* 5

> Alas! those who were shocked at my making love that way to a man are now shocked at my making love to a machine; you can't win.
>
> — Joanna Russ, *The Female Man* 200

In his recent cultural history of the genre, Roger Luckhurst astutely describes the project of science fiction as 'speculation on the diverse results of the conjuncture of technology and subjectivity' (222). In the past two decades or so, Anglo-American sf has undertaken this kind of speculative project in the most literal of ways – the concretization of metaphor being a particularly favoured sf strategy – whether exploring the impact of technoculture on the human subject as such in its many cyborg stories or attempting to trace the ontological features of our artificial progeny in stories about robots and other forms of artificial intelligences. Since the mid-1980s in particular, especially in response to the cyberpunk phenomenon, sf has almost obsessively (re)imagined the post-human subject at a variety of 'conjunctures' with the technological.[1]

But the post-human has a history, and so I will focus this discussion on pre-cyberpunk science fiction in order to examine some of sf's earlier literalizations of our increasingly intimate relations with/in the cultures of technology. In part I want to draw attention to the complex interplay between pre-cyberpunk fiction and some of sf's more recent representations of the post-human. In part I want to acknowledge the historical influence of earlier sf, especially queer/feminist sf, on cyberpunk and later science fictions about the subjects of technoculture.[2]

We can only ever know 'sex' in so far as it is implied in and expressed through the performances of gender, argues Judith Butler, so that, as she concludes, '"sex" becomes something like a fiction, perhaps a fantasy'. Sometimes, as I will argue in turn, it also becomes something like a science fiction, as fantasies of sex/gender become literalized in the discursive constructions of sf narratives. My discussion first reads several science fictions that address, with varying degrees of directness, some of the crises faced by the subject of technoculture at the intersections of sex and technology. My second section focuses in some detail on Joanna Russ's great postmodern-lesbian-feminist-utopian-satire, *The Female Man* (1975), reading it as representative of a queerly efficacious analysis and critique of some of the complexities of our (sexual) relations with technology.

1. Conjunctures of Sexuality and Technology

I want to take advantage of Andrew Feenberg's critical-philosophical work in *Transforming Technology: A Critical Theory Revisited* (2002) to outline briefly and in very broad strokes some of the quite different roles which technology can play in both theory and fiction in their various considerations of the conjunctures of subjectivities and technologies. According to Feenberg, *instrumental* theory 'offers the most widely accepted view of technology. It is based on the commonsense idea that technologies are "tools", standing ready to serve the purposes of their users' (5).[3] When this view is introduced into sf stories, it tends to result in fictions about technology as neutral prosthesis, as product and/or tool extending our physical reach into the material world – faster, farther, stronger – without any consequential impact on the subjects who use these tools.

Among the more appealing features of the instrumental position is the way in which it envisages technology as a straightforward supplement to human being in the world and its concomitant commitment to a view of human nature as authentic, coherent, and, above all, natural.[4] Consider the utopian sexual 'conjuncture' of human man and technological woman that takes place in Lester del Rey's early story, 'Helen O'Loy' (1938), a pulp classic of Golden Age sf and a cheerfully sexist fantasy about the creation of an ideal robot-woman; in my reading, del Rey's story exemplifies the instrumentalist view.

Programmed to perform femininity to perfection, Helen falls in love with one of her creators; he soon forgets she is not a 'natural' woman and they marry and live happily ever after until his death in old age – at which point she arranges for her own ending: 'Acid will burn out metal as well as flesh, and I'll be dead with Dave' (73). In 'Helen O'Loy', technoscience constructs the ultimate sexual prosthesis in a fantasy about 'woman' as the literal creation of masculinist science. As Helen insists to one of her creators, obliquely referencing her capacity to perform sexuality, 'I'm a woman. And you know how perfectly I'm made to imitate a real woman' (71).

It is not a 'real woman' that Helen imitates, of course, but rather the fantasy of 'woman' so dear to the hearts of the two techno-nerds who have transformed a rather ordinary household robot into their ideal of domestic femininity. And her imitation is completely successful: while she will never be a 'real' woman in any biological sense, she has nevertheless achieved a kind of metaphysical 'womanhood' in her perfect citation of gender. In the terms of Butler's observation about the 'fantastic' nature of sex, Helen's perfect expression of (hetero)sexuality – contrary to what common sense tells us – is the consequence rather than the impetus of (a prior performance of) gender. In 'Helen O'Loy', 'sex' is indeed a fiction, both the artificial performance of an artificial woman and the gendered fantasy of heterosexualized science fiction. Robot-Helen is 'woman' in a way that no human woman can ever aspire to be(come): the wonderful paradox in del Rey's story is that Helen is the real thing – that is, she is a real woman – exactly because she has been constructed as pure representation. In this view, the phrase 'artificial woman' is a redundancy.

Because it does not threaten the category of the human in any consequential way, technology can function in 'Helen O'Loy' as a figure for something else – in this instance, as a key element in an allegory about the construction of sexual difference. The story takes literally the notion of the construction of the gendered subject. In Butler's terms, it demonstrates very concretely the processes through which social and discursive technologies of regulation work to 'materialize sexual difference in the service of the consolidation of the heterosexual imperative' (*Bodies That Matter* 2). This is apparent from the very first words of del Rey's narrator: 'I am an old man now, and I can still see Helen as Dave unpacked her, and still hear him gasp as he looked her over... She was beautiful, a dream in spun plastics and metals' (62). 'Helen O'Loy' narrates an apparently unproblematical dream – at once a fiction and a fantasy – about the construction of the perfect artificial woman, a dream in which an active (hetero)sexuality is the mark of Helen's authenticity as a 'real' woman. At the same time, her performance is an imitation made possible through the wonders of future technoscience.[5]

In contrast to instrumental theories, as Feenberg explains, *substantive* theories of technology assume that the technoscientific project necessarily marks subjectivity (usually for the worse), that it simultaneously subjectivizes and subjugates the human, enforcing a redefinition of the human within its own 'enframing' logic (to recall Heidegger's classic theorization in 'The Question Concerning Technology'). As Feenberg explains,

> [s]ubstantive theory...argues that technology constitutes a new cultural system that restructures the entire social world as an object of control... The issue is not that machines have 'taken over,' but that in choosing to use them we make many unwitting commitments. Technology is not simply a means but has become an environment and a way of life. (6–8)[6]

To express the experience of this 'way of life' has been the particular goal of cyberpunk, which emphasizes the impact of technological transformation on its human characters as the subjects of technoculture: cyberpunk starts from the assumption that technoculture is exactly our currently all-encompassing 'way of life'. Arguably, what sets cyberpunk apart from much earlier science fiction is its relatively neutral, and sometimes even celebratory, acceptance of the ways in which technology has come to over-write innumerable features of the natural world, including human sexuality. In 'Helen O'Loy', nature is still capable of absorbing technology, but in cyberpunk it is technology that gathers both the natural world and the organic human subject into itself. We see this in the well-known metaphor with which William Gibson's exemplary novel, *Neuromancer* (1984), opens: 'The sky above the port was the color of television, tuned to a dead channel' (3). As for human sexuality, it is no coincidence – as Graham Murphy also notes elsewhere in this collection – that Gibson's console-cowboy protagonist, Case, is referred to as a 'virgin' specifically in reference to his body's almost complete lack of technological prostheses and/or enhancements: 'Some cheap dental work, is all' (*Neuromancer* 49). At the same time, *Neuromancer*'s female lead, Molly Millions, a technologically wired 'street samurai', has paid for her many prosthetic enhancements by working as a 'meat puppet', a prostitute whose mind is equipped with a 'cut-out chip' so that she remains unaware of the uses to which her body is put while she is '[r]enting the goods' to her customers (147).

I will just note the complexly gendered nature of the fictional 'sex' depicted through *Neuromancer*'s technological filters. What is of more immediate interest to me here is that the representation of sexuality – conventionally valorized for its associations with organic and embodied humanity – has also become absorbed into the discourse of technoscience.

Even Case's 'virgin' body is discursively framed by techno-metaphoricity: during sex with Molly, we read that his orgasm 'flar[es] blue in a timeless space, a vastness like the matrix' (33); there is no human subjectivity outside the technological frame which encompasses both the material and the virtual worlds of *Neuromancer*.

Sf writers who espouse substantive positions have issued many warnings about the dire consequences of burgeoning technoscience on the human subject. In fact, there has always been a strand of sf committed to this particular version of substantive theory. It would not be too far a stretch to consider that Mary Shelley's progenitor text, *Frankenstein* (1818), is 'about' the inevitability with which technoscience will come to enframe the subject who isolates himself from affective human relationships. It is unlikely to be a coincidence in Shelley's plot that the Creature takes his ultimate revenge by strangling Frankenstein's new bride on their wedding night, so that the fact of death replaces the physical promise of Elizabeth's body, and the product of Victor's own laboratory displaces all human warmth in his life. And early in the last century, E. M. Forster published his well-known fictional nightmare about totalizing technological mediation, 'The Machine Stops' (1909); this story both enacts an impassioned warning about the deadening effects of technoscience and demonstrates a fierce nostalgia for an authentically human way of life free of technology, not least in the area of sexuality:

> Cannot you see...that it is we who are dying, and that down here the only thing that really lives is the Machine? We created the Machine, to do our will, but we cannot make it do our will now. It has robbed us of the sense of space and of the sense of touch, *it has blurred every human relation and narrowed down love to a carnal act,* it has paralysed our bodies and our wills, and now it compels us to worship it... [If] it could work without us, it would let us die. (54; my emphasis)

Stories with an instrumentalist orientation tend to support a fairly unproblematic distinction between the human and the technological, especially where issues related to sexuality are concerned – human beings are human beings, and the products of technoscience are merely tools.[7] It is exactly this distinction, significantly, which is so often threatened with dissolution in stories about the substantive impact of 'technique' on the natural/human world, so that these stories as well remain committed to an ideal of the natural and the human. Often such stories, even if only through implication, call for a renewed authenticity in sexual relations, understood as a particularly 'natural' expression of the human, which should remain free from technological mediation and/or intervention. We can certainly recognize this in the desperate desire of Forster's character to be free of the Machine, to return to fully present and affectively meaningful human relations.

Stories about the threat posed by technology to the unique and authentic expression of human sexuality can sometimes (often?) be read as displacements of a prior anxiety, however repressed it might be. This is the (heterosexualized) apprehension that the supposedly clear-cut, commonsensical, and 'natural' differentiations of sex, gender, and sexual orientation may not, in fact, be so clear-cut or so natural after all. Not for nothing are they monitored, in Brian Attebery's ironic words, 'with the special vigilance reserved for instilling what a culture believes to be natural' (130). We might consider how 'vigilant' is del Rey's 'Helen O'Loy', a story in which sex, gender, and sexual desire are represented as naturally aligned in the interests of normative heterosexuality; technology's function is simply to support and replicate the natural order of things. Helen is the perfect artificial woman because her programming works exactly in this way; it seems impossible that anything might threaten such a coherent matrix of sexed bodies, genders, and sexualities.[8]

Not surprisingly, especially in the 1940s and 1950s which saw the initial developments of cybernetics as a theoretical field, it is more common to find stories about how technology poses a radical threat to (the fantasy of) normative sexuality. Many stories are structured according to an opposition between 'normal' sexuality (an essential human activity and expression) and technology (the product of instrumental reason, associated with artifice, outside the pale of nature).[9] This opposition is dramatically staged in Cordwainer Smith's early story 'Scanners Live in Vain' (1948), in which Martel, the male protagonist, is literally penetrated by technology and so rendered numb, untouchable, and physically grotesque. It is only with the removal of his loathsome prostheses that Smith's protagonist regains his full humanity, significantly figured as the renewal of his sexual capacity. In the cyberpunk future of *Neuromancer*, Case's technological virginity is a source of mild contempt, but in Smith's much earlier story, the penetration of the body by technology is figured as radically dehumanizing. Only a return to organic 'purity' can assure a return to full humanity. Martel tries desperately to explain this to his wife: 'Can't you understand what it means to me? To get out of this horrible prison in my own head? To be a man again... To *feel* again – ' (354; emphasis in original).

'Scanners Live in Vain' is an anxious narrative about the erasure of humanity under the onslaught of technology. Humanity is figured here as the organic integration of mind and body, while technology is figured as invasion, mutilation, and dehumanization. In this story's far future, the

Scanners are an elite space-faring guild of cyborgs whose bodies have been redesigned to withstand 'the pain of space'.[10] Their transformation into Scanners involves cutting off the body's sensory input to the mind and incorporating monitoring equipment directly into the flesh in compensation. Scanners must use this equipment constantly to scan their physical bodies for damage and to keep their emotions at equilibrium: except for rare occasions when they are 'cranched' – temporarily returned to direct communication with their own bodies – they can feel neither pain nor pleasure, they have lost touch and taste and hearing; in Scanner-mode, all that is left to them is sight. Not coincidentally, perhaps, in their loss of human physicality and emotion, in their reduction to mind and sight, Smith's Scanners – all of whom are male – are perfect (and parodic?) cyborg representations of Western Man, that figure whose privileged features are also rational mind and controlling sight.

As I have already implied, 'Scanners Live in Vain' dramatizes a singularly (doubled) masculine anxiety. Given that the Scanners are an all-male guild, it is not surprising that Smith figures the severance of body from mind as a kind of castration, his text referring to 'the professional requirements of [the Scanners'] mutilation' (371). Concomitantly, the text suggests that the Scanners have become feminized through the penetration of their bodies by their despised prostheses. The story directly links Martel's sense that he is no longer human, that he is 'a man turned into a machine' (360), to his conviction that he is no longer a real man because he cannot perform sexually with his wife. In the end, Martel and the other Scanners are restored to full (masculine) humanity, as Smith resolves his story through the discovery of a scientific breakthrough that renders their sacrifice no longer necessary. The direct link between body and technology – the link that has both unmanned and dehumanized the Scanners – is broken; mind and organic body are appropriately reintegrated. In the resolution of Smith's deeply humanist parable, identity returns to the (masculine) self through the self's reunification with the natural/sexual body and its renewed capacity to penetrate an appropriately feminine body.

A rather more complex cyborg subjectivity is dramatized in C. L. Moore's well-known proto-feminist story, 'No Woman Born' (1944). This is an origin story about a new technosubjectivity, an asexual hybrid of woman and machine who is also a consummate performer of 'woman' (to recall my reading of 'Helen O'Loy'). The story's obsessive focus is the mysterious nature of the cyborg Deirdre, whose (techno)body can no longer ground her ontological status as a woman, at the same time as it gives her an almost superhuman ability to perform femininity to perfection.

In a way that readers of Judith Butler's writings on gender performances and queer sexualities will recognize, Deirdre's performances for her adoring audiences confer on her a 'womanliness' that is certainly no less authentic than that which inheres in any organic body. The 'sex' implied by and expressed in her gendered performances, however, is most definitely a fiction. In marked contrast to Smith's Martel, Deirdre's gleaming metallic body is described as impenetrable, and, therefore, as necessarily removed from the unequal sexual relations of power that fix individual women and men. As if to emphasize her displacement from the heterosexual economy, she is described in terms that suggest an armoured masculinity: her head is like a 'visored golden helmet' and, considering her metallic robe, her manager remarks on her 'odd likeness to knighthood' (263). At the same time, Moore's text raises the question of Deirdre's humanity, as her manager fears that 'Deirdre was gone, and this was only machinery' (242). 'Real' women are (hetero)sexually available to 'real' men; since Deirdre is no longer a sexually available body, the text worries obsessively about her status as 'woman' and, by extension, her status as 'human'. Moore's story is a demonstration, decades *avant la lettre*, of Butler's observations about cultural 'intelligibility': 'the uncontested status of "sex" within the heterosexual dyad secures the workings of certain symbolic orders, and … its contestation calls into question where and how the limits of symbolic intelligibility are set' (*Bodies That Matter* 16).

As Butler has argued in detail, sexuality often functions metonymically as a marker of the 'human' as an intelligible category, especially when sexuality is conceived as natural, organic, expressive of the inner truth of the subject, associated with the natural body, unprogrammed and spontaneous. Technology often serves as its foil, figured in contrast as unnatural, programmed, inauthentic, and unoriginal. What differentiates Moore's story from Smith's is its refusal to reject the technobody out of hand, in spite of the anxieties it raises: as many readers will know, Moore's text ends on a note of irresolution that leaves her plot radically open: '"I wonder," [Deirdre] repeated, the distant taint of metal already in her voice' (288). 'No Woman Born' does not dream of a return to innocence, to the restored virginity of a pre-technological natural human body; instead, it looks foward to the technological future with intermingled hope and trepidation.[11]

Unexpectedly, perhaps, we find a variation on Smith's techno-repulsion in Philip K. Dick's novel *Do Androids Dream of Electric Sheep?* (1968), which I read here as a substantive-theory revision of the fantasy of technosexual satisfaction that structures 'Helen O'Loy'.[12] A long happy marriage between scientist and artificial woman resolves the conflict in del

Rey's story. Significantly, it is not a conflict about technology, but about sexuality, as the tension in the story circulates around Helen's increasingly desperate passion for Dave and his own inability to admit his love for her. In contrast, *Androids* appears to be much more conflicted about the eroticization and/or sexualization of the machine. While the novel famously identifies empathy as the definitive human quality, demonstrated most directly in its concern for the untenable enslavement of the androids, it also expresses real distaste for the kind of sexualized relationship between human and machine that is so lightly treated in 'Helen O'Loy'.

In the first instance, sex with (female) androids, which is illegal in Dick's fictional world, is associated with the repulsive bounty hunter, Phil Resch, who is so void of anything like human feeling that it is easy to suspect him of being an android himself. As he insists to Rick Deckard, Dick's bounty-hunter protagonist, 'If it's love toward a woman or an android imitation, it's sex... Don't kill [a female android]...and then feel physically attracted. Do it the other way' (126). Later, when the android Rachael seduces Deckard in order to prevent him from killing the escaped androids whom he must track down and 'retire', sexuality is once again associated with the machine. The reader has already been prepared to find the scene at least vaguely distasteful and the reader is not disappointed: as he undresses Rachael, Deckard 'expose[s] her pale, cold loins' and, in a passion of self-abjection, she insists before they have sex that '*I'm not alive!* You're not going to bed with a woman' (169). When Deckard decides to continue hunting the escaped androids after all, Rachael takes her vengeance by pushing his '*alive*' goat off the roof of his apartment building.

In the world of *Androids*, human beings are becoming indistinguishable from machines in their coldness and lack of affectivity; but while there is some indication – in Roy Baty's anguish at his wife's death, for instance – that machines are also becoming more like human beings in their capacity for empathy, this recognition does not extend to an acceptance of human/android sexuality. In spite of Deckard's final almost-mystical vision recognizing the claim to 'life' of even mechanical creatures – 'The electric things have their lives, too. Paltry as those lives are' (214) – Dick's novel does not appear to extend that 'life' to the arena of techno-sexuality.

Although *Androids* is a novel that famously problematizes any too-easy distinction between human beings and their artificial offspring, it figures the technological corruption of authentic sexuality through the character of the android Rachael.[13] This is, of course, more than appropriate in the text's own terms, given the process of rampant commodification that both defines and confines Rachael – in contrast to the domestic happy ending granted to del Rey's Helen – to the role of technoscientific product.

Notably, del Rey's text constructs Helen as unique in her fictional world – if nothing else, she enjoys a certain Benjaminian aura. 'There was only one Helen O'Loy' (73), as the narrator rather poignantly tells us, implying why it is that he has never married. In contrast, Rachael is a kind of simulacrum, one of a series of identical Nexus-Six models (so that she and Pris Stratton are physically indistinguishable), and so, ultimately, she has no identity of her own to anchor her as a subject. She is nothing more than a disposable Baudrillardian simulation, easily and endlessly replicable, the very antithesis of authentic subjectivity: '"It's an illusion that I – I personally – really exist; I'm just representative of a type." She shuddered' (165).

Dick's text seems to support the idea that to be human is not something that one automatically is; rather the human is constituted through an individual's ongoing ethical behaviour. It is, in effect, a performative process that can potentially also include androids. But the novel concludes with a scene of conventionally human/gendered warmth and tranquillity that seems to erase the androids altogether, as Deckard, watched over by his wife, Iran, sleeps after his harrowing efforts to retire the Nexus-6 escapees – all of whom are dead by now. Iran, who begins the novel as cold and unfeeling as the android Rachael, is redeemed into full humanity through her renewed concern for her husband. His sleep is 'natural', unaided by the supplementary 'mood organs' that Dick's human characters have come to rely on in the midst of the vast social depression that pervades *Androids'* grey and infertile future. For the moment, at least, Dick's characters have managed to escape the 'taint' of technology that overlays this future.

2. When It Changed[14]

In *Transforming Technology*, Feenberg recommends a position that is neither instrumental nor substantive, but takes account of both: a *critical theory* of technology – broadly speaking – recognizes the ineluctable shaping power of Western technoscience on human life while remaining committed to the possibilities of human political agency. In Feenberg's description, which owes much to the work of Frankfurt School theorists such as Adorno and Marcuse,

> [critical] theory recognizes that part of the human actor which overflows any particular network involvement and provides a basis for criticizing the construction of networks. It retains the commonsense notion that human actors have unique reflexive capacities. These capacities make it

> possible for humans to represent the networks in which they 'emerge' and to measure them against unrealized potentialities identified in thought. (34)

Although Feenberg distances his own position from Donna Haraway's cyborg theory and distinguishes his own ideas from 'various forms of postmodernism and posthumanism' (27–33), it is certainly possible to read Haraway's 'Cyborg Manifesto' (1985; rev. 1991) as a (theoretical) allegory of the post-human subject of technoculture who is at the same time the self-reflexive (techno)subject – at once agent and object – of cultural critique. As Feenberg explains, echoing what I understand to be Haraway's position as well, '[on] this view, technology is not a destiny but a scene of struggle' (15). In its role as metaphor and figure for critical technocultural hybridity, Haraway's cyborg is also the scene of an investigation: it is a theoretical object of intense interest as the new (post-human) subject of technology, one with little investment in idealized categories such as 'natural' and 'human'; it is intensely politicized.

Like 'sex', 'theory' is a kind of fantasy: for all its appeal to real differences, real bodies, real performances, and real subjectivities, queer theory is also a critical fantasy *par excellence*. It shapes its utopian dreams in theoretical abstractions and embodies them experimentally in stories – stories of the future are particularly appropriate, since the subjects, bodies, and worlds that queer theory models have yet to be materialized. Queer theories shape stories and queer stories embody the dreams of a future 'not fully determined in advance' (Butler, *Undoing Gender* 191) either by the abstractions of theory or in the activities of present-world politics. It is in this sense that story and theory sustain each other. To borrow an observation of Butler's – only somewhat out of context – theory 'takes place every time a possibility is imagined' (*Undoing Gender* 176).

This is how I understand what Haraway has in mind when she identifies writers such as Joanna Russ and Samuel R. Delany as 'theorists for cyborgs' ('Cyborg Manifesto'173). These and other sf writers, many of them active in the 1970s, already look forward to some of the possibilities of the (Harawayan) cyborg figure in stories that engage how we live our lives in technoculture, that explore new subjectivities at the technological interface. These are stories about how the 'supplement' of technology is inevitably constitutive of the (post-)humanity which it supplements.

At the same time, these writers also suggest a variety of answers – even if only in the imaginary resolutions of fiction – to the challenge posed by Butler's queer theory: 'is there a way to break out of this circle whereby heterosexuality institutes monolithic culture and monolithic culture reinstitutes and renaturalizes heterosexuality?' (*Undoing Gender*

124). Classic stories such as Delany's 'Aye, and Gomorrah…' (1967), Russ's 'When It Changed' (1972), Vonda N. McIntyre's 'Of Mist, and Grass, and Sand' (1973), and James Tiptree, Jr's 'The Girl Who Was Plugged In' (1973) mark these writers as also theorists for queer/feminists. And Judith Butler in turn can be read as a theorist of speculative futurity: 'To assume responsibility for a future,' she writes, 'is not to know its direction fully in advance, since the future, especially the future with and for others, requires a certain openness and unknowingness; it implies becoming part of a process the outcome of which no one subject can surely predict' (*Undoing Gender* 39).

Before turning my focus to *The Female Man*, I will just briefly note how interesting it is to read Delany's 'Aye, and Gomorrah…' as a queer revision of Smith's 'Scanners Live in Vain'. Delany's story is about bodies, technologies, and sexual perversion. In the story's future world, this perversion has appeared in the wake of the exigencies of space travel, recalling the agonizing 'pain of space' which necessitates the Scanners' sacrifice. The bodies of the 'spacers' in Delany's story have been altered so that they become both physically ungendered and – like Smith's Scanners – sexually neutered. Rather than longing for a return to the 'natural' body, however, Delany's story focuses on the 'plasticity' of human desire, an idea central also to *The Female Man* (as I discuss below). Inevitably, the story implies, a subculture of 'frelks' arises, individuals who are helplessly – and hopelessly – erotically attracted to the sexless spacers. As one of them explains to Delany's spacer narrator:

> *You* have no perversions at all. *You*'re free of the whole business… My love starts with the fear of love. Isn't that beautiful? … I want you because you can't want me. That's the pleasure. If someone had a sexual reaction to us, we'd be scared away. (540–41; emphasis in original)

Delany's frelks never have to test the validity of their fantasies of sex, since their desires are fulfilled only in the deferral of fulfilment – Delany's perversion is an ideal response to the notion that 'sex' is a fantasy represented in the performances of gender. The spacers are of indeterminate gender – 'You look as though you may once have been a man' (534); 'you look like you were once a woman, no?' (535) – and so they can embody the erotic fantasies of any individual frelk who desires them. Delany's story tells us that desire will continually seek out new subjects/objects through which to attain its (temporary) satisfactions. And there will always be desire that seeks elsewhere for its fulfilment.

Like 'Aye, and Gomorrah…', *The Female Man*, one of the first and still one of the most challenging critical fictions ever written about feminism and technoscience, is a particuarly appealing and effective example of cyborg fiction/theory. It is a novel about conjunctures, intersections, and sexual encounters that are monstrous, hybrid, and – inevitably – political.[15] It is also a speculative response to one of the most politically perverse of all conjunctures: 'You can't unite woman and human any more than you can unite matter and anti-matter', Russ's narrator Joanna explains to the reader; 'they are designed not to be stable together and they make just as big an explosion inside the head of the unfortunate girl who believes in both' (151).

The Female Man represents a critical turn away from both instrumentalist and substantive theories of technology and towards the kind of critically self-reflexive position championed by Feenberg. It is also exemplary of a queer turn that highlights the deeply unnatural relations among human sex, gender, and sexual orientation. At the centre of my reading of *The Female Man* is the novel's 'primal scene', in which the cyborg assassin Jael (also known as Alice Reasoner) fucks her toy-boy Davy, a scene witnessed with shock by her other selves, Joanna, Jeannine, and Janet Evason. What they think they are seeing, however, is not what is in fact occurring. As I will discuss in more detail below, the truth is even more perverse than the appearance: Russ's cyborg is fucking (with) technology and the stage is set for yet another fiction about 'sex'.

The character of Jael works exactly to disrupt the naturalized relations among sexed bodies, sexual desires, and gendered behaviours which maintain heterosexuality's psychological and social hegemony. As Susana S. Martins points out in her discussion of the novel,

> [technology] does not lend itself always and only to narratives of inevitability [the stuff of substantive theory], or to naturalized tales of evolution and progress [the stuff of instrumental theory]. Sometimes we find a completely unnatural tale of revolution and reversal... Technology can interrupt the natural and the normalized; it can make us think historically and futuristically. (419)

The main characters in *The Female Man* are four versions of the same genome who inhabit parallel worlds. Each of these worlds is quite different from the others, and so the four women – each of whom has a name beginning with 'J' – are also quite different from each other. As Jael explains their differences to the other three women:

> We ought to think alike and feel alike and act alike, but of course we don't. So plastic is humankind! ... Between our dress, and our opinions, and our habits, and our beliefs, and our values, and our mannerisms, and our manners, and our expressions, and our ages, and our experience, even I can hardly believe that I am looking at three other myselves. (162)

Or, as Judith Butler puts it, even 'Nature has a history' (*Bodies That Matter* 5).

This perspective on humanity as 'unnatural' links Russ's fiction to a range of constructivist models of the human subject, including queer-theoretical models developed in the decades since her novel's original appearance, and earlier studies such as the influential preliminary work undertaken by Michel Foucault in his histories of sexuality. Russ depicts variations in the four Js that clearly also incorporate sexual orientation, although she simultaneously disrupts any straightforward understanding of this concept. Jael, for example, considers herself heterosexual – 'Nor do I have love affairs with other women; in some things...I am a very old-fashioned girl' (192) – but, as I will return to below, sex with machines is not a form of heterosexuality that would be recognized by any moral majority. Janet Evason, on the other hand, inhabits the all-women utopia of Whileaway. In the absence of any possibility of heterosexuality, does the category 'lesbian' still retain its commonsense meaning? For Russ, as for Butler, the counterintuitive position is the more accurate one: culture produces nature, just as gender produces sex.

Unlike in 'Helen O'Loy', and as we might expect from Russ's admonitions about technology as a 'non-subject', technology does not function solely as a figure for sexual difference in *The Female Man*. Considering the dismal fate of the surgically altered youths in Manland, for example, Martins notes how '[technology] can not only *produce* subjectivities and bodies, but also exclude, foreclose, and violently transform bodies and social identities' (411). *The Female Man* tells more than one story about technology, in other words, and therefore more than one story about (the fiction of) sexuality. For example: in Jael's world, Manland, as its name suggests, is an all-male society; 'the Changed' are those who have been surgically altered to function as the 'wives' and 'mistresses' of 'real men'. The Womanlanders give the Manlanders the specifications for making 'real' women, but, as Jael tells the reader, 'I doubt if even the sex surgeons know what a real woman looks like. The specifications we send them every year grow wilder and wilder and there isn't a murmur of protest' (169). The 'women' of Manland are literal fictions of sexual difference, fantasies of the 'real men' constructed in their hopeless attempts to live up to the increasingly impossible ideals of appropriate heterosexuality.[16]

Jael has called her sisters together to support the epic conflict in which she is engaged, the ongoing war between 'the haves' and the 'have-nots' in her world, that is, between 'the men and the women' (165).[17] When she first appears, she is described in terms that construct her as both grotesque and ghostly: 'her teeth seem to be one fused ribbon of steel' (158); 'her eyes are silver, most unnatural'; 'the ends of her fingers (she says) were once caught in a press and are growing cancerous'; '[she] has hairpin-shaped scars under her ears'; when she laughs, it is 'as if some mechanical vulture on a gigantic garbage heap on the surface of the moon were giving one forced shriek for the death of all organic life' (159). These satirically over-the-top features call attention to Jael's technological enhancements, most notorious of which are the murderous blades inset into her finger-tips (weapons borrowed by William Gibson to arm *Neuromancer*'s Molly Millions).

Jael's lover is Davy, 'the most beautiful man in the world' (185). Jael gives readers a detailed first-person account of one of her sexual encounters with him, a rather unexpected scene given the importance of lesbian sexuality in the novel and of the utopian vision of an all-woman future on Whileaway. As noted above, for all her hatred of the Manlanders Jael presents herself as 'a very old-fashioned girl' (192) who does not have affairs with women. There is a punch-line, of course: it turns out that she does not have affairs with men either. Jael informs her genomic sisters that Davy, whom she refers to as her 'monster-pet' (197), is not human at all. He is an almost completely artificial construction more or less lacking in consciousness, 'a lovely limb of [Jael's automated] house'; his 'original germ-plasm was chimpanzee' (199). So horrified are the other Js by her sex with Davy that Jael is driven to her ironic lament: 'Alas! those who were shocked at my making love that way to a man are now shocked at my making love to a machine; you can't win' (200). This particular sexual activity – the female cyborg fucking her automated/subhuman lover – falls outside the Butlerian arena of cultural intelligibility. It cannot be categorized as simply and straightforwardly heterosexual; but nor it is anything like homosexuality. Retrospectively, Jael's sexuality can most easily be located within the spacious non-category of queer. And what is most notable in Russ's construction of Jael is how technology – so often figured in science fiction as anathema to human/natural sexuality – is here what enhances and supports sexuality. Not, as in 'Helen O'Loy', in a way that aspires to 'nature', but something non-normative and 'unnatural', exactly what cannot be permitted to invade most of the imagined worlds of science fiction.

In the figure of the cyborg Jael, Russ constructs a technobody that rejects sf's conventional anxiety about sexuality and technology. Russ takes up this anxiety and emphasizes it, exaggerates it, re-evalutes it, and makes it play a different role. The cheerful presentation of Jael's 'perverse' sexual relations with Davy is Russ's affirmation that technology might indeed throw (hetero)sexuality into crisis, and readers are invited to identify with the scandalized reactions of the other Js at the same time as they are invited, through Jael's own point of view, to appreciate the potential space for queerness opened up at the human/technological interface. In revising this old sf plot, Russ is doing something with what Luckhurst calls 'the materials of genre'; he describes *The Female Man* as 'a novel that thematize[s] the struggle to rearticulate generic elements for feminist ends' (181).[18]

Central to Russ's re-telling of this familiar plot is Jael's absolute refusal of any identity imposed upon her by conventional constructions of 'woman'. What is being refused here is 'woman' as both identity and subject position and it recalls other feminist refusals such as Julia Kristeva's in 'Woman Can Never Be Defined' (1974), published almost contemporaneously with *The Female Man*: 'a woman cannot "be"; it is something which does not even belong in the order of *being*. It follows that a feminist practice can only be negative, at odds with what already exists so that we may say "that's not it" and "that's still not it"' (137). Or, as we have already been informed by Joanna, 'You can't unite woman and human any more than you can unite matter and anti-matter' (151).

Under the circumstances, it is appropriate that Jael is at first an invisible presence in the novel who watches the movements of the other Js – Joanna, the author's stand-in; Jeannine, the 'feminine' J who initially wants nothing more than the rewards promised to those who successfully perform femininity (husband, children, security); and Janet Evason, the 'complete' female individual from utopian Whileaway. For Jael, all extant definitions of 'woman' are 'not it' and 'still not it': 'Look! Do you *see me?* I, I, I. Repeat it like magic. That is not me. I am not that. Luther crying out in the choir like one possessed: NON SUM, NON SUM, NON SUM!' (195; emphasis in original). Jael has no identity except her repudiation of identity. This same refusal is echoed by the beautifully named young lesbian, Laura Rose Wilding, who '[says] over and over to herself Non Sum, Non Sum, which means either *I don't exist* or *I'm not that,* according to how you feel it' (59; emphasis in original).

Jael's very first words in the text emphasize her invisibility and her unreadability: 'Who am I? I know who I am, but what's my brand name?' (19), a question she repeats several times during the course of the novel. Jeanne Corteil reads Jael's question as indicative of her limitations: she does not know what she is on the way to becoming – perhaps Janet Evason, the lucky one who inhabits the future utopia, although that seems unlikely. Jael is a cyborg and, as such, she remains poised between the organic and the machinic; in N. Katherine Hayles's words, she stands 'at the threshhold separating the human from the posthuman' ('Life Cycle of Cyborgs' 153). As a textual figure designed to support Russ's satirical critique of compulsory heterosexuality, she is a transitional subjectivitity pointing the reader toward a queer understanding of the social/cultural interpellations that shape bodies and desires. Jael's question – 'what's my brand name?' – can also be read as a challenge to the other Js, and through them to the reader as well, to think outside the conventional categories that define/confine 'woman' and 'man' and 'human', to imagine different possibilities for being in the world. Given queer theory's 'claim to be opposed to the unwanted legislation of identity', as Butler explains it (*Undoing Gender* 7), Jael's refusal of a 'brand name' seems more than compatible with queer subjectivity.

In the 'final' analysis, Russ's novel encourages readers to imagine more than one story about (post-)human ways of being in the world, including stories about how technology – so often demonized in the theories and fictions of sf writers – might support the kind of complex transformation called for in Russ's title. *The Female Man* calls ironic attention to the powers and privileges inherent in the position 'man' and the simultaneous disadvantages of the position 'woman'. The social and political constructions of gender – whether as representation or as relation – are, after all, prior to our 'fantastic' constructions of 'sex'. Russ's narrator Joanna very sensibly decides that she will occupy the more powerful of the two (gender) roles; she will become 'the female man':

> there is one and only one way to possess that in which we are defective, therefore that which we need, therefore that which we want.
>
> Become it.
>
> ... I think I am a Man; I think you had better call me a Man; I think that you will write about me as a Man from now on and speak of me as a Man and employ me as a Man and recognize child-rearing as a Man's business; you will think of me as a Man and treat me as a Man until it enters your...head that *I am a man.* (And you are a woman.)...
>
> If you don't, by God and all the Saints, *I'll break your neck.* (139–40; emphasis in original)[19]

Science fiction is, at least potentially, a 'literature of change' and, arguably, it can be a potent expression of the political imagination in its dramatizations of the technosubject.[20] The theoretical foundations of queer theory sometimes look a lot like the critical speculations of science fiction, especially in so far as they too are at work on a future 'not fully determined in advance', to recall Butler's words. In *A Genealogy of Queer Theory*, William B. Turner cites Foucault's conviction that 'what must be produced is not man identical to himself, exactly as nature would have designed him or according to his essence; on the contrary, we must produce something that doesn't yet exist and about which we cannot know how and what it will be' (qtd. in Turner 56). And Butler insists that 'a certain departure from the human...takes place in order to start the process of remaking the human' (*Undoing Gender* 3–4). The fantasies of 'sex' in critical sf speculations such as *The Female Man*, like the fantasies of queer theory, are at once textual and material, products of the imagination that suggest the potentialities of an undetermined future.

If we can only ever know sex as it is implied in and expressed through the performances of gender, then'"sex" becomes something like a fiction, perhaps a fantasy' (Butler, *Bodies That Matter* 5). And sometimes it becomes something like a science fiction.[21]

Notes

1. Academic scholarship has responded with some very good recent studies such as Thomas Foster's *The Souls of Cyberfolk: Posthumanism as Vernacular Theory* (2005) and Sherryl Vint's *Bodies of Tomorrow: Technology, Subjectivity, Science Fiction* (2007).
2. I have in mind here Takayuki Tatsumi's much quoted 1988 interview with Samuel R. Delany, one of American sf's most accomplished and influential writers. Referring to himself as 'a favorite faggot "uncle" who's always looked out for mom', Delany called cyberpunk to task for forgetting its history, for trying to erase its debts to its 'real mothers' – writers such as Joanna Russ, Ursula K. Le Guin, and Vonda McIntyre: 'It's interesting that the feminist explosion – which obviously infiltrates the cyberpunk writers so much – is the one they seem to be the least comfortable with, even though it's one that, much more than the New Wave, has influenced them most strongly... Cyberpunk is, at basis, a bastard form of writing... What it's got are mothers. A whole set of them – who, in literary terms, were so promiscuous that their cyberpunk offspring will simply never be able to settle down, sure of a certain daddy' (Tatsumi, 'Some *Real* Mothers' 9).
3. Feenberg identifies the instrumental view as 'the dominant view of modern governments and the policy sciences on which they rely' (5).
4. I will just note here Jacques Derrida's deconstructive arguments for supplementarity as constitutive of what requires supplementation.
5. But see Dominick Grace's 'Rereading Lester del Rey's "Helen O'Loy"' for a more complex view of artificiality and performance in the story; in Grace's reading, these 'artificial' features come to be associated with the humans in the story as well as with the gendered machine.
6. Feenberg suggests Martin Heidegger's 'The Question Concerning Technology' (1954) as exemplary of this particular conviction about technoculture's negative impact on the human. Jacques Ellul's *The Technological Society* (1954) is also pertinent here, arguing as it does that 'technique' inevitably forces the human into the shape of its own demanding internal logic.
7. At first glance, 'Helen O'Loy' appears to be something of an exception in

its easy acceptance of Helen as the consummate (hetero)sexual partner. But the acceptance is not of Helen's machinic artificiality, that is, of her robot ontology. Like her human husband, the text can embrace her because (a certain kind of) artificiality is what in fact identifies her as a 'real' woman: both characters and readers are allowed to forget her problematic ontological status because she so perfectly represents and she so accurately performs her creators' idealization of domestic femininity. Del Rey's story is a fantasy about the technoscientific replication of a human sexuality that remains authentic and unspoiled in spite of such replication. All that is required to 'naturalize' the artificial woman is a determined act of forgetting – 'I practically forgot, myself', del Rey's narrator tells us, that Helen 'wasn't human' (72) – which also serves to erase any suspicion that human beings as well might be 'programmed' into their performances of sex and gender.

8. At the same time,'Helen O'Loy' seems to support, as if in spite of itself, some of the arguments developed by Judith Halberstam in her discussion of the Turing Test, an imaginary imitation game devised by computer pioneer Alan Turing to test whether machines can think. Halberstam concludes that '[gender]... like computer intelligence, is a learned imitative behavior that can be processed so well that it comes to look natural. Indeed, the work of culture in the former and of science in the latter is perhaps to transform the artificial into a function so smooth that it seems organic. In other words, gender, like intelligence, has a technology' ('Automating Gender' 443). More recently, Foster has discussed Turing as 'as a queer theorist before the letter' (113).
9. Note how convincingly this opposition replicates the heterosexual binary: sexuality here takes on the features of the feminine (it is natural, affective, embodied), while technoscience takes on the features of the masculine (it is rational, unemotional, disembodied).
10. In her detailed and incisive discussion of the career of this very original writer, Carol McGuirk points out that '[the] first uses of the word "cyborg" date from 1960...; even the parent-term "cybernetics," coined by Norbert Weiner in 1948, entered the language after the writing of "Scanners." Smith sees something of the future in his emphasis on Martel's conjoining of mechanical and biological identity' (171). McGuirk also notes Martel's 'virtual castration' (176).
11. In his introduction to the 1975 collection, *The Best of C. L. Moore,* editor Lester del Rey describes 'No Woman Born' as the 'portrait of a great artist and marvelously feminine woman struggling to be true to her inner self' (xiii). In a postmodern view of the subject, del Rey's reading expresses a naively essentialist ideology of authentic selfhood. (Re)read as proto-queer cyberfiction, Moore's story is the opening act of a cyborg *Bildungsroman,* the first scene in the story of an emergent technosubject sutured together out of differences.
12. This reading concerns Dick's novel; the way in which these issues are developed and resolved in its film version, *Blade Runner* (1982), is rather different.
13. N. Katherine Hayles reads Rachael as both the sympathetic 'dark-haired girl' who appears in a range of Dick's stories and a machine-woman who coldly destroys a living animal. Hayles writes that 'her characterization oscillates wildly between a desirable, empathic partner and a cold, calculating manipulator' (*How We Became Posthuman* 172). Whether deliberately or not,

Dick's female android points us back to Fritz Lang's robot-Maria in the film *Metropolis* (1927), the evil female robot who seduces men and nearly destroys the city through her highly charged performances of sexuality. Andreas Huyssen's 'The Vamp and the Machine', a cultural-historical reading of Lang's film, provides as relevant a critical framework for Dick's novel as it does for *Metropolis*.

14. This is a reference to Russ's most celebrated sf story, 'When It Changed' (1972), one of the first and one of the most powerful manifestos for lesbian-feminist separatism. Russ's story is about a planet of women whose centuries-old way of life is threatened with destruction by the arrival of male astronauts from Earth. Intriguingly, in Gibson's third novel, *Mona Lisa Overdrive* (1988), 'When It Changed' is the phrase used by 'the old cowboys' (127) to refer to the techno-transcendent coming-into-being of mysterious intelligences in cyberspace. While this can be read as Gibson's affirmation of his literary debts to Russ, it is not necessarily so. See Delany's remarks about cyberpunk's conflicted relationship with its 'mothers' in n. 2 above; see also Graham Murphy's reading of Gibson's use of 'When It Changed' elsewhere in this collection.
15. In 1978, Russ published 'SF and Technology as Mystification', in which she referred to technology as *'a non-subject'*: '"technology"...is a consolation for and an obfuscation of something else' (27; emphasis in original). She argued that 'what is being discussed when most people say "technology"...[is] capitalism in its advanced industrial phase' (36), and that '[the] technology-obsessed must give up talking about technology when it is economics and politics that are at issue' (39). Little critical attention has been paid to the 'economics and politics' of technoscience in *The Female Man*, but see Susana S. Martins's 'Revising the Future in *The Female Man*' for a substantial discussion of the various functions of technology in the novel.
16. Analogous to the way in which 'lesbian' is disrupted as a category in the all-women utopia of Whileaway, 'homosexual' is not particularly useful as a category term for the sexual relationships in Manland's all-male society ('gay' seems even less appropriate). Manlanders on the whole remain absurdly committed to the institutions of their 'fantastic' versions of heterosexuality.
17. This war plays out a particularly malevolent version of heterosexual entrapment, with each sex trying to destroy the other, each one defined by the other who is also the ultimate enemy. As Jeanne Corteil notes in her full-length study of Russ's writing, Jael 'is the product of the very system of oppression that she fights, capitalist patriarchy' (85). While my focus in this discussion is on the more empowering features of Jael's role in Russ's text, she is neither a completely positive nor a completely coherent presence (see Corteil, esp. 81–87). See also n. 9 above, which remarks on the ease with which the heterosexual binary comes to function as a way of dividing up the world.
18. For example, Russ rewrites sf's drearily conventional 'battle of the sexes' plot in her account of Jael's 'war' against Manland. She also offers a cogent critique of this particular plot in her 1980 article, '*Amor Vincent Foeminam*: The Battle of the Sexes in Science Fiction'.
19. In Haraway's terms, Russ's title figure, 'the female man', is one of a variety of efficacious figures – the cyborg is another – through which we can begin to

imagine and explore new roles for ourselves in the world. For Haraway, the female man 'is as much a disruption of the story of the universal Female as of the universal Man. Therefore, s/he is a good participant in the nonmodern conversations we need to have about figuration and worldly practice in technoscience' (*Modest_Witness* 70).

20. 'Literature of change' is a very popular understanding of science fiction. Brooks Landon, for example, opens his history of twentieth-century sf by elaborating upon exactly this idea: 'More precisely, science fiction is the kind of literature that most explicitly and self-consciously takes change as its subject and its teleology' (xi).
21. An account of the queer 'conjunctures' of sexuality and technology in more recent science fiction might include readings of Pat Cadigan's 'Pretty Boy Crossover' (1986); Candas Jane Dorsey's '(Learning about) Machine Sex' (1988); Gwyneth Jones's *White Queen* (1991); Marge Piercy's *He, She and It* (1992); Richard Calder's *Dead Girls* (1992); Amy Thomson's *Virtual Girl* (1993); William Gibson's *Idoru* (1996); Shariann Lewitt's 'A Real Girl' (1998); Nalo Hopkinson's 'Ganger (Ball Lightning)' (2000); Maureen McHugh's *Nekropolis* (2001); Greg Egan's *Schild's Ladder* (2003); Geoff Ryman's *Air, or, Have Not Have* (2004); Tanith Lee's *Metallic Love* (2005), and Charles Stross's *Glasshouse* (2006).

'And How Many Souls Do You Have?': Technologies of Perverse Desire and Queer Sex in Science Fiction Erotica

Patricia Melzer

> I'm not asking that you change what you find sexually attractive; only that you experimentally discard the requirement for compatible fantasy when reading about sex. Remember, it's just a book. And if you *do* occasionally find yourself responding – well, that's educational, too.
>
> — Ray Davis, 'Delany's Dirt' 165

> Visiting a world where the most intriguing gender of all is 'I'm not telling'... Boys, girls, both, neither, licking, kissing, liking, loving. It doesn't matter whether you, reader, are boy, girl, straight, all or none of the above, I think you'll get along just fine.
>
> — Cecilia Tan, *Genderflex* 8

Perverse Sexualities as Queer Transgressions

Working on the fantastic in the arts means occasional trips to strange (imaginary) places. The science fiction erotica published by Cecilia Tan, and the 'pleasure' of researching queer science fiction pornography, took my experience to a new level. Tucked away on back shelves of independent science fiction bookstores and alternative erotica shops, these books are intended to be consumed in bed or while stretched out on the living room couch during an afternoon alone at home. They evoke a flushed reading satisfaction and a slight sense of guilt because they decadently provide nothing but pleasure. Reading them for 'research' earns the dedicated academic raised eyebrows from colleagues and produces slightly awkward moments at the photocopier. Literary critics do not usually regard pleasure as an analytical variable. The concept of pleasure that underlies these narratives, however, is central to queer theory, which addresses the navigations of bodies and desires in relation to subjectivity. My reading of these texts explores the pleasure politics of queer sexualities and perverse desire in queer science fiction erotica. This attempt is informed by Samuel R. Delany's observation in *Silent Interviews* that to assume that pornographic writing is purely functional, that is, task-oriented – aimed at evoking sexual arousal – is to relegate any aesthetic element to the status of mere *excess*. He concludes that 'in any given manifestation the excess can still be profoundly, ideologically informative' ('Introduction' 9). The pornographic sf narratives at hand seem exclusively aimed at getting the reader 'off'. If we shift attention to the aesthetic excess produced at the margins of their sexual encounters, however, we find comments on, and models for, new subjectivities beyond the immediate pleasure of reading them. If the task of a text gives it ideological dimensions (Delany, 'Introduction' 5), what are the ideological dimensions of the representations of hardcore queer S/M erotica in a science fiction setting?

To respond to this question, I consider the collections of sf erotica edited by Cecilia Tan, the founder and editor of Circlet Press, which publishes erotic science fiction and fantasy, including a series of anthologies of queer S/M erotica that Tan herself edits. These stories illustrate the role technology plays in the reconfiguration of sexualities and genders in representations of transgender, disabled, and otherwise altered bodies, often depicted as 'alien'. Tan's books address various intersecting reading communities; they often include queer and/or transgender characters, all are hardcore erotica, most include S/M practices, and many are written within a science fiction setting. Because of their pornographic content – and *intent*: 'to excite in such a way as to exhaust that excitement' (Delany, 'Introduction' 9) – Tan's collections are located on the fringe of science fiction discourse, similar to slash fiction (pornographic rewriting of science fiction by fans). Following the tradition of queer stories that challenge normative discourse on sexualities by writers such as Delany, Tan's anthologies create spaces for transgressive and radical sexualities and genders enacted by technologically modified and extraterrestrial bodies. This essay gives a reading of four short sf stories published in Tan's anthologies: M. Christian's 'Fully Accessorized, Baby' (1996); Raven Kaldera's 'Cyberfruit Swamp' (1996); Jana McCall's 'A Self-Made Woman' (1995); and Recondita Armonia's 'Flesh of My Flesh' (2002). All four authors are prolific science fiction erotica writers and their work exemplifies the subgenre's transgressions. I read them in a queer/transgender theoretical framework, thereby focusing on two narrative elements: prostheses that reshape bodies according to desire and cloning as a technology of autoeroticism that destabilizes sexual difference.

Perverse desire, transgender identities, and technologically enhanced or technologically produced bodies are the main narrative elements in these four stories. Intersecting with queer theory's criticism of the normalized heterosexual matrix, these erotic stories define expressions of perverse desire as politically transgressive. This is reflected in the titles of the anthologies, such as *Sexcrime* (1999, its title taken from *1984* [1949]), *Sextopia* (2001), *Worlds of Women* (1994), and *Genderflex* (1996), and in the introductions to the volumes by Tan herself, who views them as part of science fiction's comments on social orders:

> [*Sexcrime*] is a letter to all those people in the real world whose desires are marginalized, outlawed, or made taboo, to all those who fear being attacked or killed for being who they are, to anyone who has ever felt alone in their desire or who has had to hide to live it. (*Sexcrime* 8)

The technologies that (re)construct sexualities and genders enable innovative explorations of queer and transgender theories and their claiming of transgressive sexualities. Accordingly, two main concepts inform my analysis: that queer perverse desire is transgressive and inclusive of non-normative bodies (such as disabled and/or transgendered) and that in science fiction, technology reshapes desire to this end.

Necessarily Queer: Perverse Sexualities as Transgressions

To the disappointed queer reader, science fiction seems all too often to envision perverse desire (such as S/M or alien sex) exclusively within a heterosexual context. Tan's anthologies are a refreshing departure from the conventions of straight perversity. In the queer sf stories discussed here, there are no sex-slave girl-robots whipping straight businessmen in techno-Asia. Instead, the stories' transgressive moments lie in the *queer* content that places perverse desire outside heterosexual discourse.

For the purpose of my reading, 'queer' is used as a qualifier to connote sexual constellations and desires that cannot be contained within what Eve Kosofsky Sedgwick has termed the existing 'taxonomy' of categories that maintain (and rely on) a stable correlation of sex/gender/sexuality (*Epistemology of the Closet* 23–27). Furthermore, 'queer' undermines what Judith Butler calls 'the heterosexual matrix', 'that grid of cultural intelligibility through which bodies, genders, and desires are naturalized' (*Gender Trouble* 151 n. 6); it always connotes sexual practices and desires that destabilize heterosexuality.

In Tan's anthologies, the centre-staging of queer perverse desire as *subject position* produces alternative representations. The stories I examine thus represent counter-examples to mainstream pornography and problematize what Ray Davis describes as 'porn's own peculiar, problematic virtues: Desire, like art, is privileged to cut across (although not erase!) those wavering boundaries which define the power systems of the world. As such, it can, like art, be used to shore up those systems' (168). Tan's queer transgressions destabilize normative sexualities and undermine rather than '[shore] up those systems'. Perverse desire and queer sex in science fiction help envision non-regulated desire and make room for Veronica Hollinger's inquiry about a possible 'utopia of the perverse', what Jonathan Dollimore calls the 'transgressive reinscriptions' of forbidden sexualities into the future of our world (qtd. in Hollinger, 'Utopia of the Perverse' 33).[1]

Thus, what separates the sf erotica I am examining from mainstream (written) sf pornography is its use of technology to denaturalize bodies and its emphasis on queer sexual practices, especially queer S/M.[2] Here we see the intersection of queer transgender and disability studies (two areas that consider non-normative bodies and sexualities) with science fiction's explorations of technologically modified bodies. In contrast to cyberporn, the erotic encounters in these stories are based on the interactions of *material bodies,* unmediated by virtual reality.[3] Thus the disabled body does not simply signify the lack of a normative or 'real' body and the trans body is not relegated to destabilizing an otherwise stable sex/gender system. Instead, they are depicted both as objects and subjects of desires that expand and transgress the limited ways in which 'we' understand sexuality.

So what does technology have to do with queer sex? Feminist sf criticism examines how technology both denaturalizes *and* essentializes gender and sex. This is done most consistently through the deployment of Donna Haraway's cyborg metaphor. Cyber-theorists such as Allucquère Rosanne (Sandy) Stone also interrogate technology and queer sex in cyberspace and virtual reality. In a queer context, gender is often understood to be performative, suggesting its social and psychological ties to the body. Technology facilitates the disruption of unquestioned links between biology and gender, as Hollinger notes in '(Re)reading Queerly': 'gender is now disassociated from the "natural" body, and the gap between body and performance has become too great to ignore' (30). I am interested in how technology denaturalizes not only bodies (and thus gender), but also sexual *desires* and practices.

The way technology is envisioned in the narratives explored here ultimately queers desire through facilitating the creation of new bodies and non-heteronormative genders/sexualities. The cyborg is characterized by detachable extremities – the dildo and the fisting device become part of the body, not its artificial extensions. In these narratives, queer theory intersects with disability and transgender studies' explorations of prosthetics and medical intervention, which are simultaneously a response to, and a deconstruction of, the normative (sexual) body.

'That Fine Fucking Machine': Prosthetic Trans Bodies as Sexual Subjects

Of course, these narratives are not devoid of problematic elements, particularly in terms of the interactions among disabled and technologically modified bodies, pain, and sex. One needs to weigh the material realities of non-normative bodies against their imagined eroticizations. My focus is on the stories' *transgressive* elements, which I locate in the representation of these bodies as sexual agents. In the science fiction I discuss, unlike in many other texts, human trans and other non-normative bodies inhabit subject positions that are more than simply isolated metaphors for queerness: they are neither contained as fetish in a straight environment nor viewed as isolated transgressive elements. Instead, they inhabit the centre of the narratives. Technology hereby plays a central role.

In Tan's queer sf erotica, we encounter a range of technologies, including prosthetic body parts, that queer desire. A prosthesis is an artificial limb or appendage that replaces or substitutes for a body part, destabilizing the natural body by pointing to its limits. In *Narrative Prosthesis* (2000), David Mitchell and Sharon Snyder explain how disability tends to function as a 'character-making trope' in narrative representation, reducing a disabled character to a social category (10). The disabled subject becomes a one-dimensional symbol for meaning-making and cultural critique. It shares this non-normative status with the transgender subject, whose narrative presence is viewed as destabilizing gender and sexuality in its relation to a stable gendered subject, which in turn remains the normative referent for human subjectivity. Both the disabled and the transgender body are 'unfinished'; their prostheses are their 'marks' and their ultimate goal is to pass for normal.

In queer sf erotica, prostheses denaturalize *desire* through the technological enhancement of body parts, thereby disclosing the negotiations of non-normative bodies as erotic/sexual expressions. Most importantly, the non-normative body is not fetishized as that which is different, but is at the centre of erotic desire within the narrative: the 'unnatural' body is not only object (as often happens in pornography) but also *subject* of desire.[4]

M. Christian's 'Fully Accessorized, Baby' develops the trope of prosthetic sex as an example of how queer science fiction S/M erotica integrates non-normative bodies. The story is set in the familiar cyberpunk setting of 'Lower Shanghai', somewhere in the future of global capitalism. As in most pornographic writing, the plot is secondary. We meet Val and Cox at the beginning of their sexual encounter. Early on, we are led to believe that Val is a sex worker paid by Cox, only to learn as the story unfolds that the encounter was mutually ordered and purchased via an online sex-database.

Their meeting is initially set up as between two women: Val is a voluptuous fem with gorgeous legs and 'tits', equipped with suspender-belt and satin lingerie; Cox is a rugged working-class butch. At the beginning, Val's feminine body is eroticized through Cox's objectifying gaze: Val's body is on display, as she is told to strip by Cox, who hungrily scrutinizes her. A normative description of a fem's hot physique follows, when the 'bra dropped and Val's tits didn't' (144), and Cox admires her long legs. Val's body seems constructed – literally – to fit a commercialized desire: 'Val's was a milk-fed body, a pampered machine engineered and scalpeled to fit the requirement of a culture and type: hard fine legs, baby smooth yet taut stomach, tits that lifted high and fine' (145). This constructed femininity is countered by Cox's 'natural' 'worker's body', equally shaped through external factors, this time by years of hard manual work and partying: 'bones and ligaments that Cox had twisted in her worn body from running, dealing, scoring and heavy/heavy celebrations' (145). The objectifying gaze that moves in familiar heterosexual ways across the displayed body is queered by the observer's gender: Cox's hunger for soft Val disrupts the normative sexual economy we encounter in both mainstream science fiction and mainstream erotica. And this is only the beginning.

Val's cosmetic enhancements that adhere to a normatively gendered ideal are contrasted with her body's other modifications, which are much more radical: at the centre of Cox's desire is Val's arm-prosthesis. In a performative stripping, Val un-gloves her right arm and reveals a wooden Mitsubishi, that 'fine fucking machine' (146), 'a fist engineered for fisting' (147):

> The hand was a fine tooled example of the marriage in harmony of the best in Japanese prostheses and aesthetics... Set with matte-black joints, cables with undulating polymer cords, Cox could tell that it was telling Val all a real hand would have – the freckles of sensory nipples and the compound fibers that ran through the teak like veins were a sign of someone who hadn't just sold her right arm for an arm. Val had sold her right arm for something far better. (146)

Val then penetrates Cox with her 'fucking machine', fisting her until she comes.

In disability studies, the prosthesis is often understood to be a passing device, as Mitchell and Snyder explain in *Narrative Prosthesis*. A prosthesis then is an illusion, a compensation for a lack of the body that erases differences (for discourse) by making this lack invisible (6). In 'Fully Accessorized, Baby', the prosthesis does not substitute for a natural and 'better' part, but replaces a body part that was inadequate to fulfil a specific desire for the technologized body. Consequently, instead of fulfilling its common function as 'master trope for human qualification' (Mitchell and Snyder 3), Val's disabled body is what defines her desirability.

There is a fine line between eroticization and the embrace of difference on one hand and fetishization that denies the textual and material reality of disability and prosthetics on the other. The amputation of her arm in order for it to be supplemented by the prosthetic Mitsubishi places Val's physical modification in the complicated context of voluntary disability, such as is seen in fetish amputees.[5] 'Fully Accessorized, Baby' assumes the erotic potential of voluntarily modified, non-normative bodies (in contrast to merely acknowledging the erotic potential of the involuntary disabled body). Instead of isolating the prosthesis as fetish-object, however, the story integrates it into a sexual encounter dominated by non-normative bodies, not othered by them. This is further explicated in the second type of prosthesis in the narrative: one of Val's body parts turns out to be a 'bio-cock', a 'real' penis, a feature Cox included in her online order, that is contrasted with the cybercock, a penis prosthesis (commonly referred to as a dildo) used by Cox. Suddenly there are two cocks in the room and not one 'man'.

The appearance of 'the' organ on a feminized body throws the natural body, and thus 'natural' sex, into a crisis. The reader learns that Val 'had the genes for the cock, but not for those tits' (148). Yet instead of freezing Val in her (to the reader newly discovered) existence as 'transwoman' (for lack of a better term), her homegrown penis is simply viewed as a pleasure device within a choreography of body parts whose erotic attraction lies in the various combinations driven by specific desires. Unlike mainstream porn's subgenre, 'chicks with dicks', that reduces the MTF body to its trans-status, Val's penis is not the main attraction – that would be the Mitsubishi. In this instance, the trans body is simply one variant of multiple physical presentations; the 'natural' body is not our point of reference.

Val's hyper-fem body with a cock contrasts with the cybercock that Cox digs out of her utility bag. In a gesture that evokes the symbolic power of Judith Butler's 'lesbian phallus', the dyke's dildo that threatens the supreme signifier, Cox proceeds to fuck Val with the prosthetic cock.[6] While normalizing discourse establishes the problematic primary objective of the prosthesis as 'return[ing] the incomplete body to the invisible status of a normative essence' (Mitchell and Snyder 8), in 'Fully Accessorized, Baby' the aim is not to create the illusion of a natural body with natural desires, but to embrace the multidimensional manifestations of bodies and sexualities. The prosthesis is a source of sexual desire at the same time as it experiences (and makes physically possible) pleasure.

The story echoes the instability of categories in the monetary economy, creating multiple desires by insisting on their *specificity*: both characters tap into a gigantic commercial online service database to order the perfect partner based on both physique and role (bottom/top) for their one-night sexual scenario – de-coupling desire from naturalized (even though very appreciated) sexual difference. Desire also is the broker of use-value in this commercialized encounter. At the end of the story, Val and Cox are each customer *and* client, undermining the heterosexual power relations of most mainstream sex-work. It is not the desire of the subject (the one buying the service) that declares the object desirable and that determines the nature of the encounter (such as who is top and who is bottom). Instead, both parties are equally invested (literally) in specific desires, based on the needs of both subject and object (especially since it really is not quite clear who is the subject and who the object). Val and Cox both get what they want and leave satisfied (the slogan 'customer satisfaction guaranteed' here gains new meaning): 'If it was really good, who cared who paid?' (150).

When reading Tan's anthologies, it soon becomes apparent that among the most frequently used prostheses in these stories are – not surprisingly – a variety of cybercocks. The recurring play with 'the phallus [as] a transferable phantasm' (Butler, *Bodies That Matter* 86) destabilizes both bodies and desires. While much of queer science fiction (and science fiction criticism) discusses the instability of gender through the presence of gay and lesbian figures,[7] Raven Kaldera in 'Cyberfruit Swamp' focuses on transsexual and transgender bodies and their desires, subject positions that are seldom explored. As a genre interested in representations of 'posthuman' embodiment, science fiction provides a unique narrative space to envision the links of corporeal manifestations and real-life transgendered bodies. We see this in the story's pornographic depictions that circle around transmen's erotic desires.

In general, forms of gender transgression have been valorized in queer cultural productions as disclosing the instability of gender identity and the sexed body – drag, butch, and cross-dressing have become symbols for the constructedness of gender identity. The transgendered subject is reduced to 'a key queer trope' (5), as Jay Prosser states in *Second Skins: The Body Narratives of Transsexuality* (1998). Unlike many other texts, the science fiction I discuss explores transgender desire *beyond* its effect on straight sexuality – trans bodies in these stories experience pleasure for the sake of orgasmic release alone.

'Cyberfruit Swamp' explores how we imagine physical constellations outside our own bodies, echoing Butler's query in 'Imitation and Gender Insubordination' (1991): 'If a sexuality is to be disclosed, what will be taken as the true determinant of its meaning: the phantasy structure, the act, the orifice, the gender, the anatomy?' (17). These desires that transcend the body gain concrete forms in technological prostheses, so a transman's 'real-life' packing-utensils, such as the soft dress-cock and his sex-toy dildo, central to many transmen's sexuality, are animated in Kaldera's science fiction porn.

The protagonist in 'Cyberfruit Swamp' is a 'kurami', a female-to-male transgender person, whose sexual preferences are exclusively for other 'nachtlei', that is, other kurami and 'winkti', male-to-female transpeople. The futuristic technology of the story – references to a weather-dome, medcops, and medical scanners situate it in a near future – has made transitioning easy; familiar medical technologies such as hormones and surgeries are commonly available, if still expensive. Kaldera creates a political context for the story's sexual exploits: we learn that the 'Tranz-Pride movement' has made nachtlei visible and carved out safe public spaces, such as bars, as well as not-so-safe ones, such as nachtlei-cells in jail. TranzPride is countered by religious and politically conservative groups such as Nature's Front (20) and by biologically essentialist activists, such as the Cynthaians, for whom the 'natural' body is primary (15–16).

Our protagonist is about to go on a sexual prowl for the night and, as he gets ready to head out, we learn of dress-chains that indicate sexual preferences to potential sexual partners. Instead of presenting trans people (especially transsexuals) as anxious to 'fit' into a sexual binary hostile to their existence, 'natural' bodies and identities are dismissed; sexual energy is exclusively fixed on genderqueer bodies. The ambiguous and painstakingly constructed gender identities of nachtlei – winkti, kurami, and 'a few nonspecific folk right in the middle' (13) – become sources for sexual pleasure uninvested in social and cultural identities within the sexual binary: 'I just can't seem to trust people who are onlymen or onlywomyn. I mean, they can be nice people... but they just don't get it like a nachtlei does' (13). Denaturalized bodies and identities, it is implied, resist and undermine sexual regulation.

While the actual sexual encounter of the story – S/M sex with a Boy (pre-modification nachtlei) in a bar and a parking garage – begins five pages into the story, the reader's pleasure is evoked earlier, when we meet the protagonist's 'Artificial Penile Prosthetics, also known as APPles, Cybercocks, Freudbusters, and some other less flattering terms' (14). The reader familiar with queer trans sexualities appreciates the humorous nicknames and the centrality of the prostheses as part of the story's appeal, while the reader of science fiction can enjoy the intricate technological details given in the description of these versatile tools. The protagonist's seven (!) artificial penises each attach to the crotch and tap into the body's neurological system. They enable him to actually experience the physical stimulations of his gendered desire – to penetrate – a physical sensation denied to him by his 'natural' body. The greatly diverse APPles can also be exchanged based on the preferences of the sexual partner: 'Why seven of them? Different moods, different lovers, different orifices' (14). While a 'natural-flesh cock' (available through a too-expensive surgery) seems to be the narrator's preference, he is having a good time enjoying the variety of his APPles. The pleasures of prostheses in conjunction with non-normative bodies do not simply mimic the pleasures of 'natural' bodies, but are newly created.

Instead of depicting the desire born from a trans identity as either tragic – it can never be realized – or deviant – it is 'unnatural' – this queer S/M story uses technology to envision the fantasy not only as legitimate, but also as 'real'. Real-life applications of body-extensions designed to meet desires that transcend our bodies, that is, sex toys, are re-conceptualized so that they *are part of* the body. The trans body's reliance on prostheses to express sexual desires (shared by the disabled body) becomes a liberating potential, not a tragic given. Therefore, the sexual focus of the story is not reduced to the trans *body*; queer and trans *sexualities* are what get the narrator (and implicitly the reader) off. The goal of our kurami's sexual prowl is meeting 'kin', other nachtlei, independent of their bodies. When the young person he meets in a bar answers his question, 'And how many souls do you have?' with 'If I said…two…what would it…mean?' followed by 'But I'm not sure I am ready to commit to any…changes', his response is 'Neither of those…are necessary to letting me fuck you. That is, if the idea appeals' (17). Once the Boy has identified as nachtlei, the use of the female pronoun shifts to the plural 'they' – 'I think this boy deserves the plural nachtlei pronoun now' (17) – further dismissing binary forms of identification and desire.

The sex between our narrator and the submissive Boy is infused with S/M desire, which is humorously inverted when the kurami is arrested in the parking garage for 'raping' the Boy – the knife against the bottom's throat, part of the sex scene, confuses the medcops – and is bailed out by the Boy, whose mother is county commissioner. The desire to obey, which informs the Boy's sexuality, is decoupled from any social reality. We are reminded, as Davis states, that the pleasures of submission and dominance in S/M sex are not to be conflated with power, as 'in our world, power is no illusion, but *control*, mercifully, is' (173; emphasis in original). The story ends when the Boy hops onto the kurami's motorcycle and the two drive off into the figurative sunset. In addition to its pornographic intent, the narrative's political framework and the romantic undertones of the encounter between the older kurami and the nachtlei fledgling make it also both a love story and a coming-of-age tale.

'It Has Always Been My Selves, from the Very Beginning': Cloning and the Power of Autoeroticism

Cloning is another major technology used to queer desire in these stories. As the actual technology advances, human cloning increasingly evokes anxiety. Cloning, along with extra-uterine and bio-engineered reproduction, make up what Constance Ash calls the 'edge-land of human evolution' (viii). In fact, cloning's implications for our world are, as Jack Dann and Gardner Dozois put it in their introduction to the anthology *Clones*, 'old news to science fiction writers' (x), who have been speculating on this technology for thirty-five years now.

The authors in Tan's pornographic science fiction collections seem only peripherally interested in the ethical ramifications of cloning. Instead, their focus is on the new sexual pleasures this technology might bring. As a replication of the self, cloning here reflects on autoeroticism – it fuses the self and other through *doubling* the self; and we experience a collapse of voyeurism and exhibitionism as the boundaries between object and subject of desire fold into each other. Technology then enables a boundary dissolution that threatens a (hetero)sexual economy reliant on difference; the self's pleasure is the other's pleasure, a metaphorical manifestation of that rare perfectly synchronized sexual encounter. Unlike the more common sexualized fantasies about cloning women for the pleasure of men, the following stories present decidedly queer sexual fantasies about the self.[8]

In Jana McCall's 'A Self-Made Woman' (1995), Susan has not left the house in fifteen years. Hiding from the world the traumatizing effects of sexual and physical abuse she experienced as a child, she has given up on the idea of ever finding a sexual partner she can trust: as a sexual assault survivor, she cannot enjoy her inclinations as bottom in S/M relations because she does not feel safe with others. So she orders a female clone of herself with whom to have S/M sex. Initially, she identifies as heterosexual, but decides 'to pay extra and [not] have the gender changed. [A male clone] wouldn't have been "me" – it might not have felt quite as safe' (104). The author emphasizes sameness and familiarity, not fetishized difference, as the basis of S/M desire, and depicts safety, not danger, as the ground on which to enjoy the loss of control. With her-self (literally named 'Self'), Susan is able to enjoy power role-playing, as submission is decoupled from disempowerment.

In Freudian psychoanalysis, autoeroticism is considered pathological. As Judith Butler explains in *Bodies That Matter*, Freud's early theory of libido developed in 'On Narcissism: An Introduction' (1914) understands narcissism to originate in pain, which redirects desire for the object onto one's own body (560–61). Masturbation, a manifestation of narcissism, is defined by Freud as perverse in *Three Essays on the Theory of Sexuality* (1905) – as is any sexual practice whose aim is not heterosexual intercourse. In 'A Self-Made Woman', Susan's narcissism also originates in pain – in the abuse she experienced as a child. Here, though, sex with Self is therapeutic and 'masturbation' (that is, sex with Self) is not a pathology but a safe haven from violent (heterosexual) encounters.

Sidestepping heterosexual intercourse, reproduction via cloning in 'A Self-Made Woman' serves the aim of narcissism, that is, a pathology, which serves to decouple reproduction from Freud's definition of normative sexuality and to destabilize the heterosexual economy. Susan's sex with Self is a concrete form of autoeroticism, yet it also is a *projected* masturbation in that Susan is *being* masturbated. Narcissism is not cured through heterosexual romance – heterosexuality cannot repair the damage it has done. Instead, the embracing and simultaneous external projection of narcissism enables Susan's sexual autonomy.

Throughout the story, the narrator views her clone as a mirror as the behavioural patterns of her youth are repeated by her double. It soon becomes apparent that Self represents aspects of Susan's subjectivity repressed because of childhood trauma. The bedroom is 'Self's dominion', and Susan feels 'the weight of responsibility slipping away' (104) once they enter it. This sexual realm is characterized by Susan's surrender of control. In contrast, the office at the other end of the house, from which Susan conducts her business, is her space of complete control, her 'own carefully crafted real' (110). Susan's ability to recognize her-self in the person who controls her sexually enables her submission in the first place – the two spaces are fused, something that is impossible for her with anybody else.

The familiar trope of the broken but potentially whole self healing its split, which underlies the narrative, surfaces within the story's liberal framework of civil liberties. The notion of humans as defined by autonomous individual subjectivity rather than by sexual desire inevitably arises through the narrator's identification with Self: if Self is bound, Susan cannot be free. She becomes increasingly conflicted over Self's status as the property of the company from which she has leased her clone. Ultimately, the two have a confrontation over Self's self-determination. Susan blames Self for offering sexual services to gain freedom. This appals Susan because it mirrors her childhood attempts to prevent punishment through giving sexual favours. Subsequent moments of outburst and reconciliation follow the therapeutic pattern of facing and accepting the past in a safe environment:

> I fled inside to the black place, and the chaos there swirled around my thoughts. In the prison of my mind, I whimpered like a toddler. Then Self was there – her warm arms surrounding me, holding me; her words whispering calm comfort... 'You're safe', she repeated over and over again. 'You're safe, you're safe, you're safe.' (109)

The clone's healing presence during Susan's panic evoked by memories of old trauma becomes a metaphor for the feminist reclamation of the sexual abuse survivor, and resonates strongly at the end when Susan claims: 'I still loved my Self' (112).

In the end, Susan buys Self from the company to free her. In this action, she takes the risk of losing the clone, which is synonymous with the loss of sexual pleasure and autonomy. The story resolves the dilemma of proposing civil rights for clones at the expense of Susan's happiness by ending with Self's decision to stay with Susan voluntarily. Self is now named Ozma, after L. Frank Baum's character. Having gained the legal status of sister, Ozma declares: 'If I'm your sister, I'm going to act like it. And sisters take care of each other' (112). Happily undermining another psychoanalytic taboo – incest – the two women wander off towards the bedroom in their newly found relationship: 'Now that she no longer belonged to me, I belong to her and anything she wanted to do to me was fine and safe' (112).

No liberal political framework dilutes the raw, exclusively sexual energy in Recondita Armonia's 'Flesh of My Flesh' (2002). The narrative is dominated by mirrors, controlling gazes, and the interdependent erotic stimuli of scopophilia – voyeurism and exhibitionism – all combining in the collapse of self/other through cloning. An enormously wealthy and powerful woman (who remains nameless except for the generic referent 'mother') creates 78 male clones for her own sexual pleasure. The clones do not have names, only numbers – their identities are defined in perpetual reference to her, the 'original'. After she trains them sexually, they go out into the world, seeking sexual encounters that are taped for her pleasure. Significantly, the only sex the clones have, aside from the sex with their 'mother/self', seems to be with men. At the climax of the story, the protagonist connects through neural-transmitters to the brain of her favourite clone, Number 23, while he is having sex in a public bar. She fuses with his mind in his body, although they still communicate as two separate entities.

As in 'A Self-Made Woman', gender/sex transgression in 'Flesh of My Flesh' is derived from cloning and additionally through the neural-net connection between mother and clone. Both technologies symbolize a projected autoeroticism, while maintaining sexual difference through 'cross-sex cloning techniques' (49). Initially, sexual relations in 'Flesh of My Flesh' are set up to be potentially heterosexual, since sexual difference is extremely polarized in the 'original's' female body that produces and controls 78 cloned male bodies. The reader's heterosexual assumptions dissolve quickly, however, as sexual difference gradually erodes. This erosion is visible in the mirror-imagery between 'mother' and her offspring once she fuses her mind with her favourite clone:

> Her eye was caught by a shining mirror... Entranced, with 23's pretty mouth hanging slack, she stared at it and saw her face/his face staring blankly back. The same eyes, the hair, yes it was all there but subtly different – the jawline a bit harder, the chin a bit stubbled, and the shoulder set a bit wider to accommodate the male chest, broader than her own. (51)

In this story, erotic positions of subject and object do not rely on sexual difference, because power, rather than sexual difference, is the main erotic trigger. S/M roles are foregrounded: the clones mostly occupy the bottom (submissive), while 'mother' enjoys their submissiveness as top (dominant): 'Pretty, graceful, playful as kittens and self-indulgent as cats, her clones never failed to find another willing to fuck them to within an inch of their lives. Their entire beings...radiated voracious submissiveness' (49).

The story initially polarizes positions of top/bottom through access to 'real' power: mother is a powerful businesswoman who controls the male clones; her gaze 'tops' all. Mother's sexual pleasure is defined by scopophilia: her clones are under constant surveillance through a vast net of wiring that feeds into monitors in her underground lair. The tapes of the clones' sex-orgies are her main sexual stimuli and she 'run[s] her staff ragged with her requests for ever more extravagant dildoes...and has pleasured herself raw to the tapes' (48). Her autoeroticism functions through voyeuristic pleasure coupled with exhibitionism, as the clones mirror her.

Mother consumes the clones' sexual encounters – as voyeuristic top she admires how they make 'art of [their] devotion' (54). She has trained them to live for sex only and 'with her own natural appetite for sex plus the biological enhancement of testosterone, they had grown insatiable and completely sexualized in very little time' (48). They are nothing but their sexuality – 'playthings' with 'self-destructs keyed into the brains' (49), in case mother's illegal cloning of herself were to be discovered. They exist for her sexual pleasure alone and thus her pleasure is paramount at the beginning of the story. This power-polarization of top/bottom softens and shifts once mother fuses with 23.

The story builds up to the intense fusion of mother with 23 in a public bar. The technology of neuro-connections seems simply an extension of that of cloning; both erode boundaries between self and other: 'Their genotype unity made the marriage of the two neural nets almost trivial' (51). In the process, sexual difference is destabilized while maintaining its erotic potential, as mother enters 23's brain and feels his sensations, sees what he sees. Language betrays the extent of their transgression, as pronouns fail to adequately express their shared experience: 'her cock' (51), 'he – she, or *they*?' (52), 'she turned their head' (54). Pronouns become (unstable) signifiers of gendered/sexed subjectivities and their inconsistent use conveys the collapse (or fusion) of categories of sexual difference.

The new male body she inhabits is not the only challenge for mother – in a humorous moment in the narrative, 23 'teaches' her how to give a blow-job. This lesson in male queer sexual practices helps her negotiate the demands that arise from the unfamiliar position as bottom. With a peculiarly visual cue, 23 assures her, 'I'll show you how' (54). In the sex scene, mother experiences both alienation (mainly from not comprehending the sensations that assault her) and blissful union, as actual distance is bridged and the self is in two places at once (reminiscent of cybersex's crossing of geographical distances). She is simultaneously grounded in her body and transcending it: 'One of the men...had taken her cock into his mouth and she felt the head slam against the back of his throat, through an organ she never possessed before... A thousand miles away...a woman's body writhed [with pleasure]' (52). Once mother has experienced the position of bottom, the power to watch and to control is incomplete without the power of surrender. In the end, sexual satisfaction is heightened by the fusion of top/bottom and the power that defines each position, as the reader learns during the internal dialogue between mother and son: '*This is the power, Mother, 23 said silently to her. To submit, to drink in the energy of others... No,* she said silently. *I want you, I have you, and I am you. To be and to have – and to watch – that is power*' (54). She offers him the top position of voyeur – to visit her body and mind as she has sex with a woman, to watch and not simply see himself, source of both his lament and pleasure: 'It has always been my selves, from the very beginning' (54). With this we witness a collapse of dualistic voyeurism and exhibitionism as it folds into an interdependent, scopophilic autoeroticism.

How male and female bodies are experienced is central here: while sexual difference is important to the queer desire in the story, its relevance lies only in its eroticism when difference is *fused* through technology. Denaturalized through technology (anybody can experience any kind of body), sexual difference is then reframed in terms of its immediate erotic potential; its instability resists social meaning. Similar to prostheses, both cloning and neural-net connections facilitate desires that transcend our bodies' 'natural' constitution and invite their expansion.

Conclusions

In Tan's anthologies, technology not only enhances the performativity of gender, but also creates new desires and sexual practices. When viewed in the context of perverse desires and sexualities, technology in erotic science fiction does not reproduce heteronormativity by simply re-imagining enactments of heterosexual desire and male access to the commodified female body (as the technologically modified prostitute in cyberpunk and virtual pornography caters to male heterosexual desire). Instead, it facilitates the creation of radically queer and transgressive sexualities and desires.

Sf erotica primarily articulates sexual fantasies. At the same time, the narratives re-enact non-normative sexualities and bodies and the pleasures they evoke assert meanings *outside* mainstream discourses on sexuality. The fantasy enacts this new meaning through the reaction of the reader's body and creates a moment of disruption that enables us to re-evaluate and/or resist social norms that regulate desire. The act of disconnecting sexual practices from the (social) meaning affixed to them becomes a necessity for (sexual) liberation. In so doing, these writers challenge the distinction between, as Delany puts it in *Silent Interviews,*

> fantasy and agency, with the slippery and finally a-locable line of intention, of praxis, constantly called on to divide the two at some pragmatic point that puts the ethical, the moral, and the good all on the side of behavior – of those who don't actually Do Bad Things, however much they think about them. (141)

Queer sf erotica approaches technology in a way quite different from Marxist and feminist critiques that focus on bodies alienated by technology and patriarchal technoscience. These paranoid rejections of post-human subjectivity in relation to technology neglect the bodies that *already rely* on technology to express desire. Instead of insisting on normative ('natural') bodies as measures for sexuality and desire, queer sf erotica celebrates bodies and sexualities that are enabled and enhanced through technology; these stories centralize sexual subjects and their 'fine fucking machines' as agents of change. In the queer cornucopia of unpredictable body-parts and sexual practices, the 'taxonomy' of heterosexual desire collapses and is replaced by an endless variety of categories, as the naturalized body is replaced by... well... accessories. Bring your shopping list.

Notes

1. The idea that perversity can have its place in utopia is concretely (and ironically) explored in Tan's serial novel *The Velderet* (2001). In its future society, S/M sexualities are banned by the state. In the tradition of dystopian novels such as Aldous Huxley's *Brave New World* (1932) and George Orwell's *1984* (1949), *The Velderet* is a classical utopia turned dystopia, in this instance modelled after (lesbian) feminism's restrictive notions of S/M role-playing as replicating patriarchal power. The promise of liberation from violence through the regulation of desire results in oppression, reminding us of Gayle Rubin's statement that 'sex is always political' (4). The plot development centres around how the two main characters' illegal S/M practices take on dimensions of political resistance. *The Velderet* is also an ironic commentary on *1984,* whose criticism of regimes that regulate desire (hence the term 'sexcrime') is limited to the mourning of male, heterosexual desire for traditionally feminine women. Another example of queer fantastic porn that thematizes the limits of the 'politically correct' is the writing of Pat Califia, especially the novel *Doc and Fluff* (1990) and the short story 'The Hustler' (1988).
2. Such as the sf erotica line *Ellora's Cave,* which advertises itself as 'The World's largest e-publisher of Adult Science Fiction and Fantasy', presenting 'kick-ass heroines, alpha-male heroes, and all the style you'd expect from both' (see their webpage at http://www.ellorascave.com).
3. There exists considerable overlap between notions of cybersex in virtual

reality and technologically enhanced bodies having sex. In '"Trapped by the Body"?', Thomas Foster gives an overview of the discussion on prosthetic identities (and practices) in virtual reality and cyberspace. Central to this debate is Howard Rheingold's notion of 'teledildonics', the idea of sex-at-a-distance through technology. Communications technologies facilitate the physical effects within and through cyberspace usually associated with actual contact. Foster reiterates the argument for the 'dildo as sexual prosthesis' used by lesbians in relation to teledildonics (and cyberspace in general) and how it destabilizes heterosexual assumptions and normative gender identities; examples of such arguments include Cathy Griggers's 'Lesbian Bodies in the Age of (Post)Mechanical Reproduction' and Theresa Senft's 'Introduction: Performing the Digital Body – A Ghost Story'. Surprisingly, these theoretical transgressions of (hetero)sexist paradigms through 'prosthetic identities' in terms of gender and race do not include disabled bodies' parallel experiences in the 'real' world. This silence is significant, as the shared interest of re-imagining the body and sexuality in disability studies and cyberculture theory should be quite obvious. While this overlap resonates in some sf narratives, such as in James Tiptree, Jr's 'The Girl Who Was Plugged In' (1973), often the exploration of sexuality and body is limited in both fiction and theory to disabled bodies and *virtual* sex, and to assumptions of normative bodies in cyberspace, as well as to the 'overcoming' of disability through virtual bodies that reflect the 'true' subject as imprisoned in a flawed shell. This renders the materiality – and sexuality – of disabled people invisible; the metaphor of prosthesis as 'unnatural', 'attached', and 'in-place-of' identity, while transgressive in terms of gender and sexuality, is completely disconnected from its function and meaning for disabled bodies. Therefore, the focus here is on the sexual presence of the *physical* non-normative body and how it is augmented and modified by technology.

4. One example of how the non-normative body is fetishized in mainstream pornography can be found in the sub-genre 'chicks with dicks', in which male-to-female (MTF) sexuality is reduced to the 'freakishness' of a female-gendered body ('chicks') combined with a masculine-associated body part ('dicks') displayed to please heterosexual men's (illicit) homoerotic desires.
5. Amputees as fetish objects – and as sexual subjects – are at the centre of subcultural sites such as www.ampulove.com and www.deviantdesires.com/kink/amputee.html. Amputations as the source of erotic pleasure (apotemnophilia) create communities of amputees (those with amputations), devotees (those who are sexually attracted to amputated bodies and subjectivities), and wannabees (those desiring amputation). These communities voice sexual identities around amputation differently from most cultural texts, which treat the fetishizing of the amputated and disabled body as a non-normative desire used narratively to problematize technology's relationship to the body. From this perspective, the normative body remains the basis from which other bodies are exoticized and 'othered'. One example of this kind of text is J. G. Ballard's novel *Crash* (1973), which depicts the destructive eroticization of bodies damaged in car crashes. Disabled bodies become objects of fetishized desire that trouble the 'normal' sexuality of the abled body, while their characters' subject positions as sexual agents are not explored.
6. In *Bodies that Matter*, Judith Butler discusses the relationship in psycho-

analysis of the symbolic phallus to the anatomical penis. She insists that as primary signifier, the phallus is 'fundamentally transferable' (83), and that its manifestation (and displacement) in lesbian sexuality as the 'lesbian phallus' destabilizes naturalized sexual difference (87). The sexual economy of the 'wandering' phallus in lesbian sex with its function as only one of various sexual practices not only destabilizes binary sexual difference, but also dethrones the phallus as primary signifier: 'the phallus is but one signifier among others in the course of lesbian exchange, neither the originating signifier nor the unspeakable outside' (87); thus it engenders the 'possibility of deprivileging that signifier' (89). The lesbian phallus is not then an imitation of 'natural' masculinity, but it discloses masculinity as reliant on a signifier that can be displaced. Butler revisits the instability of sexual difference and her critique of Lacanian psychoanalysis's reliance on its binary structure in *Undoing Gender*. (See also Graham Murphy's discussion of 'stray penetration' elsewhere in this collection.)

7. Examples of this include Wendy Pearson's 'Alien Cryptographies', which calls on sf critics to 'queer' science fiction texts; and the collection of original sf stories edited by Nicola Griffith and Stephan Pagel, *Bending the Landscape* (1998). Griffith and Pagel explain in their introduction that their 'one rule' for contributors – which forms the common thread for the anthology's stories – was 'that the Other had to be a lesbian or gay man' (7).
8. The (hetero)sexist attitude of many male sf writers was reiterated in Damien Broderick's speech as Guest Scholar at the March 2005 International Conference for the Fantastic in the Arts. Broderick recalled Robert Heinlein's response to Ursula Le Guin's short story 'Nine Lives' (1969), the story of a clone who must reassert an individual subjectivity after the accidental death of his cloned siblings. After outlining for the audience Heinlein's fantasy of creating several female clones of himself with whom to have sex, Broderick then voiced his sympathy for Heinlein's desire, evoking in the audience the vague image of an elderly man having sex with several young women who looked like his daughters. This familiar 'old-boys' understanding of issues of sexuality is undermined in McCall's 'Self-Made Woman', where the clone is the same sex as the 'original', as well as in Armonia's 'Flesh of My Flesh', where gendered power is complicated, autoeroticism eludes the boundaries of self and other, and sexual differences are newly aligned in queered relations.

BDSMSF(QF): Sadomasochistic Readings of Québécois Women's Science Fiction

Sylvie Bérard

> For the first time in my life, I was living in the world where my fantasies – what I once considered perversions – were fully accepted, even encouraged.
>
> — Chelsea Shepard, *Worthy of a Master* 110

Sexual themes are quite common in science fiction, demonstrated for instance in the many entries in sf dictionaries and encyclopaedias and in the many anthologies that revolve around speculative sexuality.[1] Interestingly, sexual representations in sf stories often suggest a certain level of sadism, or at least of cruelty. From the impossibility of sexual encounters between the mutually alien bodies of human beings and Others (for example, in Octavia Butler's 'Bloodchild' [1984]) to the mind's entrapment in a machine that prevents any sexually induced exultation (for example, in Anne McCaffrey's *The Ship Who Sang* [1961]); from psychologically painful mutations (as in Samuel R. Delany's 'Aye, and Gomorrah…' [1967]) to the loss of the corporeal envelope in cyberspace (as in Pat Cadigan's *Mindplayers* [1988]), science fiction has not always been kind to the physical body in the stories that it tells. Beyond even these conjunctures of sf and sadomasochistic fantasies, however, there is an active subgenre that combines sf and sadomasochism – or BDSM.[2] Its fictions depict scenes of domination and submission, of consensual (and sometimes not so consensual) torture and bondage, of BDSM established as a system. Books such as Cecilia Tan's *The Velderet* (2001), Chelsea Shepard's *Two Moons* series (2003–2004), and K. M. Frontain's *Bound in Stone* series (2005) fall into this category. John Norman's sadomasochistic-fantasy series *Gor* (1966–2001) made such a strong impression on the BDSM community that it led to a new set of material practices: real people, calling themselves *Goreans*, actually live their fantasies within the rules created by Norman for his novels (see Macintyre). Moreover, the fetish or SM scene and the sf milieu seem to some extent to attract the same audience:

> I am no longer surprised when I go to a play party at someone's house and find their book collection looks very similar to mine. A small shelf of Pat Califia, Anne Rice, *The Story of O*, of course, but also shelves and shelves of science fiction and fantasy. I am no longer surprised when I meet people at Renaissance fairs or science fiction conventions, and discover I already know them from the S/M community. Or vice versa. 'There's so much crossover', people say. But I think there is no 'crossover'. We have always all been one. (Tan, 'Sadomasochism and Science Fiction')

In 'The Pornographic Imagination', Susan Sontag links pornography to science fiction and explains how the Marquis de Sade envisions 'the body as a machine and...the orgy as an inventory of the hopefully infinite possibilities of several machines in collaboration with each other' (52). As well as the mechanistic conception of the body, Sontag observes some similarities in the relative importance of space to both genres: 'The ahistorical dreamlike landscape where action is situated, the peculiarly congealed time in which acts are performed – these occur almost as often in science fiction as they do in pornography' (46). It is easy to argue that Sontag has a limited preconception of science fiction, one based on the most current prejudices about the genre – that it presents one-dimensional characters evolving in a paper world – but what she observes in a deprecating way may nevertheless be relevant to the present analysis if we phrase it in a more neutral fashion. The science-fictional commodification of the body may indeed suggest some similarities to pornography, not least in the creation of the same kind of 'mechanical' or 'clinical' organism that Leo Braudy finds in what he calls 'bad sexuality' (23).[3] Scientifically motivated torture of the body, the reduction of the body to its most technical responses – these are prevalent images in science fiction. In a way, the fact that science fiction, like science itself, is a conjectural discourse based on the 'what if factor' (see Wright) also contributes to the reification (*thingification*) of the body, for the body itself becomes the object of the scientific/literary experiment. The cold Sadean 'demonstrative ability' as described by Gilles Deleuze (1967) might just as accurately be applied to science fiction.

In this essay, I concentrate on several sadomasochistic sf fictions by Québécois women writers of the fantastic, leaving aside for now consideration of poetics or of sociological aspects of the links between sf and BDSM. Observing how and, more importantly, from which perspective sadomasochistic scenes develop in these fictions, I aim to show how the narrative analysis of these texts and perhaps of science fiction as a whole can benefit from such new conceptual input. Not only does science fiction have a lot to say about sexuality and sadomasochism, but BDSM as an analytical framework also has much to tell us about science fiction.

Mapping ... the Rougher

I have chosen three contemporary sf narratives based on a BDSM dynamic. Each features, in the first place, someone (some instance) in charge whom we can call the *Top*; second, there is a compliant object, the *Bottom*; and, finally, there is a favourable situation, the *Scene*. It does not seem so important for the fictions to be pornographic or openly sexual as long as they depict a BDSM interaction. 'La carte du tendre' (The Map of Tender, 1986), a short story from well-known Québec sf writer Élisabeth Vonarburg, provides a fictive Scene in which a Bottom, simply called the 'Subject', is being literally carved up onstage by another character, a Top called the 'Operator'. In Esther Rochon's *Lame* (Blade or Wave, 1995), Lame is condemned to eternal damnation after her death, condemned to the humiliating degradation of her body. The Scene is set in 'Hells' – which evokes not the Judaeo-Christian site of eternal punishment but perhaps a more down-to-earth Pagan or Buddhist or Hindu version of the afterlife. Rochon's eponymous protagonist plays the role of the Bottom; the Top is the King of Hells, who is accompanied by his delegates. *La mue de l'hermaphrodite* (The Moulting of the Hermaphrodite, 2001), Karoline Georges' first novel, is also about humiliation through the reification of the human body. In this narrative, hermaphrodite Hermany, our Bottom, after committing a crime, chooses a subtle but cruel form of punishment instead of a jail sentence: she agrees publicly to confess her whole story through the electronic media and to allow herself to be judged according to the ratings of this public confession.[4] The Top here is the artificial intelligence that controls her confession, and the electronic media provide a convenient set-up for the Scene.

The most acclaimed of these three writers is Élisabeth Vonarburg. She has published more than ten novels, many short-story collections, numerous short stories, and dozens of articles, reviews, and other unclassified texts. Her most ambitious projects, to date, have been her *Tyranael* pentalogy (1996–1997) and her *Reine de Mémoire* tetralogy (2005–2006).[5] Vonarburg's short stories and novels are often thematically and narratively interlinked through common characters and motifs. The short story

'La carte du tendre', however, is not part of this literary fabric. It was originally published in *Aimer* (To Love, 1986), an anthology of ten short stories revolving around the theme of love.

The most recent story included in this present study is by new writer Karoline Georges. *La mue de l'hermaphrodite* is her first novel, published by a mainstream house. The fact that the cover blurb identifies Georges' novel as the '[premier] roman de la génération techno' [first novel of the techno generation] may not only have been prejudicial to the reception of the book, but also shows the extensive ignorance of the editor about science fiction and cyberpunk. At the same time, however, this is indeed an sf story that uses many cyberpunk images and tropes, including omnipotent technology, dominance of informational systems, degradation of the social fabric, loss of identity, and so on.

Esther Rochon's *Lame*, the third story I have chosen, is probably the most problematic of the three and one might question its inclusion in a discussion of science fiction. Of course, the mere fact that the novel is set in 'Hells' might push it towards the fantasy genre. Rochon's writing is famously difficult to classify, however, and this is probably why her present publisher Alire has created a whole new series – called 'Zen Fiction' – with her as its only author. Rochon defines herself as an sf writer, however, and most of the themes she develops belong to the genre. She is also studied as an sf writer more than as a writer of fantasy (see Bozzetto and Ketterer, for intance). As to whether the *Chroniques infernales* (Hells' Chronicles) cycle (1996–2000) – of which *Lame* is the prologue – belongs either to sf or to fantasy, the author herself addressed this question when, as guest speaker at an Italian conference, 'Au cœur de l'avenir: Littérature d'anticipation dans les textes et à l'écran' (In the Heart of the Future: Anticipation Literature in Texts and on Screen), she gave a presentation on *Lame* as science fiction. In any case, the Hells described by Rochon are not so much a fantasy world as a parallel universe; the magic it contains may not be scientifically explained, but it is set in such a rational context that it can pass for a realistic element.[6]

Of course, I cannot ignore the gender component of these texts, of these fictions written by three women writers and depicting (self-identifying) female characters. When one talks about sadomasochism, one must address the gender issue very carefully, because it has been heavily charged in the past, both in the vocabulary of Freudian psychoanalysis and in the discourse(s) of feminist theory.

Experiencing the Pain

The main characters in *La mue de l'hermaphrodite*, 'La carte du tendre', and *Lame* share the same kind of discomfort, a discomfort linked to the body. One important trait that these stories have in common is the fact that this suffering is an elected state – this is crucial to understand. Indeed, consent is the basis of the BDSM dynamic, for the lack of it, of course, implies abuse:

> Trust is an integral part of SM. There's no denying this statement. After all, in today's loosely knit, enormous network of people we call the SM community, we fiercely adhere to the credo of 'Safe, Sane and Consensual'. It's taught in all the classes and it's in all the books. Underlying this very sensible motto is the assumption of trust. We trust that the person we play with has safe techniques. We trust that they are in their right mind. We trust that they will respect our limits and seek our consent. (Midori 82)

In Rochon's novel, Lame is sentenced to eternal torment, but this proves to be only the perpetuation of the way she used to live when she was alive. In Georges' novel, Hermany undergoes her public humiliation only because she chooses such a punishment over more traditional chastisement. The most obvious case of consent appears in Vonarburg's short story, in which both the Subject and the Operator are performers and playing the sadomasochistic game is how they entertain their audiences. In 'La carte du tendre', not only is the exchange based on a consensual contract, but it is also based on trust between the two actors – an essential component of the Top/Bottom dynamic.

The sadomasochistic Scene in Georges' *La mue de l'hermaphrodite* is an imposed yet elected public confession. The novel is set in an unspecified country in the near future. Hermany, the main character, was born a hermaphrodite, child of a mother who submitted herself to scientific experiments. When her mother died four months after she was born, Hermany was sent to a scientific facility where she became an object of observation. She gradually became asexual as her penis and testicles, then vulva and ovaries were amputated for medical reasons:

> At the age of ten years and seven months, the most famous bisexual being in the world mutated into an asexual carcass. I felt like keeping my female identity. Nobody raised an objection. Don't get me wrong: I didn't necessarily want to be a girl. All I wanted was to keep the feminine gender. For I had lost almost everything. [A dix ans et sept mois, l'être bisexué le plus célèbre du monde s'est transmuté en carcasse asexuée.

> J'ai voulu conserver mon identité féminine. Personne ne s'y est opposé. Entendons-nous: je ne désirais pas nécessairement être une fille. Je voulais simplement conserver l'accord du féminin. Parce que j'avais presque tout perdu.] (Georges 45)

Nearly dead from the deterioration of her body, she was rescued by a scientist who offered her the artificial happiness of a powerful psychotrope and helped her utilize her extrasensory abilities. Eventually, she rebelled against the whole of society, not excepting her ambiguous benefactor (has psychiatrist Nay Mésange helped or utilized her?). She used her psi powers and mentally injured thirty-three people. Then, using the very tools he taught her to master, she almost killed Nay.

The discursive dimension is very important in the novel. Throughout her testimony, Hermany speaks in the feminine, because she has chosen to keep her feminine gender even when she becomes an asexual being. The novel's prologue begins with Hermany's trial. Given a choice between a life sentence in jail or submission to a judicial experiment, Hermany chooses the latter. In any case, as she says, 'The profession of guinea pig. That sounds familiar enough' [Et la profession de cobaye, je connais] (Georges 12). A first explicit allusion to SM appears at the very beginning of the book. Before she chooses, the hermaphrodite asks if there will be torture involved. The judge replies: 'This is not the Middle Ages' [Nous ne sommes pas au Moyen Age] (Georges 12). But the punishment, in fact, will be a subtle kind of torture: as Hermany tells her story for the benefit of the audience, her jailer keeps her informed of the ratings or 'captations'. She has to behave if she does not want to be punished. Not only does she have to expose herself, but she has to put on a show, a show over which, as a Bottom, she has no control. For example, when the hermaphrodite tries to be funny, the cybernetic Top tells her: 'We suggest that you avoid being cynical. That is unless your behaviour is dictated by some masochistic program' [Nous te suggérons d'éviter toute forme de cynisme. À moins qu'un programme masochiste ne dicte ton comportement] (Georges 15).

Esther Rochon's *Lame* also tells the story of a character who suffers a condemnation. After her supposed death (which takes place outside the novel's narrative space), Lame is sent to a parallel world called 'les enfers' [the Hells] where she has to live in a body modifed to endure eternal damnation. The novel, told in the third person but focusing on Lame, begins as the main character has been at work in this disgusting world – where '[the] ground was made of clay and shit' [Le sol était en glaise et en merde] (Rochon 1) – for quite some time; in contrast to her fellow sufferers, she has not yet lost too much of her human appearance. Lame is still a functional being and she works at the gate of Hells as a receptionist. Eventually, Vaste, fencing master to the King of Hells's hermaphrodite son, will rescue her and bring her to the doctors and submit her to intense training so that she may regain a sane body. She then becomes the leader of a reform that will change Hells drastically.

The beginning of the novel, which describes the Scene I will study more closely in the next few pages, shows Lame's degradation before she has started recovering. The narrative begins after Lame is sent to Hells and opens with the description of the main character's agony: 'She did not know whether she was dead or living' [Elle ignorait si elle était morte ou vive] (Rochon 1), says the incipit. She is condemned to see her body gradually swell up as it is subject to an inextinguishable appetite and sexual craving. Like the other damned who are confined to that part of Hells, she must constantly seek sexual gratification for a body which has become insatiable – this is precisely her punishment. The other damned souls masturbate constantly, but Lame tries to resist her cravings because she knows that giving in to them will only cause her body to decline more rapidly. The first pages of the book are about pain, the estranged body, humiliation, degradation.

In such a state of debasement, she is exposed to everyone's contemplation: 'Newcomers were horrified when they saw her' [Les nouveaux arrivants étaient horrifiés en l'apercevant] (Rochon 4). Lame has called for such a chastisement, for her immortal life is only an exaggeration of the mortal existence she used to live:

> Back there, she had preferred to hurt herself. To injure her own belly, for instance, or her sex. To seek self-humiliation by wearing clothes that were too tight for her and to observe the marks they left behind. It seemed she deserved suffering: she was ugly, undesirable, unworthy to be alive. [Là-bas, elle avait préféré se faire mal. Se blesser le ventre, justement, ou le sexe. S'humilier en portant des vêtements trop serrés et en regardant ensuite les marques qu'ils laissaient. Il lui avait semblé mériter de souffrir, puisqu'elle était laide, indésirable, indigne de vivre.] (Rochon 16)

Lame, like Hermany, is a masochist: 'She liked her prickles' [Elle aimait ses épines] (7), the narrator tells us about her mortal life. She contemplates her own punishment in the same way that her torturers observe her agony, in a similarly cold fashion, with an equivalent distance and morbid fascination.

In contrast to the novels by Georges and Rochon, in Vonarburg's short story suffering is not a punishment but a vocation – a profession. Her story describes a spectacle that features a Subject and an Operator.

The reader does not know much about the fictive place where this is occurring except that it is some kind of amphitheatre with a stage in the middle of a large room; there are tables and benches and waitresses or hostesses. An external narrator coldly tells the story and the narrative's centre of attention alternates between the onstage performance and the briefer passages in italics which feature a spectator and a hostess who are absently following the show. As the story progresses, the reader gradually realizes that this is not a live spectacle but the hologram of a previously broadcast performance.

In this fictive Scene, the Top, simply called 'l'Opérateur' [the Operator], is slowly carving up and revealing a Bottom, 'le Sujet' [the Subject]. He removes layers from what at first apppears to be a black cube, then a crystal, and then finally a naked young girl. The atmosphere in the theatre is cold and aseptic and the performance is described as a 'jeu' [game]. As soon as the Subject takes a human form, there is a shift in the performance and the Operator himself begins to experience pain. What occurs next becomes 'le Grand Jeu' [the Great Game] (Vonarburg, 'Carte' 175). Gradually, the Subject's skin is detached from her body. Every pain that the Bottom's body receives, however, must be reproduced on the Operator's, so that he too gradually loses his skin:

> With a small sound of discreet ripping, nails are torn away from the extremity of the phalanges that usually remain hidden under layers of skin. Another small suction disc comes and sticks to each finger, like a little mouth sucking the blood from around the nail. Then it injects a local slow-acting anaesthetic and cauterises the blood vessels. Thus the Subject's screams soon end. [Avec un petit bruit de déchirement discret, les ongles sont arrachés de l'extrémité des phalangettes invisibles sous l'épaisseur de la chair. Une autre petite ventouse vient se coller à chacun des doigts comme une bouche, aspirant le sang qui sourd de la circonférence de l'ongle, puis cautérisant les vaisseaux sanguins après avoir injecté dans le même mouvement un analgésique local à effet retardé. Le hurlement du Sujet s'interrompt donc bientôt.] (Vonarburg 175)

Everything in the Scene is meticulously controlled: how many incisions to make, how to take off the skin, how to proceed with every part of the body, and especially the sexual organs:

> Some areas are particularly delicate, those where the skin is thinner (the inner side of the wrist, the fold of the arm, the axilla, the areolas… Or, of course, on the other side, the popliteal, the groin, and, when the Subject is a man, the penis, when it is being treated as a finger: then one must follow the path to the root of the penis, starting with the head, pass the prepuce, and manage to overcome the limpness of the

> scrotum. [Il y a des zones particulièrement délicates, celles où la peau est plus fine (face interne du poignet, creux du bras, aisselles, aréoles... Ou, bien sûr, de l'autre côté, le creux poplité, l'aine et, lorsque le Sujet est un homme, le pénis, lorsqu'il est traité initialement comme un doigt: il faut remonter du gland à la racine en passant le surplomb du prépuce, et venir à bout de la mollesse du scrotum).] (Vonarburg 177)

In fact, as the narrative progresses the reader discovers that everything in this sadomasochistic spectacle is indeed about control, which is inherent to BDSM play (see Hart 151). It is also about beauty and savoir-faire! The story ends after the performance is over, when it is replaced by the next one, and as the two principal observers are also leaving.

How sexual are these BDSM Scenes? At the least, all three contain some sexual components and all depict some form of erotic gratification. For example, towards the end of *La mue de l'hermaphrodite*, Hermany's adoptive father (the psychologist who has rescued her from the hospital) invites her to a see a sexually explicit performance:

> Three women. Pregnant women. A white one, a black one, and an Asian. All bearing enormous bellies. All scalped. Each head black with dried blood. Each head like a rose ready to bloom... /and Larcan is groaning his head off, just as they do,/and then,/Larcan arched his back,/he offered the world his enormous penis/and the abject surged up/in three little gushes. [Trois femmes. Enceintes. Une Blanche, une Noire et une Asiatique. Toutes nanties d'un ventre énorme. Toutes scalpées. Le crâne noir de sang séché. Le crâne pareil à une rose sur le point d'éclore... /et Larcan gémit à tue-tête, comme elles, pareil/et, là,/Larcan s'est cambré,/ il a offert à l'univers son énorme verge/et l'immonde a surgi/en trois petits jets.] (Georges 88)

After this dramatic performance that suggests death and mutilated bodies – are they holograms or real beings? – Nay asks her: 'Did you experience the visceral fascination, the complex marriage of repulsion and curiosity, the empathy wrapped in estrangement?'[As-tu ressenti cette fascination viscérale, ce mélange complexe de répugnance et de curiosité, cette empathie nappée de distanciation?] (Georges 90). And Hermany resumes her narrative and replies, not to her adoptive father, but to herself and to her audience: 'Yes, I had experienced such a complex amalgamation. Yes, it was a unique, powerful experience. And this is exactly why I was so upset' [Oui, j'avais éprouvé ce mélange complexe. Oui, c'était une expérimentation d'une puissance unique. Et c'était exactement ce qui me perturbait] (Georges 90). Sexuality is obviously something that the character fears, but also something that the narrator depicts rather complacently.

Sex is also very much present in *Lame*. The main character is aroused by her own humiliation and is kept in a constant state of sexual desire and frustration. As the nude receptionist of that part of Hells called 'les enfers mous' ['Limp Hells'] she is exposed to newcomers. Because of her job, her sexual pleasure is deferred: 'If she had let go, and preferred her pleasure over her duty, she would have lost her job.' [Si elle avait laissé faire, et préféré sa jouissance à son devoir, elle aurait perdu son poste] (Rochon 10). In the logic of that world, her climax would become her complete surrender, and the minute she succumbs completely to her desire, she will lose the last remains of her dignity: 'With terror, but also with a perverse desire, she envisioned the day when she would not be able to resist any more, when she would become as stupid as all the others. She would finally let go!' [C'est avec terreur, mais aussi avec un désir pervers, qu'elle envisageait le jour où elle ne pourrait plus tenir le coup, où elle deviendrait imbécile comme tous les autres. Elle se laisserait enfin aller!] (Rochon 1995, 11). That 'perverse desire' linked to the postponement of pleasure contributes to Lame's sexual arousal also evokes the BDSM exchanges in which delayed gratification of the bottom plays a crucial role (see Brame et al. 110–11).

In 'La carte du tendre', the focus remains outside the characters, and the reader does not access their stream of consciousness but only their actions. The narrator suggests, however, that there is some satisfaction in the Scene: 'the way he moves around the Subject's envelope, then his own, clearly shows how satisfied he is with the outcome of the confrontation: somehow, they have been worthy of each other' [sa façon de tourner autour de l'enveloppe du Sujet, puis de la sienne, indique assez clairement sa satisfaction devant l'issue de la confrontation: ils ont été, en quelque sorte, dignes l'un de l'autre] (Vonarburg 179). In fact, the kind of Scene depicted in Vonarburg's text falls into the category of 'Safe, Sane, and Consensual' play that is the basis of BDSM (see Miller and Switch): it occurs as a pre-negotiated interaction between consenting adults and it implies that no participant will be harmed beyond what they have agreed upon. There is also another central sexual element. As I have said, the narrative develops on two discursive levels, the second being that of the two spectators, a man and a woman, who are inattentively watching the show; this is the embedded level. The relationship between these two characters is obviously sexual: they are kissing, caressing each other, interacting in a very intimate fashion. Now as the Scene progresses, it becomes more and more evident that this couple may be watching their own performance:

> People exclaim here and there, showing that the [artists'] names sound familiar to many spectators. For a little while, in some of the alcoves, tongues are speculating at a good pace about what might have convinced the Manager to present what is probably a dozen-years-old performance; the artists long ago parted to follow their individual destinies and to explore more modern forms of art. [Des exclamations indiquent ici et là que leurs noms sont familiers à plusieurs spectateurs. Pendant un moment, dans certaines alcôves, les spéculations vont bon train sur ce qui a bien pu pousser le Gérant à présenter un spectacle vieux déjà, si on se rappelle bien, d'une dizaine d'années; les artistes sont depuis longtemps partis chacun de son côté vers d'autres destinées et d'autres formes d'art plus modernes.] (Vonarburg 80)

The end of the story supports that effect by making it clear that some members of the audience know the couple who have been kissing in their alcove throughout the performance. That, of course, reinforces the sense of intimacy developed throughout the narration between the Operator and the Subject.

Performing the Pain

Although these narratives depict sadomasochistically inspired games in quite different fashions, they share an interesting and significant common thread: in all three texts, a Top inflicts pain on a Bottom in the context of a performance. That is, the SM-like Scene develops in a situation where the body is represented in a space that is already a stage, and characters have predefined roles and predefined interactions. In the broadest sense, we can read this as the dramatization of human desire itself, for as Lynda Hart declares, 'desire is always in some sense "theatrical"' and '[desire], like theatre, takes place in the fantasy one constructs with others' (8–9). The principle of the performance is also interesting because it insists on the deed as process rather than as end, contributing both to the dynamic of the representation and to the construction of a 'subject in process'.[7]

Moreover, in the three stories I read here – even in *Lame* and *La mue de l'hermaphrodite* in which the Scene is a chosen punishment – there is a vivid realization by the characters that they are, in fact, *putting on a show* – the Operator and the Subject for their audience, Lame for the newly damned, and Hermany for the sake of the ratings.

In Esther Rochon's novel, the main goal of the punishment is to chastise the damned. It becomes clear through Lame's stream of consciousness, however, that her torturers also expose her degradation for the *benefit* of the newcomers, to frighten them and to show them their fate. It is also obvious that Lame's chastisement is a remake of her past life: for example, one day her torturers give her a piece of blue fabric that might add comfort to her life but that only acts as a reminder of her past life:

> Back then, blue was the favourite colour for the ones who would have preferred to have no body and no belly, no sexual parts and no desire, to blend somewhere with space, to become pure spirits. This blanket was that blue; in other words, it did not help her escape from the mud of her concrete life. This celestial blue was the underside of Hells. [Le bleu était alors la couleur en voque chez tous ceux-là qui auraient bien préféré ne pas avoir de corps ni de ventre, de sexe ou de desires, mais se fonder quelque part dans l'espace, devenirs de purse sprits. Cette sorte de couverture était de ce bleu-là; en somme il ne lui faisait pas du tout échapper à la fange du contret. Ce bleu céleste était le côté face de l'enfer.] (Rochon 13)

In Georges' novel, the performance is in fact a central element of the narrative: the reader accesses Hermany's confessions only because she must publicly tell her story. Ratings or 'captations' punctuate the narrative, which is also interrupted by warnings from the cybernetic jailer whenever the hermaphrodite does not comply or behave. Hermany's sentence is a show that is constantly reoriented by/to the audience's will and whims:

> Indulging in silence during the performance is forbidden. / I am pondering.No reflection period is allowed during the performance. / I am here, I speak, and words climb up my throat. [Il est interdit de se vautrer dans le silence pendant la performance. / Je réfléchis. / Il n'y a pas de période allouée à la réflexion pendant la performance. / Je suis là, je parle, les mots grimpent dans ma gorge] (Georges 80)

At stake here is not the reality of her story, but its potential as entertainment.

Vonarburg's story too includes references to the entertaining quality of the performance. The whole narrative is about the fact that *tonight's* performance is subject to infinite variations, especially because the audience has an impact on the effect of the performance: they applaud, they exclaim, and they even talk to the Manager via the communication network:

> On the fifth terrace, a spectator, cleverer than the others, immediately begins to applaud; a few seconds later, others understand too and soon the whole audience is clapping – whether they are mimicking him or had a sudden epiphany, no one can tell. [Un spectateur plus perspicace que les autres se met à applaudir dans le cinquième gradin; d'autres

> comprennent aussi, quelques secondes plus tard, et bientôt le reste de l'assistance en fait autant – par effet d'entraînement ou soudaine illumination, impossible d'en décider.] (Vonarburg 179).

The fact that these stories are based on narrative strategies that imply more than one level of discourse creates a distance and reminds us that this is a game (Vonarburg), a piece of entertainment (Vonarburg, Georges), an exemplum (Georges, Rochon), and a re-enactment (Vonarburg, Georges, Rochon). In all three stories, the performance is, indeed, a remake or a rerun. Lame's punishment is the repetition of the life of humiliation she lived on Earth. Hermany's sentence reproduces the kind of existence that her society has imposed on her. As a hermaphrodite with psychic abilities, she has always been perceived as some sort of guinea pig. It becomes clear that the Scene between the Operator (Top) and the Subject (Bottom) of Vonarburg's story is the rerun of a hologram that was featured years ago. Additionally, all three performances are *one among many*. There are numerous levels to Hells (many parallel worlds) and Lame is just one of many damned. Likewise, the Scene performed in 'La carte du tendre' follows another performance and precedes the next one. When Hermany asks if there are other criminals like her who are punished in the same fashion at the same time, her cybernetic jailer remains eloquently silent. That reinforces the importance of the motif of the performance, which is then mirrored by the dozens of other performances that are implied in these texts.

Why is the presence of a performance – of multiple performances – in these fictions so noteworthy? First, performance is a significant element of the sadomasochistic power exchange and, as a structuring force in these narratives, it acts as a BDSM trope. Narratively, it is a way to keep the fiction alive and the representations dynamic. It is, of course, a literary artifice, but it helps project the idea of fiction as a process instead of a finite object. References to the audience also help to include the reader in the discursive situation even though she knows that the actual enunciatee (receiver), in the course of the narrative, is the fictive receiver or spectator. In the context of the representation of gender and sexuality, reference to and actualization of the performance can also prove very fruitful, for, according to Judith Butler, performance 'may preempt narrative as the scene of gender production' ('Performative Acts' 281) and, as opposed to narrative, is more apt at expressing sexuality. These three stories also develop around gender issues: gender exchange in Vonarburg's short story; female body image in Rochon's novel; hermaphroditism and asexuality in Georges' story. The inclusion of the performance in the very fabric of narrative discourse is a way to emphasise its political power in regard to the construction of new gender expressions – and active representations of them, because the literary text bears a performative value.[8] In a BDSM Scene, gender is not a given and nor is sex; '[even] the reactions of the participants are anticipated and prepared for as much as possible' (Hart 151). Performance favours the exploration of various roles in the context of a sexual encounter – which roles, paradoxically, allow the BDSM *players* to go deeper into their psyches and help them establish a more profound interaction – as well as the constant re-creation of sex:

> Sadomasochistic, or any kind of 'perverse' sexuality is about *doing*. Whereas 'straight' sex (whatever the preference of the people involved) is about *having*. Now, this is an obvious but, I think, crucial and fascinating difference. For, the notion of 'having sex' signifies at once that 'sex' is something one can own, and that it (sex) was there *prior to the performance*. The s/m sensualist, quite contrarily, in *doing* a scene *makes* sex in the performance. (Hart 148)

Polymorphing the Perversity

If there is a sadomasochistic interaction in these three narratives, or a BDSM-flavoured exchange, and if the Scene is included in the context of a performance, where does the discursive subject (the main enunciator) stand? When Vonarburg, Rochon, and Georges, as female writers, picture suffering female/feminized bodies, exactly what message are they sending to their readers? Are they simply perpetuating the image of females as martyrs and thus supporting the inequities of the patriarchal system or, at the opposite end of the spectrum, are they seeking more empowerment, at least on the level of imagination, through the shameless expression of such extreme fantasies and fears?

According to a vision first expressed by Freud (see 'Sadism and Masochism') and perpetuated in contemporary psychoanalytic theory (see, for instance, Lacan and Deleuze; see also Schaeffer), women get only the meanest share of the sadomasochistic fantasy. Men have access to what Freud calls a 'female masochism', such as can be found in Sacher-Masoch's *Venus in Furs* (1870). Supposedly, however, this position cannot be achieved by a woman – for it arises from the perverse pleasure of suffering... as a woman:

> Freud did claim that masochism was essentially feminine, which did *not*, in his theory, mean that men could not be 'feminine masochists'. Ironically, however, it did come to mean that *women* were presumed to be

> inherently masochistic, and thus women were symbolically barred from assuming erotogenic masochism actively. (Hart 50–51)

Such a conception implicitly leads, as in Michelle Massé's analysis of masochism and the Gothic, to linking masochism in women to a past trauma instead of associating it with an early sexual gratification – which is usually how it is interpreted when experienced by male subjects. Hart (89), borrowing John Austin's words, concludes that female masochism can only be 'constatative' for a woman, whereas it is 'performative' for men.

Some aspects of the three narratives certainly seem to reinforce the female masochist/male sadist dichotomy. In 'La carte du tendre', the Operator is male while the Subject is female. The Scene, for the most part, contrasts an active male character with a passive female object, apparently emphasizing the stereotypes. At the level of the two principal observers, there are also many signs of female submission to the male: 'the man takes her face in his hands' [(l)'homme lui prend le visage] (Vonarburg 73); 'the man's hand envelops the hand of the woman' [la main de l'homme enveloppe la main de la femme] (Vonarburg 73); 'the woman's head is tilted on the man's shoulder' [la tête de la femme est inclinée sur l'épaule de l'homme] (Vonarburg 173–74). Likewise, in *Lame*, Hells are run by a male leader, King Har, and Lame is first rescued from Limp Hells by Vaste, another male. This seems only to perpetuate the sexist dynamic: even as she is saved, it looks as if she will remain her lover's property and will be submitted to his cruelty, just as she used to be Hells' common property. Finally, in *La mue de l'hermaphrodite*, it is significant that Hermany chooses to present herself as a female or, at least, in the feminine grammatical form. This then appears to be the story of a self-identified grammatically female character who suffers at the hands of a cybernetic jailer who identifies with the masculine grammatical form.[9]

Both Esther Rochon and Karoline Georges seem to adopt the masochistic perspective, but a close reading of these fictions complicates this conclusion. The three narratives, as enunciative, creative systems, largely supersede the binary oppositions implying female masochism and male sadism. Actually, an interesting chiasm or inversion appears between the first two stories on the one hand and Vonarburg's on the other hand. Rochon's narrative is told in the third person, but the story is focused through Lame, the masochist, the female Bottom. Likewise, *La mue de l'hermaphrodite* is based on a dialogue between the jailer and the prisoner, but most of the narrative is dedicated to female self-identifying Bottom Hermany's testimony. On the contrary, in Vonarburg's short story, while the description is in the third person and is based on external focus, the emphasis is on the Operator's (the sadist's, the Top's) actions – because the Subject appears to be simply a cube for the greater part of the performance, it is hard to perceive it/her as a conscious/sentient character.

Considering the implacable power of the Law in these three texts – what Lacan refers to as the 'Nom du Père' [Name of the Father] – some fascinating crossings between sadism and masochism can be observed. In his comparative study of de Sade and Sacher-Masoch, Deleuze remarks that the masochist seeks out and underlines the law of the contract while the sadist tends to subvert the law (cf. Deleuze 79). When such a perspective is applied to these stories, they appear under a new light. Vonarburg's short story, for instance, the one that insists on the sadistic or the Top's position, is curiously the one in which the Law is the key element: both the Operator and the Subject perform their sadomasochistic Scene *by the book*, within the state of the art, in a fashion that Deleuze might describe as masochistic. On the contrary, although the other two narratives seem to adopt the point of view of the masochist, of the Bottom, they depict the unwritten, unpredictable, sadistic Top's rules. This chiasm shows that identities, even in the most apparently binary context, are not what they appear to be on the on the surface and are never completely univocal.

Such an ambivalence or ambiguity contradicts, at least partially, the vision of science fiction as a mechanistic system. The BDSM Scene is based on predetermined roles in a negotiated structure, which indeed may reinforce the idea of a 'congealed' time and space as described by Susan Sontag above. This is, however, precisely a game in which participants freely choose to engage in a performance in which the process is at least as important as the result. Besides, the mere fact that subjects choose to engage in a game puts some distance between the pre-established, somehow 'congealed', roles (the rules of the game) and the social selves that play those roles (if there is such a thing as selves in fiction!). Likewise, the body, in these fictions, may be treated as a machine and reduced to its most automatic responses, as in what Leo Braudy describes as 'bad sexuality' (23). That idea is conveyed in Rochon's novel in the way that Lame's body is modified to suit her torturers' needs, in Vonarburg's short story in the way that the Operator chooses the proper instruments to carve his Bottom's body, and in George's novel in the way that the body is manipulated by the electronic media. Still, BDSM interaction is also a means of subverting natural responses, of short-cutting the defence reaction and transforming pain into an ambiguous pleasure. Again, the fact that this is a performance, something planned and carefully set up, but also something subject to the fuzzy logic of a process, challenges the principle of a basic mechanistic interaction.

Walking the thin line between sadism and masochism, topping and bottoming, dominance and submission, these fictions also seem to sit on the frontier between exhibition and voyeurism as writers expose their most intimate and extreme fantasies and readers voyeuristically peer into them from the safety of their favourite reading spots. The principle of the performance, and especially the presence of a *mise en abyme*, introduces a distance between the sadomasochistic Scene and the reader, but it also insists on fiction as a creation and it reveals the presence of the author as both the creator and the spectator of her own Scene.[10]

The analytical framework I have developed for this essay may suggest that sf writers in general, like the three writers studied here and exactly like Freudian children, are genuine polymorphous perverts. *La mue de l'hermaphrodite*, 'La carte du tendre', and *Lame* depict extreme images that only science fiction can render possible. Even when they adopt the perspective of the Bottom, or when they establish masochistic rules, these stories show how sadistic an author can be toward her characters and, above all, they reveal what kind of sadomasochistic thoughts can cross the mind of a writer. And when these stories are told from the point of view of the Top, or when they base their world on a sadistic, perverse, and unruly law, their writers expose themselves by revealing some of their most intimate images. They give readers access to an imagery that might or might not be their own fantasies (in the same way that writers of crime fiction are not necessarily assassins and do not even necessarily have secret murderous fantasies!), but which they assume as writers. Somehow, as they write and expose their most intimate and extreme images and fantasies, these writers place themselves in the same state of vulnerability that they impose on their characters when they throw them onto the stage of a fictive BDSM performance.

Notes

1. See, for example, the Tiptree Award collection, Debbie Notkin et al., eds, *Flying Cups and Saucers: Gender Explorations in Science Fiction and Fantasy* (1998), as well as the following anthologies: Joseph Elder, ed., *Eros in Orbit: A Collection of All New Science Fiction Stories about Sex* (1973); Pamela Sargent, ed., *Women of Wonder, the Classic Years: Science Fiction by Women from the 1940s to the 1970s* (1995) and *Women of Wonder, the Contemporary Years: Science Fiction by Women from the 1970s to the 1990s* (1995); and Ellen Datlow, ed., *Off Limits: Tales of Alien Sex* (1997).
2. 'BDSM' is a polysemic acronym that stands for bondage and discipline, domination and submission, and sadomasochism. It appeared around 1990 and was created to advantageously replace the expression S/M (or simply SM) that

tends to insist only on the sadomasochistic components of 'non-normative' sexuality.

3. 'If the word "machine" summons up ideas contrary to our general beliefs about human nature, it is even more inimical to our ideas of the erotic, either in life or literature. Bad sexuality is "mechanical" or "clinical", that is, devoid of life and feeling and emotion. Pornography is bad because it stimulates "mechanistic" responses, that is, responses without the alloy of either mind or will' (Braudy 23).
4. Why is there no explicit BDSM science fiction in my corpus? Because there is none in the professional contemporary female Québécois sf repertoire. There are representations of blatant sexuality in Québec sf, however: Daniel Sernine's *Boulevard des étoiles I* and *II* (1991), for example, describe a decadent Earth where anything sexual, even the deadliest scenes, might happen. Some of the performances depicted in these two collections of stories might well be included in an eventual (perhaps comparative) analysis of the problematic developed in this present discussion, but more broadly applied to Québec sf.
5. Of the five novels in Vonarburg's *Tyranael* sequence, only two have been translated into English: *Book I: Dreams of the Sea* (2004) and *Book II: A Game of Perfection* (2006).
6. One more issue that should be addressed here is the lability of generic frontiers in the Québec sf and fantasy milieu. Most literary awards (Prix Boréal, Grand prix de la science-fiction et du fantastique, and even the Solaris short award) are dedicated to both science fiction and fantasy. Many writers (Joël Champetier, Daniel Sernine, Elisabeth Vonarburg) work in both genres. The annual francophone convention Boréal also does not make a clear distinction between the two genres and often includes guest speakers who specialize in horror, espionage, and/or detective fiction.
7. According to Janelle Reinelt,'"[p]erformance" has been used to differentiate certain processes of performing from the products of theatrical performance, and in its most narrow usage, to identify performance art as that which, unlike "regular" theatrical performances, stages the subject in process, the making and fashioning of certain materials, especially the body, and the exploration of the limits of representation-ability' (Reinelt 200).
8. In linguistics, the word 'performative' refers to an utterance that does something as it is being uttered. Literally, to say is to do, the most common example being the verb 'to swear' (see Austin).
9. This seems similar to the choice made by Ursula K. Le Guin when she wrote *The Left Hand of Darkness* (1969) and used the masculine pronoun to refer to her hermaphrodite Gethenian characters; she later examined and justified this choice in her essay, 'Is Gender Necessary?' (1976) and returned to the subject yet again in 'Is Gender Necessary? Redux' (1976). Whereas the use of pronouns is fairly unreflective in Le Guin's novel, it is explained and justified in Georges' more recent novel.
10. Lynda Hart remarks that the fact that the performance is based on *the real stuff* is crucial in a BDSM scene. The audience wants to know that the game is not faked, that there is real suffering and real blood. She has studied the work of a few performers and she notes that this tends to be the first question a spectator asks: is it for real? The referent is, somehow, necessary (Hart 241).

Because they are performing with their own bodies, their own selves, the fictive performers in these three stories, like the S/M performers described by Hart, draw attention to the referential process instead of to the constructed illusion.

Part IV

Embodying New Worlds

'Happy That It's Here': An Interview with Nalo Hopkinson

Nancy Johnston

> Oho. Like it starting, oui? Don't be frightened, sweetness; is for the best. I go be with you the whole time. Trust me and let me distract you little bit with one anansi story:
>
> It had a woman, you see, a strong, hard-back woman with skin like cocoa-tea. She two foot-them tough from hiking through the diable bush, the devil bush on the prison planet of New Half-Way Tree. When she walk, she foot strike the hard earth *bup!* Like breadfruit dropping to the ground. She two arms hard with muscle from all the years of hacking paths through the diable bush on New Half-Way Tree. Even she hair itself rough and wiry; long black knotty locks springing from she scalp and corkscrewing all the way down she back. She name Tan-Tan, and New Half-Way Tree was she planet.
>
> — Nalo Hopkinson, *Midnight Robber* 1

Nalo Hopkinson, a Jamaican-born Canadian author, has become in less than a decade a critically acclaimed novelist of speculative/science fiction and an original voice in the critical and political debates about speculative fiction, feminism, and afro-futurism. For her three novels, *Brown Girl in the Ring* (1998), *Midnight Robber* (2000), *The Salt Roads* (2003), for her collection of short fiction, *Skin Folk* (2001), and for her three edited anthologies, she has received wide critical recognition, including winning the Locus First Novel Award, the John W. Campbell Award for Best New Writer, the Sunburst Award for Canadian Literature of the Fantastic, and the World Fantasy Award, among others. Her most recent novel, *The New Moon's Arms* (2007), is published by Warner/Hachett. Hopkinson attended the Clarion Science Fiction and Fantasy Writers Workshop as a student in 1995; now she is one of its teachers.

I first met Nalo Hopkinson in 1999 when she agreed to read from her new novel, *Midnight Robber*, at a small academic sf conference in her home city, Toronto. But that was after I had seen her in a 30-second video clip on Canada's *Space Channel* introducing her first novel: she was the hippest and sexiest writer I'd ever seen in my ten years of science fiction convention-going. I bought *Brown Girl in the Ring* and found an intelligent, inventive style and compelling characters. Hopkinson's first novel was the sort of sf that keeps the reader anticipating each new book – and her prolific output lives up to expectations, not simply because it is inventive and original, but because it brings to sf a fresh perspective on social and political issues, especially those involving questions of race, gender, sexuality, and life in a diasporic culture.

In her on-line essay 'Dark Ink: SF Writers of Colour', Hopkinson asserts that sf is a malleable genre which has the potential to subvert political and social boundaries: 'Speculative fiction has reinvented itself repeatedly at the hands of the new wave, feminist, cyberpunk and queer writers. Perhaps idealistically, I believe that it will also open up to fantastical expressions from communities of colour.' Her own characters are most often of African diasporic cultures who face conflict with Western power structures, institutions, and future technologies. As editor of several fiction collections, including *Whispers From the Cotton Tree Root: Caribbean Fabulist Fiction* (2000) and *Mojo: Conjure Stories* (2003), and co-editor of *So Long Been Dreaming: Postcolonial Science Fiction and Fantasy* (2004), she has acted on this potential by drawing attention to postcolonial science fiction and to the work of writers of colour. Hopkinson describes her groundbreaking anthology, *Whispers from the Cotton Tree Root*, as a collection of Caribbean 'fabulist' fiction which uses 'the fantastical as its central theme' and 'dips into archetype and otherworldiness' (xiii):

> Northern science fiction and fantasy come out of a rational and sceptical approach to the world: That which cannot be explained must be proved to exist, either through scientific method or independent corroboration. But the Caribbean, much like the rest of the world, tends to have a different worldview: The irrational, the inexplicable and the mysterious exist side by side each with the daily events of life. Questioning the irrational overmuch is unlikely to yield a rational answer, and may prove dangerous. Best instead to find ways to incorporate both the logical and the illogical into one's approach to the world, because you never know when life will just drop you down in that hold, into a ceiba space where none of the rules you know operate. (*Whispers from the Cotton Tree Root* xi)[1]

That same impulse to bend and play with the genre's conventions defines her work: embracing and refusing to dismiss the irrational in one's 'approach to the world' (*Whispers* xiii). Her most recent novel, *The New Moon's Arms*, revolves around a woman at a time of painful emotional and physical change. Hopkinson's Calamity Lambkin suspects that her feverish hot flashes are somehow responsible for the sudden appearance of objects from her past, even a grove of cashew trees in her backyard. But she stops her daughter from explaining away this magic: 'Plenty in this world don't make sense… Don't do like everybody else around me doing. Don't try to come up with a story to explain it, then talk yourself into believing the story' (194).

This is an apt metaphor for the question of sexuality: culturally, we tend to come up with stories to explain it and then talk ourselves into believing those stories. Thus issues of sexuality in sf have become central themes for expressing questions of subjectivity, power, and the representation of otherness. One of Hopkinson's innovations as a writer is also to trouble conventional limits of sexuality and desire – to denaturalize heterosexual norms and to challenge dominant stereotypes about desirable bodies. Her frank and often humorous engagement with the complexities of desire, subjectivity, and sexuality is a defining trait of her fiction. She employs myth, archetype, speculation, and potential technologies to imagine worlds where her characters can transform or transcend their bodies and invent futures where individuals are not alienated by race, colour, sex, gender, or class. In her early story 'Ganger (Ball Lightning)' (2000), two lovers, Issy and Cleve, playfully swap 'skins' – suits which enhance sensuality and stimulation – to vicariously experience an alternative gender identity, but find that the 'skins' themselves are electrified by the exchange and take on a life of their own. In *Midnight Robber*, the central character, Tan-Tan, a young girl grappling with her father's sexual abuse, identifies with and masquerades as a powerful figure from Trinidadian carnival, a traditionally male trickster figure who regales his audience with tales of his exile from African royalty, his escape from slavery, and his survival. In *The Salt Roads*, Hopkinson creates a narrative perspective which shifts through the consciousnesses of three women, from eighteenth-century Haiti, nineteenth-century France, and ancient fourth-century Egypt as they are embodied by the African goddess of love and sexual desire, Ezili. Each of the women – Jeanne Duval, a mixed-race entertainer and mistress of Charles Baudelaire, Mer, a slave 'doctress' and lover of women, and Thais, a young prostitute of Nubian and Greek background – embrace their passionate sexuality and share common struggles for an identity transcending misogyny and brutality.

The persistence of non-normative sexualities throughout Hopkinson's work seems ripe for exploration in an anthology on queering sf. Hopkinson agreed to be interviewed for *Queer Universes* in the first hot days of summer 2005. As charismatic and gracious as ever, she took time away from two novels in progress for the interview over cool drinks. Over the course of the summer, she expanded on her initial responses to questions about the intersections of sex, race, and gender in her work. While she has done several provocative interviews in the past, critical attention has focused on her engagement with race issues, literary influences such as Samuel R. Delany, and her emergence as a black writer of speculative fiction. By focusing on related issues of sexuality and on her reading of queer theory, this interview asks what connections Hopkinson makes as an author between and among expressions of sexuality, subjectivity, power, and the representation of otherness.

Nancy Johnston (NJ): One of my attractions to your work is the 'newness' – the originality and energy of your short fiction and novels, from *Brown Girl in the Ring* to *Midnight Robber* to *The Salt Roads*. (Sandra Jackson-Opoku has admired your 'conjurer's art'.) For readers, I think particularly for queer readers, you offer some radical and challenging perspectives, futures, and worlds. In much of your fiction, you seem to resist the conventions of a normative heterosexuality: the idea that one form of sexuality and gender performance is or should be the norm. I'm thinking of your subtle representation of pairings or group partnerships of queer men and women in *Midnight Robber*, Issy and Cleve's playful and electric role reversals in 'Ganger (Ball Lightning)', and the fluid sexualities and the expression of complex desires of Mer and Jeanne Duval in *The Salt Roads*. What motivates or inspires you to challenge your readers?

Nalo Hopkinson (NH): Sexuality gets binarized too often. Not only do I resist the idea of one form of sexuality, but the assumption that there are only two forms, and you do one, the other, or both, and those are the only possible behaviours. It sometimes seems to me – and perhaps whimsically so – that the people who are courageously non-normative in their sexualities are doing in the real world some of the work that speculative fiction can do in the world of the imagination, that is, exploring a wider range of possibilities for living.

I've realized recently that the commonly accepted spectrum of gay-bi-straight doesn't work for me, either, though in a pinch, I'll describe myself nowadays as bisexual if no other word that will be understood is available, and if I don't have time to give the long answer, which is one I'm still figuring out, but which seems to have to do with an attraction to queering gender, and to overt and principled sexual transgression. For a long while it was very painful to me to feel like I had no name for what

I am. But I eventually realized that there are more options than straight/gay and almost as an afterthought, oh yeah, those bisexual people; that there are more than two binary poles around which most people cluster like magnetic filings with a few people wandering around in the middle, supposedly waiting for one or the other pole to draw them in.

When I write, I want to present as wide a spectrum as I can of the ways in which people can choose to behave sexually and in relationships, and I like representing those where possible as visible, acceptable behaviours. Because they should be, and because science fiction is about conceiving new possibilities. So yes, I find I'm constantly resisting both monoliths and binaries because I find them limiting for myself. It took a while for me even to be able to understand myself as queer, because monoliths and binaries obscured me from seeing it. Gay/straight/bisexual are all important to represent, but they aren't the only possible axes along which to sort human sexual attraction.

NJ: You have counted many sf writers as early and current influences on your work. Whose writing stimulates or challenges your work in the depiction or representation of sexuality or sexual politics? Which sf writers do you find the most demanding and rewarding?

NH: Science fiction is and has been ripe to discuss other possibilities for sex and relationships: multiple marriages, communal structures, different genders. Writers like Theodore Sturgeon, Samuel R. Delany, Octavia Butler, Elizabeth Lynn, Nicola Griffith, Élisabeth Vonarburg, Candas Jane Dorsey, Eleanor Arnason, Storm Constantine have been my touchstones.[2]

NJ: When you talk about your early influences, you have often mentioned Samuel R. Delany. Critics have also pointed to Delany (as well as Octavia Butler), one of the most prominent black writers in the genre, as an important model for many writers of colour. He is also one of the most prominent queer writers in the genre and one who dramatically troubles all kinds of boundaries, including sex and gender. Has his work influenced your approach or opened up the field for queer writing?

NH: Yes – his work makes me see the world, including blackness and sexuality and class, in ways that have not occurred to me before.

From Chip Delany's writing (I think that's where I originally encountered it, though I can't be certain), I got the notion that identity labels aside, if you were to look at the specific particularities of what or who people enjoy sexually, or how they end up structuring their intimate lives and their families, you'd see a lot more variance than we're led to believe is there. And I've certainly found that to be true as I meet more and more people. Hanne Blank (*Virgin: The Untold History*, 2006) calls identity boxes 'umbrellas', because she says, as with umbrellas, they don't completely cover you; there'll often be a part of you that's left out in the rain.

NJ: In your fiction, including *Midnight Robber* and stories like 'Fisherman' in *Skin Folk*, you portray female characters that choose to cross-dress or to disguise themselves to take up the traditional roles of men.

NH: I do? I hadn't realized that. I wouldn't call the protagonist of 'Fisherman' 'female'. Kelly just lives in a community where there is no concept of being transgendered. Tan-Tan in *Midnight Robber* isn't wearing men's clothing, she's wearing trousers; no more remarkable in her world than in mine. You could make the weak case that Kelly in 'Fisherman' is acting 'like a man', but the things that Tan-Tan does are considered transgressive in her world because she's chosen to be an outlaw, and because she's emotionally out of control, even by the standards of a world where life is cheap and whole communities are way dysfunctional. It's not because she's female. But I am intrigued by the stories of women and men in history who have cross-dressed.

NJ: Are there historical models or folk stories in which women take on the dress or gender roles of men? Are you responding to traditional stories, in which protagonists are forced to abandon various kinds of disguises (or take up their old 'skins') to reintegrate into their societies or return home? Can you discuss the significance of impersonation and cross-dressing in your own stories?

NH: I'm not sure that I can, because I haven't written the story yet. I am planning to, though. I'm not sure why it interests me so much. Gender-bending's sexy, so maybe that's one reason. And limiting people's actions based on their genitalia is kinda asinine, so maybe that's another reason. But I don't want to psychoanalyse myself on this topic too much before I actually write the novel.

NJ: In describing 'Fisherman' to readers, some critics are challenged by the 'graphic' depiction of sexuality. Do you intentionally challenge descriptions of sexuality? Do you view your stories, especially those depicting same-sex or alternative sexualities, as 'graphic' or explicit?

NH: I hope that my vanilla and het sex scenes are graphic and explicit, too! I write. It's an art form. Why would I make the effort to describe a meal or a sunset in a way that's detailed and responds to all the senses, but not do so for a sex scene? Why are 'graphic' and 'explicit' good in descriptions of walking through a field of lavender in full bloom, but not for a character coming so hard that his eyes roll back in his head? I don't make a distinction between porn and erotica; I use the words interchangeably. I do make a distinction between well-written stories meant to turn the reader on, and poorly written stories meant to turn the reader on. And that's to some extent a subjective judgement. I don't try to make the same-sex or alternative sex scenes more striking than the het or vanilla scenes (and it even kinda bugs me that I'm implicitly pairing 'het' and 'vanilla' by wording them the way I just did). Science fiction and fantasy are about looking at the world through a different lens. So whatever I write, including sex scenes, I may first think, 'how can I cause myself, and the reader, to see this differently? What can I do to challenge, delight, surprise, unsettle?'

NJ: Your fiction offers a breadth of female and male characters, and sexy, desirable women populate your fiction. The characters who most embrace their bodies and sexuality seem to exhibit the most power, whether personally or fantastically. I'm thinking, for example, of your early story, 'A Habit of Waste', where you draw attention to how culturally prescribed Western representations of ideal female beauty are. How important are these questions of body image and representations of beauty, as themes?

NH: The prevailing mass culture message that the only beautiful female body is young, white, straight-haired, and thin with a flat behind can destroy a woman's healthy body image. The protagonist in 'A Habit of Waste' started out black, kinky-haired, and curvy, and has internalized a lot of self-hatred. She has undergone a procedure to discard her voluptuous dark-skinned body for a more acceptable thin, white one; however, she finds herself jealous of how a stranger wearing her cast-off body is broadcasting confidence and self-love. So many women live in a state of induced neurosis around our bodies. I know how damaging it is, because I have to fight it daily. I once belonged to a health club at my university. The first time I used the changing room there was the first time I saw women of all ages, sizes, and shapes walking around naked. There was beauty all around me, and only a small proportion of it was conventional beauty. It finally occurred to me that the wide range of human body shapes, heights, and sizes can in no way be expected to fit into the narrow range of 'acceptable' body types and clothing sizes. And perhaps that's the point; if everybody can be one of the in crowd, how in the world would we know who's on the outs? It would be a disaaaaster! (Yes, I am speaking tongue-in-cheek.)

I know – we all know – women who have become emotionally and physically ill, sometimes to the point of death, trying to fit their societies' narrow beauty and behavioural standards. We know of women who have been hurt or killed because they have not. It's happening increasingly to men, too. It's criminal and wasteful that that should be so. So if I can present all kinds of bodies in a positive light in my writing, perhaps it's a way of modelling another point of view. There are any number of ways I could do that, but science fiction and fantasy excel at it.

NJ: In your introduction to 'Riding the Red' in *Skin Folk*, you used the metaphor of shedding the skin: 'Throughout the Caribbean, under different names, you'll find stories about people who aren't what they seem. Skin gives these skin folk their human shape. When the skin comes off, their true selves emerge'. Can you elaborate perhaps on how your characters in this collection are 'people who aren't what they seem'?

NH: Those stories all got written and in most cases published independently of each other, with no thought to collecting them. I didn't write them with any connection amongst them in mind. When my editor said she would like to collect some of my short stories into one volume, I then had to figure out what to call the collection. So I looked at all the stories and tried to discern a common thread from which I could generate a title. I thought I was being so clever when I noticed that a lot of the characters change from one thing into another. But I later realized I hadn't come up with anything novel. Fiction is about taking a protagonist through some life-changing moments, and science fiction and fantasy can literalize that change into actual bodily transformations. In any case, I went with something I'd found in a few African diasporic folk tales; when the soucouyant can't get back into her skin because someone has rubbed the inside of it with hot pepper, she says to the skin, 'Kin-kin, you don't know me?' (something like, 'skin of mine, don't you recognize me?'). I liked the idea of kin and skin being the same thing. I liked the idea that people changed into different things by taking off their skins. Hence, *Skin Folk*. It was after the collection was published that I discovered the black American proverb, 'All my skin folk ain't my kin folk', which adds some more layers to the imagery.

NJ: In both *Brown Girl* and *Midnight Robber*, your protagonists are young women at the point of a transition into adulthood roles (or rites). This transition is ultimately liberating, and opens their access to a potent sexuality and even supernatural power. What interests you in this transitional moment for adolescent and young women to adulthood?

NH: Mostly because I was one once, and it sucked. It's like a message back in time to my twenty-two-year-old self, to let her know that it'll get better.

NJ: How does sexuality as a thematic thread inform *Midnight Robber* or *Brown Girl in the Ring*?

NH: Not so much, I don't think. At least, nowhere near as much as *The Salt Roads*, or some of my short stories. But even though they're my first two published novels, some of my natural bents are already evident: in *Brown Girl in the Ring*, the grandmother is an older woman who's not written as asexual; I believe (can't quite remember) that one of the gang members is queer – and male, and macho, and black, and Caribbean – because I wanted to push at the misapprehension that the first attribute cannot or shouldn't co-exist with the remaining four. The characters come in a few different sexualities, and I portray that pretty matter-of-factly. Still, I was too shy to actually write a sex scene between the protagonist and her ex-boyfriend. People reading my current work might be surprised to know that I was once shy about writing sex scenes. I do a similar stirring up of sexual conformities in *Midnight Robber*, with the addition of a couple of different versions of polyamory. I don't make it front-and-centre, but I was interested in creating a world in which there wasn't a monolithic expectation for how sex/love/marriage relationships would be constructed. I wanted a world in which people co-created the individual relationship structures that seemed to suit them. Whatever you wanted out of a relationship you had to articulate and negotiate for, including monogamy. It felt risky to use Caribbean characters to examine different kinds of sexualities and sexual relationships. I think that we (Caribbean people) are so used to protecting our sexualities from prurient gaze that we've built up these huge taboos against many types of sexual expression. I've been affected by those taboos, too. So for me, the fact that I was finding it so difficult to depict two black Caribbean men publicly wining each other down (the only translation that comes to mind is 'dirty dancing') meant that I *had* to portray it, as an act of freeing up my own mind, as an acknowledgement that it happens in the real world, as an expression of my joy in the knowledge that human beings love and lust after each other. For me, it's part of my avowal that black people and Caribbean people are human, in the face of a world that continually tries to convince us that we are not.

NJ: Are you interested in troubling notions of desire, or portraying unconventional relationships and sexualities?

NH: Yes. It's fun to do. And it's scary to do. It makes me push at some of my own biases. When I wrote *Brown Girl in the Ring*, I was, as far as I knew, straight. I was also younger and less aware than I am now. When I told an acquaintance that I had just had my first novel published, he said, 'Oh, yeah? And how many queer people are in it?' I had a moment of sheer panic until I mentally went through the roster of characters and came up with, I think, seven. Or five. I can't remember all the characters any more. Then at some point, a sweetie of mine pointed out that one of those characters dies as his boyfriend holds him, and they could be seen as the stereotypical tragical queers; you know, well of loneliness stuff. Up until then, I hadn't been consciously aware that there was a trope. I was mortified to think that I might have replicated it as a result of not examining my own unconscious assumptions. Weighed against the handful of other queer characters in the book, two of whom are partnered and having quite happy lives together, I don't think I did play into the trope, but I only avoided doing so by happy accident, not by intention. Sometimes I've not been so fortunate; some years ago, I lost a friend over an argument we had about a male whore-cum-thief I had written into an earlier version of *Brown Girl in the Ring*. I hadn't the first idea what the life of someone like that might be like; the closest thing I had in mind was a character from the 'Thieves' World' series; not a great idea to try to create a fully rounded character by basing him on a fictional one! It's sort of like making a third-generation photocopy. I thought he was fun, but what I wrote was hugely offensive. My friend did know people working in the sex-trade industry. He chewed me out, and I got huffy, and though we both made nice a few days later, our friendship has never recovered. Interesting, though; a few days after that, I complained to a fellow writer about the incident. He, trying to reassure me, told me that he'd read what I'd written and he wasn't offended; he said that he was a straight, white male, and he figured people like him would form most of my audience, so it didn't so much matter what this other person thought. That was when I began to feel uneasy. Because it very much did matter to me. I had more in common with the guy who got angry with me – a politicized First Nations man – than with someone for whom identity politics were irrelevant. Perhaps straight white men are the largest part of my audience. Fair enough, but I already knew that I had no interest in contributing further to the erasure of people whose experiences are already marginalized; quite the opposite, in fact, if only because doing so would be to do psychic damage to myself. I still didn't understand why my (ex) friend had gotten so upset. But if I didn't know how to fix the offending character, I could do the next best thing; I took him out altogether. A few years and a bit more experience and wisdom later, I understood that that man had had every reason to be furious. I had the occasion a few years ago to tell him that he'd been right and I'd been wrong. Every time I put my work out into the public, I risk putting something out there based in my unexamined and unrecognized assumptions. That's part of the game.

NJ: In *The Salt Roads*, you avoid idealizing or sentimentalizing same-sex partnerships. Your haunting depiction of Mer, an enslaved woman and plantation doctor, and her love for Tipingee, is followed, in the same novel, by the more casual lovers, entertainers Jeanne and Lisette, in nineteenth-century Paris. Why is that important to you?

NH: I think my reasoning goes a little like this: people will love each other, no matter what circumstances they are in. Some of those loves will be of a type not commonly accepted. How might that play out? Mer and Tipingee have this horrible life that can injure or kill them at any moment, and that deliberately works to break their spirits, yet they find ways to love each other and other people, because that's what keeps human beings going. Everyone in their community of slaves knows that they are making *z'anmi* (an old Trinidadian expression for women in an intimate sexual relationship with each other; the root word is *amie*, i.e., friend), but because they are necessary to a community in chronically dire straits, and because they preserve outward appearances, they are pretty much left alone. It's not that people necessarily approve. It's that they know they may need Mer and Tipingee's medical services some day. And because the two women have the compliance of Tipingee's husband Patrice, so they can all partially shelter under the 'umbrella' of the convention of polygyny, which is a familiar one to their community. Tipingee, Patrice, and Mer aren't exactly doing polygyny (Mer and Patrice aren't lovers), but it looks enough like it from the outside that they're able to preserve appearances. There's also the convention of homosociality, which means that their community accepts and expects that people of the same sex will form strong friendship and social bonds; again a partial umbrella, since those bonds aren't expected to be sexual in nature. But since any of the slaves on that plantation can see that Mer and Tipingee are good friends, they may not question the nature of the friendship.

In nineteenth-century Paris, Jeanne and Lisette aren't exactly having a picnic either; they are essentially sexual servants who know that the only way out is to use their beauty – while they still have it – to attract the attentions of rich gentlemen; and Jeanne knows quite well that because of her blackness and her lack of 'breeding', none of those gentlemen will ever make her his legitimate wife. Jeanne and Lisette love each other – perhaps Jeanne loves more than Lisette – but they never question that their love can only ever be casual; it's simply not possible in their place and time, for women of their station. If they were both independently wealthy, white society women, perhaps. So yes, I'm trying not to be simply reactionary in the way I portray same-sex relationships, but I'm also trying to be realistic about what's possible for the characters in their context.

NJ: You have written candidly about sexuality and sex in short stories and especially in your recent fiction. In *The Salt Roads*, you linger delightfully over one woman's frank appreciation and intimate pleasure in the taste and smell of her female lover. Has this openness been received well by readers and critics?

NH: By some, not by others. Some people find it disgusting. Some people find it liberating. My mother's just alarmed. Generally reception has been fine. A few readers have been offput by the explicit sexuality in *The Salt Roads*, and I suspect it's at least partly because the sex is non-normative. The other part of what people may find shocking about the non-normative sexuality is that I involve a respected historical literary figure in it (Charles Baudelaire), and I also show black people doing kinky sex. There are all kinds of reasons why it feels particularly taboo to do the latter. For one thing, we ('we' in this instance meaning 'black people') are too often the victims of having white sexual fears projected onto our bodies, often in dangerous ways. So we can be cautious about making any room for that to happen. But I think there's a cost when black communities keep too opaque a veil over the fact that black people's desire and sexual inclinations are as varied and human as anyone else's. I was thinking about that when I wrote *The Salt Roads*. So I show a black man and woman who both enjoy dressing him up in women's clothing when they have sex. I show a famous white poet in bondage, bottoming to his black female lover. I show two nineteenth-century women, one black, one white, having oral sex. I wouldn't have thought that would be particularly shocking; by contrast to the other two, it's pretty daily sex. But I do tend to try to evoke all the senses in my descriptions, and that may be more than some people are comfortable dealing with. I use explicit words for sex. A lot of the characters in the novel are sex-trade workers, so they have bawdy, streetworthy, specific language for sex and sexual acts. That's the kind of language I tried to put into their mouths. *The Salt Roads* has received a more mixed reception than my other books; for all kinds of reasons, not just the sexualities. The novel is also non-linear with multiple viewpoints, and there are differences of opinion as to how successful that was. But even so, the overall response has been positive. I haven't heard a lot of Caribbean response yet; a hardcover book priced to the American market is an expensive thing in the Caribbean, so I suspect that it hasn't been that widely read there.

I am aware, though, that there is no accounting for how people will perceive what I've written. One reader was disturbed by what he saw as my depicting black women as indiscriminately ready for sex with anyone, any time. He wondered at my playing into the stereotype of the rapacious black or mixed-race woman. That reading surprised me, because I was actually trying to write against the stereotype by depicting the characters as people with full lives who find ways to make choices, good, bad and indifferent, no matter how constrained their circumstances.

NJ: You said that you had wanted to tackle Saint Mary of Egypt…

NH: Yeah. I also wanted to play against the traditional depiction of Saint Mary of Egypt, who has struck me powerfully from the first time I encountered stories of her. She's sometimes called 'the dusky saint' or 'Gypsy Mary' ('gypsy' as in 'Egyptian'). So here was an expression of Africanness that I had not seen before in Catholic orthodoxy – an African saint! (I'm deliberately not saying a 'black' saint. Egyptianness does not necessarily indicate blackness.) Her Africanness and her 'duskiness' were intriguing, that potential for a rare reflection of self in mainstream mass culture. But when I investigated the stories about her, she was depicted as so consumed with sexual desire that she became a prostitute at the age of twelve so she could have sex with a lot of men. Seems to me that the last thing you would do as a means of enjoying sex is get sold into prostitution. So I had a look at what was happening in North Africa in that general time period. There were a lot of famines, and farmers in particular often ended up selling themselves and/or their families as bondservants because drought had destroyed their livelihoods. If you were female, you could end up working as a serving girl in a tavern, where you could be expected to turn tricks. It made much more sense to me that Gypsy Mary might have ended up a prostitute because she was bloody well hungry.

The Catholic lore further goes that Gypsy Mary became sanctified when she accepted shame and not only gave up her sexual self, she gave up appetite entirely; she stopped eating. These were the times of ascetic Christianity, where there were people who were mortifying the flesh in order to glorify the spirit: people who lived in caves and never bathed; people who climbed to the tops of pillars and lived exposed to the elements for years. Intriguingly enough, I found that one ascetic practice was to have sex with anyone who asked. That too was a way to mortify the flesh. So looked at through one lens, prostitution was the ultimate in self-indulgent debauchery. But through another lens, it was a practice of subduing the wills of the flesh in order to elevate those of the spirit. The hypocrisy made me kinda cranky on poor Gypsy Mary's behalf, even though she may never have existed. So I tried to interpret her story in a way that felt more grounded in how a human being might experience the events that she experiences. And I decided that the redemption she finds for herself would not be one based in self-loathing. She never does think that it's demeaning to be a prostitute. It's not her choice, and it's difficult, and not particularly pleasant, and sometimes risky. It's not fun. But it's her job, and she feels about it the way that many of us feel about our jobs. It's a means to an end, and when she knows that she's going to have to somehow earn her way back home, she quite matter of factly decides that she's going to whore to do so.

NJ: The tone in the Jeanne Duval section is humorous, even bawdy.

NH: Yes, it is. I'm glad you see it that way. Not everyone does. I was going for a bawdy humour, comic in the more antique sense of the word. I think the cover artist captured the comic sensibility really well (though I still have issues with him having given nineteenth-century Jeanne straightened hair. And she was much lighter-skinned than the cover image shows). Nineteenth-century Paris was very sophisticated, but it was also a big city, and as with any big city, management of water and waste was a challenge. You had to draw water from wells, which meant going outside, which (particularly if you were a woman) meant the bother of getting decently enough dressed to do so. The catalogue of the layers of clothing that went into dressing a nineteenth-century French woman made my head spin. So I could absolutely see why you would use your chamber pot until it was overflowing, and put off bathing until it was absolutely necessary. I didn't want to so romanticize the time and place that I omitted dirt and piss-pots.

NJ: Do you see your work, or a particular work, as addressing or redressing negative stereotyping of queer issues or people?

NH: I do enjoy using my work to challenge unexamined norms and binarized conceptions of human sexuality and gender identity (and race, and class, and...). Does doing so address or redress negative stereotyping? I don't know. For readers who are ready to be convinced, or who are hungering to see themselves represented, or who like having their assumptions challenged, maybe I can provide some of that. But for others, people can react negatively to anything if they're determined to do so. For some people, the mere fact that a story of mine contains a description of Baudelaire's black mistress tying him up and butt-fucking him – to both their enjoyment, I might add – is disgusting simply because it's there. In fact, someone tried to have my novel *The Salt Roads* banned from an American public library system on the basis of that scene. Apparently, women and especially black women would never do something so depraved. I'm probably not going to change the mind of someone like that. Though I do note that the scene is halfway through the book, which meant that she'd gotten past the scene where Baudelaire is clumsily mauling his mistress about during sex and she's not much liking it; the scene where a plantation master skins a slave alive; the one where Jeanne is listening helplessly while Baudelaire's mother mocks Jeanne's dark skin; the one where a woman loses a baby in childbirth and two other women help her bury it; and the lesbian cunnilingus scene accompanied by hashish smoking, tampon removal, blood, and pissing. She didn't complain about any of those things, but the scene of a man and a woman enjoying the (admittedly kinky) sex they're having with each other was apparently 'filth'.

NJ: Can you tell me something about your new novel, *The New Moon's Arms*?

NH: I was thinking about the story of the Green Children of Woolpit, which was originally written down as history, not a folk tale. And about the 'aquatic ape' theory of evolution. I was also thinking about poltergeists, and the theory that it's not caused by ghosts; that it's telekinetic energy driven by the sublimated sexual expression of a young girl about to enter menarche. I decided that if menstruation can be magic, then menopause can be magic, too. My protagonist Calamity is a 53-year-old woman whose mother disappeared when Calamity was ten. Calamity's life from that point on has been hard and full of trouble. Now, without realizing it, she's going into menopause, and every time she has a hot flash, something from her past materializes. Not always something she's happy to confront.

NJ: Finally, some parting thoughts. You said in your earlier essay, 'SF Writers of Colour', that you found sf to be a malleable genre, one that has the potential to subvert political and social boundaries. You said, 'Speculative fiction has reinvented itself repeatedly at the hands of the new wave, feminist, cyberpunk and queer writers. Perhaps idealistically, I believe that it will also open up to fantastical expressions from communities of colour'. Do you still have the same idealism about speculative fiction's potential to subvert or bend boundaries and categories? How open do you find the genre, especially readers, to presenting diverse perspectives on sexuality and queer identities?

NH: Well, I find that we in the sf community sometimes like to think of ourselves as more progressive than other people. And while there's a lot of fodder for that argument, I'd say it's also true that we are reflective of the larger communities to which we also belong, and as those communities struggle with sexism, racism, queerphobia, classism, ableism, ageism, etc., so do we. And it shows. Sometimes the sf community can be quite oppressive and close-minded. But it's also a place that values openness and critical thought and exploration and the notion of diversity (even though we still have a long way to go to practise that last one more). SF/F/H [Science Fiction/Fantasy/Horror] is perhaps the only community I know where an editor can put out a call for submissions for a queer anthology and have straight writers wanting to submit stories largely without the defensive posture of 'I'm straight, but...'. Science fiction as a literature probably helped to save my life. I suspect I would have self-destructed without it, and without the people I have met because of it. So even when I'm critical of it, I'm very happy that it's here.

Notes

1. Hopkinson writes: 'The cotton tree, or silk cotton tree, is also called the ceiba; it's a tall spreading tree with thick roots around which pits and caves form. Spirits are supposed to live in these places, and people will be cautioned to avoid the roots of the ceiba tree' (*Whispers from the Cotton Tree Root* xi).
2. Theodore Sturgeon (*God's Body*), Samuel R. Delany (*Dhalgren*), Octavia Butler (the *Xenogenesis* trilogy), Elizabeth Lynn (*The Chronicles of Tornor*), Nicola Griffith (pretty much anything), Élisabeth Vonarburg (*The Maerlande Chronicles*), Candas Jane Dorsey (*Black Wine, A Paradigm of Earth*), Eleanor Arnason (*A Woman of the Iron People*), Storm Constantine (the *Wraetthu* books).

Queering Nature: Close Encounters with the Alien in Ecofeminist Science Fiction

Helen Merrick

[Q]ueering what counts as nature is my categorical imperative...
— Donna Haraway, 'A Game of Cat's Cradle' 60

'Queering nature' seems an appropriate theme for enquiries into sexuality in science fiction, especially from the perspective of feminist and queer theories. While it may not immediately suggest an overt comment on sexualities, it is inarguable that 'nature' as well as 'culture' is heavily implicated in our understandings and performances of sexuality.[1] Indeed, just as our constructions of sexuality (and the strictures of normative heterosexism) infuse every aspect of our culture/s, so too do sexualized assumptions underpin our constructions of 'nature'. And further, the ways we think about 'nature' impact upon and constrain our notions of sexuality. Wendy Pearson observes that science fiction has the potential to 'interrogate the ways in which sexual subjectivities are created as effects of the system that sustains them' ('Alien Cryptographies' 34). I want to further her argument to suggest that the variety of discourses and 'knowledges' that have come to stand for (or take the place of) 'nature' are one such system.

Attention to nature is an important facet of critical considerations of sexuality, particularly considering the pre-eminence of the biological sciences in (over)determining the category or categories of 'sex', and the fact that 'for many people...sexuality – and particularly heterosexuality – can be envisioned only within the category of the "natural"' (Pearson, 'Science Fiction' 149). I want to re-visit the loaded space of 'the natural' and consider how 'queering nature' might further question normative notions of sexuality and gender. While queer theory obviously engages with 'nature' on the level of regulatory discourses around notions of biology, feminist science studies and ecofeminist theory have a particular (and different) investment in the discursive positioning and uses of nature. Such theories are engaged in critiquing a broad range of biological and life sciences in which the construction of 'human nature' and 'nature' are implicated in often unstable and contradictory ways. Similarly, feminist sf texts may reflect on the ways in which we constitute and reproduce 'human' and 'nature', most strikingly through the familiar sf figure of the alien. In this essay, I focus on sf stories which feature a central (and often sexualized) female/alien encounter; I explore, in particular, how an 'othering' of the human might 'queer' nature through a close reading of Amy Thomson's *The Color of Distance* (1995). In concluding, I consider how certain notions of 'kinship' (as recently deployed by Donna Haraway and Judith Butler) might help advance the challenges to heteronormativity that are implicated in 'queering nature'.

Queering Ecofeminism

The notion of kinship is also a useful way of reconceptualizing the relations among the three theoretical threads informing my reading of 'queered nature'. Ecofeminism might appear unlikely 'kin' to feminist science studies and queer theory, not least because many within the academy continue to view ecofeminism with some suspicion as being overly essentialist (Sandilands, 'Mother Earth'; Soper). And although ecofeminism and feminist science studies arguably both stem from Carolyn Merchant's classic *The Death of Nature* (1980), they have developed along divergent discursive and political paths.[2] Yet, partly in reaction to tensions between ecofeminism's cultural and constructivist trends, critics such as Greta Gaard and Catriona Sandilands have argued the need for a 'queered' ecofeminism. An important driver for 'cross-fertilization' between ecofeminism and queer theory has been the failure of much ecofeminist and environmental politics to recognize its heterosexism – not least in its figuration of 'a nature that is both actively de-eroticized and monolithically heterosexual' (Sandilands, 'Unnatural Passions' 33).

A queer ecofeminist perspective, in contrast, argues that 'the naturalization of heterosexuality has been historically accompanied by the heterosexualization of nature' (Sandilands, 'Unnatural Passions' 34); the very nature/culture relation itself, which is mapped as feminine/masculine, 'becomes one of compulsory heterosexuality' (Gaard, 'Toward a Queer Ecofeminism' 131). When nature is feminized it is also, Gaard notes, eroticized, an argument that appears to contradict Sandilands' characterization of nature as 'de-eroticized'; this tension highlights the internal contradictions and instabilities of such regulatory discursive regimes. That is, our 'knowing' of nature is de-eroticized through the mediation of the mechanized, objective, 'disembodied' discourses of traditional Western sciences, even as the 'domination' and subjugation of nature allowed (even encouraged) through such knowledge puts it in the realm of the (eroticized) feminine half of the nature/culture binary. Not surprisingly, such tensions are constantly evoked and expressed through science fiction, most famously in what many consider its founding text, *Frankenstein* (1818): true to its Romantic influences, the text sets Victor's pursuit of technoscientific dominion against an ideological commitment to the 'natural sublime'.

The work of Gaard and Sandilands (among others) suggests an ecofeminist approach that aligns with queer theory on a number of levels, particularly in the need to move beyond the restrictive binaries of feminine/masculine and hetero/homosexual. As with queer theory, 'gender' is not situated in ecofeminist theories as the 'privileged' category of oppression. Rather, ecofeminism calls for a non-reductionist, interdisciplinary, and synthesizing understanding of a whole series of interlocking relations, from gender to race, sexuality, economics, globalism, and, of course, the environment. Both queer theory and ecofeminism have as political goal and analytical method the assumption that (gender) identity is not fixed, but is unstable, mutable, and fluid. Sandilands, for example, identifies the importance of what she terms 'performative affinity' for a political project such as ecofeminism, where material ecological goals, and an emphasis on a multiplicity of political affinities with numerous 'others', result in a recognition of the failure of the term 'woman' to act as a 'content-filled subject position' (Sandilands, 'Mother Earth' 29). A queered ecofeminist 'performative affinity' relies, Sandilands argues, 'on the insertion of a strongly parodic understanding of nature and its discourses' ('Mother Earth' 33). Such 'performative affinities' between women and nature – which 'allow for the possibility of each to disrupt the other' (Sandilands, 'Mother Earth' 36) – recall the kinds of 'subversive repetition' that Butler suggests might 'call into question the regulatory practice of identity itself' (*Gender Trouble* 32). Subverting or disrupting gendered and sexed identity and the category 'woman' thus requires, in a queer ecofeminism, a disruption – or queering – of nature: 'To queer nature, in this context, is to question its normative use, to interrogate relations of knowledge and power by which certain truths about ourselves have been allowed to pass without question' (Sandilands, 'Mother Earth' 37).

At the heart of a queer-ecofeminist reading, then, is a sustained attention to the ongoing reinscriptions of the nature/culture binary in our understandings of sexed and gendered subjectivities (and embodiments), particularly as regulated and constrained through the narratives of Western scientific discourse.

Constructing Nature, Regulating (the) Human

One of the many paradoxes inherent in our use of 'nature' is emphasized by a queer ecofeminist view: that in any series of binary oppressions, 'each characteristic of the other is seen as "closer to nature" in the dualisms and ideology of Western culture. Yet queer sexualities are frequently devalued for being "against nature"' (Gaard, 'Toward a Queer Ecofeminism' 119). As Gaard points out, the (ab)use of the concepts of 'natural' and 'unnatural' in regulating queer sexualities stems from the fact that 'natural' is invariably associated with 'procreative' ('Toward a Queer Ecofeminism' 120). The difficulty with picking apart such notions is that the 'natural' is on the one hand used to enforce normative social strictures dressed up as self-evident imperatives; while on the other hand, 'nature' is a subjugated object that is dominated by 'culture' and Western science.[3]

'Nature' is, of course, a very slippery term, which shades from descriptions of the world to symbols of 'wilderness', homilies on 'natural' (pre-given, normalized) behaviour, or a way of signifying that which is 'outside' culture. The 'human' figures in a strange and shifting relation with these series of signifiers. It is at once a part of 'nature' (the organic) and what is 'natural' (god- or biology-ordained), but is also apparently separate from it as the purveyor and originator of 'culture' and discourse. The ways in which we define 'human' are obviously complexly intertwined with our definitions and codifications of 'nature' and how we separate the 'human' from non-human/other. Human/other boundaries are also, of course, prime sites for contestations and reinforcements of notions of sexuality.

Kate Soper usefully distinguishes among three differing uses of 'nature': as a metaphysical concept used to signify humanity's 'difference and specificity', which can either signal human continuity with the non-human or its irreducible difference; as the realist concept of the physical structures and processes studied by the natural sciences; and finally as the 'lay' reference to the non-urban environment or 'wilderness' (Soper). Of most relevance here are the first and second uses, which tend, however – even within the sciences – to blur at the edges. This is partly due to the way the relatedness of human/non-human is either confirmed or sharply delineated. The appearance of this contradictory impulse in even the 'realist' concept of nature becomes clearer if we look to Bruno Latour's characterization of scientific modernity, which has at its heart a paradoxical dynamic generated by two opposing practices:

> The first set of practices, by 'translation', creates mixtures between entirely new types of beings, hybrids of nature and culture. The second, by 'purification', creates two entirely distinct ontological zones: that of human beings on the one hand; that of nonhumans on the other. (Latour 10–11)

That is, much of the work of the life sciences (and, recently, of biotechnologies) produces continuity between humans and other organisms (through, for example, DNA or genetically modified products) while the distinctiveness and 'purity' of 'human' as ontological category continues to be enforced in other discourses. Thus despite the force of this human/other opposition, which is normalized through reference to both 'nature' and 'culture', it is at heart inherently unstable. If the very category of 'human' is open to question, with what authority can this fictive genus continue to substantiate and regulate the excision of 'human'-generated culture from its other, nature?

Just as sf in general has the potential to escape the 'reincorporation' of the 'Cartesian subject of realist fiction' (Pearson, 'Alien Cryptographies' 18), I want to explore the possibility that ecofeminist and feminist science studies might resist the reinscription of mechanistic scientific narratives around 'nature/s' by destabilizing the traditional 'subject' of both 'science' and 'nature': the paradoxically 'translated yet purified' human. In order to unpack discourses around 'nature/s' it is helpful to turn to fictions and narratives where – if only momentarily – 'the human' (like the 'straight' or 'masculine') perspective is neither centralized nor normalized. Such fictions may be found, I suggest, in feminist sf texts which involve 'close encounters' with 'alien ontologies', where questions about 'nature' and 'human' are brought to the fore, including how both are variously sexualized.

Queer Bodies: 'Doing' the Alien

Alien encounters are of course a very charged trope in sf history. As Istvan Csicsery-Ronay, Jr observes, '[a]nxiety over sexual power and purity underlies most articulations of alien–human contacts'; significantly, the alien 'has always disturbed the deep-lying connection between biology and human culture' ('Dis-Imagined Communities' 228–29). Even if it is ultimately defused or recontained, the science-fictional alien is immanently disruptive – suggestive of the multiple sexualized and racialized binaries which inflect the category 'human', inevitably invoking the other, even as it may be registered as undesirable. However, it is when the alien is deployed as tool for thinking through both (human) nature/s and culture/s that such binaries might be destabilized. If the alien differs from us 'only' in terms of its biology, it potentially does little to advance us beyond the realms of the metaphysical anti/pro-naturalist differentiation between human and non-human. That is, to recall Csicsery-Ronay again, if the alien figures primarily as biologically rather than ontologically Other, then (as when dealing with racial difference) it is often too easy to 'conflat[e] cultural difference with putative natural difference' ('Dis-Imagined Communities' 229).

I want to turn now to some sf examples that are open to readings that 'queer nature'. Of course many sf texts lend themselves to a queered understanding of nature in one aspect or another, from Mary Shelley's *Frankenstein* to Ursula K. Le Guin's *Left Hand of Darkness* (1969), Samuel R. Delany's *Stars in My Pocket like Grains of Sand* (1984) and *Triton* (1976), John Varley's *Gaean* trilogy (1979–84), and more recently, Nalo Hopkinson's *Midnight Robber* (2000) and *The Salt Roads* (2003). In this essay I have deliberately chosen to focus on a number of lesser known authors, for two reasons. Firstly, I believe it is important to widen the scope of our reading beyond the usual canon, to explore the different forms of 'feminism' that might be recognized or produced through ecofeminist and queered readings, and to recognize the potential for 'queered' readings of what might appear fairly traditional sf treatments. Secondly, I want to look specifically at female–alien encounters, which are less easily mapped as masculinized culture versus feminized nature, or as reminiscent of (heterosexually) eroticized immersion in 'alien' culture and relations.

The texts discussed below all in some way resonate with an ecofeminist perspective and have a number of themes in common. There is at base a concern with the environment and human relations to 'nature' which encompass the ways we represent nature. Concomitantly, these texts are concerned with alternative understandings of 'being in' and knowing 'nature', which demand the construction of different scientific discourses and often imagine new biotechnologies, usually represented through an alien culture. One way of encapsulating these themes is through the notion of 'alien biologies', which signify not just biologically different species (and ontology), but also different practices and systems of knowledges (alien biological technosciences), and finally the intersections (too easily dissolved in the 'human–nature/human–culture' split) between physical being/matter and sociocultural discourses. Unlike more traditional sf readings which parallel the human/alien with a gendered dichotomy, in these texts the problematics of difference and otherness are located around the dualism of human/non-human, thus suggesting the possibility of escaping the heterosexual bind. For as Hollinger warns, '[an] emphasis on gender risks the continuous reinscription of sexual binarism', that is, the 'reinscription of an institutionalized heterosexual binary' ('(Re)reading Queerly' 24). In the texts discussed below, gender is not the most significant marker of the human–alien relation. Rather, the tensions in human–alien relations reflect the 'purifying' practices of scientific (and colonialist) discourses which contribute to the delineation of human from other.

In Marti Steussy's *Dreams of Dawn* (1988), a sentient alien race stands in the way of human colonization of a planetary environment; this colonizing approach is contrasted to the potential of alternative human–other relations which are represented by an empathetic female–alien bond. Disa, a human, is the youngest member of a 'First-In' team (first to explore new planets) made up of human and alien members, including the crab-like Kargans whose home planet is under threat. Having grown up with the Kargans, Disa sees them as 'family', not alien, and is both fluent in their language and at home in their damp cave environs. The crisis on Kargan has been precipitated by the presence of a human colony which has co-existed with the Kargans for years by ignoring their existence. However, the humans' non-native husbandry, agriculture, and imported foods are poisoning the Kargan young. Eventual resolution is brought about, primarily through Disa's ability to understand and connect with the aliens by changing human biochemistry so they can survive on native Kargan proteins. Overturning the xenophobic speciesism of humans thus effects a radical change in the human–nature relation, such that instead of changing the world to suit humans, human biological and environmental practices are altered to suit their new environment.

Such interventions into scientific and cultural discourses around nature and human are intensified in texts where the boundaries between human and alien are destabilized through a much more intimate encounter: where 'acting like' the alien, 'performing' an 'other' subjectivity equates – as in queer theory – with 'being' the alien. Intimate and eroticized encounters with alien others are a recurring motif in Naomi Mitchison's classic *Memoirs of a Spacewoman* (1962), which tells of the space-faring communications expert and xenobiologist, Mary. The world of *Memoirs* is a tolerant one, and acceptance of others encompasses race, species, and terrestrial fauna and animals. All life, even only potentially sentient life, must be treated with respect (to the extent that scientists communicate with and obtain permission from animals such as dogs who consent to cooperate in experiments) (31). *Memoirs* may be read very productively through a queer/ecofeminist lens: not only does the spacewoman Mary have a 'sexualized' relation with a Martian, she also twice becomes 'pregnant' through alien encounters. As part of an experiment with self-generating alien tissue to test for potential intelligence, Mary offers to host a graft of this particular alien. Her body responds as if she were pregnant, and she perceives the graft (which she calls Ariel) in very intimate terms, as 'flesh of [her] flesh'; she receives sensual enjoyment from their interactions: 'It liked to be as close as possible over the median line reaching now to my mouth and inserting a pseudopodium delicately between my lips and elsewhere' (54). Her second alien 'pregnancy' is 'activated' by the Martian, Vly, producing the haploid 'not entirely human' child Viola (67). Viola is a 'queer' progeny indeed, 'fathered' by a hermaphrodite alien (who later becomes a mother itself [143]) through a primarily communicative act – the standard sexed and gendered heteronormative system is certainly 'skewed' in this particularly unfaithful re-productive event.

These intimate encounters with other natures also significantly contaminate the boundaries between human and non-human. Other intimate and 'impure' alien encounters are found in Octavia Butler's *Xenogenesis* trilogy, *Dawn* (1987), *Adulthood Rites* (1988), and *Imago* (1989). Unlike Mitchison's text, becoming other in these novels is not really a matter of choice, although the resulting symbiosis of human and alien is much more extensive. Having rescued humans from an Earth which they have finally destroyed, the alien Oankali become midwives to a new hybrid human/non-human species. From the 'organic' and embodied nature of Oankali biotechnology with which they effect this transformation, to the nature of the Oankali–human relation itself, *Xenogenesis* exemplifies the destabilization of Latour's transforming/purifying practices signalled by hybrids, cross-species confusions, and 'monstrous' bodies. As a species, the Oankali are, as Haraway notes, compelled to cross and blur boundaries, engaging in 'dangerous intimacy across the boundaries of self and other' (*Simians* 227). On the surface, this boundary-crossing narrative seems to remain rigidly wedded to a procreative heterosexuality, with no evidence of either human or alien homosexual relations. However, the Oankali interventions into human reproduction, survival, and indeed human subjectivity (as both individuals and species) constitute an overt critique of the 'othering' tendency encapsulated by our human/nature/culture distinctions. In this way, the *Xenogenesis* trilogy suggests the contours of a 'queered nature': the 'naturalness' of human dominion over its world is revealed as nonsense when there is no world left (only an Oankali reconstruction to return to); while the product of a 'natural' human reproduction has been replaced (through what initially resembles a 'breeding experiment') by a literal 'construct' of human and alien. In this alien encounter (at least for those who remain on Earth), future survival necessitates both (sexually) 'being with' and becoming the 'Other'.

Othering (the) Human

Traditionally, sf narratives have been part of the 'proliferation' of cultural narratives which have 'demonized the Other' (Pearson, 'Alien Cryptographies' 20). In contrast, many ecofeminist sf texts turn this narrative on its head, employing aliens as a way of normalizing the other and, conversely, 'demonizing' the human. Amy Thomson's *The Color of Distance* (1995) is one such text that invites us to take an 'othered' perspective. It opens with the discovery of what appear to be two strange-looking animals in the forest by one of the central characters, Ani:

> underneath the masklike head-covering was a flat, uninteresting face with a fleshy nose like a bird's beak, and a small mouth with fat, swollen lips... [S]tripped the creature was ugly and clumsy-looking... Its thick, awkward feet had tiny, weak toes, useless for climbing... It lay there, laboring for breath like a dying fish. How could such a poorly adapted animal manage to survive? (2)

We quickly realize that this ugly creature is in fact a human, Juna, and that our viewpoint is that of the alien 'Tendu'. Within the context of Tendu 'nature', the human is immediately 'othered' as useless, 'poorly adapted' and 'unnatural'. Humans cannot survive exposure to this alien environment and so in order to save Juna, the Tendu make changes to her body to bring it into alignment with what they perceive as right and 'natural'. Ani's teacher, Ilto, changes Juna's body to enable her to live as the Tendu do – growing a protective 'skin' over her whole body, which undergoes other physiological alterations such as the colour of her skin (now a 'brilliant orange'), the replacement of fingernails by claws, and the growth of fleshy spurs on her forearms. The Tendu are expert healers and also, as Juna comes to realize, have highly advanced skills in bio-manipulation, using their own bodies rather than external technologies to monitor and effect changes on a cellular level.

Juna's transformation – and her initial fears – clearly recall demonized 'alien invasion' narratives. As Pearson observes of John Campbell's story,

'Who Goes There?', the 'conversion from human to alien is figured in bodily terms that are reminiscent of the sexual act', with the takeover 'figured in terms of both consumption and consummation' ('Alien Cryptographies' 22). Although Juna is not initially aware of it, the Tendu's means of healing and transformation involve processes that reflect a similar consumption/consummation. They penetrate her body with their 'fleshy red spurs' in the process of 'linking' or 'allu-a', the form of intense communication used by the Tendu both with each other and to explore other genetic and cellular beings and information. Not surprisingly, Juna's first conscious experience of allu-a terrifies her:

> Then its wrist spur pricked her arm, and she was unable to move... She could feel a presence moving through her like a chill in the blood. It felt as if slimy hands were fingering her flesh from the inside. Enmeshed in a cocoon of passivity, she could only sit in paralyzed terror as an alien presence took over her body. (25)

The resonances with sexualized penetration/consumption are reinforced as Juna immediately links this 'alien violation' to a childhood memory of being raped, the whole experience made even more abhorrent to her as the Tendu subsume her fears and replace them with feelings of euphoria. Juna's perceptions of allu-a change gradually throughout the book, as she becomes more attuned to Tendu culture and world. While the sexualized undertones remain, they come to signify more a 'becoming alien', rather than invasion.

This process of 'becoming alien' is highlighted by Thomson's use of alternating narrative voices: Ani refers to Juna continually as 'the new creature' and is initially hostile and dismissive of her clumsiness and lack of intelligence, while from Juna's perspective the need to survive by living in trees, eating raw food, and sleeping in leaf 'nests' signals the dissolution of her humanity. From her changed body to the daily rhythms of her new life, the narrative charts a progressive and increasing alienation as Juna sheds (or loses) her 'humanness'. To survive, understand, and participate in this world, she must become part of it, must become 'alien'. But from the perspective of the Tendu's world, this is a 'reverse' othering – Juna moves from a state of 'otherness' and disharmony as human to that of 'oneness' and harmony.[4] The rendering of Juna as alien is made explicit when the human 'Survey' finally returns for her after four years, and she is mistaken for one of the aliens.

An ecofeminist perspective on this process of alienation emphasizes the fact that it functions not just to reveal or privilege the 'other', but to recognize and indeed valorize a very different way of 'being in the world' –

specifically, a non-hierarchical and non-colonizing way of thinking about 'nature'. Gaard argues that a primary thread linking ecofeminism and queer is 'the observation that dominant Western culture's devaluation of the erotic parallels its devaluations of women and of nature' (Gaard, 'Toward a Queer Ecofeminism' 115). That is, a queer ecofeminist perspective alerts us to both the gendered and 'natured' character of the reason/eroticism binary. In ecofeminist sf, 'alien ontologies' often suggest more eroticized, involved, and non-differentiated understandings of nature – and thus different 'life' or biological (techno)sciences.

For the Tendu, knowledge is enacted through – and in – the body: they literally 'write' on their bodies (communicating through 'skin speech'), and 'taste' and communicate cellular and genetic information within their bodies. Their biotechnology is embodied, intimate, tactile – indeed sensual. Because of the way they know their world or apprehend the 'natural' (in both its metaphysical and realist senses), the Tendu do not employ 'purifying practices' to delineate themselves from other species or 'actors' in their world. They live in a carefully managed system of environmental sustainability and responsibility, with themselves as only one part of a system that must exist in balance. Indeed this managerial responsibility extends to severe self-correction in their own species: at some time in their past, when their numbers threatened the environment, they released a bio-engineered virus which eliminated half the Tendu population (336). The Tendu's responsibilities to the ecosystem are formalized through the central cultural notion of 'atwa'. Every adult Tendu must choose a portion of their world – whether it be a group of plants or animals, or a particular tree-based ecosystem – to be their atwa, and must 'make sure that their part of the word is in harmony and balance with all of the other parts' (206).

Ani's atwa becomes Juna and the other humans, which gives rise to an exchange which dramatizes the still-lingering differences between human and Tendu notions of self/other, culture/nature. Juna does not understand how she can be the subject of an atwa: 'I'm not a plant, or animal. I'm a person'. Ani replies:

> 'What you say is impossible! You eat, you drink, you shit. How can you say that you're not an animal?'
>
> 'Yes,' Eerin [Juna] told her, 'I am an animal, my people are animals, but we are different from other animals. We change the world we live in. We make things.'
>
> Anito's [Ani's] ears spread even wider. The new creature seemed to believe that it was separate from the world it lived in. (206)

This exchange clearly dramatizes the difference between traditional scientific objectivity – the belief that 'we know reality because we are separated from it' – and the Tendu perspective, which answers N. Katherine Hayles's question, 'What happens if we begin from the opposite premise, that we know the world because we are connected to it?' ('Searching for Common Ground' 16).[5] Thomson's critique of this differentiating, externalized, and dominating approach to nature is stated even more overtly in the sequel to *The Color of Distance, Through Alien Eyes* (1999), as Ukatonen compares his people's worldview to ours: 'How strange to look at the world as humans did, as a thing to fight against, to alter, as though it were made of clay and could be molded without consequences' (360).

Alien Sex?

So what are the consequences of this 'othering' of humans and the move towards more intimate, 'eroticized' encounters with others and nature? As noted above, allu-a – the process of linking – is one of the most sexualized encounters between human and alien in Thomson's two novels: 'The link made her feel incredibly vulnerable, as though there were no boundaries between herself and the aliens... Her loins throbbed with sexual heat' (*Color* 197). In all her years on the alien planet Tiangi, Juna's only physical, sensual, and emotive connections come through allu-a with the Tendu; thus allu-a substitutes for or functions as the only form of sexuality available to her. As linking most often incorporates her friend/'mentor' Ani, the enkar male Ukatonen, and her bami/adopted 'son' Moki, it escapes and confounds any easy hetero/homo divide. These intimate encounters with 'nature' (in the form of both Tiangi and the Tendu) are thus far from being 'de-eroticized and monolithically heterosexual' (Sandilands, 'Unnatural Passions' 33). Crucially, the 'eroticization' that takes place here is not the objectivist subjugation of 'nature' by the masculinized (heterosexist) 'culture' criticized by Gaard ('Toward a Queer Ecofeminism' 131). In becoming the 'other', Juna's perceptions, understandings, and very physiology challenge traditional notions of what counts as 'human' and what counts as 'nature'.

Indeed the intimate, multiple, and non-heterosexual links Juna shares with the Tendu are contrasted unfavourably with human heterosexual acts: Juna reflects that while she enjoys sex with (human) Bruce, she wished 'they could have linked so she could share how good it felt' (*Through Alien Eyes* 447). We are left with the strong impression that Juna's emotional and physical linking with the Tendu is more intense and ultimately more satisfying than (human heterosexual) copulation. And while the Tendu are two-sexed, intimacy and sensuality are disconnected from reproduction, producing very different familial and social ties. Juna's own experiences when with the Tendu in many ways render her gender irrelevant in terms of her status as othered/alien human (although there is a subtextual suggestion that her male equivalents, especially male alien-contact specialists, would not have been able to take on a sufficiently non-normative subjectivity to integrate into and understand Tendu society).

In the sequel, however, Juna returns to Earth (with her bami Moki and the enkar Ukatonen) and both she and the narrative appear to be reinscribed into dominant heteronormative, rational, mechanistic, and patriarchal norms. This is most evident in the changed relationship between Juna and Bruce. In *Color*, Bruce is an empathetic character, who does not react in a xenophobic way either to Juna's alien body or to the Tendu themselves; he provides some 'good sex', but also and more importantly he provides some comfort and support. In the sequel, he becomes one of the more xenophobic, removed, and unlikeable characters. Back on Earth, Juna's only human sexual encounters are with Bruce and, indeed, beyond examples of strong homosocial bonds between women, only heterosexuality seems in evidence. It appears that the 'othering' of the human and renegotiated relation with nature cannot be sustained once Juna (and perhaps the author herself) leaves Tiangi: in travelling back to Earth the narrative is constrained and reincorporated into a (straight, male, scientific) human-centric perspective on nature, sex, and sexuality.

However, there are still possibilities in the text for reading against the traditional heterosexual grain of the narrative, if we turn our attention to the intersections of gendered sexuality with relations of sociality, specifically with ideas and structures of family and kinship.

Alien Kin? Queered Kinship and Companion Species

> I tend to think in terms of kinship systems more than oppositions. It is a kinship system that does damage to our notions of nature, surely, but also to our notions of culture, so that neither nature nor culture emerges unscathed from our meditations on these modes of being.
>
> — Haraway, 'Birth of the Kennel'

In this final section, I want to consider briefly the idea of 'queered kinship', and how it might function as a metaphor for thinking through a queered ecofeminist perspective on 'naturecultures' (in Haraway's words in 'Birth of the Kennel'). Certainly from an ecofeminist as well as a queer perspective it seems more appropriate to think in terms of the 'translation' mode of kinship, rather than the 'purifying' mode of oppositions, to recall Latour's distinction.

Recently, spurred by heated and difficult debates over gay marriage and childrearing, Judith Butler has argued that it is politically and theoretically necessary to attend to notions of kinship as we negotiate contemporary changes in family structures away from the 'heterosexual norm' towards what she describes as 'post-Oedipal kinship' (Kirsten Campbell 645). As Butler notes, debates on gay marriage and kinship 'have become sites of intense displacement for other political fears... fears that feminism...has effectively opened up kinship outside the family, opened it to strangers' ('Kinship' 21). Indeed, drawing on Haraway, we might reflect that certain feminists have indeed opened up 'kinship' to include even non-human strangers.

Butler traces the radical changes in contemporary anthropological practice and resulting theories of kinship, which have moved from the concept of a 'natural' relation to the more performative notion that 'kinship is itself a kind of doing', a practice of self-conscious assemblage:

> Debates about the distinction between nature and culture, which are clearly heightened when the distinctions between animal, human, machine, hybrid, and cyborg remain unsettled, become figured at the site of kinship, for even a theory of kinship that is radically culturalist frames itself against a discredited 'nature' and so remains in a constitutive and definitional relation to that which it claims to transcend. (Butler, 'Kinship' 37)

There are obvious resonances here with Haraway's more recent approach to such questions, which she figures under the rubric 'companion species'; this is her replacement for the cyborg as figure for telling her 'story of co-habitation, co-evolution, and embodied cross-species sociality' (*Companion Species* 4).[6]

A narrative for 'cross-species sociality' which might result in 'queered kin' seems a highly appropriate aid for re-reading and potentially destabilizing the heteronormative surface of ecofeminist stories of alien–human encounters. From this perspective, even those texts where the 'demands' of reproduction produce reinscriptions of heteronormativity might offer alternatives to, or a break in, 'oedipal' heterosexual kinship patterns, especially where they cross species boundaries. For, as Butler notes, the breakdown of traditional kinship 'not only displaces the central place of biological and sexual relations from its definition, but gives sexuality a separate domain from that of kinship' ('Kinship' 37).

Alternative kinship patterns are of course a familiar theme in sf, featuring in the well-known work of Le Guin, Delany, and Octavia Butler, among many others.[7] In *Color* and *Through Alien Eyes* (1999), extended kinship patterns amongst humans are evident: group marriages of at least six people (and often more) are apparently the norm in Thomson's future and are not confined to internal monogamous male/female partnerships. By the close of *Through Alien Eyes*, Juna's daughter Mariam is emerging into a very queer set of kin indeed. As well as numerous human parents, there are her alien 'brother' Moki and Tendu 'uncle' Ukatonen, a kinship which is formalized when Juna, Mariam, and the Tendu are accepted into a group marriage (that includes Juna's brother). And while she is purely human born, Mariam certainly does not recreate the 'image of her father'; having been linked with the Tendu since the womb, she is, if not 'some half-alien thing' as her father fears (161), certainly not 'just' human. Group marriages blending different species are also a common feature of the society depicted in Steussy's *Dreams of Dawn*, which can include pairs and single humans of either sex, and in the specific case of 'Dawn circle' a non-gendered alien 'sheppie' and two female Kargans plus their 'groundlings'. In *Dawn*, companionable and even loving relations between human and alien are seen as a normal consequence of such 'queered' families: 'such attachments weren't unusual for children raised in the multispecies kinship of a First-In circle' (Steussy 2).

Thinking about queered notions of 'kinship' that involve human and non-human others also provides different perspectives on Octavia Butler's *Xenogenesis* series. Not for nothing are the ooloi, the Oankali third sex, known as 'treasured strangers' (104). One crucial function of the Oankali 'third sex' in the reproductive/genetic mixing of Oankali young is to ensure that sufficient diversity emerges from the very close male/female dyad who are often siblings. A strangely compounded two-sex system this may be, but even in this small fact it challenges familial notions of kinship and sexuality; even more so when humans are added to form the five-person, three-sexed, two-species 'construct' family. Quite apart from the very different conjugal or reproductive functioning of this queer family, traditional social and emotive relations are also disrupted. For the human couples, as for the Oankali, the intense emotional and psychological male–female relation enabled and mediated by the ooloi essentially disallows heterosexual intercourse – or indeed any kind of touching. In an interesting homosocial spin on human–Oankali kinship, the only people who can in fact touch each other are children or same-sex relatives. Pearson's reading of the figure of the hermaphrodite as a Derridean 'supplement' to the two-sex system in a number of sf texts is of interest here ('Sex/uality'). Even when dealing with texts where the primacy of apparent reproductive need drives a reinforcement of a biologically 'necessary' heterosexuality, the introduction of 'supplements' – in the case of Butler's trilogy, the ooloi – as necessary to complete or bridge the reproductive heterosexual system might, as Pearson notes, invite us to question 'whether the apparent plenitude of the two-sex system...does not also need supplementation...in the so-called real world' ('Sex/uality' 118). Indeed, as Judith Butler writes, 'when the relations that bind are no longer traced to heterosexual procreation, the very homology between nature and culture...tends to become undermined' ('Kinship' 39).

What might these 'alien biologies' and encounters suggest about the potential for undermining or destabilizing the 'naturalized' reinscription of heterosexual bio-social systems? Most of the texts I have discussed do not seem to upset significantly the conventional sexualized binaries for their human characters, who are ultimately reinscribed into the heterosexual code. However, the possibility of different forms – both biological and cultural – of sexed and gendered structures and societies is developed though the figure/s of the alien. Thus, even if not entirely successful, the conjunction of alien possibilities with human re-containment perhaps literalizes or figures the difficulty of escaping this binary within our current human forms of thought, codes, social forms, and sciences.

Science fiction has, in a sense, always occupied the fault line between the 'two cultures'. Its potential for queered ecofeminist disruptions offers ways of telling new stories about nature, humans, and others that might disrupt traditional and restrictive binaries of thought infecting our notions of nature/culture, human/non-human, epistemology, and ontology. Feminist and sf stories of 'queer nature' might, if nothing else, help progress our 'difficult labor of forging a future from resources inevitably impure' (Judith Butler, *Bodies That Matter* 241).

Notes

1. The use of the 'natural world' to justify heterosexism has of course been under challenge from research which emphasises diversity and difference in the mating behaviour and social groupings observed in nature. Such critiques emerge not only from queer and feminist theorists, but also from within the sciences in what Bagemihl calls the 'quiet revolution' in biology, which challenges traditional biology by documenting 'the diverse range of sex "differences," and sexual activities in strong species and ecosystems' (Hird 14). See for example Bagemihl; Roughgarden; Lancaster; Short and Balaban; and Margulis and Sagan. My thanks to Wendy Pearson for drawing my attention to some of these key texts.

2. See Noël Sturgeon for a brief overview of this issue; for further discussion of the intersections between the two, see my 'Alien(ating) Naturecultures'.
3. This is, of course, a very long-standing paradox in Western thought; as Haraway notes, in the West nature 'has been the key operator in foundational, grounding discourses for a very long time... [N]ature is the zone of constraints, of the given, and of matter as resource; nature is the necessary raw material for human action, the field for the imposition of choice, and the corollary of mind. Nature has also served as the model for human action; nature has been a potent ground for moral discourse' (*Modest_Witness* 102).
4. Indeed, the success of *Color*'s alienating positioning for Juna and the reader is highlighted by the sequel, which, being situated on Earth and centred in human culture, loses much of the cognitive dissonance provided by this radically alternative perspective.
5. It is also a central concern in many of Joan Slonczewski's stories, one of the few feminist sf authors who is also a practising scientist (in molecular biology). See, for instance, *A Door into Ocean* (1986) and *The Children Star* (1998).
6. As Hird points out, findings from non-linear biology itself challenge traditional cultural understandings of kinship, along with the 'new materialist' feminist studies of science, which have 'expanded analyses of the ways in which culture influences biological notions of kinship' (79).
7. See, for example, Le Guin's Ekumen and Hainish stories (such as those in *A Fisherman of the Inland Sea*), Delany's *Triton*, Butler's 'Bloodchild', and Russ's *The Female Man* (1976). Group-type marriages were also famously explored by Robert A. Heinlein, although unlike many of the feminist reworkings, they demonstrate that not all alternative kinship systems work to destabilize heteronormativity.

Queering the Coming Race? A Utopian Historical Imperative

De Witt Douglas Kilgore

1

Must any future order, whether on Mars or elsewhere, recapitulate a racialized heteronormativity? Can we imagine a peaceful and just society only as the outcome of a reproductive order that requires a firmly rooted hierarchy of racial and sexual identities? Are we to assume that an ideology combining white supremacy with patriarchy must serve as the limit condition of any viable future? Do the new races imagined in science fiction simply recreate the habits of dominance and submission that structure current social realities? These are my guiding questions as I consider whether it is possible to 'queer' the utopian subgenre of a coming race.

Over the past two centuries, science fiction has persistently asked us to imagine futures inhabited by human beings radically different from ourselves. For a literature that claims Mary Shelley's *Frankenstein* (1818) and H. G. Wells's *The Time Machine* (1895) as its founding documents, this persistence is determined by tradition. The task of imaging a queer futurity, therefore, requires that we confront closely held generic assumptions about human nature and destiny. From sf's utopian and dystopian roots we inherit our evolutionary speculations about the advent of a new human race. In the history of the genre race is both a corporate term including all humanity and an exclusionary rhetoric that naturalizes possessive investments in heteronormative whiteness. My interest here is in whether narratives of new human species can resist extending the political logic of this tradition.

I take my title from Edward Bulwer-Lytton's *The Coming Race* (1871), a utopian novel that distilled mid-nineteenth-century beliefs about race and gender into the conventions that subsequent sf writers have either reinforced or resisted. In the following pages I briefly account for the limitations of coming race narrative and then investigate how we can evaluate its potential for evoking a queer futurity. My particular focus is on how Kim Stanley Robinson, a celebrated contemporary practitioner, tropes the idea of a coming race in his *Mars* trilogy – *Red Mars* (1992), *Green Mars* (1993), and *Blue Mars* (1996) – as he works to show the way to a better future. I will argue that although it is not Robinson's primary intention to show us a queer future, he suggests the conditions under which it could appear. In doing so he engages past utopian hopes while challenging our conventional images of the future.

In contemporary science fiction it is easy enough to present futures in which our conflicts around sexuality and race have disappeared. This gesture may be as transcendent as the ending of Arthur C. Clarke's *Childhood's End* (1953) or as pragmatic as the uniformed discipline imposed in Jerry Pournelle and S. M. Stirling's *Prince of Sparta* (1993).[1] The genre can accommodate at one pole a mystic-evolutionary liberalism and at the other a militant neo-conservatism. Both positions are bound together by a faith that retains whiteness and heterosexuality as the core of any future social norm. Both dismiss historical alternatives that would de-centre this faith as either non-existent or perverse inversions of the truth. Both leave us with the certainty that either history will end or it will produce endless and ever more glorious iterations of our present.

The genre is also adept at generating futures that are recognizably queer. Samuel R. Delany's ambitiously conceived and realized *Trouble on Triton* (a.k.a. *Triton* [1976]) and *Stars in My Pocket Like Grains of Sand* (1984) come immediately to mind. In the former, Tritonian social custom treats gender and sexuality as malleable terms, independent of any simple biological determinism. In the latter the dichotomies that structure our own feeling for social hierarchy undergo a radical deconstruction, allowing Delany to present a culture that is not organized around heteronormative expectations nor even human racial biology. In other words, the idea of a queer future has been imaginable in science fiction for quite some time.[2]

To ask if the universe may be queered is to inquire whether humankind's understanding of itself and its place in the world can undergo a radical change. Can we imagine futures in which our descendants differ profoundly from ourselves while existing with us in a shared history? The question requires that we consider an epistemic change, a new structure of feeling incommensurate with the currently dominant hegemony. From a point of view that finds possibility in the prospect of a queer humanity, it is that incommensurability that represents political hope. This perspective allows us to imagine that the current configuration of society and life is neither stable nor permanent, and that a new social order, an alternative to what is now 'straight', is well within the horizon of social thought and action. But as I define it, a queer futurity, however much it must proceed from our present, nevertheless is incommensurate with our own circumstances as a predictable end. It is a process in which the complex imbrication of race and gender with hierarchy shifts into a shape we cannot anticipate. It would emerge from the practices of what Kim Stanley Robinson calls 'the great work of the bulk' of humanity and not as a formula prescribed by a single writer/prophet or social/political group (Szeman and Whiteman 183). The central problem, as I see it, is not in imagining what a queer future would look like but how we might get there from where we are.[3] How can a writer or a scholar come to grips with such a change or believe that such thought experiments presage liberation instead of disaster?[4]

For scholars of science fiction this may mean, as Eve Kosofsky Sedgwick has suggested, ceasing to rely on 'paranoid' habits of reading, and instead searching for a 'reparative' mode that looks for hope in unexpected places (Sedgwick, *Touching* 146). Sedgwick argues that paranoia is a way of reading that seeks to reveal the oppressive truth behind even the most seemingly benign cultural expressions. It is a powerful critical strategy driven by the hope that revelation will expand the freedoms we enjoy. Sedgwick notes, however, that 'paranoia knows some things well and others poorly' (*Touching* 130). One of the things that paranoia is not good at knowing is surprise. It tends, in other words, to be ahistorical, assuming that the future will be much like the past and that an oppressive past must produce an oppressive future. The 'reparatively positioned reader', on the other hand, may think it 'realistic and necessary to experience surprise' (*Touching* 146). This is nothing less than the rediscovery, in critical terms, of the future.

Readings sensitive to unanticipated futures can be achieved only if the critic is willing to embrace a future different from his/her own past. For Sedgwick, such intuition requires a shift of evaluative priorities from the emotive stance of suspicion to that signified by hope. She argues:

> Hope, often a fracturing, even a traumatic thing to experience, is among the energies by which the reparatively positioned reader tries to organize the fragments and part-objects she encounters or creates. Because the reader has room to realize that the future may be different from the present, it is also possible for her to entertain such profoundly painful, profoundly relieving, ethically crucial possibilities as that the past, in turn, could have happened differently from the way it actually did. (*Touching* 146)

A reparative reading strategy thereby acknowledges oppressive pasts but recovers their utopian potential, allowing for the possibility of futures that are 'pleasurable' and 'ameliorative' (*Touching* 141).

Sedgwick gestures towards a history that is never simply a repository of oppressions to be repeated endlessly but is also a chorale of voices that have not achieved harmonious closure. Such a model of history is very much in tune with certain strands of progressive, anti-capitalist science fiction. For our present purposes, Sedgwick opens a space in which we may reconsider the legacy of certain calcified ideas in science fiction and their reconstitution by writers for whom Fredric Jameson's difficult injunction, 'always historicize', is the catalyst for new stories. For such writers historicizing means that the past may be understood as, in Carl Freedman's words, 'a locus of radical *alterity* to the mundane status quo' (Freedman 55).[5]

Since the publication of Edward Bulwer-Lytton's *The Coming Race*, stories about the emergence of a superhuman race have been a persistent feature of this past century's fantastic literature. As Brian Stableford notes, stories sympathetic to a new human species tend to be written by writers 'harshly critical of the contemporary human condition and wholly in favor of "progress"' (1180). For the most part tales of new species of men or women or robots are evolutionary narratives. Whatever the physical or mental enhancements of the new races they invent, most sf narratives are organized around a heteronormative whiteness that limits thought experiments on species that truly differ from us or on social relations that diverge radically from our own. Bulwer-Lytton sets a standard with his race of physically, mentally, and politically superior women and men. In the pecking order his utopian race considers women (called Gy-ei) to be, in fact, the superior sex, though they happily support patriarchal social relations (Bulwer-Lytton 283–87). As the Gy-ei are superior to their men (called Ana), so their race is superior to others on and under the Earth. But while it is important to his narrative to set the Vril-ya above the rest of humanity, Bulwer-Lytton makes it possible for his Anglo-American narrator to wander around their utopia 'without exciting unpleasant curiosity' (300). In novels that follow Bulwer-Lytton's example, the coming race is revealed not as a new species living in a new society, but only as a glamorously improved extension of an enfranchised white, bi-gendered, and heterosexual race – a racial elite, that is, by natural endowment, superior to all other peoples. To be other than Vril-ya is to be always and inevitably inferior. The critical value that Stableford identifies in tales of the 'superman' is undercut by the oppressions consequent to any one group's assumption of ineluctable superiority.

The great public crises of the twentieth century should make us wary of ideologies heralding the advent of a superior human race. They emerge time and again in Western political culture as part of the ideological superstructure of white supremacy. Crystallized within a history of imperialism and colonialism, black codes and anti-miscegenation law, social Darwinism and eugenics, they have served as an imaginative way of securing the subjugation of peoples seen as moronic, savage, or unfit. In Kurd Lasswitz's *Auf zwei Planeten* (1897), for example, when European explorers meet a technically superior Martian culture their claim to equality is based on their distance from Earth's 'backward,' 'degenerate' races – such as the Inuit (Lasswitz 59–60, 103–104). White terrestrial and Martian equality is confirmed by romantic entanglements between Martian women and European men. The meeting of these races signals the arrival of a patriarchal future in which the cream of Europe transcends earthly limitations.

Such tacit approval of heteronormative whiteness as the dominant social relation of the future has been a central feature of this past century's science fiction.[6] A future that seems queer from our perspective – that is, one not implicated in our experience of race, gender, and sexuality – would result from a resignification of the sexual customs we consider natural. Since our sexuality has as much to do with pleasure and power as with reproduction, such resignification inevitably calls into question our possessive investments in race and gender, culture and nation – institutional structures by which we define what is natural and good or perverse and evil.

2

At first glance Kim Stanley Robinson's *Mars* trilogy is a curious choice for demonstrating the possibility of a queer futurity. The author's primary philosophical engagement is with the social transformations theorized by a Marxist historiography (Szeman and Whiteman, 182, 188). Ideally such an engagement does not foreclose a queer future, but it also does not make its imagining a priority. For example, Robinson exhibits little interest in the psychoanalytic and poststructuralist debates dominant in aspects of queer critical thought. His philosophical commitments are more Habermasian, deeply engaged with the political thought of social ecologists such as Murray Bookchin (Robinson, *Future Primitive* 10–11, *Green* 6). Nevertheless, the series of planetary revolutions that mark the turn from capitalism to radical democracy in the *Mars* trilogy can be read as queer from the perspective of structures of feeling now dominant.

Robinson insists that the quest to create truly new stories is central to his theory and his practice. His concern with rescuing utopia both as a political tool and as an artistic form presupposes that literary thought experiments are essential in altering our understanding and habitation of the public sphere. More provocatively, he champions the imagination of the science-fictional utopia as an art that can transform our feeling for the present and, therefore, the future. This advocacy aligns his work with the utopian strand of British scientific romance, especially the critical utopian tradition we inherit from the reinvention of science fiction in H. G. Wells's *The Time Machine*.[7] Although the *Mars* trilogy presents a highly detailed future history it is also an interrogation of the capitalist teleology dominant in Campbellian science fiction.[8] Robinson recasts and complicates the tradition of the coming race tale within the larger political aesthetic of utopian sf. The result is not the kind of queer futures (or mythopoeic pasts) we find in, for example, Delany's stories – temporal imaginaries removed from our immediate experience. Rather it is a queer futurity, a historical projection of our present emerging from a reparative reading of modern history. Robinson's narrative meets the reader half-way with a thought experiment grounded in a reading of sf conventions that restores or reinvents their liberatory potential in an attempt to create something new from old and, perhaps, vinegary wine.[9]

Robinson posits a future in which a grand revolution propels humanity out of an era dominated by bourgeois capitalism and into a series of socialist attempts to theorize and realize the promise of democracy. If this change also marks the progression of a queer futurity it is because the colonization and terraformation of Mars are posited as the fostering agents. Robinson's exhaustive portrayal of economic and political change is inseparable from the physical transformation of the Red Planet; this is a change matched by the physiological innovations created and accepted by its inhabitants. As Mars colonists create a Martian biota like and yet unlike that of Earth, their children become post-earthly Martians, a new race shaped by a planet that carries terrestrial memory but charts a new destiny. In Robinson's historical scheme, as a public sphere that *can* support democracy emerges, a new human race is born that inhabits it in ways unavailable to the old model. The facticity of birth, breed, race, sexuality, and gender is transformed and made multiple. Thus, previous social meanings are almost always queered. Robinson offers Mars as the site of a new mode of production that radically displaces what Judith Butler, in another context, has termed 'a specific mode of sexual production and exchange that works to maintain the stability of gender, the heterosexuality of desire, and the naturalization of the family' ('Merely Cultural' 42).

Robinson allows mild, rather than radical, physiological changes to stand for the changes that Mars would make to the meaning of biology. His native Martians are physical giants who tower over their earth-bred parents and peers. It is fairly easy to see the roots of Robinson's evolutionary speculation in the giant children of H. G. Wells's *The Food of the Gods* (1904), Olaf Stapledon's philosophical metahistory in *Last and First Men* (1930), and Bulwer-Lytton's *The Coming Race*. These novels provide an extant vocabulary, a tradition within which to find models for a superhuman and/or post-human future. To understand what Robinson accomplishes with his Mars we can refer to the precedent established by Ray Bradbury in the late 1940s and early 1950s. The Mars of Bradbury's *The Martian Chronicles* (1950) is a fabulous projection of the American middle-west as it seemed in the early twentieth century. It is also both a powerful evocation of the frontier rhetoric that popularized US expansion into the west and a sign of a national expectation that required the perpetual opening of new frontiers. Bradbury's early success at making Mars visible to a non-science fiction reading public, as a place to be inhabited emotionally and physically, lay in his highly sentimental projection of middle America onto the Red Planet. Thus Mars, an exotic landscape that owed much to the imaginations of both Percival Lowell and Edgar Rice Burroughs, took on a habit of simple homespun.

Often overlooked is the importance of race to Bradbury's evocation of a homespun Mars. His native Martians serve as the aboriginals who must be supplanted by white and black American settlers. They disappear, following an old Western pattern of resistance and inevitable defeat. The racial conflict between humans and Martians is amply illustrated in stories such as 'Ylla' and 'The Third Expedition' (2–14, 32–48). Bradbury's Red Planet is also a liberal critique of a segregated America: 'Way in the Middle of the Air', for instance, confronts the social traditions of racism and offers the hope of salvation on the Martian frontier (89–102). Not surprisingly, these stories of racial conflict and resolution resonated in an America embarking on several decades of debate, conflict, and transformation around race.

The final story of *The Martian Chronicles*, 'The Million-Year Picnic', reads as the collection's definitive statement on hope and human destiny (172–81). It follows a settler family, exiles from a dead Earth, who land on a Mars emptied of its aboriginal population. During their trek to a new home a child sees his family's image in a canal and discovers a new identity:

> The Martians were there. Timothy began to shiver. The Martians were there – in the canal – reflected in the water. Timothy and Michael and

> Robert and Mom and Dad. The Martians stared back up at them for a long, long silent time from the rippling water. (181)

Seeing themselves as Martians instead of Americans (or Terrans), the members of Timothy's family take on an alien guise. At the end of a collection that imagines, with sympathy and despair, the destruction of the planet's indigenes, Bradbury hails the birth of a new race, a new nation on Mars.

'The Million-Year Picnic' follows 'There Will Come Soft Rains', the tale of an automated house whose California family was destroyed by nuclear war (166–72). This is the end that Timothy's family escapes. Mars is, therefore, the site of a second chance; it is a new frontier that offers the possibility of 'common sense, good government, peace, and responsibility' (173). The family stands for what is threatened and what must survive. If 'Rains' is the stick, then 'Picnic' is the carrot, with the latter offering salvation for an American family otherwise faced with oblivion. The book's closing pages suggest an opening to an expansive future in which the self and community may be reinvented. But the reflective moment that ends 'Picnic' places symbolic limits on the social order that will be saved. The wonder-struck appearance of the new Martians is constrained by our recognition of them as familiar: patriarchal, heterosexual, middle-class, and white. Bradbury's coming race is the same old race on new ground. The power of this image should not be underestimated. It tends to overwhelm the good intentions of its author, presenting us with a future that claims particular social relations as immutable, natural and, therefore, good. Here, stripped of an explicit imperialism or racism, we find where the notion of a coming race resists the idea of a queer universe.

In designing his Martian future, Robinson is well aware of Bradbury's precedent, going so far as to end his own epic with a family picnic on a Martian beach complete with seagulls, ice cream, sand castles, ancient adults, and energetic children (*Blue* 755–61). The picnic echoes the image of naturalization and human renewal produced by 'The Million-Year Picnic'. Robinson's homage would be nostalgic if not for the radically different circumstances and political conditions that produce the moment:

> A brush reminded one what was important. Oh yes, very pretty! And why not admit it. Nowhere on this world were people killing each other, nowhere were they desperate for shelter or food, nowhere were they scared for their kids. There was that to be said. (*Blue* 761)

Robinson's Mars, however, does not restate the domestic salvation narratives familiar to us from mid-century stories of atomic apocalypse and planetary conquest. On his Mars the nuclear family has already been fractured, and the racial and sexual implications of its fragmentation challenge the assumptions of Bradbury's fifty-year-old vision. His new Martian race can live with terrestrial humans in a cultural geography that is international rather than parochial. By narrating the emergence of a new world from the still living ruins of the old, Robinson suggests that new futures might evolve from our present without destroying it.

Robinson's *homo ares* (also called *homo martial*) develops in a four-generation-long narrative that begins with an agonized debate about whether the first Martian colonists should reproduce. This conflict, and the science that allows one colonist to begin an illicit, non-consensual breeding programme, leads to the denaturalization of the nuclear family as regulator of sex and race on Mars. It is important that the rogue Japanese genetic engineer, Hiroko Ai, as the only registered non-white member of the first colonists, is the catalyst for this change. The result of her interventions is a community whose kinship is radically reconfigured and a social network that discourages proprietary rights over children. Individuals affiliate with one another through networks defined by social affinities and parenting, instead of through reproductive units focused on heterosexual pairs. Maya, a member of the pioneering generation, considers the resulting complex family structure and genealogies:

> To accompany her...she requested the company of one of their areologists, a young woman named Diana, whose reports had been coming in from the east basin. Her reports were terse and unremarkable, but Maya had learned from Michel that she was the child of Esther's son, Paul. Esther had had Paul very soon after leaving Zygote, and as far as Maya knew, she had never told anyone who Paul's father was. So it could have been Esther's husband Kasei, in which case Diana was Jackie's niece, and John and Hiroko's great-granddaughter – or else it could have been Peter as many supposed, in which case she was Jackie's half-niece, and Ann and Simon's great-granddaughter. Either way Maya found it intriguing, and in any case the young woman was one of the yonsei, a fourth-generation Martian, and as such interesting to Maya no matter what her ancestry. (*Green* 396)

As a fourth-generation Martian, however, Diana doesn't return that curiosity and belongs to a peerage that does not 'give a damn about Earth' (*Green* 408). This is in direct contrast to the intense sentimentality that Bradbury's Martian settlers feel towards Earth. Theirs is an attachment to family that prompts them to go 'back home' despite a nuclear holocaust (Bradbury 132, 144–45). Few, if any, of Robinson's Martians would feel such instinctual self-abnegation. While it is Robinson's intent to demonstrate that the fates of Earth and Mars are inextricably conjoined (if one planet dies so will the other), not giving a damn is important to the structure of feeling that creates a new race and a different sexuality. Robinson's characters build a new world that both extends and fundamentally differs from the old. Maya, who is white Russian, is drawn to Diana because of the difference the latter embodies: 'With her great size (over two meters tall, and yet very rounded and muscular) and her fluid grace, and her high-cheekboned Asiatic features, she seemed a member of a new race, there to keep Maya company in this new corner of the world' (*Green* 496).

To queer a race means to shift not only what a body means in culture but also the kinds of acts it may perform in relation to others. This involves reconsidering other components of contemporary social hierarchy, including the allocation of rights and wrongs, winners and losers. For Robinson, rethinking race requires the simultaneous resignification of sex and sexuality as categories of difference. Our attention is drawn time and again to the giant women who occupy the new Martian terrain. In *Blue Mars,* after a Martian government has been formed in the aftermath of the second revolution we find our long-lived heroes considering further the nature of their radically othered descendants. We are taken to an Olympiad sponsored by one of the islands in the new Hellas Sea. Maya, who functions as our viewpoint character in the coming race sections, watches the games with something between pleasure and jealousy of 'the new species... *Homo martial*'. Watching a female discus thrower she notes:

> This Annarita was very tall, with a long torso and wide rangy shoulders, and lats like wings under her arms; neat breasts, squashed by a singlet; narrow hips, but a full strong bottom, over powerful long thighs – yes, a real beauty among the beauties. And so strong; though it was clear that it was the swiftness of her spin that propelled her discus so far. (*Blue* 592)

This physical description focuses our attention on a body that breaks with the soft, curvy ideal traditional for women characters in sf.[10] This is not a body that current cultural mores prompts us to regard as 'womanly'. For our purposes it represents another element of racial difference between Martian and terrestrial humanity. Robinson emphasizes that over time it becomes difficult to differentiate between Martian men and women on the basis of physical strength or skill. The representatives of terrestrial humanity who are our point-of-view characters articulate the hypothetical reader's surprise:

> In the late afternoon they held the sprints. As with the rest of the events, men and women competed together, all wearing singlets. 'I wonder if

> sexual dimorphism itself is lessened in these people', Michel said as he watched a group warm up. 'Everything is so much less genderized for them – they do the same work, the women only get pregnant once in their lives, or never – they do the same sports, they build up the same muscles'. (*Blue* 593)

Therefore, a new species is recognized through bodies that might sustain a transgendered social order. Other members of the first settlers cannot help but contrast the treatment of women on Mars with customs in the old world. The trilogy's scientist-inventor hero, Sax Russell, reflects: 'On Earth men had abused women; on Mars, never. Was that true? Sax did not know for sure, but he felt it was true. This was what it meant to live in a just and rational society, this was one of the main reasons it was a good thing, a value' (*Blue* 722).

Thus one of the goods of an emergent queer futurity on Mars is the end of patriarchy. It is important to remember that this is a political end, for which a possibly queer biology stands as a sign. It does not, by itself, determine the nature of social relations or their direction. There is no preordained recession of the heterosexuality mandated by patriarchy. The presence of antagonists to the new Martian order indicates that though Robinson's Mars aspires to a utopian condition it is not isolated from other, perhaps retrogressive constitutions. By imagining perpetual immigration between the old and the new worlds and continuing exchange between racial present and future, Robinson stages constant movement between social orders defined as straight and queer. The consequence is anything but peaceful, particularly around the practice of a Martian androgyny. Many immigrants bring neither sympathy nor tolerance for the new order on Mars. And native Martians find little to like in the behaviour of new settlers:

> '[The] new comers can't cope. They cluster in immigrant ghettos, or new towns entire, and keep their traditions and their ties to home, and hate everything here, and all the xenophobia and misogyny in those old cultures breaks out again, against both their own women and the native girls.' [Maya] had heard of problems in the cities, in fact, in Sheffield and all over east Tharsis. Sometimes young native women beat the shit out of surprised immigrant assailants; sometimes the opposite occurred. 'And the young natives don't like it. They feel like they're letting monsters into their midst'. (*Blue* 594)

This passage moves us toward understanding what is at stake in envisioning a queer humanity. From the Martian point of view the old species makes monsters, creatures that are hampered by stunted bodies, enslaved to atavistic impulses. Here Robinson neatly reverses a dominant convention in colonial narrative in which the twin spectres of miscegenation and homosexuality produce racial and sexual horror.[11] Terrestrials who cannot accommodate the new Martian reality seek to reinstate heteronormative practice through social and political violence, and thereby to reinstate a 'straight' relationship between baseline humanity and any other race or culture. The danger here is that the social and political conflicts of twentieth-century history resurface in new guises on Mars. The coming of a new race holds the promise of a new racism as well as racial transcendence.

The new Martian species, the 'natives', supply the foundation of Martian difference. It is on and in these bodies that Robinson founds his Martian constitution, his recapture of a utopian hope for a very different future. There is a delicate balance to be achieved here; a razor's edge lies between utopian hope and dystopian nightmare. The superhuman scale at which Robinson's Martians work invokes the Victorian dream of a humanity perfected through its ability to reshape its environment. This old promise of physical and moral progress is leavened by our knowledge of its human cost. That precedent, perhaps, is why one of the founding mothers of the new race is Asian, Hiroko Ai, and one of its founding fathers, Coyote (a.k.a. Desmond Hawkins), is black. Robinson's coming race is not the emanation of a straight white male elite; it is the creation of two sexes and many races and cultures. In this way, perhaps, a queer futurity might avoid the racist assumptions that underlay the techno-utopian dreams of recent history.

3

The notion that humanity might change as a species by moving to another world or by gaining control over biological nature is a familiar feature of astrofuturist speculation. Astrofuturist writers promise that we will evolve beyond the conditions and places that continually produce our misery. Their underlying assumption is that only by changing human biology and its environment can we hope to reform human behaviour. Robinson, however, recognizes the danger in assuming that a healthier, wealthier, smarter human race will automatically follow benign political and cultural paths. The coming race could become a new ruling class, a caste physically and politically separate and dominant over common humanity even if queer in some physical or social way. Reassigning the roles accorded by race and gender or sexual preference does not, on its own, make a utopia. At best it is a technological fix that calls for a magical change in human history and culture. It must be accompanied by the will to create political and economic arrangements uninflected by possessive investments in a status quo defined by a heteronormative whiteness.

Hence Robinson gives us the elements of a queer future but not its full realization. What he does offer is a work in progress in which participants are enabled continually to queer their present as they pursue a better future. His queer futurity is a historical artefact that emerges from how we currently conceive and practise sex and race. With this in mind it is worth reading Robinson to discover whether the racialized sexuality that he presents makes for a difference beyond the heterosexuality in which it is expressed. A partial answer is found in Robinson's representation of sex between an old-species male and a new-species woman: Sax Russell, the pioneering father of Martian terraforming, and Zoya Boone, a fourth-generation Martian. Our attention is drawn to the power ascribed to differences in bodily scale and certain organs. Here the nature of heterosexual desire is revised to open up social relations based on feminine rather than masculine power:

> She stopped once to look [at] herself, big rich taut curves, and saw that the space of her hips stood nearly as high as his shoulders. Then back to it, vagina dentata, so absurd those frightened patriarchal myths, teeth were entirely superfluous, did a python need teeth, did a rock stamp need teeth? Just grab the poor creatures by the cock and squeeze till they whimpered, and what were they going to do? They could try to stay out of the grip, but at the same time it was the place they most wanted to be, so that they wandered in the pathetic confusion and denial of that double bind – and put themselves at the risk of teeth anyway, any chance they got; she nipped at him, to remind him of his situation; then let him come. (*Blue* 517)

Sex, as a social act, is the relation between predator and prey. Here racial difference is directly conjoined to sexuality: the new-species woman has what the old-species male lacks, and, therefore, must have.

The differences are underscored when Sax notices that Zoya purrs during intercourse. In other hands that would be a traditionalist feline metaphor, but here it is a physical fact: she displays an ability normal to a non-human species.

> 'The genes are from cats?'
> 'From tigers.'
> 'Ah.'
> 'It turns out to be a minor change in the larynx and vocal cords. You

> should try it, it feels really good.'
> He was blinking and did not answer. (*Blue*, 517–18)

This ordinary hard-science wonder leaves the old species paramour, the trilogy's ideal scientist, speechless. To redesign the human body is to reconsider its status as an object of fixed social and political meaning that can be described in language. To embrace the animal is (in some sense) to leave language behind, to raise questions about whether the result is more or less than human. It might also lead us to question a linguistic construction that assumes humanity as a stable referent. Since Sax is the trilogy's articulate, ultra-rational inventor-scientist, his inability to respond opens the text to a reading that breaks with our investment in a humanity defined over and against the animal and, therefore, over and against nature. The pendulum of power and desire swings but – unlike the precedent set by Bulwer-Lytton – implies something radically new. The focus, in other words, is not on the preservation of an ideal flattering current prejudices but on anticipation of what our descendants might achieve through unprecedented choices. In context, Zoya's self-fashioning is of a piece with the great public work of terraforming Mars, a technological process for which there are ready rationales but that also outstrips attempts at rhetorical and political control.[12]

It is here that we come to the crux of Robinson's engagement with the utopian tradition he treasures. Literary precedent in the American branch of this tradition – from Edward Bellamy and Charlotte Perkins Gilman to Ernest Callenbach and Marge Piercy – leads us to futures alienated from historical progression. Their good societies depend on our sympathy for the alienated visitor to utopia, our only narrative point of view. Even the most anti-racist and 'queer' of them, Piercy's *Woman on the Edge of Time* (1976), is what Jameson would call existential ('Politics' 39–40), for it focuses more on realizing the hopes of an aggrieved individual than in presenting a field on which aggrieved communities might act. Unfortunately, this means that a text intending a critique of the present could demobilize its audience. We are left with nothing to do but wait for the desired future to appear. Robinson takes a different tack in his revision of the utopian tradition. His future emerges from myriad voices and choices, not from the desires of a single visitor to utopia.

Robinson shows us a future that emerges from the present as a public work in progress. The vast ensemble of societies, corporations, parties, and individuals who make up the Martian nation is his model of a future that mirrors our own world in its complexity, but is optimistic about outcomes. Robinson's critique of our present implies, therefore, that the labour of making the future is within the power of his readers. It does not emerge as the product of some biological or environmental determinism, but from a determined, self-conscious effort by races old and new. The basis of his utopian vision is, in other words, a series of hegemonic shifts that eschew the top-down resolution of political grievances.

Towards the end of his trilogy Robinson gives us a Martian revolution that aspires to the political/historical conditions necessary for a queer futurity. He posits an optimal cultural turn in which the structure of feeling undergoes a radical change, producing a better world. Though accomplished without bloodshed, the ongoing revolution does not nullify all tensions nor does it resolve all disagreements. Rather, it establishes a democratic episteme that finally disposes of the feudal social relations sustained by capitalism (*Blue* 482). The result is a democracy not predicated on the violent suppression of dissent or on a winner-takes-all system of political representation. Robinson's intention, however, is to make plausible a way of looking at history, and ourselves in it, that allows us to see it as open-ended, influenced by ungovernable gestalts, and as contingent on the actions of various disputatious groups as it is on the behaviour of individuals typed as heroic or villainous.[13] When he writes the revolution that creates a new historical reality, he reaches for metaphors quite different from the strident rhetoric of our time. It is '*so complex and nonviolent that it was hard to see it as a revolution at all, at the time; more like a shift in an ongoing argument, a change in the tide, a punctuation of equilibrium*' (*Blue* 743; italics in original).

This Gramscian hegemonic shift gains credibility from its attempt to resignify the racialized, nationalistic dichotomies that attend even the most liberal earlier iterations of the coming race convention in science fiction. Robinson's multi-racial, newly raced Martians are presented as 'natives', the incarnation of utopian 'scientist primitives', many of whom roam the newly created lands of Mars as nomadic 'ferals' (*Blue* 471).[14] They face an invasion that possesses the military and economic might needed to forcibly settle and exploit the new Martian wilderness. This scenario sets the stage for what, in other hands, would be inevitable and exciting bloodshed. Robinson, however, imagines a close to that expectation and the opening of a new set of possibilities:

> *On the coast of Tempe, the new Kampuchean settlers got out of their landers and went to the little shelters that had been dropped with them, just as the First Hundred had, two centuries before. And out of the hill came people wearing furs, and carrying bows and arrows. They had red stone eyeteeth, and their hair was tied in topknots. Here, they said to the settlers, who had bunched before one of their shelters. Let us help you. Put those guns down. We'll show you where you are. You don't need that kind of shelter, it's an old design. That hill you see to*

> *the west is Perepelkin Crater. There's already apple and cherry orchards on the apron, you can take what you need. Look, here are the plans for a disk house, that's the best design for this coast. Then you'll need a marina, and some fishing boats. If you let us use your harbor we'll show you where the truffles grow. Yes, a disk house, see, a Sattelmeier disk house. It's lovely to live out in the open air. You'll see.* (*Blue* 744; italics in original)

This account of first contact works to overturn our expectations. The Martians are presented as 'natives' in the classic, imperial sense. They come with all the signs of racial difference that we have been conditioned to recognize: the topknot, the bow and arrow, furs, and 'red stone eyeteeth' (Robinson's invention). But though the Martians have 'gone native', they are the bearers of a higher scientific and technical culture than the settlers. The gifts they bring include the most crucial knowledge: how to live well off the land. The Kampuchean settlers overturn our expectation that the conquest of space is a project proper to white Europeans. The Martians themselves make no claim to racial purity in the sense that we would understand it. And the implied savagery of their raiment is a lifestyle choice of some people who chose to live with, rather than against, the land. Robinson invokes the modern history of colonialism to indicate both stability and advance in this historical movement.

By describing his new Martians as a new human species, Robinson forces the issue of what we mean by a human future. Occupation of a new land, physical difference, cultural change, economic alternatives, and political dissent are signs of a future in which humankind could proliferate and adapt to ecological niches quite different from those occupied by terrestrial humanity. The limits in such speculation are our unexamined commitments to the status quo, to those possessive investments in race and sex that we inherit from older stories of conquest and settlement. Our theoretical and political leanings notwithstanding, we remain suspended in networks of kinship and places that we cherish. Exchanging these communities for the prospect of a queer futurity requires paying attention to detailed thought experiments that make what is conceivable but unexperienced emotionally resonant, even attractive. Perhaps this is why Robinson chooses to end his trilogy in a way that hails the 'sentimentalism' of Bradbury's half-century-old precedent: 'Waves broke in swift line on the beach, and she walked over the sand toward her friends, in the wind, on Mars, on Mars, on Mars, on Mars, on Mars' (*Blue* 761). It is through this Steinbeckian evocation of a race in place that Robinson's Mars emerges as an emotional reality. The text opens out to offer a future that is unfinished, a work in progress. It is a place, in other words, that a new humanity could grow into.

Robinson has said that it is necessary to rescue utopia as a word and as a way of 'working toward a more egalitarian society' (Foote 56). An integral part of the utopian tradition inherited by science fiction is the idea that humanity might transcend its weaknesses and become something stronger, finer. By framing the *Mars* trilogy in the light of precedents set by writers such as Bulwer-Lytton, Wells, and Bradbury, we gain some purchase on the tradition and consider whether it can be queered to entertain new possibilities. This frame does, however, make Robinson's accomplishment vulnerable to sceptical readings that could fault him for not completely discarding a gender-structured sexuality in his *homo ares*. A paranoid reading would emphasize how, despite his best intentions, Robinson undermines his desire to visualize 'true democracy', reinforcing contemporary investments in heteronormative whiteness. The reparative reading that I have attempted in these pages suggests that intimations of queer futurity can be read even in texts that are otherwise closed to radical reconfigurations of social relations. Given our own possessive investments, we will find it impossible to draft a complete blueprint for a queer future. We are left anticipating it through theories and practices that are resistant, minority, or marginal, but always only partial, momentarily and fleetingly experienced.

Robinson offers our anticipatory project a thought experiment rich enough to prompt an evaluation of possible strategies and strong enough to permit discussion of how to proceed. A reparative reading of his engagement with the coming race subgenre reveals the hopes and dangers it carries. We do not, as a result, find the future. Instead we discover a text that invites us to dream of escaping from heteronormative whiteness. In this way we get an inkling of how a queer futurity might be lived.

Notes

1. Pournelle and Stirling are important figures in the flowering of military science fiction in the 1980s and 1990s. This fiction is a self-conscious extension of the most militaristic of Robert A. Heinlein's space juveniles, *Starship Troopers* (1959). Politically conservative when not completely reactionary, this fiction reinstates a race-based, heteronormative patriarchy even as it provides versions of gender equity and cultural diversity. For a detailed analysis of Pournelle's work, see chapter 7 of my *Beyond Earth*.
2. Jeffrey Allen Tucker's *A Sense of Wonder* presents this argument with well-chosen and convincing evidence.
3. Robinson argues that it is easy 'to imagine a radically different society', but hard to '[imagine] any plausible way of getting from here to there' (Szeman and Whiteman 187). In this Robinson follows Fredric Jameson's insight,

in 'Progress versus Utopia', on the impossibility of imagining the future as something that emerges from our present.

4. Jameson argues that utopia brings fears of loss as well as hopes of gain. As an example, he notes that we are 'addicted' to the sexuality we experience. 'What would it mean', he asks, 'from within our own sexualized existentiality, to imagine a human sexuality that was so unrepressed, yet so utterly divested of the multiple satisfactions of meaning as such?' Invoking Ursula K. Le Guin's *The Left Hand of Darkness* (1969), he answers, '[it would be] an appalling experience' ('Politics' 52–53).
5. Freedman presents with approval Jameson's argument in 'Progress versus Utopia' that science fiction offers no simple prophecy of 'real' social futures (Freedman 55). Rather it makes 'our own present into the determinate past of something yet to come' (Jameson qtd. in Freedman 55 n. 25). If the past is repositioned, so must be the present and therefore any future we might describe.
6. This expectation is so much a part of the operating system of contemporary sf that S. M. Stirling has made a career of lightly ironizing it in a series of alternative-history military adventure novels featuring the Draka. They are the descendants of Confederate expatriates who proceed to enslave all of humankind while turning themselves into a master race through good diet, proper exercise, and genetic engineering (see Stirling's *Marching Through Georgia* [1988] and *Under the Yoke* [1989]). For a more directly satiric fiction of master-race ideology, see Spinrad's *The Iron Dream* (1972).
7. Carl Freedman makes this point as he cites and recasts Tom Moylan's term 'critical utopia'. Thus he establishes the formal issues at stake in the confluence of literary utopia and science fiction (81). See also Moylan's *Demand the Impossible*.
8. With the exception of Ursula K. Le Guin's *The Dispossessed* (1974), it is the British tradition of utopian writing that provides inspiration for Robinson's work ('Kim Stanley Robinson: Green Thoughts' 70). This literary genealogy puts him at odds with the imperialist historiography crafted by Robert A. Heinlein and John W. Campbell in the 1940s. For more on the formulation of future history in American sf, see my *Astrofuturism* (88–90).
9. In an interview with David Seed, Robinson finds that the use of American history as a direct analogue for the future, as in fiction by Heinlein and others, is 'usually unhelpful'. Practically, he explains, this means constructing his futures from the ground up, from 'one moment to the next', avoiding the undoubted attraction of rehearsing familiar stories. In other words, he is concerned that his intellectual and aesthetic projects serve the aim of creating new stories. Robinson indicates this as an abiding feature of his thought in, for instance, Szeman and Whiteman (182, 185, 186). Robinson's specific critique of 'the coherent future history' is given in 'Kim Stanley Robinson Answers Your Questions' and in his interview with Gevers. For Robinson, writing stories about the future has more to do with art than with science or, at least, than with predictive analogies.
10. See Harry Harrison's survey of sexuality in science fiction art, *Great Balls of Fire*.
11. The horror is more than simple repulsion, as a simplistic reading of Joseph Conrad's *The Heart of Darkness* (1899) would imply. Robert Young's examina-

tion of mid-nineteenth-century scientific racism presents the idea of miscegenation as a complex that embraces race mixing as both essential to the creation of civilization and the danger that might lead to its destruction (Young 108). In his analysis of Joseph-Arthur Gobineau's *Essay on the Inequality of Races* (1853–55), Young reveals a theory of sexual relations between races that trades on an analogy with accepted gender roles: whites are figured as 'pre-eminently male groups' and non-whites are 'female or feminized races' (109). In other words, for Gobineau, the fundamental relationship between whites and other races is organized around the pre-scripted roles of male and female. Young elucidates that relation as one in which 'an inter-racial homo-eroticism' is never foregrounded but always implicit (109). Robinson, therefore, attempts to break with this racialist logic by creating a human race for which the analogy between race and sex exists but is neither silent nor horrible. For more on the disciplinary analogy between race and sex in late nineteenth- and early twentieth-century scientific racism, see also Nancy Leys Stepan (5–21).

12. Technological intervention is one of the things that 'makes the body queer', according to Halberstam and Livingston (16). See also Donna Haraway's 'A Cyborg Manifesto', perhaps the paradigmatic celebration of the technologically queered body.
13. In *Blue Mars*, for example, Robinson lists the political parties and interests represented by delegates to the congress that drafts a Martian constitution. The implication is that the future will not be made by a singular authority but will evolve through the collective effort of antagonistic parties to govern together (*Blue* 120–21). Without conflict there can be no democracy.
14. For more on Robinson's thoughts about the reintroduction of 'primitive' habits in 'rethinking the future', see his introduction to *Future Primitive*.

Works Cited

Ahmed, Sara. *Queer Phenomenology: Orientations, Objects, Others*. Durham: Duke UP, 2006.

Aiken, Joan. *The Wolves of Willoughby Chase*. New York: Doubleday, 1962.

Aldiss, Brian W. *Billion Year Spree: The True History of Science Fiction*. 1973. London: Corgi, 1975.

—— Review of James White's *The Watch Below*. *Zenith Speculation* 13 (July 1966): 28–31.

—— *The Shape of Further Things: Speculations on Change*. 1970. London: Corgi, 1974.

Aldiss, Brian W., with David Wingrove. *Trillion Year Spree: The History of Science Fiction*. 1986. New York: Avon, 1988.

Allyn, David. *Make Love, Not War: The Sexual Revolution, An Unfettered History*. New York: Routledge, 2001.

Anderson, Poul. 'Les Amants'. *Startling Stories* 29.1 (Feb. 1953): 134–35.

Armonia, Recondita. 'Flesh of My Flesh'. *Mind and Body*. Ed. Cecilia Tan. Cambridge, MA: Circlet, 2002. 47–55.

Ash, Constance, ed. *Not of Woman Born*. New York: Penguin, 1999.

Ashley, Mike. *Transformations: The Story of the Science-Fiction Magazines from 1950 to 1970*. Vol. 2. *The History of the Science-Fiction Magazines*. Liverpool: Liverpool UP, 2005.

Attebery, Brian. *Decoding Gender in Science Fiction*. New York: Routledge, 2002.

Austin, J. L. *How to Do Things with Words*. Cambridge: Harvard UP, 1962.

Bagemihl, Bruce. *Biological Exuberance: Animal Homosexuality and Natural Diversity*. New York: St Martin's, 1999.

Ballard, J. G. *Crash*. London: Jonathan Cape, 1973.

Barnett, Chad P. 'Reviving Cyberpunk: (Re)Constructing the Subject and Mapping Cyberspace in the Wachowski Brothers' Film *The Matrix*'. *Extrapolation* 41.4 (2000): 359–74.

Baudrillard, Jean. *The Consumer Society: Myths and Structures*. London: Sage, 1998.

Bellamy, Edward. *Looking Backward: 2000–1887*. 1888. New York: Signet, 2000.

Benedikt, Michael, ed. *Cyberspace: First Steps*. Cambridge, MA: MIT, 1994.

Benjamin, Walter. 'The Storyteller'. 1936. *Illuminations*. Trans. Harry Zohn. London: Fontana, 1973. 83–109.

Berger, Albert I. 'Love, Death, and the Atomic Bomb: Sexuality and Community in Science Fiction'. *Science Fiction Studies* 8.3 (Nov. 1981): 280–96.

Berlant, Lauren, and Michael Warner. 'What Does Queer Theory Teach Us About *X*?' *PMLA* 110.3 (May 1995): 343–49.

Bersani, Leo. 'Is the Rectum a Grave?' *AIDS: Cultural Analysis/Cultural Activism*. Ed. Douglas Crimp. Cambridge, MA: MIT, 1988. 197–222.

Bérubé, Allen. 'Marching to a Different Drummer: Lesbian and Gay GIs in World War II'. *Hidden from History: Reclaiming the Gay and Lesbian Past*. Ed. Martin Bauml Duberman, Martha Vicinus, and George Chauncey, Jr. New York: New American Library, 1989. 383–94.

Birken, Lawrence. *Consuming Desire: Sexual Science and the Emergence of a Culture of Abundance, 1871–1914*. Ithaca, NY: Cornell UP, 1988.

Blank, Hanne. *Virgin: The Untouched History*. London: Bloomsbury, 2007.

Boyer, A. Philippe. Review of Robert A. Heinlein's *I Will Fear No Evil*. *Renaissance* 3.1 (Winter 1970): 13–14.

Bozzetto, Roger. '*Esther Rochon*: L'Emergence d'une écrivaine de SF au Québec dans les années 80'. *Au cœur de l'avenir: Littérature d'anticipation dans les textes et à l'écran*. Actes du Séminaire international de L'Aquila (29–30 septembre 2000). Angelus Novus Edizioni, 2002. n.p.

Bradbury, Ray. *The Martian Chronicles*. 1950. New York: Bantam, 1979.

Bradley, Marion Zimmer. *The Shattered Chain*. New York: DAW, 1976.

—— *Thendara House*. New York: DAW, 1983.

Brame, Gloria G., William D. Brame, and Jon Jacobs. *Different Loving: The World of Sexual Dominance and Submission*. New York: Villard, 1995.

Braudy, Leo. 'Fanny Hill and Materialism'. *Eighteenth-Century Studies* 4.1 (1970): 21–40.

Brazier, Donn. 'Stop Shaking the Boat – You're Making a New Wave'. *Godless* 4 (July 1973): 5, 12.

Broderick, Damien. *Reading by Starlight: Postmodern Science Fiction*. New York: Routledge, 1995.

Broege, Valerie. 'Technology and Sexuality in Science Fiction: Creating New Erotic Interfaces'. *Erotic Universe: Sexuality and Fantastic Literature*. Ed. Donald Palumbo. Westport, CT: Greenwood, 1986. 103–29.

Brunette, Peter, and David Wills. 'The Spatial Arts: An Interview with Jacques Derrida'. *Deconstruction and the Visual Arts*. Ed. Peter Brunette and David Wills. Cambridge, MA: Cambridge UP, 1993. 9–32.

Brunner, John. 'Interference on My Wavelength'. *Niekas* 18 (Spring 1967): 23–28. Originally given as a speech at the 1966 Worldcon in Cleveland, Ohio.

—— 'We're Glad Too'. *Startling Stories* 29.1 (Feb. 1953): 129–31.

Bukatman, Scott. *Terminal Identity: The Virtual Subject in Postmodern Science Fiction*. Durham, NC: Duke UP, 1993.

Bulmer, Pamela, and Ken Bulmer. Review of Harlan Ellison's *Dangerous Visions*. *Speculation* 22 (Apr.–May 1969): 8–14.

Bulwer-Lytton, Edward. *The Pilgrims of the Rhine* and *The Coming Race*. Boston: Estes and Lauriat, 1892.

Burdekin, Katherine (as Murray Constantine). *Proud Man*. 1934. New York: Feminist Press, 1993.
Butler, Judith. *Bodies That Matter: On the Discursive Limits of 'Sex'*. New York: Routledge, 1993.
—— 'Critically Queer'. 1993. *Playing with Fire: Queer Politics, Queer Theories*. Ed. Shane Phelan. New York: Routledge, 1997. 11–29.
—— 'The End of Sexual Difference?' 2001. *Undoing Gender*. New York: Routledge, 2004. 174–203.
—— *Gender Trouble: Feminism and the Subversion of Identity*. New York: Routledge, 1990.
—— 'Imitation and Gender Insubordination'. *Inside/Out: Lesbian Theories, Gay Theories*. Ed. Diana Fuss. New York: Routledge, 1991. 13–31.
—— 'Is Kinship Always Already Heterosexual?' *differences: A Journal of Feminist Cultural Studies* 13.1 (2002): 14–45.
—— 'Merely Cultural'. *New Left Review* 227 (Jan.–Feb. 1998): 33–44.
—— 'Performative Acts and Gender Constitution: An Essay in Phenomenology and Feminist Theory'. *Performing Feminisms: Feminist Critical Theory and Theater*. Ed. Sue-Ellen Case. Baltimore, MD: Johns Hopkins UP, 1990. 270–82.
—— *Undoing Gender*. New York: Routledge, 2004.
Butler, Octavia. *Adulthood Rites*. 1988. New York: Warner, 1989.
—— 'Bloodchild'. 1984. *Women of Wonder, The Contemporary Years: Science Fiction by Women from the 1970s to the 1990s*. Ed. Pamela Sargent. New York: Harcourt Brace, 1995. 123–40.
—— *Dawn*. 1987. New York: Warner, 1988.
—— *Imago*. 1989. New York: Warner, 1990.
Cadigan, Pat, ed. *The Ultimate Cyberpunk*. New York: ibooks, 2002.
Cadora, Karen. 'Feminist Cyberpunk'. *Science Fiction Studies* 22.3 (Nov. 1995): 357–72.
Califia, Pat. *Doc and Fluff: The Dystopian Tale of a Girl and Her Biker*. Los Angeles: Alyson , 1990.
—— 'The Hustler'. *Macho Sluts*. Los Angeles: Alyson, 1988. 177–210.
Campbell, John W. 'The Nature of Literature'. *Analog* 76.2 (Oct. 1965): 6–7, 159–62.
—— [as Don A. Stuart[. 'Who Goes There?' 1938. *Science Fiction: The Science Fiction Research Association Anthology*. Ed. Patricia S. Waugh, Charles G. Waugh, and Martin H. Greenberg. New York: HarperCollins, 1988. 84–124.
Campbell, Kirsten. 'The Politics of Kinship'. *Economy and Society* 31.4 (2002): 642–50.
Cavallaro, Dani. *Cyberpunk and Cyberculture: Science Fiction and the Work of William Gibson*. London: Athlone, 2000.
Chan, Edward K. '(Vulgar) Identity Politics in Outer Space: Delany's *Triton* and the Heterotopian Narrative'. *JNT: Journal of Narrative Theory* 31.2 (2001): 180–212.
Charnas, Suzy McKee. *Motherlines*. New York: Putnam, 1978.
—— *Walk to the End of the World*. New York: Ballantine, 1974.
Christian, M. 'Fully Accessorized, Baby'. *Genderflex: Sexy Stories On the Edge and In-Between*. Ed. Cecilia Tan. Cambridge, MA: Circlet, 1996. 143–50.

Clarke, Arthur C. *Childhood's End*. New York: Harcourt, Brace and World, 1953.

Cogswell, Theodore R., ed. *PITFCS: Proceedings of the Institute for Twenty-First Century Studies*. Chicago: Advent, 1992.

Colwell, Chauncey. 'Deleuze and Foucault: Series, Event, Genealogy'. *Theory and Event* 1.2 (1997): pars 1–28. 27 Oct. 2007 http://muse.jhu.edu.proxy2.lib.uwo.ca:2048/journals/theory_and_event/v001/1.2colwell.html.

Congregation for the Doctrine of the Faith. 'Considerations Regarding Proposals to Give Legal Recognition to Unions between Homosexual Persons'. 3 June 2003. 7 July 2006 http://www.vatican.va/roman_curia/congregations/cfaith/documents/rc_con_cfaith_doc_20030731_homosexual-unions_en.html.

Copjec, Joan. 'The Phenomenonal Nonphenomenal: Private Space in *Film Noir*'. *Shades of Noir: A Reader*. Ed. Joan Copjec. London: Verso. 167–97.

Corley, Edwin. 'Re-Enter the Sarge'. *Thrilling Wonder Stories* 41.3 (Feb. 1953): 130–31.

Corteil, Jeanne. *Demand My Writing: Joanna Russ/Feminism/Science Fiction*. Liverpool: Liverpool UP, 1999.

Csicsery-Ronay, Jr., Istvan. 'Dis-Imagined Communities: Science Fiction and the Future of Nations'. *Edging into the Future: Science Fiction and Contemporary Cultural Transformation*. Ed. Veronica Hollinger and Joan Gordon. Philadelphia: U of Pennsylvania P, 2002. 217–37.

—— 'The SF of Theory: Baudrillard and Haraway'. *Science Fiction Studies* 18.3 (Nov. 1991): 387–404.

Curtain, Tyler. 'The "Sinister Fruitiness" of Machines: *Neuromancer*, Internet Sexuality, and the Turing Test'. *Novel Gazing: Queer Readings in Fiction*. Ed. Eve Kosofsky Sedgwick. Durham, NC: Duke UP, 1997. 128–48.

Dann, Jack, and Gardner Dozois, eds. *Clones*. New York: Ace, 1998.

Davis, Ray. 'Delany's Dirt'. *Ash of Stars*. Ed. James Sallis. Jackson, MS: UP of Mississippi, 1996. 162–88.

De Grazia, Edward. *Girls Lean Back Everywhere: The Law of Obscenity and the Assault on Genius*. New York: Vintage, 1993.

Delany, Samuel R. 'Aye, and Gomorrah…'. *Dangerous Visions*. Ed. Harlan Ellison. 1967. New York: Berkley, 1983. 534–44.

—— 'Introduction: Reading and the Written Interview'. *Silent Interviews: On Language, Race, Sex, Science Fiction, and Some Comics*. Hanover, NH: Wesleyan UP, 1994. 1–17.

—— *The Motion of Light in Water: Sex and Science Fiction Writing in the East Village, 1960–1965*. New York: Richard Kasak, 1993.

—— *1984: Selected Letters*. Rutherford: Voyant, 2000.

—— 'Science Fiction and "Literature"'. *Analog* 99 (May 1979): 59–78.

—— 'The Second *Science-Fiction Studies* Interview: Of *Trouble on Triton* and Other Matters'. *Shorter Views: Queer Thoughts and the Politics of the Paraliterary*. Hanover, NH: Wesleyan UP, 1999. 315–49.

—— 'The Semiology of Silence: The *Science-Fiction Studies* Interview'. 1987. *Silent Interviews: On Language, Race, Sex, Science Fiction, and Some Comics*. Hanover, NH: Wesleyan UP, 1994. 21–58.

—— 'Shadows'. *The Jewel-Hinged Jaw: Notes on the Language of Science Fiction*. New York: Dragon, 1977. 51–134.

—— *Silent Interviews: On Language, Race, Sex, Science Fiction, and Some Comics.* Hanover, NH: Wesleyan UP, 1994. 1–17.

—— *Starboard Wine.* New York: Dragon, 1984.

—— *Stars in My Pocket Like Grains of Sand.* New York: Bantam, 1984.

—— 'A Tale of Plagues and Carnivals, or: Some Informal Remarks Towards the Modular Calculus, Part Five'. *Flight from Nevèrÿon.* New York: Bantam, 1984. 181–360.

—— *Trouble on Triton.* 1976 [as *Triton*]. Middletown, CT: Wesleyan UP, 1996.

Delap, Richard. 'SF/Sex Compendium'. *SF Review* 37 (Apr. 1970): 28–29.

—— 'Tomorrow's Libido: Sex and Science Fiction'. *The Alien Critic* 8 (Feb. 1974): 5–12.

Deleuze, Gilles. *Présentation de Sacher-Masoch.* Paris: Minuit, 1967.

del Rey, Lester. 'Art or Artiness?' *Famous Science Fiction* 8 (Fall 1968): 78–86. Originally given as a Guest of Honour speech at the 1968 Lunacon in New York, NY.

—— 'Helen O'Loy'. 1938. *The Science Fiction Hall of Fame.* Ed. Robert Silverberg. New York: Avon, 1970. 62–73.

—— 'Introduction: Forty Years of C.L. Moore'. *The Best of C.L. Moore.* Ed. del Rey. New York: Ballantine, 1975. ix–xv.

D'Emilio, John. 'Capitalism and Gay Identity'. *The Lesbian and Gay Studies Reader.* Ed. Henry Abelove, Michèle Aina Barale, and David Halperin. New York: Routledge, 1993. 167–76.

Dick, Philip K. *Do Androids Dream of Electric Sheep*? 1968. New York: Ballantine, 1982.

—— 'The Story to End All Stories for Harlan Ellison's Anthology *Dangerous Visions*'. *Niekas* 20 (Fall 1968): 47.

Disch, Thomas. 'The Embarrassments of Science Fiction'. *Science Fiction at Large.* Ed. Peter Nicholls. London: Gollancz, 1976. 141–55.

Donawerth, Jane. *Frankenstein's Daughters: Women Writing Science Fiction.* Syracuse, NY: Syracuse UP, 1997.

Dorsey, Candas Jane. 'Letter'. *Extrapolation* 44.2 (2003): 250–51.

—— *A Paradigm of Earth.* New York: Tor, 2002.

Dozois, Gardner. 'Beyond the Golden Age – Part II: The New Wave Years'. *Thrust: Science Fiction in Review* 19 (Winter/Spring 1983): 10–14.

Dubey, Madhu. *Signs and Cities: Black Literary Postmodernism.* Chicago: U of Chicago P, 2003.

Easterbrook, Neil. 'State, Heterotopia: The Political Imagination in Heinlein, Le Guin, and Delany'. *Political Science Fiction.* Ed. Donald M. Hassler and Clyde Wilcox. Columbia: U of South Carolina P, 1997. 43–75.

Ebert, Patricia. 'The Convergence of Postmodern Innovative Fiction and Science Fiction: An Encounter with Samuel R. Delany's Technotopia'. *Poetics Today* 1.4 (1980): 91–104.

Echols, Alice. *Daring to Be Bad: Radical Feminism in America, 1967–1975.* Minneapolis: U Minnesota P, 1989.

Edelman, Lee. *Homographesis: Essays in Gay Literary and Cultural Theory.* New York: Routledge, 1994.

—— 'The Mirror and the Tank: "AIDS", Subjectivity, and the Rhetoric of Activism'.

Homographesis: Essays in Gay Literary and Cultural Theory. New York: Routledge, 1994. 93–117.

—— 'Seeing Things: Representation, the Scene of Surveillance, and the Spectacle of Gay Male Sex'. *Inside/Out: Lesbian Theories, Gay Theories*. Ed. Diana Fuss. New York: Routledge, 1991. 93–116.

—— 'Tearooms and Sympathy: Or, the Epistemology of the Water Closet'. *Homographesis: Essays in Gay Literary and Cultural Theory*. New York: Routledge, 1994. 148–70.

Edwards, Malcolm. Review of Robert A. Heinlein's *I Will Fear No Evil*. *Quicksilver* 1 (Dec. 1970): 28–31.

Eisenstein, Gabe. Review of George Shaw's *Astrosex*. *BeABohema* 10 (Aug. 7, 1970): R4–5.

Ellison, Harlan. 'I Have No Mouth, and I Must Scream'. *If* 17.3 (Mar. 1967): 24–36. Repr. with restored text in *I Have No Mouth and I Must Scream*. New York: Ace, 1983. 1–22.

—— 'Introduction'. Tom Reamy, *San Diego Lightfoot Sue and Other Stories*. New York: Ace, 1983. ix–xxviii.

—— 'Introduction: Thirty-Two Soothsayers'. *Dangerous Visions*. Ed. Harlan Ellison. New York: Doubleday, 1967. xix–xxix.

—— 'Letter to the Editor'. *SF Review* 30 (Apr. 1969): 48–50.

—— 'A Time for Daring'. *Algol* 12 (Mar. 18, 1967): 27–34. Originally given as a Guest of Honour speech at the 1966 Westercon in San Diego, California.

Ellul, Jacques. *The Technological Society*. 1954. Trans. John Wilkinson. New York: Vintage, 1964.

Elshtain, Jean Bethke. 'Against Androgyny'. *Feminism and Equality*. Ed. Anne Phillips. Oxford: Blackwell, 1987. 139–59.

Eskridge, Kelley. 'Alien Jane'. *Century* 1 (1995): 88–102.

—— 'And Salome Danced'. *Little Deaths*. Ed. Ellen Datlow. London: Millennium, 1994. 265–78.

—— 'Dangerous Space'. *Dangerous Space*. Seattle, WA: Aqueduct, 2007. 144–230.

—— 'The Eye of the Storm'. *Sirens and Other Demon Lovers*. Ed. Ellen Datlow. New York: HarperPrism, 1998. 204–34.

—— *Solitaire*. New York: Eos, 2002.

Ewald, François. 'Norms, Discipline, and the Law'. *Representations* 30 (1990): 138–61.

Fairbairns, Zoë. *Benefits*. London: Virago, 1979.

Farmer, Philip José. 'A Letter to Mr. Lem'. *SF Commentary* 25 (Dec. 1971): 19–26.

—— 'Reap'. *SF Review* 28 (1968): 4–16. Originally given as a Guest of Honour speech at the 1968 Baycon in Berkeley, California.

Fausto-Sterling, Anne. 'The Five Sexes: Why Male and Female are Not Enough'. *The Sciences* 33.2 (1993): 20–25.

Feenberg, Andrew. *Transforming Technology: A Critical Theory Revisited*. 1991. Rev. 2nd ed. Oxford: Oxford UP, 2002.

Fekete, John. '*The Dispossessed* and *Triton*: Act and System in Utopian Science Fiction'. *Science Fiction Studies* 6.2 (July 1979): 129–43.

Fernbach, Amanda. 'The Fetishization of Masculinity in Science Fiction: The Cyborg and the Console Cowboy'. *Science Fiction Studies* 27.2 (July 2000): 234–55.

Firestone, Shulamith. *The Dialectic of Sex: The Case for Feminist Revolution*. London: Women's Press, 1970.

Floyd, Kevin. 'Making History: Marxism, Queer Theory, and Contradiction in the Future of American Studies'. *Cultural Critique* 40 (1998): 167–201.

Foote, Bud. 'A Conversation with Kim Stanley Robinson'. *Science Fiction Studies* 62.1 (Mar. 1994): 61–66.

Forbes, Caroline. *The Needle on Full*. London: Onlywomen, 1985.

Forster, E. M. 'The Machine Stops'. 1909. *Science Fiction: The Science Fiction Research Association Anthology*. Ed. Patricia S. Warrick, Charles G. Waugh, and Martin H. Greenberg. New York: Harper & Row, 1988. 41–63.

Foster, Thomas. *The Souls of Cyberfolk: Posthumanism as Vernacular Theory*. Minneapolis: U of Minnesota P, 2005.

—— '"Trapped by the Body"? Telepresence Technologies and Transgendered Performance in Feminist and Lesbian Rewritings of Cyberpunk Fiction'. *Modern Fiction Studies* 43.3 (1997): 708–42.

Foucault, Michel. *The History of Sexuality, Vol. 1: An Introduction*. Trans. Robert Hurley. 1978. New York: Vintage, 1980.

—— 'Nietzsche, Genealogy, History'. *Language, Counter-Memory, Practice: Selected Essays and Interviews*. Ed. D. F. Bouchard. Ithaca, NY: Cornell UP, 1977. 139–64.

—— 'On the Genelogy of Ethics: An Overview of Work in Progress'. *Michel Foucault: Beyond Structuralism and Hermeneutics*. Ed. Hubert Dreyfus and Paul Rabinow. 2nd ed. Chicago: Chicago UP, 1988. 229–52.

—— *The Use of Pleasure: The History of Sexuality, Vol. 2*. 1984. Trans. Robert Hurley. New York: Vintage, 1986.

Freedman, Carl. *Critical Theory and Science Fiction*. Hanover, NH: Wesleyan UP, 2000.

Freud, Sigmund. 'On Narcissism: An Introduction'. 1914. *The Freud Reader*. Ed. Peter Gay. New York: Norton, 1989. 545–62.

—— *On Sexuality: Three Essays on the Theory of Sexuality and Other Works*. 1905. The Pelican Freud Library. Vol. 7. Trans. James Strachey. Ed. Angela Richards. New York: Penguin, 1953.

—— 'Sadism and Masochism' [excerpted from *Three Essays on the Theory of Sexuality*. 1905]. *S & M: Studies in Dominance and Submission*. Ed. Tomas S. Weinberg. Amherst, NY: Prometheus, 1995. 33–35.

Frontain, K. M. *Bound in Stone*. [n.p.]: Thinkharder Press, 2005.

Gaard, Greta. 'Toward a Queer Ecofeminism'. *Hypatia* 12.1 (1997): 114–38.

Gaard, Greta, ed. *Ecofeminism: Women, Animals, Nature*. Philadelphia: Temple UP, 1993.

Gagnier, Regenia. *Idylls of the Marketplace: Oscar Wilde and the Victorian Public*. Aldershot: Scolar, 1987.

Gallagher, Catherine. 'George Eliot: Immanent Victorian'. *Representations* 90 (2005): 61–74.

—— 'The Trouble With Characters'. *British and American Fiction to 1900* 9.2 (Winter 2002): 283–302.

Garber, Eric, and Lyn Paleo, eds. *Uranian Worlds: A Guide to Alternative Sexuality in Science Fiction, Fantasy, and Horror*. 1983. Rev. 2nd ed. Boston: G. K. Hall, 1990.

Gearheart, Sally Miller. *The Wanderground: Stories of the Hill Women*. 1978. New York: Persephone, 1980.

Geis, Richard E. 'Delusions'. *Psychotic* 25 (May 1968): 17–19.

Georges, Karoline. *La mue de l'hermaphrodite*. Montréal: Leméac, 2001.

Gevers, Nick. 'Wilderness, Utopia, History: An Interview with Kim Stanley Robinson'. *Infinity Plus* (May 2001). 19 April 2005 http://www.infinityplus.co.uk/nonfiction/intksr.htm.

Gibson, William. 'Academy Leader'. *Cyberspace: First Steps*. Ed. Michael Benedikt. Cambridge, MA: MIT, 1991. 27–29.

—— *Count Zero*. New York: Ace, 1987.

—— 'Johnny Mnemonic'. 1981. *Burning Chrome*. New York: Ace, 1987. 1–22.

—— *Mona Lisa Overdrive*. New York: Bantam, 1989.

—— *Neuromancer*. New York: Ace, 1984.

Gilliland, Alexis A. 'The Pornography of Science Fiction'. *Outworlds* 5 (Sept.–Oct. 1970): 141–42.

Gillis, Stacy, ed. *The Matrix Trilogy: Cyberpunk Reloaded*. London: Wallflower, 2005.

Gordon, Joan. 'Yin and Yang Duke It Out'. 1990. *Storming the Reality Studio: A Casebook of Cyberpunk and Postmodern Science Fiction*. Ed. Larry McCaffery. Durham, NC: Duke UP, 1994. 196–202.

Goto, Hiromi. *The Kappa Child*. Edmonton: Red Deer, 2003.

Grace, Dominick M. 'Rereading Lester del Rey's "Helen O'Loy"'. *Science Fiction Studies* 20.1 (Mar. 1993): 45–51.

Gray, Chris Hables. *Cyborg Citizen: Politics in the Posthuman Age*. New York: Routledge, 2001.

Greenland, Colin. *The Entropy Exhibition: Michael Moorcock and the British 'New Wave' in Science Fiction*. London: Routledge & Kegan Paul, 1983.

Greyson, John, dir. *Zero Patience*. Normand Fauteux, John Robinson. Zero Patience Productions, 1993.

Griffith, Nicola. *Always*. New York: Riverhead, 2007.

—— *Ammonite*. New York: Del Rey, 1993.

—— *The Blue Place*. New York: Avon, 1998.

—— 'Living Fiction, Storybook Lives.' Oct. 1998. 1 Nov. 2007 http://www.nicolagriffith.com/storybook.html.

—— *Slow River*. New York: Del Rey, 1995.

—— *Stay*. New York: Nan A. Talese, 2002.

Griffith, Nicola, and Stephen Pagel. 'Introduction'. *Bending the Landscape, Science Fiction: Original Gay and Lesbian Writing*. Ed. Griffith and Pagel. New York: Overlook, 1998. 7–10.

Griffith, Nicola, and Stephen Pagel, eds. *Bending the Landscape, Science Fiction: Original Gay and Lesbian Writing*. New York: Overlook, 1998.

Griggers, Cathy. 'Lesbian Bodies in the Age of (Post)mechnical Reproduction'. *Fear of a Queer Planet: Queer Politics and Social Theory*. Ed. Michael Warner. Minneapolis: U of Minnesota P, 1993. 178–92.

Grosz, Elizabeth. *Volatile Bodies: Toward a Corporeal Feminism*. Sydney: Allen and Unwin, 1994.

Gudding, Gabriel. 'The Phenotype/Genotype Distinction and the Disappearance of the Body'. *Journal of the History of Ideas* 57.3 (1996): 525–45.

Hacking, Ian. 'Making Up People'. *Reconstructing Individualism*. Ed. Thomas C. Heller, Morton Sosna, and David E. Wellbery. Stanford, CA: Stanford UP, 1986. 222–36.

Halberstam, Judith. 'Automating Gender: Postmodern Feminism in the Age of the Intelligent Machine'. *Feminist Studies* 17.3 (Fall 1991): 439–60.

—— *Female Masculinity*. Durham: Duke UP, 1998.

Halberstam, Judith, and Ira Livingston, eds. *Posthuman Bodies*. Bloomington: Indiana UP, 1995.

Haldane, J. B. S. *Possible Worlds and Other Essays*. London: Chatto and Windus, 1927.

Hall, Sandi. *The Godmothers*. London: Women's Press, 1982.

Hallas, Roger. 'The Genealogical Pedagogy of John Greyson's *Zero Patience*'. *Canadian Journal of Film Studies* 12.1 (Spring 2003): 16–37.

Hambly, Barbara. *The Armies of Daylight*. New York: Del Rey, 1983.

—— *The Time of the Dark*. New York: Del Rey, 1982.

—— *The Walls of Air*. New York: Del Rey, 1983.

Hand, Elizabeth. *The Glimmering*. Scranton, PA: HarperCollins, 1997.

Haney II, William S. *Cyberculture, Cyborgs and Science Fiction: Consciousness and the Posthuman*. Amsterdam: Rodopi, 2005.

Hanson, Ellis. 'Undead'. *Inside/Out: Lesbian Theories, Gay Theories*. Ed. Diana Fuss. New York: Routledge, 1991. 324–40.

Haraway, Donna J. 'Birth of the Kennel: A Lecture by Donna Haraway.' Aug. 2000. 9 Apr. 2007 http://www.egs.edu/faculty/haraway/haraway-birth-of-the-kennel-2000.html.

—— *The Companion Species Manifesto: Dogs, People, and Significant Otherness*. Chicago: Prickly Paradigm, 2003.

—— 'A Cyborg Manifesto: Science, Technology and Socialist-Feminism in the Late Twentieth Century'. 1985. Rev. *Simians, Cyborgs, and Women: The Reinvention of Nature*. New York: Routledge, 1991. 149–81.

—— 'A Game of Cat's Cradle: Science Studies, Feminist Theory, Cultural Studies'. *Configurations* 2.1 (Winter 1994): 59–71.

—— *Modest_Witness@Second_Millennium. FemaleMan©_Meets_OncoMouse™*. New York: Routledge, 1997.

—— *Simians, Cyborgs and Women: The Reinvention of Nature*. New York: Routledge, 1991.

Harrison, Harry. *Great Balls of Fire: An Illustrated History of Sex in Science Fiction*. London: Pierrot, 1977.

—— 'Letter to the Editor'. *Granfalloon* 6 (Jan. 1969): 51–52.

—— 'We Are Sitting on Our…'. *SF Horizons* 1 (Spring 1964): 39–42. Originally given as a speech at the 1963 Eastercon in Peterborough, England.

Hart, Lynda. *Between the Body and the Flesh: Performing Sadomasochism*. New York: Columbia UP, 1997.

Harvey, David. *The Condition of Postmodernity: An Enquiry into the Origins of Cultural Change*. Oxford: Blackwell, 1989.

Hayles, N. Katherine. *How We Became Posthuman: Virtual Bodies in Cybernetics, Literature, and Informatics*. Chicago: U of Chicago P, 1999.

—— 'The Life Cycle of Cyborgs: Writing the Posthuman'. *A Question of Identity:*

Women, Science, and Literature. Ed. Marina Benjamin. New Brunswick, NJ: Rutgers UP, 1993. 152–70.

—— 'Searching for Common Ground'. *Reinventing Nature? Responses to Postmodern Deconstruction*. Ed. Michael E. Soule and Gary Lease. Washington, DC: Island, 1995. 47–53.

Heidegger, Martin. 'The Question Concerning Technology'. 1954. *The Question Concerning Technology and Other Essays*. Trans. William Lovitt. New York: Harper & Row, 1977. 3–35.

Heinlein, Robert A. *I Will Fear No Evil*. New York: Ace, 1970.

—— *Starship Troopers*. 1959. New York: Ace, 1987.

Hemmingson, Michael. 'An Interview with Earl Kemp'. *Sin-a-Rama: Sleaze Sex Paperbacks of the Sixties*. Ed. Brittany A. Daley. Los Angeles: Feral House, 2004. 36–39.

Heuser, Sabine. *Virtual Geographies: Cyberpunk at the Intersection of the Postmodern and Science Fiction*. New York: Rodopi, 2003.

Hill, Douglas, ed. *The Shape of Sex to Come*. London: Pan, 1978.

Hird, Myra J. *Sex, Gender, and Science*. Basingstoke: Palgrave Macmillan, 2004.

Hollinger, Veronica. '(Re)reading Queerly: Science Fiction, Feminism, and the Defamiliarization of Gender'. *Science Fiction Studies* 26.1 (Mar. 1999): 23–40.

—— 'The Utopia of the Perverse: An Exercise in "Transgressive Reinscription"'. *Femspec* 2.1 (2000): 30–37.

Hollinger, Veronica, and Joan Gordon. 'Introduction: Edging into the Future'. *Edging into the Future: Science Fiction and Contemporary Cultural Transformation*. Ed. Hollinger and Gordon. Philadelphia: U of Pennsylvania P, 2002. 1–8.

Hopkinson, Nalo. *Brown Girl in the Ring*. New York: Warner, 1998.

—— 'Dark Ink: SF Writers of Colour.' 1998. 10 February 2008 http://www.nalohopkinson.com/writing/on_writing/dark_ink/essay_dark_ink.html.

—— 'Fisherman'. *Skin Folk*. New York: Warner, 2001. 119–46.

—— 'Ganger (Ball Lightning)'. *Dark Matter: A Century of Speculative Fiction from the African Diaspora*. Ed. Sheree R. Thomas. New York: Warner, 2000. 134–51.

—— 'The Glass Bottle Trick.' *Whispers From the Cotton Tree Root: Caribbean Fabulist Fiction*. Ed. Nalo Hopkinson. Montpelier, VT: Invisible Cities, 2000. 257–72.

—— 'A Habit of Waste'. 1996. *Skin Folk*. New York: Warner, 2001. 183–202.

—— *Midnight Robber*. New York: Warner, 2000.

—— *The New Moon's Arms*. New York: Warner/Hachett, 2007.

—— *The Salt Roads*. New York: Warner Books, 2003.

—— *Skin Folk*. New York: Warner, 2001.

Hopkinson, Nalo, ed. *Mojo: Conjure Stories*. New York: Warner, 2003.

Hopkinson, Nalo, and Uppinder Mehan, eds. *So Long Been Dreaming: Postcolonial Science Fiction and Fantasy*. Vancouver, BC: Arsenal Pulp Press, 2004.

Huxley, Aldous. *Brave New World*. 1932. New York: Harper & Row, 1989.

Huyssen, Andreas. 'The Vamp and the Machine'. *After the Great Divide: Modernism, Mass Culture, Postmodernism*. Bloomington: Indiana UP, 1986. 65–81.

Ingraham, Chrys. 'The Heterosexual Imaginary: Feminist Sociology and Theories of Gender'. *Sociological Theory* 12.2 (July 1994): 203–19.

Irwin, William, ed. *The Matrix and Philosophy: Welcome to the Desert of the Real*. Chicago: Open Court, 2002.

Jackson, Earl. *Strategies of Deviance: Studies in Gay Male Representation*. Bloomington: Indiana UP, 1995.
Jagose, Annamarie. *Queer Theory: An Introduction*. New York: New York UP, 1996.
Jameson, Fredric. *Archaeologies of the Future: The Desire Called Utopia and Other Science Fictions*. London: Verso, 2005.
—— 'The Politics of Utopia'. *New Left Review* 25 (Jan.–Feb. 2004): 35–54.
—— *Postmodernism, or, the Cultural Logic of Late Capitalism*. London: Verso, 1991.
—— 'Progress versus Utopia; or, Can We Imagine the Future?' *Science Fiction Studies* 9.2 (July 1982): 147–58.
Jenkins, Henry. 'Out of the Closet and Into the Universe: Queers and *Star Trek*'. *Science Fiction Audiences: Watching* Doctor Who *and* Star Trek. Ed. John Tulloch and Henry Jenkins. New York: Routledge, 1995. 237–65.
Jesser, Nancy. 'Blood, Genes, and Gender in Octavia Butler's *Kindred* and *Dawn*'. *Extrapolation* 43.1 (2002): 36–67.
Jones, Gwyneth. *Divine Endurance*. London: Allen and Unwin, 1984.
—— *Escape Plans*. London: Allen and Unwin, 1986.
—— *Kairos*. London: Unwin Hyman, 1988.
Jones, Langdon. 'I Remember, Anita…'. *New Worlds* 144 (Sept.–Oct. 1964): 69–80.
Kaldera, Raven. 'Cyberfruit Swamp'. *Genderflex: Sexy Stories on the Edge and In-Between*. Ed. Cecilia Tan. Cambridge, MA: Circlet, 1996. 11–24.
Kerr, Peg. *The Wild Swans*. New York: Warner, 2001.
Ketterer, David. *Canadian Science Fiction and Fantasy*. Bloomington: Indiana UP, 1992.
Kilgore, De Witt Douglas. *Astrofuturism: Science, Race, and Visions of Utopia in Space*. Philadelphia: U of Pennsylvania P, 2003.
—— *Beyond Earth: Popular Science, Science Fiction, and the Cultural Construction of an American Future in Space*. Ann Arbor, MI: UMI, 1994.
Kinsman, Gary. *The Regulation of Desire: Homo and Hetero Sexualities*. Montreal: Black Rose, 1996.
Kolko, Beth E., Lisa Nakamura, and Gilbert B. Rodman, eds. *Race in Cyberspace*. New York: Routledge, 2000.
Kristeva, Julia. 'Woman Can Never Be Defined'. 1974. Trans. Marilyn A. August. *New French Feminisms: An Anthology*. Ed. Elaine Marks and Isabelle de Courtivron. New York: Schocken, 1981. 137–41.
Lacan, Jacques. *Écrits*. 1966. Paris: Éditions du seuil, 1999.
Lancaster, Roger. *The Trouble with Nature: Sex in Science and Popular Culture*. Berkeley: U of California P, 2003.
Landon, Brooks. *Science Fiction after 1900: From the Steam Man to the Stars*. New York: Twayne, 1997.
Larbalestier, Justine. *The Battle of the Sexes in Science Fiction*. Middletown, CT: Wesleyan UP, 2002.
Lasswitz, Kurd. *Auf zwei Planeten*. 1897. Carbondale, IL: Southern Illinois UP, 1971.
Latham, Rob. *Consuming Youth: Vampires, Cyborgs, and the Culture of Consumption*. Chicago: U of Chicago P, 2002.
—— 'The New Wave'. *A Companion to Science Fiction*. Ed. David Seed. London: Blackwell, 2005. 202–16.

—— '*New Worlds* and the New Wave in Fandom: Fan Culture and the Reshaping of Science Fiction in the Sixties'. *Vector: The Critical Journal of the British Science Fiction Association* (July/Aug. 2005). Rpt. *Extrapolation* 47.2 (Summer 2006): 296–315.

Latour, Bruno. *We Have Never Been Modern*. 1991. Trans. Catherine Porter. Cambridge, MA: Harvard UP, 1993.

Leblanc, Lauraine. 'Razor Girls: Genre and Gender in Cyberpunk Fiction'. *Women and Language* 20.1 (1997): 71–76.

Lefort, Claude. *Democracy and Political Theory*. Trans. David Macey. Cambridge: Polity, 1988.

Le Guin, Ursula K. 'American Sf and the Other'. *Science Fiction Studies* 2.3 (1975): 208–10.

—— *A Fisherman of the Inland Sea*. New York: Harper Prism, 1994.

—— 'Is Gender Necessary?' 1976. *The Language of the Night: Essays on Fantasy and Science Fiction*. Ed. Susan Wood. New York: Putnam, 1979. 161–69.

—— 'Is Gender Necessary? Redux.' 1976/1987. *Dancing at the Edge of the World: Thoughts on Words, Women, Places*. New York: Grove, 1989. 7–16.

—— *The Left Hand of Darkness*. New York: Ace, 1969.

—— 'Nine Lives'. 1969. *Clones*. Ed. Jack Dann and Gardner Dozois. New York: Ace, 1998. 1–30.

—— 'Thea and I'. *Entropy Negative* 5 (1972): n.p.

Lem, Stanislaw. 'Sex in Science Fiction'. *Quarber Merkur* 9.1 (July 1971). Trans. Franz Rottensteiner. *SF Commentary* 22 (July 1971): 2–10, 40–49.

Lewis, Steve. 'Editing or Censorship? An Open Letter to John W. Campbell and His Reply'. *Granfalloon* 5 (Nov. 1968): 13–16.

Lindskold, Jane. *Marks of Our Brothers*. New York: Avon, 1995.

Lipsitz, George. *The Possessive Investment in Whiteness: How White People Profit from Identity Politics*. Philadelphia: Temple UP, 1998.

Livia, Anna. *Accommodation Offered*. London: Women's Press, 1986.

Luckhurst, Roger. *Science Fiction*. Malden, MA: Polity, 2005.

Lukács, Georg. *The Theory of the Novel*. 1920. Trans. Anna Bostock. London: Merlin, 1971.

Lupton, Deborah. 'The Embodied Computer User'. *Cyberspace/Cyberbodies/Cyberpunk: Cultures of Technological Embodiment*. Ed. Mike Featherstone and Roger Burrows. London: Sage, 1995. 97–112.

Lynn, Elizabeth A. *The Dancers of Arun*. New York: Berkley, 1979.

—— *A Different Light*. New York: Berkley, 1978.

—— *The Northern Girl*. New York: Berkley, 1981.

—— *The Watchtower*. New York: Berkley Putnam, 1979.

Macintyre, Ben. 'Of human bondage: books can lead to a novel sort of enslavement'. *The Times* (UK) (27 May 2006): 20.

Mahon, Michael. *Foucault's Nietzschean Genealogy: Truth, Power, and the Subject*. New York: SUNY UP, 1992.

Margulis, Lynn, and Dorian Sagan. *What is Sex?* New York: Simon and Schuster, 1997.

Martins, Susana S. 'Revising the Future in *The Female Man*'. *Science Fiction Studies* 32.3 (Nov. 2005): 405–22.

Massé, Michelle. '"All you have to do is know what you want": Individual Expectations in *Triton*'. *Coordinates: Placing Science Fiction and Fantasy*. Ed. George Slusser, Eric Rabkin, and Robert Scholes. Carbondale: Southern Illinois UP, 1983. 49–64.

—— *In the Name of Love: Women, Masochism, and the Gothic*. Ithaca, NY: Cornell UP, 1992.

McCaffery, Larry, ed. *Storming the Reality Studio: A Casebook of Cyberpunk and Postmodern Fiction*. Durham, NC: Duke UP, 1991.

McCall, Jana. 'A Self-Made Woman'. *Color of Pain, Shade of Pleasure*. Ed. Cecilia Tan. Cambridge, MA: Circlet, 1995. 103–12.

McGuirk, Carol. 'The Rediscovery of Cordwainer Smith'. *Science Fiction Studies* 28.2 (July 2001): 161–200.

McIntyre, Vonda. *Dreamsnake*. Boston: Houghton, Mifflin, 1978.

—— *The Exile Waiting*. New York: Nelson Doubleday, 1975.

McQuire, Scott. 'Space for Rent in the Last Suburb'. *Prefiguring Cyberculture: An Intellectual History*. Ed. Darren Tofts, Annemarie Jonson, and Allesio Cavallaro. Cambridge, MA: MIT, 2002. 166–78.

McRae, Shannon. 'Flesh Made Word: Sex, Text and the Virtual Body'. *Internet Culture*. Ed. David Porter. New York: Routledge, 1997. 73–86.

Merchant, Carolyn. *The Death of Nature: Women, Ecology, and the Scientific Revolution*. San Francisco: Harper & Row, 1980.

Merrick, H. 'Alien(ating) Naturecultures: Feminist SF as Creative Science Studies'. *Reconstruction: Studies in Contemporary Culture* 5.4 (Fall 2005). 9 April 2007 http://reconstruction.eserver.org/054/merrick.shtml.

Merril, Judith. 'Books'. *The Magazine of Fantasy and Science Fiction* 32.3 (Mar. 1967): 20–27.

—— 'Books'. *The Magazine of Fantasy and Science Fiction* 33.6 (Dec. 1967): 28–34.

Midori. *Wild Side Sex: The Book of Kink*. Los Angeles: Daedalus, 2005.

Miller, Elaine, and Gary Switch. 'Safe, Sane, and Consensual – SSC – Risk-Aware Consensual Kink – RACK – VancouverLeather.Com.' *Vancouver Leather*. 2002. 28 October 2004 http://vancouverleather.com/bdsm/ssc_rack.html.

Mitchison, Naomi. *Memoirs of a Spacewoman*. 1962. London: Women's Press, 1985.

Mines, Samuel. 'The Ether Vibrates'. *Startling Stories* 27.1 (Aug. 1952): 6, 8, 130–45.

—— 'The Reader Speaks'. *Thrilling Wonder Stories* 42.1 (Apr. 1953): 6, 134–45.

—— 'Those Four-Letter Words'. *Luna Monthly* 2 (July 1969): 9, 18.

Mitchell, David T., and Sharon L. Snyder. *Narrative Prosthesis: Disability and the Dependencies of Discourse*. Ann Arbor, MI: U of Michigan P, 2000.

Mohanraj, Mary Anne. 'Nalo Hopkinson'. *Strange Horizons*. 1 Sept. 2000. 6 May 2007 http://www.strangehorizons.com/2000/20000901/NaloHopkinson_Interview.shtml.

Mohin, Lilian, and Sheila Shulman, eds. *The Reach and Other Stories*. London: Onlywomen, 1984.

Moorcock, Michael. 'Introduction'. *New Worlds: An Anthology*. Ed. Moorcock. London: Flamingo, 1983. 9–26.

—— 'A New Literature for the Space Age'. *New Worlds* 142 (May-June 1964): 2–3.

—— 'Play with Feeling'. *New Worlds* 129 (Apr. 1963): 2–3, 123–27.
—— 'Symbols for the Sixties'. *New Worlds* 148 (Mar. 1965): 2–3, 25.
Moore, C. L. 'No Woman Born'. 1944. *The Best of C. L. Moore*. Ed. Lester del Rey. New York: Ballantine, 1975. 236–88.
Morehead, Rev. C. M. 'And More'. *Thrilling Wonder Stories* 42.3 (Aug. 1953): 135.
Moylan, Tom. *Demand the Impossible: Science Fiction and the Utopian Imagination*. New York: Methuen, 1986.
Mulvey, Laura. 'Visual Pleasure and Narrative Cinema'. 1975. *The Sexual Subject: A Screen Reader in Sexuality*. London: Routledge, 1992. 22–34.
Nelson, Alondra. '"Making the Impossible Possible": An Interview with Nalo Hopkinson'. *Social Text* 20 (Summer 2002): 97–113. Special issue on Afrofuturism.
Nixon, Nicola. 'Cyberpunk: Preparing the Ground for Revolution or Keeping the Boys Satisfied?'. *Science Fiction Studies* 19.2 (July 1992): 219–35.
Notkin, Debbie, and the Secret Feminist Cabal, eds. *Flying Cups and Saucers: Gender Explorations in Science Fiction and Fantasy.* Cambridge, MA: Edgewood, 1998.
Odzer, Cleo. *Virtual Spaces: Sex and the Cyber Citizen*. New York: Berkley, 1997.
Offutt, Andrew J. 'Extrapolation Problematical'. *Energumen* 9 (Sept. 1971): 26–28.
—— 'Grumlin'. *Citadel* 5 (Winter 1972): 4–5.
—— 'SF & F for the Big Kids'. *Double:Bill* 21 (Fall 1969): 35–38.
Olsen, Lance. 'The Shadow of Spirit in William Gibson's Matrix Trilogy'. *Extrapolation* 32.3 (1991): 278–89.
Orwell, George. *1984*. London: Secker and Warburg, 1949.
Palmer, David R. *Emergence*. New York: Bantam, 1984.
Palumbo, Donald, ed. *Eros in the Mind's Eye: Sexuality and the Fantastic in Art and Film*. Westport, CT: Greenwood, 1986.
—— *Erotic Universe: Sexuality and Fantastic Literature*. Westport, CT: Greenwood, 1986.
Panshin, Alexei. *Rite of Passage*. New York: Ace, 1968.
Pearl, Monica B. 'AIDS and the New Queer Cinema'. *New Queer Cinema: A Critical Reader*. Ed. Michele Aaron. New Brunswick, NJ: Rutgers UP, 2004. 23–37.
—— '*Zero Patience*: AIDS, Music, and Reincarnation Films'. *Musicals: Hollywood and Beyond*. Ed. Bill Marshall and Robynn Stilwell. Bristol: Intellect, 2000. 141–46.
Pearson, Wendy. 'Alien Cryptographies: The View from Queer'. *Science Fiction Studies* 26.1 (Mar. 1999): 1–22.
—— '"I, the Undying": The Vampire of Subjectivity and the Aboriginal "I" in Mudrooroo's *The Undying*'. *Mongrel Signatures: Reflections on the Work of Mudrooroo*. Ed. Annalisa Oboe. Amsterdam: Rodopi, 2003. 185–202.
—— 'The Queer as Traitor, the Traitor as Queer: Denaturalizing Sexuality, Gender and Nationhood'. *Flashes of the Fantastic: Selected Essays from the Nineteenth International Conference on the Fantastic in the Arts*. Ed. David Ketterer. Westport, CT: Greewood, 2004. 77–91.
—— 'Science Fiction and Queer Theory'. *The Cambridge Companion to Science Fiction*. Ed. Edward James and Farah Mendlesohn. Cambridge: Cambridge UP, 2003. 149–60.

—— 'Science Fiction as Pharmacy: Plato, Derrida, Ryman'. *Foundation: The International Review of Science Fiction* 85 (Autumn 2002): 66–75.

—— 'Sex/uality and the Hermaphrodite in Science Fiction, or, the Revenge of Herculine Barbin'. *Edging into the Future: Science Fiction and Contemporary Cultural Transformation.* Ed. Veronica Hollinger and Joan Gordon. Philadelphia: U of Pennsylvania P, 2002. 108–23.

Perry, Tom. 'Cardshark Campbell Meets Sex and the Common Man'. *Trumpet* 4 (Apr. 1966): 6–10.

Pierce, John J. 'The Devaluation of Values'. *Algol* 16 (Dec. 1970): 4–11.

—— 'Letter to the Editor'. *SF Review* 29 (Jan. 1969): 44–45.

Piercy, Marge. *Woman on the Edge of Time.* New York: Fawcett Crest, 1976.

Platt, Charles. 'Non-Category Fiction'. *Speculation* 23 (July–Aug. 1969): 22–26.

—— 'The Strange Relations of Philip José Farmer'. *Zenith Speculation* 7 (Dec. 1964): 34–38.

Polhemus, Ted. 'In the Supermarket of Style'. *The Clubcultures Reader: Readings in Popular Cultural Studies.* Ed. Steve Redhead, Derek Wynne, and Justin O'Connor. Oxford: Blackwell, 1997. 148–51.

Pollack, Rachel. *Unquenchable Fire.* London: Century, 1988.

Porter, Theodore M. *The Rise of Statistical Thinking, 1820–1900.* Princeton: Princeton UP, 1986.

Pournelle, Jerry, and S.M. Stirling. *Prince of Sparta.* New York: Baen, 1993.

Pringle, David. '*Bug Jack Barron*: A Review'. *Speculation* 20 (Jan.1969): 3–6.

Prosser, Jay. *Second Skins: The Body Narratives of Transsexuality.* New York: Columbia UP, 1998.

Purdom, Tom. 'Censorship, Money, and Crazy Ideas'. *Niekas* 6 (Sept. 1963): 9–14.

Reamy, Tom. *Blind Voices.* 1978. New York: Berkley, 1979.

—— 'San Diego Lightfoot Sue'. 1975. *San Diego Lightfoot Sue and Other Stories.* New York: Ace, 1983. 40–66.

—— 'Under the Hollywood Sign'. 1975. *San Diego Lightfoot Sue and Other Stories.* New York: Ace, 1983. 94–141.

Reinelt, Janelle G. 'The Politics of Discourse: Performativity meets Theatricality'. *SubStance* 31.2-3 (2002): 201–15.

Rheingold, Howard. *Virtual Reality.* New York: Summit, 1991.

Robinson, Kim Stanley. *Blue Mars.* New York: Bantam, 1997.

—— *Green Mars.* New York: Bantam, 1994.

—— 'Kim Stanley Robinson Answers Your Questions'. *Science Fiction Weekly* 23.2 (17 June 1996). 3 March 2000 http://www.scifi.com/sfw/issue23/interview.html.

—— 'Kim Stanley Robinson: Green Thoughts'. *Locus* 28.2 (Aug. 1992): 4, 69–70.

—— *Red Mars.* New York: Bantam, 1993.

Robinson, Kim Stanley, ed. *Future Primitive: The New Ecotopias.* New York: Tor, 1994.

Rochon, Esther. *Lame.* Montréal: Québec-Amérique, 1995.

—— 'Présentation subjective des Chroniques infernales.' *Au cœur de l'avenir: Littérature d'anticipation dans les textes et à l'écran.* Actes du Séminaire international de L'Aquila (Italy), 29–30 septembre 2000. Angelus Novus Edizioni, 2002. n.p.

Rosen, Ruth. *The World Split Open: How the Modern Women's Movement Changed America*. New York: Penguin, 2000.

Roughgarden, Joan. *Evolution's Rainbow: Diversity, Gender, and Sexuality in Nature and People*. Berkeley: U of California P, 2004.

Rubin, Gayle. 'Thinking Sex: Notes for a Radical Theory of the Politics of Sexuality'. *The Lesbian and Gay Studies Reader*. Ed. Henry Abelove, Michèle Aina Barale, and David M. Halperin. New York: Routledge, 1993. 3–44.

Russ, Joanna. '*Amor Vincent Foeminam*: The Battle of the Sexes in Science Fiction'. 1980. *To Write Like a Woman: Essays in Feminism and Science Fiction*. Bloomington: Indiana UP, 1995. 41–59.

—— *The Female Man*. New York: Bantam, 1975.

—— 'The Image of Women in Science Fiction'. *Vertex* 1.6 (1974): 53–57.

—— 'SF and Technology as Mystification'. 1978. *To Write Like a Woman: Essays in Feminism and Science Fiction*. Bloomington: Indiana UP, 1995. 26–40.

—— 'When It Changed'. *Again, Dangerous Visions*. Ed. Harlan Ellison. 1972. New York: Berkley, 1983. 253–60.

Ryman, Geoff. *The Child Garden*. London: Unwin Hyman, 1989.

—— *Lust, or No Harm Done*. New York: St Martin's, 2001.

—— *Was*. New York: Penguin, 1992.

Sandilands, Catriona. 'From Unnatural Passions to Queer Nature: Common Assumptions Linking Urban-Artificial-Queer in Opposition to Rural-Natural-Straight Deserve Closer Attention'. *Alternatives Journal* 27.3 (2001): 30–35.

—— 'Mother Earth, the Cyborg, and the Queer: Ecofeminism and (More) Questions of Identity'. *NWSA Journal* 9.3 (1997): 18–40.

Saxton, Josephine. *The Travails of Jane Saint & Other Stories*. London: Women's Press, 1986.

Schaeffer, Jacqueline. 'Une perversion au féminin? A la folie!' *Filigrane* 12.2 (Fall 2003): 66–79.

Schweitzer, Darrell. 'Dangerous Peekaboo'. *Renaissance* 2.1 (Winter 1970): 10.

Scortia, Thomas N., ed. *Strange Bedfellows: Sex and Science Fiction*. 1973. New York: Pocket, 1974.

Scott, Jody. *I, Vampire*. London: Women's Press, 1984.

——*Passing for Human*. London: Women's Press, 1977.

Sedgwick, Eve Kosofsky. *Epistemology of the Closet*. Berkeley: U of California P, 1990.

—— 'How to Bring Your Kids up Gay'. *Fear of a Queer Planet: Queer Politics and Social Theory*. Ed. Michael Warner. Minneapolis: U of Minnesota P, 1993. 69–81.

—— *Tendencies*. Durham, NC: Duke UP, 1993.

—— *Touching Feeling: Affect, Pedagogy, Performativity*. Durham, NC: Duke UP, 2003.

Seltzer, Mark. *Bodies and Machines*. New York: Routledge, 1992.

Senft, Theresa. 'Introduction: Performing the Digital Body – A Ghost Story'. *Sexuality and Cyberspace: Performing the Digital Body*. Ed. Theresa Senft and Stacy Horn. Special issue of *Women and Performance* 9.1 (1996): 9–33.

Sernine, Daniel. *Boulevard des étoiles*. Montréal : Publications Ianus, 1991.

—— *Boulevard des étoiles 2: A la Recherche de Monsieur Goodtheim*. Montreal: Publications Ianus, 1991.

Shelley, Mary. *Frankenstein*. 1818 [1831]. Ed. D. L. Macdonald and Kathleen Scherf. 2nd ed. Peterborough, ON: Broadview, 2001.
Shepard, Chelsea. *Two Moons. Book One: Worthy of a Master*. Lincoln: iUniverse, 2003.
—— *Two Moons. Book Two: The Freeman's Captive*. Lincoln: iUniverse, 2004.
Short, Roger V., and Evan Balaban, eds. *The Differences between the Sexes*. Cambridge: Cambridge UP, 1994.
Silverberg, Robert. 'My Life as a Pornographer'. *Sin-a-Rama: Sleaze Sex Paperbacks of the Sixties*. Ed. Brittany A. Daley. Los Angeles: Feral House, 2004. 10–17.
—— 'The Throwbacks'. *Galaxy* 30.4 (July 1970): 26–54.
—— 'Who is Tiptree? What is He?' *Warm Worlds and Otherwise* by James Tiptree, Jr. Ed. Silverberg. New York: Ballantine, 1975. ix–xviii.
Sinfield, Alan. *Cultural Politics – Queer Reading*. Philadelphia: U of Pennsylvania P, 1994.
Singleton, Peter. 'Letter to the Editor'. *Scottische* 51 (Feb. 1969): 4.
Slonczewski, Joan. *The Children Star*. New York: Tor, 1998.
—— *A Door into Ocean*. New York: Arbor House, 1986.
Slusser, George, and Tom Shippey, eds. *Fiction 2000: Cyberpunk and the Future of Narrative*. Athens: U of Georgia P, 1992.
Smith, Cordwainer. 'Scanners Live in Vain'. 1948. *The Science Fiction Hall of Fame*. 1970. Ed. Robert Silverberg. New York: Avon, 1971. 354–90.
Sobchack, Vivian. 'The Virginity of Astronauts: Sex and the Science Fiction Film'. *Shadows of the Magic Lamp: Fantasy and Science Fiction in Film*. Ed. George E. Slusser and Eric S. Rabkin. Carbondale: Southern Illinois UP, 1985. 41–57.
Somay, Bülent. 'Towards an Open-Ended Utopia'. *Science Fiction Studies* 11.1 (Mar. 1984): 25–38.
Sontag, Susan. 'The Pornographic Imagination'. 1969. *Styles of Radical Will*. New York: Anchor, 1991. 35–73.
Soper, Kate. 'Feminism and Ecology: Realism and Rhetoric in the Discourses of Nature'. *Science, Technology and Human Values* 20.3 (1995): 311–31.
Spinrad, Norman. *Bug Jack Barron*. 1967/68. New York: Avon, 1969.
—— 'The *Bug Jack Barron* Papers'. *Algol* 15 (Spring 1969): 9–14.
—— *The Iron Dream*. New York: Jove/HJB, 1972.
—— 'Totem and Taboo'. *Psychotic* 24 (Mar. 1968): 7–11.
Sponsler, Claire. 'William Gibson and the Death of Cyberpunk'. *Modes of the Fantastic: Selected Essays from the Twelfth International Conference on the Fantastic in the Arts*. Ed. Robert A. Latham and Robert A. Collins. Westport, CT: Greenwood P, 1995. 47–55.
Springer, Claudia. *Electronic Eros: Bodies and Desire in the Postindustrial Age*. Austin: U of Texas P, 1996.
Springer, Sherwood. 'A Nod to Sturgeon'. *Thrilling Wonder Stories* 42.3 (Aug. 1953): 134–35.
Stableford, Brian. 'Superman'. *The Encyclopedia of Science Fiction*. 2nd ed. Ed. John Clute and Peter Nicholls. London: Orbit, 1993. 1180–83.
Stapledon, Olaf. *Last and First Men* and *Star Maker*. 1931, 1937. New York: Dover, 1968.
Steele, Colin. 'Sex is a Strange Mistress'. *Vector* 38 (Mar. 1966): 2–6.
Stepan, Nancy Leys. 'Race and Gender: The Role of Analogy in Science'. *Science,*

Race and Ethnicity: Readings from Isis and Osiris. Ed. John P. Jackson, Jr. Chicago: U of Chicago P, 2002. 5–21.

Sterling, Bruce. Preface. *Mirrorshades: The Cyberpunk Anthology*. Ed. Sterling. New York: Ace, 1988. ix–xvi.

Stirling, S. M. *Marching Through Georgia*. New York: Baen, 1988.

—— *Under the Yoke*. New York: Baen,1989.

Steussy, Marti. *Dreams of Dawn*. New York: Ballantine, 1988.

Stockton, Sharon. '"The Self Regained": Cyberpunk's Retreat to the Imperium'. *Contemporary Literature* 36.4 (1995): 588–612.

Stone, Allucquère Rosanne. *The War of Desire and Technology at the Close of the Mechanical Age*. Cambridge, MA: MIT, 1995.

—— 'Will the Real Body Please Stand Up?: Boundary Stories about Virtual Culture'. *Cyberspace: First Steps*. Ed. Michael Benedikt. Cambridge, MA: MIT, 1994. 81–118.

Stuart, Donald A. [John W. Campbell, Jr]. 'Who Goes There?' 1938. *Science Fiction: The Science Fiction Research Association Anthology*. Ed. Patricia S. Waugh, Charles G. Waugh, and Martin H. Greenberg. New York: HarperCollins, 1988. 84–124.

Sturgeon, Noël. 'Re-inspiration, Recommitment, and Revolution: Revisiting *The Death of Nature* by Carolyn Merchant'. *Environmental History* 10:4 (2005). 9 April 2007 http://www.historycooperative.org/journals/eh/10.4/rr_1.html.

Sturgeon, Theodore. 'The Sex Opposite'. *E Pluribus Unicorn*. 1952. London: Abelard-Schuman, 1959. 108–30.

—— 'Taboos Need Breaking'. *Thrilling Wonder Stories* 42.1 (Apr. 1953): 138–39.

—— 'The World Well Lost'. *E Pluribus Unicorn*. 1953. London: Abelard-Schuman, 1959. 53–68.

—— *Venus Plus X*. New York: Pyramid, 1960.

Suvin, Darko. *Metamorphoses of Science Fiction: On the Poetics and History of a Literary Genre*. New Haven, CT: Yale UP, 1979.

Szeman, Imre, and Maria Whiteman. 'Future Politics: An Interview with Kim Stanley Robinson'. *Science Fiction Studies* 31.2 (July 2004): 177–88.

Tan, Cecilia. 'Sadomasochism and Science Fiction: Connections and Parallels'. 10 October 1995. 15 February 2007 http://www.ceciliatan.com/smsf.html.

—— *The Velderet: A Cybersex S/M Serial*. Cambridge, MA: Circlet, 2001.

Tan, Cecilia., ed. *Color of Pain, Shade of Pleasure*. Cambridge, MA: Circlet, 2004.

—— *Genderflex: Sexy Stories on the Edge and In-Between*. Cambridge, MA: Circlet, 1996.

—— *Mind and Body*. Cambridge, MA: Circlet, 2002.

—— *Sexcrime: An Anthology of Subversive Erotica*. Cambridge, MA: Circlet, 1999.

—— *Sextopia*. Cambridge, MA: Circlet, 2001.

—— *Worlds of Women: Sapphic Science Fiction Erotica*. Cambridge, MA: Circlet, 1994.

Tatsumi, Takayuki. 'Some *Real* Mothers: An Interview with Samuel R. Delany'. *Science Fiction Eye* 1 (March 1988): 5–11.

Taylor, Gordon Rattray. *The Biological Time Bomb*. London: Thames and Hudson, 1968.

—— *Sex in History: The Story of Sexuality's Changing Attitudes to Sex Throughout the*

Ages. 1954. 2nd ed. New York: Harper Torchbooks, 1973.

Theall, Donald. 'The Art of Social-Science Fiction: The Ambiguous Utopian Dialectics of Ursula K. Le Guin'. *Science Fiction Studies* 7.2 (Nov. 1975): 256–75.

Thomson, Amy. *The Color of Distance*. New York: Ace, 1995.

—— *Through Alien Eyes*. New York: Ace, 1999.

Tiptree, James, Jr [Alice Sheldon]. 'The Girl Who Was Plugged In'. 1973. *Her Smoke Rose Up Forever: The Great Years of James Tiptree, Jr*. Sauk City, WI: Arkham House, 1990. 44–79.

—— 'Houston, Houston, Do You Read?' 1976. *Science Fiction: The Science Fiction Research Association Anthology*. Ed. Patricia S. Waugh, Charles G. Waugh, and Martin H. Greenberg. New York: HarperCollins, 1988. 434–74.

—— *Out of the Everywhere*. New York: Del Rey, 1981.

—— *Star Songs of an Old Primate*. New York: Ballantine, 1978.

—— *Ten Thousand Light Years from Home*. New York: Ace, 1972.

—— *Warm Worlds and Otherwise*. New York: Ballantine, 1975.

—— 'The Women Men Don't See'. 1973. *Warm Worlds and Otherwise*. New York: Ballantine, 1975. 131–64.

Tucker, Jeffrey Allen. *A Sense of Wonder: Samuel R. Delany, Race, Identity and Difference*. Middletown, CT: Wesleyan UP, 2004.

Turkle, Sherry. *Life on the Screen: Identity in the Age of the Internet*. New York: Touchstone, 1995.

Turner, William B. *A Genealogy of Queer Theory*. Philadelphia, PA: Temple UP, 2000.

van den Wijngaard, Marianne. *Reinventing the Sexes: The Biomedical Construction of Masculinity and Femininity*. Bloomington: Indiana UP, 1997.

Van Gastel, Louis E. 'Letter to the Editor'. *New Worlds* 146 (Jan. 1965): 125–26.

Varley, John. *Demon*. New York: Berkley, 1984.

—— *Titan*. New York: Berkley, 1979.

—— *Wizard*. New York: Berkley, 1980.

Vint, Sherryl. *Bodies of Tomorrow: Technology, Subjectivity, Science Fiction*. Toronto: U of Toronto P, 2007.

Vonarburg, Élisabeth. 'La carte du tendre'. 1986. *Aimer*. Ed. André Carpentier. Montreal: Quinze, 1986. 163–81.

—— TYRANAEL, Book I: *Dreams of the Sea*. Trans. Élisabeth Vonarburg and Howard Scott. Edmonton, AL: Tesseracts/Edge, 2003.

—— TYRANAEL, Book II: *A Game of Perfection*. Trans. Élisabeth Vonarburg and Howard Scott. Edmonton, AL: Tesseracts/Edge, 2003.

Wakeford, Nina. 'Cyberqueer'. *The Cybercultures Reader*. Ed. David Bell and Barbara M. Kennedy. New York: Routledge, 2000. 403–15.

Waldby, Catherine. *The Visible Human Project: Informatic Bodies and Posthuman Medicine*. London: Routledge, 2000.

Warner, Michael. 'Introduction.' *Fear of a Queer Planet*. Ed. Warner. Minneapolis: U of Minnesota P, 1993. vii–xxxi.

Wells, H. G. *The Food of the Gods*. 1904. New York: Berkley Highland, 1967.

—— *The Island of Doctor Moreau*. 1896. Athens, GA: U of Georgia P, 1993.

Wiegman, Robyn. 'Introduction: Mapping the Lesbian Postmodern'. *The Lesbian Postmodern*. Ed. Laura Doan. New York: Columbia UP, 1994. 1–20.

Wilson, Anna. *Altogether, Elsewhere*. London: Onlywomen, 1985.

Wittig, Monique. *Les Guérrillères*. 1969. Trans. David LeVay. Boston: Beacon, 1985.

—— *The Straight Mind and Other Essays*. Boston: Beacon, 1992.

Wollheim, Donald A. 'Guest of Honour Speech, Lunacon 1968'. *Niekas* 20 (Fall 1968): 24–29.

Woodiwiss, Kathleen E. *The Wolf and the Dove*. New York: Avon, 1974.

Woolf, Virginia. *Orlando*. 1928. New York: Penguin, 1946.

Wright, Sean. *New Wave of Speculative Fiction: The What If Factor*. London: Crowswing, 2005.

Wylie, Philip. *The Disappearance*. London: Victor Gollancz, 1951.

Young, Robert J. C. *Colonial Desire: Hybridity in Theory, Culture and Race*. New York: Routledge, 1995.

Index

www.ingramcontent.com/pod-product-compliance
Lightning Source LLC
Chambersburg PA
CBHW050401231225
37194CB00024B/601

9781846315015